LEGACY OF THE ARCANIN FLAME

AJ McMullen

Published by Ascension Publishing

First Edition

Paperback ISBN: 978-1-955254-12-0

Hardcover ISBN: 978-1-955254-14-4

eBook ISBN: 978-1-955254-13-7

Library of Congress Control Number: 2024924120

Cover Design, Interior Design by the author Ascension Design

Typeset in Times New Roman; Arcanin

Printed in the United States of America

Books By AJ McMullen

Arcanin Calamity series

- Legacy of the Arcanin Flame (S0B1)
- (S0B2) Name Reveal Coming Soon
- (S0B3) TBA
- (S0B4) TBA
- (S0B5) TBA
- (S0B6) TBA
- (S0B7) TBA
- (S0B8) TBA
- (S0B9) TBA
- (S0BX) TBA

Dark Chaos Series
(Arcanin Calamity Companion Stories)

- The Darkest Day (S0B1.5) [Coming Soon]
- The Darkest Hour (S0B5.5) [TBA]
- The Darkest Minute (S0B7.5) [TBA]

Titles accompanied by a stock number (i.e. S0B1) are novels or short stories that fall under the Aether Comics Universe.

Dedication

I hardly ever know what to say in this section as I am always unsure what the perfect message is. But I am going to consider this an opportunity to be transparent in hopes that I inspire anyone whose fingers should graze the pages of this story. But I would like to dedicate this book to the dreamer in you. The person who screams inside of you when they want to release the winner within. The spark that imagines you at your best and fills the mind with images that makes you the most ecstatic about the things you are passionate about.

Occasionally, I imagine it like the moment I win the World Heavyweight Championship and listening to the crowd roar over my theme music. The moment I play the last note at my concert and get a standing ovation. Hearing the people chant my name as I walk across the stage and receive the award I've worked so hard for. No matter what the story is or how you imagine it, keep it in mind as you work toward the goal.

Let this book be the prime example that things that were once born in chaos can be beautiful. I'll discuss that in the Author's note at the end of the book. But for now, just keep working on your story! When you make the decision to create and add value to the world, there will always be a group there to deter you. They will say that your value is not enough. They will tell you that you need to follow the course of those before you. But I'm here to tell you the truth. The people before you will attempt to keep you on the *"right track"* because they do not know how to pioneer a course to success. Being the only one with an idea can be discouraging when placed in the wrong circles. Do not let it!

Be brave, Dreamer! Step out into the world and create, motivate, and inspire the world in the way you know how! I plan to do that, using this book as the first step to getting that championship, winning that award, and hearing the crowd chant, *"Aether, Aether!"*! If I'm going to have big dreams and you're going to read about them, the least you could do is live up to your fullest potential. Remember, there is no life without balance, my dear reader. If you are going to work hard in life, find a way to enjoy every step of the way.

Legacy of the Arcanin Flame is an action-packed, thrilling adventure set in a futuristic Idaho, U.S. In a world deceptively appearing like our own, but one with a dark secret. This story includes elements regarding war, mass genocide, man-hunting, burning, graphic language, intense violence, blood, fatal injury and dismemberment, grief, loss of life, murder, and sexual activity. Readers who may be sensitive to these elements, please take note and continue at your discretion.

Prologue

"3, 2, 1, rolling."

"World War III left us without a spine to stand on, it seems. I am not here to spread conspiracies. I am here to shine a light on the truth and be a beacon of hope for our future. Welcome back to the Observer Chronicles. If you don't know me by now, I am your host—the one formerly known as Tawnie. You can call me The Oracle because I saw what was, and I am enlightened on what is to come.

Humankind claimed to be on top because we had opposable thumbs, something they thought we were the only ones to have. They said that no being nor species could stand up to us. But only if you folks knew what that war really did to us. Not a single technological advancement has occurred in decades. Not a person willing to step up and break free of the norm. The secrets they keep from you are dark, and what they have in store for you is even darker.

They wanted me to quiet down, don't say everything that was on my mind. But I realize now that longevity and peace is not the agenda, as they once told me it was. Just as they lied to use me for my gifts, they robbed you of your sentience and mortality. Whether you want to stand against the tyranny, or be held down by their boots, the choice is yours. I just want to present the option. Keep seeing the unseen, Observers."

Chapter I

It was 109 degrees Fahrenheit in Idaho in February. On live television, local news reporters stared at Doppler radars and maps in wonder. They displayed an unfamiliar level of incompetence before their viewers.

"It's the first time it has been this hot anywhere during winter in history." One meteorologist insisted. "Yes, it is peculiar. Yesterday, Idaho Falls got a foot of snow. But somehow, we are in triple digits today!" The female anchor added. Little Milo sat at the kitchen table of his family home, watching in awe as he ate his breakfast—a small plate with a sausage link and French toast sticks. As usual, he had more food around his mouth and on the table than he could have possibly eaten. His mother, Tawnie, was in the kitchen cleaning dishes. Her wild, curly, black hair bounced around her face as she bent over to pick up something she dropped on the floor. Her medium-toned skin turned red due to the heat. With a similar complexion and straighter yet curly hair, Milo watched her with much fascination. As most kids would at the age of five.

"Mommy, I don't want anymore." The little boy said. Tawnie stood upright and looked at him. Her brown eyes stared at his plate, wondering how much he'd eaten. Only a few bites were taken out of the sausage link. His French toast sticks were barely touched.

"Baby, are you not hungry?" She asked as she entered the dining area and touched his upper back. "How are you feeling?"

The young one looked up at her, "I don't feel good." He whined.

"Okay," Tawnie responded as she palmed her scalp through her buoyant hair. "Why don't you lay on the couch and get some rest until it's time to leave."

The boy nodded and climbed down from the seat. As he stumbled toward the front of the house, raking his eyes with the back of his hands, Tawnie watched him. She clenched her jaw and looked away. As he was told, he climbed onto the giant sectional couch and placed himself in front of the television. It didn't take long for him to fall asleep.

Tawnie finished her chores and grabbed her phone from the counter. After looking through it for a moment, she made a call. She quietly walked through the living room, looking at her son before walking up the stairs.

"Of course, you're not answering!" She grumbled into the phone. "Milo, I want to remind you that you have a household to maintain and a son who needs his father. I'm tired of talking to your voicemail."

Little Milo Jr. heard his mom rambling and woke up. After ten minutes of rest and no true sense of time, the boy forgot he was tired altogether. He waited on the couch for a moment, staring at the television. A cartoon that he was hardly interested in. He heard something upstairs and slid to the sofa's edge to get down. Quietly, he made his way to the stairs and ascended upon them. The large, two-story foyer allowed him to see the door to Tawnie's office from where he stood. It was slightly ajar, and the light was on inside. He could hear her talking but couldn't understand what she was saying. When he reached the top, Milo approached the door and stood outside.

"Time will clash as future, past, and present threaten to destroy all chronological balance!" she yelled into a camera in front of her desk. Blinding lights shined at her as she spoke. "While everyone is distracted by things they can't control, reality itself will start to collapse, marking the end of humanity as we know it."

"Mommy," Milo called as he opened the door. Tawnie was already up, turning off the camera.

"Hi, Spud. Did you enjoy your nap? You weren't sleeping for long," she said with an unnatural glee.

"Yeah, I did." The little boy answered as he looked around the room that he was hardly allowed in. He noticed the minimalist desk with sheets of words, graphs, and drawings all over. In front of it were two light boxes that shined toward her. The rest of the room was bare. Plain white walls surrounded them except for the wall behind the desk. A black tarp covered the window but had a large whiteboard hanging. The boy became captivated by the hundreds of unrecognizable symbols she had drawn.

"What language is that, mommy?" He asked with his finger pointed at the board.

"Uh," Tawnie said as she looked at the board again. "It's called Arcanin."

"Like… people from Arcania?"

Tawnie chuckled as she walked toward him. "Sure, Spud." She said with a smile as they left the room. She walked behind her kid down the stairs and headed to the front door. Milo, however, ran to the kitchen, assuming they would leave from the garage.

"Wait a second, Spud!" She called out as she pulled out her phone to see if she had received any calls. She sighed upon realizing that Milo's father had not called back. She looked up to the ceiling, biting her bottom lip. Milo playfully stomped into the foyer, apologizing for going the wrong way. Tawnie smiled as she guided him to the door. She opened it, and the bright sun reflected from the mounds of snow on the ground, causing her to squint.

"It's so bright!" The boy impishly snarled.

"I know!" She said as she closed the door behind them. Milo ran toward the car, treading through the slush on the ground. She watched him, ensuring he didn't get distracted and run off. She pressed the unlock button on the car remote, and he ran to the door that his car seat occupied.

"Mommy, I'm going to do it all by myself!" He boasted.

"Good job, Spud!" The woman cheered as she saw her neighbor across the street. She was taller with brown hair and glasses, peering at Tawnie. As they made eye contact, the woman smiled and waved. Tawnie looked around the beautiful subdivision where all the sizable houses were uniformed. Many of the neighbors stood outside their homes, and Tawnie noticed glares from most of them. As Milo got into the car and closed the door, she started the car with the remote and went across the street.

"Tawnie, good morning!" Her neighbor greeted her.

"Mariah, what the hell has everyone staring at me?" Tawnie asked.

The woman chuckled. "Sweetie, don't even mention it. Everyone is just wondering if you spoke on this weather in those videos you do."

Tawnie relaxed her body, looking off into her thawing lawn.

"I guess that makes sense." Tawnie nodded. "Well, I have to get Milo off to school. I'll talk to you later."

"Tawnie, hold up!" The woman called. She stopped walking only to turn her head and peek over her shoulder. "Do you really believe that people will take your little social media channel seriously? Is that really the best way to help your cause?"

"Hmph," Tawnie grunted as she allowed her chin to fall.

"I'm only asking 'cuz–"

"I know what you're asking me," Tawnie said as she spun around to confront the woman. "You're saying my stance is not valued because I don't look like everyone else in this neighborhood!"

Mariah shook her head. "Tawnie, no! Nobody is judging you because you're…" She paused.

Tawnie cocked her head to the side and stared into the woman's eyes.

"Maybe I'm not aware these days. It's 2079, and everyone is offended by everything," Tawnie joked. "But does the word black offend you?"

The woman turned red and looked away for a slight second.

"No, Tawnie! It's not like that?" She pleaded. "Many of us believe that your videos upset people, and we want to keep the peace."

Tawnie put on a pair of sunglasses and stepped away.

"You know what, Mariah?" She said. "I usually don't like to coast on my reputation, but remember who you're talking to."

With one final grin and side-eye, Tawnie left the woman in shock as she headed back to her car. She opened the door and got inside.

"Alright, Spud, let's split!" Tawnie cheered as she fastened her seatbelt.

"You left an infant in the car on a day as hot as this?" She heard a woman ask.

"What the hell?" Tawnie looked back at Milo, who shrugged his shoulders in ignorance. But when she looked forward, she noticed her mother-in-law's name on the dash. The call had been going for nearly four minutes. Tawnie sighed, "First of all, he's not an infant. Secondly, the car was running with the AC on."

"Hmm," the woman responded. I am trying to get in touch with Milo. Is he off the grid again?"

"Not to my knowledge." She answered. "I was told he had to get to Yellowstone for some reason. I haven't heard from him for two days either."

The line went silent for a moment. Tawnie turned around to check on her son, who seemed preoccupied with a toy he had found in the back seat.

"Well, I'm not sure why he would be going to Yellowstone at a time like this!" The woman complained. "When you get some information, could you let me know what's happening?"

Tawnie nodded. "Yes, ma'am. I will."

The call ended, and Tawnie buckled her seatbelt.

"Mommy, where are your mommy and daddy?" Milo asked as the car began to roll backward.

Tawnie slammed on the brake as the car began to roll. She was stunned at his question, "I don't have a mommy and daddy anymore, Spud."

The kid's eyes grew large, and his mouth opened as he gasped. "What happened to them, mommy?" He questioned, full of curiosity. His mother smiled and shook her head. "I lost them to that special place I told you about."

"Oh." He muttered. "I'm sorry, mommy. Do you miss them?"

Tawnie nodded. "As much as I possibly can."

The car cleared the driveway, and the woman began to drive down the road, turning the radio on. The first thing they heard was a report about the cause of the heat.

"After mass hysteria over the current temperature, researchers feel that they now know why the heat is so high on this winter day." The anchor announced.

"This should be interesting," Tawnie said. "Let's see if they're even close."

Chapter II

Tawnie sped down the highway, periodically looking at her phone. Her chest was heavy. She attempted not to look into the rearview mirror because Milo might see the rage in her swollen eyes. The traffic was dense on the I-15, and the radio personalities continued to address the heat. Done hearing their banter, she turned it off. Again, she looked down at her phone when the car before her slammed on the brakes. As she looked up, she saw the stop and did the same.

"What the hell?" She asked. "Why would anyone want to stop in this heat?"

She waited a moment for traffic to start moving. But it never did.

"Mommy, why is Daddy not coming home?" Milo asked.

Tawnie sighed. "You already know that Daddy is working, Spud."

The kid growled. "You guys work too much!"

Tawnie spun around in her seat and glared at him, grinding her teeth in the heat of the moment. The boy flinched as the horn sounded from the car behind them. Tawnie immediately turned around to find that traffic had started moving again. She put the car back in drive and crept forward. Her eyes were wet, and she used the back of her hand to dry them.

"Milo, I'm sorry." She said, "I didn't mean to snap at you like that. Mommy is just struggling right now."

The boy still clutched the arm of his car seat, listening to his mother sniffling. He wanted to speak but didn't, fearing that he would only worsen things.

"I'm alright, Spud." She said as she took a deep breath.

The phone began to ring.

"It's your dad, finally!" She said as she pressed the steering wheel button to answer.

"Milo, what the hell?" Tawnie answered.

"Tawnie, I'm sorry, but there has been a lot going on here, and I haven't been able to call." The man responded in a deep voice. "I've been trying to get a hold of you, but I had no signal."

"Milo, we could have avoided this by you staying home!" Tawnie screamed as she slammed her fists against the steering wheel.

He sighed. "Tawnie, I can't neglect my job."

She slammed on the brakes, almost hitting the car in front of her. The sudden stop caused little Milo's body to jolt forward.

"You were home for two days last time, weeks ago, Milo! We didn't agree to this!"

The little boy tried covering his ears to drown out the hostility. He even tried making noises with his mouth, but that still didn't work.

"Tawnie, random occurrences against the laws of nature have happened worldwide! It is my job to investigate them!"

Tawnie shook her head in disbelief. "I don't care about any job other than the one you committed to at the altar!"

"Yeah, I'm on the phone with—her. Give me a moment." They could hear him saying to someone in the background. Tawnie shuddered at the slight hesitation and the reluctance to acknowledge her. But, despite his request, the woman continued to talk. Furious, she attempted to ignore the woman, but she must have been close.

"We have lost control of the energy and need to shut it down," she explained. Tawnie shook her head in disbelief.

"Alright, I'm coming," Milo responded to them. "I have to go."

"Oh, hell no!" She yelled at him. "Milo, don't hang up on me!"

But the man continued to say his salutations and hung up. Tawnie's face turned red as she wrapped herself around her steering wheel. Her lips rolled over her teeth to bite back a scream. She stopped the car again and leaned forward to take another calming breath.

"Mommy, is Daddy not coming home tonight?" Milo asked.

Her mouth clicked. "No, Spud, I don't think he is."

The little boy's face drooped as his head fell.

"Shit!" Tawnie yelled as she started to go through her phone again.

"Mommy, what's wrong?" Her son asked.

"Nothing, sweetie," She assured. "I just have to handle something."

Tawnie's eyes bounced between her phone and the traffic ahead. Milo attempted to see what was going on outside the vehicle. A semi-truck trailer blocked the view in front of them. A large truck with over-sized tires was on the right, making it sit high. The driver, a young, white man with a scruffy beard, and his skinny arm out the window of his truck. He kept looking into their car as if he wanted to get Tawnie's attention. Milo made eye contact with him, and the man pointed to the front of the vehicle. Milo looked ahead, his mother still stewing over the phone call with his father.

"Mm…mommy," the boy muttered. Tawnie looked over her shoulder at him and saw Milo pointing at the vehicle next to them.

"What is it?" she asked as she glanced out the window to see the man waving to her. Tawnie looked back at her window switch on the driver's door. Then, the temperature readout on the gauge cluster reading 109 degrees Fahrenheit. Reluctantly, she tapped the switch to roll the passenger window down.

"Can I help you with something?" she asked the man.

He shook his head out of his window. His eyes squint to shield them from the harsh sunlight.

"No, ma'am." He said with his deep southern accent. I just wanted to let you know you left your gas cap open."

The man pointed back to it, still keeping his eyes on Tawnie. She leaned forward to see the gas door in the passenger side mirror. Surely enough, it was wide open.

"Yeah," She said. "I guess it is."

Tawnie opened her car door and stepped out into the burning heat. She walked around the front end of the vehicle toward the gas cover. The man in the truck tried to strike up a conversation as he locked his eyes on her. Sitting in the back, Milo could see the predatory look in his eyes as he scanned his mother's body. The boy hid his face and waited for her return.

"Yes, I'm married with a five-year-old who's right in the car," Tawnie said to the man.

"Well, I apologize for offending you, ma'am." He said as he tipped his hat to her. "But if that kid there is five years old, I can't believe he's yours. Did you have him at fourteen?"

Tawnie laughed as she returned to the driver's side of her car.

"Thank you for the compliment. I—" she paused and looked around her. Other than the traffic ahead moving slightly, she saw nothing. Her eyes sharpened, and her brows furrowed.

"Everything alright?" the man in the truck asked as the vehicles behind them started beeping their horns. He hung out of his window to scream at the cars behind them. Tawnie looked for her son but saw him tucked in the backseat. His head was down, and he rocked back and forth, covering his ears with his palms.

"Oh shit!" Tawnie yelled as she opened the door to get inside. "Milo, baby, breathe! Everything is fine!" She began to console him from the front seat.

"Mommy!" The boy screamed, "It's coming!"

"Nothing is coming, Milo," she said with impatience. You know that, Spud!"

But the boy still buried his head in his lap. She tried lifting him back up. But Milo broke away from her and curled up again.

The man in the truck looked forward, and his eyes grew large. Tawnie saw the fear in his face as he looked around for a way out.

"Mommy, it's coming!" Milo screamed. "Mommy, stop it!"

"Milo, what's coming?" Tawnie yelled. Suddenly, she felt a tremor. A cracking sound emanated from the distance and echoed over the land. Her heart sank.

"What?" She looked around as she heard people screaming all over. The semi-truck in front of them looked like it was sinking into the ground. People started to run past her from the front, but she couldn't see what they were running from. The truck next to Tawnie began to sink as well. The southern man tried to get out, but his door was jammed at the frame by the fissures in the road. It wasn't long before his tall truck had brought him to eye level with Tawnie's short car. Suddenly, the woman saw the car's dome light switch on, and a wave of heat swiped at her. She looked back to Milo's car seat, realizing it was empty and the door was wide open.

Tawnie jumped back out of the car.

"Milo!" She called out to her son as she looked around. Her view ahead was now clear as she stood between the lanes. A bright light appeared ahead as if the sun was sitting on the Earth just a few cars away. Tawnie looked up at it and realized that it domed at the top and was wide enough to cover all four lanes of the highway and much more.

Tiny cracks appeared all over the ground, and light shined through like illuminated veins in the road. The southern man began to scream in agony. Tawnie followed a fissure with her eyes to his truck as it and the other vehicles ahead of them fell into the ground. She wanted to try to help him, but the fiery energy was spreading.

"Shit!" She yelled as she started to run away. As she dodged around the cars, she cried for her son. But she couldn't hear anything over the humming of the running vehicles and screams. Suddenly, there was an explosion behind her. The force knocked her down, and she slid across the concrete. Immediately, she looked around and saw Milo hiding underneath a semi-truck yards away. The boy was in a tucked position on his knees with his hands behind his head. But as soon as she saw him, the crowd thickened as they escaped the catastrophe. For a moment, the heels of the fleeing civilians repeatedly trampled Tawnie as she lost sight of her son.

Anger filled her, and she was able to roll to her feet again. But the panicked crowd pushed her away from the boy. She looked over to the truck that Milo hid under and screamed for the people to get out of her way. But it was no use. Tawnie looked back to find the wall of light getting closer. It was bright, giving off a strange, reddish glow. Motivated to get her child away from it, she swung her elbow forward, knocking down a man beside her. His falling disrupted the group behind him, and the plowing people tripped over him like dominoes. Recognizing the opportunity Tawnie skipped across their backs to get to Milo. "Milo, I'm here, Sweetie!" she screamed for him.

"Mommy!" He yelled back as he lifted his head. His little face was red and soaked from tears.

She reached for his arm underneath the vehicle. "Come on!"

Cautiously, he made his way over to his mother. But cracks spread underneath his feet and light shining up from the ground distracted him. Immediately, the air pressure around them became much denser.

"MILO!" Tawnie screamed again. Snapping out of his stupor, he continued to run to her. Once he touched her hand, she snatched and tossed him over her shoulder. She ran away from the approaching energy. Milo looked into the veil as vehicles and debris ascended into the mysterious power.

"MOMMY!" He screamed to Tawnie, but the energy contracted like a shoreline before a giant wave.

"Milo, close your eyes, sweetie!" Tawnie yelled to him. "It'll be okay!"

Milo could hear the cracking in her voice and did the opposite of what Tawnie told him. The energy expanded again, and Milo watched as the vertical wall of flames approached. He and his mother were stuck in its path.

Chapter III

Moments later, Milo awakened with his ears ringing. He was so disoriented that he couldn't see. He panicked.

"Mommy!" He screamed. "Mommy, where are you?" But there was no answer. It seemed quiet around, and he stopped feeling the harsh heat. Eventually, his vision returned, and he was able to look around. He saw that he was on the opposite side of town. The sunken highway was far in the distance, and flames were blazing around the entire area. The city was filled with the sounds of sirens and faint screaming. But nearby, Milo could see his mother lying on the ground. Her clothes were all tattered, and her body was bruised. Milo ran to her side and grabbed her hand. He lifted it and shook it, hoping she'd awaken. He could see the grayish tone of her face and the blue tint of her lips.

"MOMMY, WAKE UP!" He screamed as he leaned over top of her and shook her entire body. "MOMMY!"

Miraculously, the woman gasped for air and rolled to her side. Milo patted her back as she came to. Over time, her color returned to normal.

"What?" She asked as she reached for her head.

"I'm here, Mommy!" Milo assured her as she flipped up to sit on her butt. The ground was still cold, sending a slight chill up her spine.

"Milo." She muttered, staring at him with concern. The kid looked terrified as they locked eyes.

"Mommy." He said as he looked her in the eyes. "I thought you were dead."

Tawnie reached for him and wrapped her arms around him.

"Oh, Spud." She said with tears in her eyes. "I'm so sorry." The young woman embraced her son before getting up from the ground. She looked ahead at the dark cloud cast over Idaho Falls. The highway had all but vanished under the smoke and flames.

"Mommy?" Milo called to her as he grabbed her hand. He looked up at her, trying to shield his eyes from the sunlight above. "How did we get over here?"

Tawnie paused momentarily and blinked sporadically. "I don't know, Spud." He looked out at the carnage once more. "But I'm glad we made it here."

"Do you think the other people got away too?" He asked.

Tawnie's heart skipped a beat. She gulped, thankful that he never looked up to see the look on her face. "I hope so."

At that moment, she looked around and noticed people standing nearby. They were all cautious of her and Milo. Looking around at everyone, she could feel the temperature decreasing drastically.

"What the hell?" She mumbled before pulling her son. "Come on, Milo."

As his mother pulled him along, Milo could see the fear in everyone's eyes as they passed through the crowd.

"Hey!" A man yelled from the distance. "You!"

The two of them looked at him—a large white male with a bulky, muscular build.

"Sir, I don't want any trouble," Tawnie told him as she kept walking. But the man persisted and jogged toward her. Milo seemed to slow down, but Tawnie pressured him to walk faster. The man behind her was now yelling, and other bystanders kept him from getting to her.

"Let her go," One person yelled. "She's okay!"

"But did you see that?" The man asked. "She must be one of them!"

Tawnie stopped for a moment and looked over her shoulder. She caught most of the crowd's eye. Expressions of shock and disgust were displayed on many of them. She sighed deeply, trying her best not to show any emotion. Instead, she continued to walk.

"Mommy, what's wrong with them?" Milo asked.

"I wish I knew, Spud."

Tawnie left the area and pulled out her phone. She wanted to see if she had reception, but the screen didn't turn on.

"Dammit!" She barked as she looked around. There was a convenience store nearby, and the two of them headed there. Outside the small shack was a motorcycle fleet belonging to a biker gang. Tawnie froze, weighing her options before proceeding into the unknown.

"What's wrong, Mommy?" The little boy asked.

"Nothing, Sweetie." She smiled at him. "We're just going to go to this store so I can get a phone charger."

"Is your phone dead?" He asked as Tawnie pulled him toward the building.

Tawnie reached the store and pushed the door open. A small bell sat atop the threshold, jingling as they entered. Inside, Tawnie recognized the bikers by their vests. There were plenty of them standing in line, waiting to checkout. The rest still paced around the store, grabbing their items. There were men and women in their group, all of the Caucasian variety. They all stared at her as she tiptoed through the aisles, cautious of her surroundings. Tawnie found the electronic accessories and faced the shelving. Milo looked to the end of the aisle and saw a man heading toward them. He clutched his mom's hand and inched toward her leg. Tawnie continued to look at the selection, and the man came to stand next to them. The section beside her carried a few snack options, and he stared at them. Tawnie readied herself for the worst-case scenario. But the man grabbed a bag of beef jerky and walked away. Her body shook with fear as she took a deep breath. She picked up the phone charger she needed and stepped toward the front of the store. There was a line at the register full of the gang members. Tawnie stood behind them, staring at the back of the black leather vest the man in front of her wore. A large patch on the back carried a human skull and a picture of a motorcycle engine behind it. The name on the vest read Road King Motorcycle Gang.

One member came to stand in line behind Tawnie, and she glanced at her. The woman was taller than her. She was muscular and bordered the line of femininity. Underneath her vest, she wore only a tight halter top. She had tattoos all over and a Mohawk hairstyle. Tawnie spotted a 1% patch on the front of the vest as she turned around. Her heart pounded as she waited for the line to move. A television was on behind the counter, capturing everyone's attention. A breaking news report of the incident was showing. An aerial view of the devastation. It was the first time Tawnie could see how much damage was caused.

"Authorities are not sure how this happened," the reporter said. "We are in the helicopter hovering over miles of damage from the I-15 and the western part of Idaho Falls."

The fires still blazed the area that appeared to be a giant sinkhole. It seemed like a fire pit with magma underneath.

"Man, what the fuck is going on, Idaho?" One of the cyclists asked as the store clerk rang him up. "This is putting a kink in our plan."

"I bet." The cashier responded. "It's good you guys weren't near that when it happened."

Tawnie stood by, listening to the conversation and hoping to remain inconspicuous. The men stood aside to continue watching the broadcast after buying their goods. Their presence caused a congestion by the door. Her eyes cautiously counted the number of people around her. She held Milo in front of her to keep an eye on him as she paid for the charger. Tawnie pulled out her phone, which had her card wallet attached. As she fumbled with her bank card on the keypad near the counter's edge, strange bruising revealed on her arms. The store clerk stared at it, making her self-conscious.

"Ma'am, is that a burn on your arm?" The cashier asked.

"Uh." She answered, unsure how to proceed.

"What the hell? Were you there?"

Tawnie pulled her arms back and gave him a slight nod. Blown away, he raised a fist to his mouth and looked back at the television.

"That's wild!" He said, causing the others in the room to start commenting.

"Thank you," Tawnie said. She grabbed her belongings and headed outside. The jingling door made it evident that someone was coming out. People were standing by the motorcycles, heads turning to look at the door. In the middle of their conversation, they paused upon seeing her.

"Alright, sweetie. We have to go find some jackets before it gets too cold." Tawnie said to her son.

"Okay, Mommy." The boy answered as they walked across the parking lot.

"Hold up!" A man yelled at Tawnie. She kept walking, pretending not to hear him.

"Ma'am!" He yelled again. But Tawnie kept going. Milo, however, looked back and slowed his pace to look at the guy. But his mother only pulled him along.

"We see the unseen." The man said. Finally, Tawnie stopped dead in her tracks. Slowly, she turned around. The man could see the look of discomfort on her face. The other gang members exited the store and crowded around as she stared at him. All of them stared at her with intense expressions. The man who called her held up a card. Tawnie gasped, pulling out her wallet. She immediately noticed that her bank card was missing.

"Oh, dammit." She said as she stepped toward him. Generously, he handed it back. But the others seemed to be crowding around her. She paused again, staring at the man before her as he crossed his arms. His vest was similar to the others. However, his was lined with silver and carried a lot more patches. He was tall, around six-foot-three inches, and muscular. His eyes seemed so sunken on his face that light hardly penetrated them. He was bald with the tattoo of a familiar symbol on the side of his head, just above his left ear. Tawnie recognized the symbol because she was the one who created it. It was the Oracle symbol that helped her gain notoriety. A simple ring with an upside-down cross inside.

"You guys would hurt a woman in front of her child?' She asked.

"Absolutely not, Madame Oracle." He responded. Tawnie's eyes widened from shock as she stepped backward. "You are not alone." He assured her. Tawnie looked around at the crowd. Many of them nodded in agreement to his statement. At that moment, it appeared they had all suddenly submitted. Tawnie awaited her acknowledgment. She looked back at Milo, who was confused, looking around at all the big, scary men and women. Tawnie nodded as she turned to look at the man before her.

"It's gettin' cold, Madame Oracle." He said to her, nodding his head to another group member. A woman broke away and headed to the area where the motorcycles were parked.

"You may know this already," the man said as he pointed at the smoke in the sky. "But that stuff won't be an accident, and those people are about to be all over this mess."

Tawnie grinned and crossed her arms as well.

"I figured," She responded as she looked over her shoulder. "So where are you folks headed?"

"We were heading out East before this explosion happened," the man said. The woman came back with a couple of coats for Tawnie and Milo. Tawnie graciously took them away. She held them at arm's length to get a good look at them. One was a white pea-coat that made her smile while she examined it. The other was a black bubble coat for Milo. Tawnie looked back at the woman with an eyebrow raised.

"Are you sure?" She asked the woman.

"Yeah, honey!" She responded. "I have a lot of stuff in that trunk of mine. And my kid outgrew that years ago."

"Milo!" Tawnie called. Cautious, the kid stepped forth, looking around at all the bikers. Tawnie reached down and wrapped the coat around the young one. He quickly slid his arms inside and zipped it up himself.

"Thank you," Tawnie said to the woman. She only nodded as she stepped back into the group.

"It is our pleasure, Oracle." The leader added. "You've helped a lot of us here already. It is my honor to serve you."

Tawnie smiled and nodded slowly. "You guys have a safe trip."

The bikers quickly put the side of their right hands to the center of their faces. Their thumbs and pinky folded to their palms. Their remaining three fingers pointed straight up. In unison, they dropped their hands.

"Let's roll out!" The leader roared. The group broke and started walking back to their respective rides.

"Hey!" Tawnie called the man. He looked back at her with a grin.

"What's your name?" She asked.

The man turned back to her and cleared his throat.

"Most people know me as Thumper, Ma'am." He answered. Tawnie smiled again and crossed her arms.

"See you around, Thumper." She said.

"If you need us, check the pockets."

She turned around with a grin and directed Milo away from the store.

"Mommy, where do you know all those people from?" Milo asked.

With a smile, Tawnie simply answered, "From the internet."

Chapter IV

Tawnie found herself outside the store in the cold. She and Milo sat at an electrical outlet on the side of the building. She leaned against the brick wall with Milo snuggled up next to her. Her phone sat on her lap, and her fingers twitched in anticipation to turn it on again. Milo was sleeping, drooling on her chest. The wind started picking up, and the temperature seemed to drop rapidly. But, despite how cold it was, snuggling up to Milo produced enough heat to keep her warm.

Patrons visiting the store had to step around them to maneuver down the sidewalk awkwardly. She carefully watched her surroundings, staring at the red traffic light down the road and wondering why she didn't feel the temperature as much as everyone else. People were suddenly bundled in multiple coats, scarves, and gloves, but she didn't feel like it was frigid enough for that. Suddenly, she heard an odd sound coming from her right. It was a young man standing outside his car and appearing to reach into his center console. Subconsciously, Tawnie gripped her son tighter. The man stepped away from the vehicle and closed it before stepping onto the sidewalk. He had one hand holding the crotch of his pants, and the other swung as he walked.

"Here you go, Sweetheart." He said as he approached her, holding his clenched fist out. Tawnie waved her palm at him.

"I appreciate you, but I'm not homeless." She said.

The man paused and nodded. "You good though?" He asked.

"Yeah." Tawnie nodded. "I'm just charging my phone." The man walked away, leaving her alone again.

She watched the remaining charge time on the phone screen

and pulled the cable out when it finished. She held the button to turn it on, hoping to see an update from her husband. But as the phone booted, there were no new notifications from him. However, there was an unread message from Abigail Calloway, her assistant. She opened it, and her eyebrows immediately sharpened with anger. Instead of responding to the message, she hit the call button.

"Hi, Ms. Everwood!" the woman said, picking up on the first ring. "Thank God you're okay!"

Tawnie sighed. "Abbie, it's Simms." She corrected her. But there was silence on the line.

"When he finally decides to do right and end your separation, I will say his name."

"Just remember," Tawnie added. "I'm your boss, and I don't feel much respect coming through this phone."

Milo awakened and roared as he yawned. He looked up at his mother and immediately placed a hand over his mouth after realizing she was on the phone. Tawnie put a thumb up, and he nodded before getting up.

"I called you to tell you what I found on the Primotech case."

Tawnie grinned.

"You were right about their involvement in Saudi Arabia." Abbie continued. "The Prime Minister has issued multiple warnings concerning Primotech's infestation of Riyadh."

Tawnie scratched her chin. "It has caused some hostility between the other countries."

"Hostility?" Tawnie asked. "You mean, like, war?"

Abbie went silent for a moment. But Tawnie could hear her assistant sighing.

"Saudi Arabia is one of many countries pissed about the invasion." She answered. "Everyone else is concerned about what they found."

"Hmm," Tawnie said as she stood from the ground. "Is there any record of what they found?"

She could hear the sound of rustling papers over the phone.

"I have to read through all of this stuff," Abbie answered. "But it doesn't look like it."

Milo could see that something was wrong as he stared at Tawnie.

"Are you still in Idaho Falls, by chance?" she asked. Tawnie looked in the direction of the explosion. She could still see the cloud of smoke looming over the city.

"I am," she answered. "And I witnessed the explosion."

The city was still in arms as emergency workers attempted to restore order. Everything seemed loud and chaotic, and the screams of the crowds and sirens filled the area.

"Where are you, Abbie?" Tawnie asked.

"I'm attempting to leave the city. But traffic on all the exit routes seems to be gridlocked. Nobody is leaving anytime soon."

Tawnie's eyes grew large as she continued to look around the environment.

"Miss Tawnie, I have a bad feeling about all this."

Tawnie nodded. "Yeah. Me too."

She stepped forward and took Milo's hand in hers. "Come on, Milo." She said as she pulled the boy across the parking lot. Tawnie removed the phone from her ear to search for news updates. However, she couldn't find anything.

"Your suspicions may be correct, my friend," Tawnie said as she returned the phone to her ear. "How often does a highway explode, and there's no news about it in the government database?"

"Uh…" The woman started to say, creating awkward silence. "Hey, now that I'm looking around here, I don't see anything."

"Wait, what?" Tawnie asked. "What's keeping the traffic from leaving the city?"

In the right lane of a two-lane highway, Abbie opened the door of her car and stepped out. She looked around, first noticing no incoming traffic in the opposite direction. She continued examining the situation, giving Tawnie a play-by-play of what she saw. People sat in their cars, outraged at the standstill, anxiously awaiting the end of the jam. But looking ahead, she saw nothing stopping traffic in the distance.

"What the hell?" She said as she began to walk toward the cause of the jam.

"Abbie, what do you see?" Tawnie asked as she stopped walking.

"I'm not sure, boss. Hold on."

Tawnie looked around her, noticing the dozens of people

entering a nearby school. Police officers stood around guiding traffic and herding the people inside.

"Ma'am!" An officer yelled to her from across the street. "Let's get off the streets, please!" The man was wearing his uniform underneath a bulletproof police vest. He held a rifle in his arms, pointing it at the ground and ready to shoot. He pointed to the school, but she became curious about what he was preparing for. Tawnie stepped off the sidewalk in a rush. Her son's little legs struggled to keep up as she tugged on his hand. The officer continued to direct foot traffic, removing focus from the curious mother. That is until she got close and examined the man from the ground up.

"Ma'am, I need you to follow instructions and move along!" He roared. The middle-aged Caucasian man wore a hat that hardly revealed his eyes. Nonetheless, Tawnie felt he looked familiar. The instant shock on his face only showed he had the same thought. The man's eyes grew large, and she could see his shoulders stiffen and jaw clench.

"Sir, I'm sure we can have a civilized conversation as you inform me what's going on, right?" she asked, stepping closer to him. The man growled, "Move, now! Disobey my orders, and you're going to lock up!"

Tawnie put her palms up, stepping away from him. Upset, she looked down at Milo, anger overcoming her spirit. "Come on, Milo."

The two of them continued along the sidewalk. Tawnie reached for the pocket holding her phone but thought twice about pulling it out. Just before blending in with the crowd, she stopped walking.

"Mommy, what's wrong?" Milo asked, looking up at his mother with concern. She turned around, staring at the officer with hatred in her eyes. Abbie yelled her name on the phone stuffed in her pocket, but she couldn't possibly hear it over the crowd. Tawnie turned around and marched back toward him. As he continued to direct the people, Tawnie approached him again, waving a finger in front of his face.

Tawnie and the police officer began to argue as Abbie listened on the line. But in front of her was something bone-chilling. Her eyes widened as she watched a convoy of black military-grade vehicles enter the city.

"What the hell?" She asked as she followed them with her eyes. Other drivers started getting out of their cars to see what was happening. Every vehicle halted, causing the people to start asking questions.

"You know what's going on over there?" A man asked Abbie. She shook her head to respond.

"What's happening?" A woman asked from inside his vehicle.

"I don't know, honey." He answered. "It looks like the military's coming through or something." Abbie stared across the vast, grassy median as the vehicles came to a stop in the right lane. Bright lights shined on her from the side of the cars as more trucks passed in the second lane. As Abbie threw her arm over her face to shield herself from the light shining her way, she could see men jumping out.

"Hey, what the hell?" The older man asked as he tried to look across the median. As Abbie squinted, attempting to make out what she was seeing, she saw something that made her heart race. Suddenly, the lights turned off, and Abbie turned around to run between the cars. At that moment, she heard the first gunshot. It was explosive, sounding like a dynamite cracking in the sky. Then, the same sound multiplied as the entire platoon of soldiers began to shoot into the cars. Bullets spilled into the Westbound corridor, ripping through vehicles with ease. Abbie hit the ground and covered her head with her hands. Tawnie heard the gunshots on the phone and placed it to her ear again.

"Abbie?" She called. But there was no answer. Thunderous noise filled Tawnie's ear as bullets began to spray across the highway median. The worst part is that Tawnie could hear the gunshots in the distance. Everyone around her stopped where they were, curious about the noise.

Tawnie could hardly breathe, and her chest became heavy. She glanced at the police officer, noticing he was just as concerned about the sound. Tawnie yelled for Abbie again, but seconds later, the call ended. She pulled the phone away, staring at it in horror. The police officer urged Tawnie to get inside the school again.

"Why the hell should I?" She asked.

"That's the safest place for you right now, ma'am." He responded. Tawnie grabbed Milo's hand and turned around to leave. But the man reached forward and yanked her back.

"Hey!" She screamed at him.

"Get off of my mommy!" Milo yelled. The kid stood in front of his mother and clenched his fists. The officer looked down at him with amusement. A smug grin crossed his lips for a moment. Milo lunged forward and punched him in the groin. With a grin of pride on Tawnie's face, she pulled Milo along as the man reeled in pain. Moving in the opposite direction, Tawnie walked against the crowd, away from the school. But before she made it an entire block away, she saw the same convoy of black vehicles driving through the city. She stopped walking and watched as they passed through the intersection before her. They started to take their routes, breaking their convoy. One vehicle turned at the intersection and traveled toward the school. Tawnie held her breath, watching it traverse about one hundred yards in and then stop. The vehicle's lights went out, adding to the suspicion.

"Mommy, who's that?" Milo asked. But Tawnie didn't answer. All she could do was stare in fear. Suddenly, she saw a man jump down from the large vehicle. She could hardly see anything but his silhouette from where she stood. But as he turned to face her, she could see the rifle he held in his arms.

"Oh shit!" She said as she turned to walk back toward the school again. The officer saw her returning and reached for the handcuffs on his belt. Tawnie shook her head as she hurried past him.

"Now is not the time for that," she said to him, jutting her head toward the armed vehicle. Tawnie ran into the school with her son, hoping it would keep them safe.

The interception of power by mankind is inevitable. For as long as the eleven Servines are bound to the Midworld, humanity will always be at risk of discovering something they never should.

-Excerpt of the Arcanin Prophecy; Translated by the Oracle

Chapter V

The following day in Washington, D.C., the President of the United States sat in the Oval Office of the White House. The halls just outside his door were chaotic and disorderly. He was joined by his vice president, Hawthorne McTierman, and chief of staff, Henry Waddell. The two men sat in wait as they watched a now angry Commander and Chief as he stared at the paperwork on his desk.

"How did this happen?" President Nathaniel Wesley asked, shooting up from his chair. He was out of his suit. His blazer was haphazardly thrown on the back of his chair. His tie was loosened, and his shirt was untucked in the front but not the back. His face burned red, and he clenched his jaw so tight that it looked as if he had a Charlie Horse on his face. His shirt was covered with sweat stains, and large bags sat underneath his puffy eyes. The president was usually a dashing man with a chiseled jaw and perfect teeth. His typically flawless, side-parted, black hair was messy and unkempt.

"Mr. President, there is no need to worry. This experiment was conducted to ensure our victory in the arms race." Hawthorne McTierman answered. His three-piece suit was still clean and sharp. He sat on a sofa perpendicular to the President's desk. Hawthorne was a Caucasian man with short, straight brown hair.

He was tall and also had a slender build. His skinny legs crossed as he side-eyed the president from his seat.

"Arms race? This implies we are going to war. What war are you referring to exactly?" Wesley asked.

McTierman cleared his throat, recognizing that his boss was still mid-thought. "Mr. President—"

"And who the hell authorized biochemical research?" The President cut him off.

McTierman sighed. "Sir, I assure you, this research was more a necessity for the growth of mankind."

The President stared intensely at Allan Waddell, angry and red, undoing his necktie. McTierman stared at a glass of scotch in his hand and pretended not to listen to the conversation.

"I don't give a shit about that, Hawk!" The President exploded, punching the surface of the desk. "Do you know how much damage has been done because of this issue? How many people's lives will change for the worse?"

McTierman nodded.

The President looked at his Chief of Staff. But the heavy-set man seemed to stare into the distance.

"Henry, you seem lost to all of this," Wesley stated.

But the grayed, elderly gentleman shook his head. "No, Sir," He said as he and McTierman made eye contact. "What are we talking about here? It's a potato-carving, rural city in the middle of nowhere. Anything that goes in disappears." The man was stocky; once an armed forces soldier, he still had his size. However, a bit short in stature, he was still intimidating. He had a short, squared haircut with black tones but primarily gray. He also had no facial hair. His sunken gray eyes moved over to the desk as he approached to review the paperwork. After scanning over it, he chuckled. The angered president waited for him to give more context.

"President Wesley, I am not particularly opposed to this idea," Waddell announced. The president scoffed.

"Not opposed? There are lives at stake here!" He yelled, stepping from behind the desk. "When I was elected, I promised to protect the people of the United States. I served this country for all my life, and I won't stop serving them now!"

McTierman smiled. "That was a good speech, Nate. But you

are missing the big picture."

The man raised an eyebrow as he looked at the two of them. "This isn't about your pride or your time in service. Your reputation here is protected as always."

The man snapped as he walked toward his Vice-President. The anger in his eyes forced Waddell to step in front of him.

"Hold up, Wes!" He yelled as he pushed on his shoulder. "You have to control your anger!"

"I'm sick of these back-handed reaches for power!" He yelled as he shoved his Chief of Staff out of his path. Hawthorne stood from his seat and tugged on the lapels of his blazer.

"Nate, you remember that those same back-handed reaches got you here in the first place, right?"

The president grunted and punched the air before him. He looked away, running his hands through his hair. Waddell and McTierman looked at one another. Their eyes alone seem to have an entire conversation.

Waddell almost seemed uncomfortable as he looked at the vice president. But the man nodded at him with a grin.

He cleared his throat and nodded back as he shut his eyes.

"Mr. President, Sir." He called. "This isn't happening to put the American people at risk. We never intended to get here in the first place."

Wesley spun around and faced him. "So what?" He roared. "What's the end game here? You are seriously about to quarantine these people in their homes?"

"It's a temporary solution, Sir." He answered as he stepped backward. "Primotech is currently working to fix the issue now."

The president shook his head, attempting to make the connection independently. The room got quiet. Waddell looked back at Vice-President McTierman. His arms were crossed, and he was staring at the president.

"What the hell does Primotech have to do with a bio-engineering accident?" He asked.

"Good question, sir," Waddell answered. "Jacob Maxwell has discovered the flaws in the testing and his company –"

"Jacob Maxwell?" Wesley cut him off. "Son of Corbin Maxwell? The twenty-four-year-old kid running a multi-billion dollar company, Jacob Maxwell?"

"Yes, sir," Waddell answered. "He is our point of contact for this issue."

"The Legendary Playboy made another mistake that the American People have to clean up."

Waddell's head fell as he stared at the floor.

"Look, Wesley," Hawthorne interrupted. "No matter how pissed you are, this situation is happening and needs to be rectified before it gets worse." The president threw his arms up and walked behind his desk.

"Tell me, how could this get any worse?" He asked as he spun his chair around to take a seat. Hawthorne approached the desk, putting his knuckles down on the surface as he looked at Wesley. A grin appeared on his face as the president leaned forward in anticipation.

"If we are not granted the resources to respond to this situation, everyone on the planet becomes a target. The biochemical agent known as Kaitricodex will spread until we meet our demise."

"Kaitricodex?" He asked for clarification. "What the hell is that?"

"Mr. President, this research has allowed Primotech to build a device that can scan life energy," Waddell explained. "They call this energy Kaitrons."

"And what is Codex?" He asked. "Is this all some kind of development for a weapon?"

McTierman shook his head. "The Codex is the act of manipulating the cells that produce energy in the body. We are dealing with the Codex Virus, an unintentional byproduct of the current research."

Suddenly, there was a knock on the door.

"Mr. President, Sir?" A Secret Serviceman said as he opened the door, allowing the noise pollution to seep inside. "You have a Jacob Maxwell here for you."

Angered all over again, he looked back at his Chief of Staff. Waddell turned to the door. "Let him in, Baxter." He answered the man. President Wesley stood from his seat and stared out into the hall. The agent disappeared outside, and a dapper young man entered with a costly designer suit. He raised his hands to run through his short, brown hair. The President clenched his jaw, just watching him enter the room. His pasty white skin reflected the pale light as he walked toward the President's desk. McTierman and Waddell both stepped aside and allowed him to approach.

"Mr. President, I am at your service." He said as he extended his hand across the desk. President Wesley stared at it, then looked up at Maxwell.

"Hmph." Was all he could say as he sat in his chair again. "You made sure you were the only service available here as well. Didn't you, kid?"

Maxwell turned his head to the side as the remark generated a smile due to discomfort. After realizing the stoic look on the President's face, he pulled his hand back and placed it in his pocket.

"Mr. President," said Waddell. "Jacob Maxwell is here to give us our options on resolving the current issue in Idaho."

The President leaned back in his seat. His elbows were on the armrests, and his fingertips pressed together before him.

"I'm listening." The man said to Maxwell. The young man looked at both Waddell and McTierman before clearing his throat.

"Yes, uh…" He paused. His usually deep voice trembling under the weight of the pressure. "About that, uh."

McTierman began to look annoyed as he side-eyed the young man. "What now?"

"So you guys may want to sit for this one, too," Jacob said as he looked back at the door. "There's been a new development in this case."

Chapter VI

Back in Idaho, Tawnie awakened on the gymnasium floor, full of people. Daylight shone in from the high windows at the top of the room, but the sky looked cloudy and gray. She held Milo, who had been in her lap throughout the night. They could see everyone moving around the room as they opened their eyes. Tawnie motioned for Milo to get up, and the two stood.

"You okay, Spud?" she asked as she rested her hand on his head. He nodded as he looked up at her. Fear sent chills through his tiny body.

"I'm hungry." He answered.

"Yeah, me too." Tawnie smiled as she began to pull him across the gym floor. People still seemed riled up and afraid. They were moving fast, but nobody seemed to be leaving. There was a lot of hostility and panic in the atmosphere. Tawnie reached the entrance to the gym and slammed her body against the door. She attempted to open it, but a man stood on the opposite side, pushing it closed. A large window allowed her to see outside into the hallway. A team of unknown soldiers stood outside, keeping everyone inside. Tawnie was able to see their uniforms. They were wearing all black. An unknown crest was embroidered on the shoulders. The men held rifles, all modified with buttons and switches. White light pulsated from the barrels, giving off an ominous glow throughout the hall.

"Who the hell are they?" One civilian asked.

"Why are they even here?" asked another.

"Maybe it's the army." suggested someone.

But Tawnie knew that these people weren't government

soldiers. She noticed the armor the men were wearing. She had never seen anything like it. Their chest plates were glossy. In the center of the pectoral section was a control panel. They sported an armored spine on the suit made with what looked like hundreds of metal pieces. On their heads, they wore what looked like motorcycle helmets from the back. But the face was like a gas mask with two large evil-looking lenses that covered their eyes. A respirator sat on their cheeks with a tube that swooped to the side of the helmets, underneath their ears. The respirator glowed with the same light as the rifles in their hands. The technology was unlike anything Tawnie had ever seen.

She reached to pick Milo up. The soldier in front of the door had his back turned, and she kicked it open, temporarily knocking the men out of the way. They all turned toward her.

"Well," She said. "I wasn't expecting that to work."

Tawnie looked up at the men, hoping to see their faces. But their masks made it impossible. Their eyes were dark, and canister-like filters sat on their cheeks. A ring of blue light circled the end of their respirator canisters.

"Woah, you guys are geared up, aren't you?" Tawnie asked.

"Ma'am, we need you to stay in the gymnasium," one man said in a voice that sounded like it was coming through a speaker. Tawnie raised an eyebrow and looked around the hallway again. She realized that other soldiers continued to shove civilians into the building.

"Ma'am, get back inside now!" He yelled at her. Milo responded by burying his head in his mother's neck. Her hair covered him momentarily. As she stepped back into the room, she saw Abbie enter the building. She recognized her as the men began to shut the door.

"Wait," she blurted. Abbie!" The blond looked toward the gymnasium, shocked to hear her name being called. Once she locked eyes with Tawnie, she ran for her.

"Hey!" The soldiers barked. One man grabbed her by the arm, throwing her against the lockers. Tawnie yelled as she stepped into the hallway, hoping to intervene.

"Get off of her!" She roared. But the soldiers at the door pointed their long, glowing rifle barrels at her.

"What the hell?" She said as she grabbed the barrel of one rifle with her free hand and shoved it away. Another soldier, holding a small device in his hand, approached Abbie. The item looked like a phone or a small computer. It made a strange, eerie sound as he pressed buttons on it.

"Hey, what is that?" Abbie asked. She flailed and jerked to get away from the man. But the more she did, the tighter he squeezed. "Let me go!"

"She's good." The soldier with the electronic device said as he held a thumb up. The strange device beeped, and a green light appeared at the top of it.

Just down the hall, another soldier scanned another man using the same device. But this time, the device made a different sound. Tawnie watched the interaction as Abbie struggled again to break the man's grip on her. The civilian pleaded for the soldier to allow him through. His family cried for him as they were pushed through the hall. He attempted to get to his wife and his two little children, but the soldiers continued to drive a wedge between them. A red light gleamed at the top of the device, and the masked soldier yelled for his comrades. "I got one!" He yelled. His wife tried to go back for him, but the chaos grew louder by the second, pushing them away.

"Ma'am, get into the gym before you lose your life!" A soldier yelled as he shoved her toward Tawnie at the door. "Honey!" Her husband began to panic. "Honey, it's going to be alright!" The kids started to screech as they saw their father get shoved in the opposite direction. The man continued to fight them, but a soldier raised the barrel of his glowing gun and pointed it at the man's head. The light in the barrel changed from blue to red, and the gun went off. A vicious red laser left the barrel and hit the man in the chest. His terrorized screams transitioned into a dying, agonizing medley of sounds that made Tawnie sick to her stomach.

The man let her friend go, and she paused against the locker, feeling violated. Abbie looked down at her arm, seeing a bruise on her right bicep. The gatekeepers at the gymnasium still didn't allow Tawnie to come out, so she called for Abbie again. She slowly walked to the door, holding herself timidly and looking around at the soldiers.

"Abbie, come on!" Tawnie yelled again. The woman started moving a little faster to get to the gym. Tears rolled down her face as she stepped through the threshold and ran to Tawnie. The doors closed behind them as they hugged. Milo threw his arm out to tap Abbie on the head. She pulled away to find the little boy gasping for air.

"Dammit." She muttered as she reached for her eyes and wiped her tears away. "I'm sorry, Milo."

"Abbie, what the fuck is going on out there?" Tawnie asked as she put her son down.

The woman shook her head. Her blond hair whipped out of the hairpins she wore on top of her head.

"Mrs. Simms, I don't know what's going on." She cried out. "These guys invaded the city and are rounding up civilians into random spots."

Tawnie tilted her head to the side as she stared at her colleague. "I guess that's not too far-fetched," she responded. "What about the gunshots I heard over the phone?"

Abbie covered her mouth with clasped hands as tears rolled down her face again.

"You always tell us to visualize the outcome, Mrs. Simms," she cried. "But I didn't see this coming."

Tawnie reached for her hand. "It's okay." The woman pulled away.

"It's not!" She shrieked. "It was so much death...so much blood."

Tawnie walked Abbie to the bleachers, finding a place to rest for a moment. Abbie stared at the floor, attempting to regain her bearings. Milo looked up at his mom, seeing the look of worry on her face. The two women sat silently, allowing her to calm down. The room was loud and full of chatter. Milo could hear all sorts of scary things listening to the other civilians.

"Jesus has returned, and we're all going to hell for our sins." An older woman claimed, not far from them.

"Maybe this is a sign of war!" another person said. The constant negativity caused the boy to latch onto his mother's leg. He squeezed against her thigh for comfort, and she rubbed the top of his fluffy mane.

"We're all going to die." Abbie cried out. Tawnie reached for her hand on her lap and gently squeezed it.

"Mommy, I don't want to die!" Milo yelled, causing others to look in their direction. Tawnie rubbed her son's back with one hand and shook Abbie's arm with the other.

"Nobody's dying today!" Tawnie growled. "You two cut it out."

Abbie sniffled and wiped her face. She shook her wild, curly hair and ran her fingers through her scalp.

"Abbie, what did you see on the way here?" Tawnie asked.

The woman sighed deeply before saying anything. "This group has set up boundary lines out there," Abbie answered. "It almost looked like they were setting up concentration camps."

Tawnie looked away, nodding and muttering something.

"What about the tech?" She asked. Abbie winced with confusion.

"The weapons and that weird gadget they scanned you with."

Abbie shook her head, "I have no clue what that was. But on the way, I saw it being used a lot. Every situation was similar to what happened in the hallway just now."

"What the hell?" Tawnie scoffed. "What could they be looking for is the real question."

Abbie looked back at the entrance of the gym. Again, people started to flood inside.

"Why are they still stuffing people in here?" She asked.

Still stuck on the big picture, Tawnie paused and stared into the distance. Abbie sighed and turned to her.

"Is this the thing you saw coming?" She asked Tawnie. "The event that is going to—"

"Abigail!" Tawnie barked as she pointed at Milo. She looked down to find the boy staring at her in wonder.

Abbie turned forward as her mouth clicked. "I'm sorry." She said. "Between the new Warrior of Justice, you told us about and the catastrophe that… you know."

Tawnie nodded her head. "Let's not jump to conclusions.

Suddenly, Tawnie cried out as she reached for her head. A throbbing pain had returned.

"Mommy!" Milo yelled as he stood up and hugged her free arm.

"Mrs. Simms?" Abbie yelled. "Are you okay?"

Tawnie nodded. "Do you have your medicine?"

Tawnie started to shake her head as she allowed her arms to

fall. Tears streamed down her face as she stared up at the ceiling to wait out the pain.

Abbie continued as she reached for Tawnie's hand. "It seems to be getting worse."

"It is." She whined in response. "Because of that, I had to stop the meds. Feels like a thousand blades tearing at my scalp."

Abbie's mouth fell open as she stared at her friend.

"What the hell?" she began to ask. But Tawnie jumped to her feet and ignored her. She patted Milo's head and looked down at Abbie.

"Can you watch him while I go to the restroom?" Tawnie asked. Nervous about her abrupt urge to leave the conversation, Abbie nodded. She grabbed the boy's hand, tugged him toward her, and wrapped him in her arms. The two watched as Tawnie worked toward the restrooms at the back of the gymnasium.

Chapter VII

Tawnie walked across a crowded basketball court and looked back at her son and assistant. They watched her, seeming nervous about the situation. But momentarily, her feet seemed to move differently than she intended. Tawnie's grogginess caused her to slip and fall to a knee in the middle of the monotony of the chaos.

"Dr. Simms?" Abbie gasped.

"Mommy!" Milo screamed. Strangers approached to help her from the ground, but the woman snapped, causing everyone to step back. The sudden quiet shook the crowd as they stared and began their sidebar conversations, speculating what may be wrong with her. Abbie headed to her boss, but Tawnie was back on her feet when she reached her side. Still holding her head, she let her hands drop and watched Abbie approach.

"Dr. Simms, you okay?" Abbie asked.

"Yeah, I had to stop those meds, though. I think they were messing with my brain." Tawnie responded. Abbie's eyes widened, and her mouth opened slightly. Milo buried his head into Abbie's neck to hide his face.

"Hey Spud, I'm okay, I promise," Tawnie said as she grabbed his hand. "I just need to go to the restroom for a moment."

Abbie stepped backward, and Milo snatched his hand away from her. Tawnie took one look at the concern on Abbie's face and gasped. Her neck bobbed as her mouth opened to ask a question she dreaded.

"Did I do it again?"

Abbie simply nodded as she swayed to calm Milo. Tawnie glanced at her son and cursed herself for a moment. She rattled her head and sighed. Her shoulders relaxed, and her chin lifted. Her eyes closed for a moment,

"Today's date is February 14th, 2079. Nathaniel Wesley is the current president." Tawnie lowered her eyes at Abbie, who looked at her with pity. She turned away and headed into the crowd.

"Do you want to talk about it?" Abbie yelled. Tawnie stopped walking, shifting her hip as if she was going to turn around. But she shook her head and proceeded to the restroom.

She reached the restroom threshold and looked around for any other visitors. The bathroom was in shambles. There was trash everywhere, and water covered the entire floor. The putrid smell of old urine was enough to make her gag. As she approached one of the sinks, Tawnie took a deep breath, trying not to get sick due to the scent and her excruciating headache. She rested her hands on the cold porcelain and hung her head. Looking up at herself, she noticed a glimpse of light on the wall behind one of the stalls. Suspiciously, she scanned every stall in the mirror, seeing that all were open except for one. The last stall in the back of the restroom was the only one with a closed door.

"Is someone there?" Tawnie asked aloud. But nobody answered. She turned around and looked for feet underneath the stall opening. There was no obvious sign of anyone, but she felt something.

She turned the water on and splashed a handful into her face. She raised her hand to her head, feeling her elevated pulse at her temples, then again as her hand slid to her neck.

"What the fuck?" She asked herself, wincing due to the pain. Until she heard a tapping sound behind her. Again, she looked, but still, she didn't see anyone.

"Hello?" She called out. Again, there was no answer. Tawnie turned the faucet off and shook her hands dry. She looked at the wall at the paper towel dispenser. It was empty.

"Figures." She said as she shook her hands again. Cautious, Tawnie walked to the end of the restroom. Her eyes locked on the space underneath the stall dividers. She stopped in front of the door and raised her hand to knock. Another flash of light filled the stall as she readied her fist to slam into the door.

"Leave me alone!" She heard a woman scream. Tawnie jumped backward.

"Yeah, I should have seen that coming!" She said.

The woman began to sniffle. "Stay away from me… please."

Again, Tawnie sighed as she took a step back.

"You got it." She responded. "Anything I can do to help?"

There was a brief silence. Tawnie looked to the entrance, wondering if anyone heard the scream.

"It's too late to help me."

She looked back at the door to the stall, wishing the woman would come out.

"Is there anyone I can get for you, at least?"

"No!" The woman yelled. "I just want to be left alone!"

Tawnie walked away and leaned against the wall across from the door. She sighed as she considered everything she could say.

"You know, I don't want to assume anything, but you sound young," Tawnie said. "You're what, sixteen or seventeen years old?"

Another flicker of light followed a few sniffles.

"I'm seventeen." She answered. "How did you know?"

Tawnie smiled. "There was a certain inflection in your voice. It made it easy to tell you were still a minor."

The girl got quiet. Tawnie could hear her rummaging around in the stall.

"What's your name, miss?" Tawnie asked. Hesitant to answer right away, the girl stayed quiet.

"That would be you, Stall Girl." She pestered. "What is your name?"

The slide lock on the stall was undone and slowly pulled open. Tawnie looked at a gorgeous young woman who was even shorter than her at about five-foot-one. Her blue eyes were puffy and red from crying. Her long hair was dark and straight. She had a fair complexion that showed the blushing on her face, arms, and chest. Tawnie examined her from her feet up and noticed her arms and hands were charred. Apathetic, she looked away momentarily after seeing her damage.

"Well, Kid, looks like you had one hell of a morning," Tawnie told her.

The girl's head fell, and she began to focus on her charred hands. Tawnie watched her for a moment in silence. She quickly ran to a sink and vigorously washed her arms and hands. There was hardly anything she could do to get them cleaned. The blackness on her hands did not come off.

"You mind telling me how that happened, sweetie?" Tawnie asked as she crossed her arms. Instead of answering, she started crying again. She continued smashing her hand against the soap dispenser and lathering herself. Tawnie noticed that the soap was not tainted with debris at all. She stepped closer to the woman, verifying that she wasn't getting clean.

"Hey, I think you can…" Tawnie started, placing her hand on the girl's shoulder. But she didn't stop as she continued to sob.

"You need to stop!" Tawnie screamed as she pulled the woman away from the sink. Still, the girl only stared at her hands as her back slammed against the stall dividers.

"Please!" She cried. "Make it stop!"

"I know it hurts," Tawnie said as she placed her palm in the center of her chest. "But nobody can stop that but you. Breathe with me."

Tawnie started taking deep breaths, looking the girl in the eyes. After a few long breaths, she finally joined. The two of them breathed in unison for about thirty seconds.

"What's your name?" Tawnie asked again.

The girl nodded, "Lydia she answered as she continued her deep breathing.

"Lydia, huh?" Tawnie reached to scratch her chin. "And I suppose you have a light burning inside of you."

The girl's eyes grew wide in horror.

"No, no, no! I'm not judging you at all! Don't worry!" Tawnie said. "I was obviously sent here for a purpose."

Again, the girl looked afraid. "Did someone send you here to arrest me?"

Tawnie smiled and shook her head with a smile. "My name is Tawnie Simms. I'm just here to help."

The teen stared at the woman before her.

"Wait, are you The Oracle?" She asked. Humbly, Tawnie nodded. "I am."

The young girl gasped and grappled her mouth with her palm as she stepped backward. Tawnie watched her as she attempted not to panic.

"Oh my god!" The girl shrieked. "You're famous. How are

you even here?"

Tawnie's head tilted to the side as she stared.

"Ms. Oracle, I'm so sorry I didn't recognize you." The girl said, clasping her hands in front of her face. "I thought you seemed familiar, but–"

"We're all good, Lydia." She responded. "I just want to make sure you're okay right now. Is there anything I can do for you?"

Lydia relaxed and looked away for a moment.

"Maybe I can go find your family?"

Lydia sighed. Suddenly, the young woman seemed to be saddened.

"I don't have a family anymore." She responded.

Tawnie raised an eyebrow. "Did something happen to them during the explosion yesterday?"

Tears began to fall from her eyes as she shook her head.

"No, they—" she hesitated. Lydia raised her hands, looking at them with sadness in her eyes. Tawnie approached her, touching her arm for comfort. "They don't want anything to do with me," she said.

Tawnie allowed the girl to sulk for a moment as she watched her.

"This situation is rough. I'm sorry you have to go through this—alone especially," she said, guiding the girl back to the sink. "But the bright side is that soon enough, the world will accept everything that you are."

The girl looked at her, baffled. "How could you possibly know that?" She asked.

"Because the world discards things it fears and doesn't understand. But it is difficult to discard something that is helping."

The girl stepped away, folding her arms. "You don't even know me!"

"Yeah," Tawnie said. "I don't. But I know you were hiding here to keep from hurting others." Lydia slowly turned, looking over her shoulder at the woman before turning to face her fully. "I know that despite how much you hate your powers, you wish you could have used them to save those people yesterday."

Lydia's head fell as she stared at the floor.

"Hmm." She grunted. "How do you know that?"

Tawnie's mouth clicked as she stepped to the sink and looked in the mirror at herself.

"I used to be a psychiatrist," she answered as she started to flip her hair. "I just happen to be really good at my job."

Tawnie took a moment to fix herself up, remembering why she entered the restroom. She looked herself in the eyes, realizing the pain had subsided. She turned to face the door.

"Wait!" Lydia yelled. Tawnie stopped. She turned her head slightly and waited for the young girl to continue.

"Thank you." She said.

"You are only as big as your biggest problem, Lydia," Tawnie announced. "Once you understand that you are all you need to succeed, you will overcome anything."

Tawnie continued to the door.

"Wait, can I help you find out what happened?" she asked, but Tawnie continued walking.

"We will meet again, don't worry," she responded as she waved to the young girl.

Tawnie left the restroom and entered the crowd to return to her son and assistant. Somehow, the crowd appeared to be even more riled up than before. She scanned the bleachers before her, forgetting where she left Abbie and Milo. Milo spotted her first, pointing when he found her walking through the crowd. Abbie smiled when she saw her.

"Dr. Simms!" She yelled as she stood to wave. Tawnie spotted them and made her way up the stairs that divided the bleachers into sections. People ran up and down, seemingly in a panic. All the small woman could do was brace herself as they shoved her to get past. Tawnie clasped her hand on the support rail in the center of the steps to keep herself upright. Foot traffic was so jammed on the bleachers that people even jumped the benches to get down. After several minutes of getting shoved around, she finally reached her group's row.

"What the hell?" She asked aloud as she moved toward them. Excited for her return, Milo ran to her and grabbed the woman's leg. His face buried into her hip, and he hugged her with joy.

"What the hell is wrong with these people?" She asked. Suddenly, Abbie looked away.

"Abbie, you have that look again." She said.

"What look?" Abbie asked. "I always look like this when I'm

in a high school surrounded by mercenaries!"

Tawnie shook her head quickly. "Mommy, what's a mercenary?" Milo asked. Tawnie held her finger up to him as she shook her head.

"Abbie, what the fuck?" She asked.

"Dr. Simms, those men out there are here to kill us all!"

Tawnie looked down at the gymnasium entrance. A man stood in the viewing glass of the door, peering inside. To Abbie's point, Tawnie could see the man press a button on a communicator to speak into it. Without a doubt, Tawnie sensed the danger and looked down at her son in fear.

Chapter VIII

Tawnie felt nauseous, staring at the entrance to the gymnasium. The man outside the door was preparing to rush in.

"Dr. Simms!" Abbie cried out, taking her attention away from the door. "What are we going to do?"

Tawnie clenched her jaw and fist as she looked around. She looked for exit signs or alternative routes from where she sat. But only found one emergency exit sign at the back of the room. Atop the bleachers were large windows that everyone seemed to crowd around. Tawnie pushed Milo back to Abbie.

"I'm gonna go check this out." She said as she stood and headed for the center stairs.

"Mommy!" Milo called out.

"It's okay, Spud!" She responded. "I'll be right back!"

She headed toward the window, trying not to be mauled by the civilians moving around. Despite going against the crowd heading down the steps, she reached the top and had a full view out the window.

"What the fuck?" She asked as she gazed out into Idaho Falls. Black, military-like vehicles covered the nearby streets. Armored men with illuminated guns marched around the school, still rounding up civilians. There was a tent base nearby that she could see men taking civilians there as well. A sense of doom swept over. Her mouth became wet as the nausea returned. Cold sweat excreted the pores of her forehead as she could do nothing but watch. She could see black smoke rising into the sky in the distance. But glancing at the local firehouse proved that no first responders were coming. Tawnie turned around. A few rows down, she recognized a man in a dark blue t-shirt sitting and watching the chaos. Tawnie slipped down the stairs again and entered the row where the stranger sat. As she got closer, she recognized the fire department crest on the breast of the shirt. The word, volunteer on the back.

Tawnie sat beside him, tapping his shoulder before asking him a question. The man looked at her with a defeatist demeanor. His shoulders slumped, and his head hung low.

"Excuse me." She said, "The world is literally burning. What are you doing here?"

"I know." He cut her off. "But these men showed up and started throwing everybody inside the school."

Tawnie ran her hand over her head, taking a moment to think. She looked around again and saw police officers in the gym as well.

"All these first responders are in here, too?" She asked. "Is this not a crisis?"

"I'd say so." The firefighter answered. "But there's some top secret, Area 51-type crap going on here. All because of that explosion yesterday."

"Area 51, huh?" Tawnie asked. She stood up, looking down at the man with a grin. "Thank you so much, Sir." She said as she returned to her friend and son. By this time, an older woman, appearing to be around seventy years old, with dark skin and curly gray hair, sat nearby. She fanned herself with a thin pamphlet. Tawnie assumed she pulled it from the gigantic, black leather purse she held on her arm. A glance at Abbie made the young woman uncomfortable as she held onto Milo. Tawnie sat next to them, looking around at everyone. The woman had people with her who appeared to be her family. She looked at Tawnie. The woman stopped fanning and tilted her head downward to peer at her over her glasses.

"You alright, sweetheart?" The woman asked with a grimace.

"Yeah, so far so good." Answered Tawnie as she looked over to Milo.

"I asked you that because it's rude to insert yourself into folk's conversation without introducing yourself." The woman clarified. Tawnie took a deep breath.

"Yeah, yes, ma'am," Tawnie said with a smile as she shifted in her seat to make herself comfortable. "My name is Tawnie, and this is my best friend, Abigail, and my son, Milo."

The woman's eyes grew. "Lord, that baby yours?"

Tawnie nodded. "Yes, ma'am."

The woman burst into hysterical laughter. "Honey, I thought that was your son!" The woman pointed at Abbie.

"Yeah, I see," Abbie said, sinking into her seat.

"Wait," The woman disrupted the conversation. All the laughter stopped, and all attention was on her. "Y'all not some sort of lesbians, are you?"

Tawnie and Abbie both looked at one another in horror.

"Mommy, what's a lesbian?" Milo asked.

"Not now, spud." His mom answered as she shook off the disbelief of the woman's question.

"What does that even mean?" Tawnie asked. The older woman raised an eyebrow as she stared at Tawnie. "And what exactly would it change if we were a lesbian couple?"

"Oh, Lord Jesus." She said as she buried her face in her palm. The two women who were with the elder turned their attention to Tawnie.

"Who she think she talking to like that?" One woman asked another as they both stood.

"Will y'all sit down?" The woman said to them. They looked at one another again, then back at Tawnie as they slowly took their seats. "Don't cause a scene in here in front of all these white folk!"

Appalled, Tawnie and Abbie closed their eyes, turned their heads, and took a deep breath.

"Ma'am, don't you think our current situation is critical enough without involving racism?" Tawnie asked. "There are people of all colors in here."

The woman paused again, raising an eyebrow as she stared at her.

"You know what? You are absolutely right, young lady." She responded as she continued to fan herself and rock from side to side. Tawnie looked at Abbie, preparing to speak.

"No matter what happens here, God will protect us," the woman interrupted as she smiled at Milo. "He will always lay his hand over us and protect us from evil."

"Hey!" Tawnie yelled at the woman as she jumped to her feet. The two women with the old lady did the same, staring at Tawnie.

"Who this lil' bitch think she is?" One of the women said as she clenched her fists.

"I know you don't think you gone yell at my momma like that!" said the other.

"Keep your God away from my kid!" Tawnie snarled.

"You don't know God, Sweetheart?" The woman asked. "No wonder you so rude! Do you not have faith?"

"Plenty of it," Tawnie responded, crossing her arms. "I don't have any trouble teaching that to my kid. But you need to keep that manufactured religious stuff to yourself!"

"That's it!" One of the woman's daughters said as she stepped up the bleachers.

"Dr. Simms!" Abbie called out.

"Eh!" The old lady yelled at her daughter as she blocked her with her arm. "So doctors really do think they are above the Lord's will."

The woman stood up, staring at Tawnie. "You think that because you went to medical school, you don't have to follow the good book?"

Tawnie chuckled and shook her head as she placed her hands on her hips. "PhD, not MD. I operate on the mind, not the body."

The old lady's eyes bulged. "Well, excuse me!" She said. "I can't even–"

Tawnie held up a finger, interrupting the woman. "This conversation will solve nothing." She assured the woman. "Right now, there are men outside about to kill all of us in this gymnasium. The best part of it, your God isn't here to protect you! I am!"

People nearby turned to look at the group, intrigued by the commotion.

"What did she just say?" She heard a man ask nearby.

"Is that the Oracle?" A woman asked. Tawnie looked around at everyone, noticing that she had the crowd's attention. She stepped up onto the bench and whistled.

"Alright, ladies and gentlemen, listen up!" She yelled. "We are in danger!"

"Dr. Simms, I have a bad feeling about this!" Abbie yelled up to her.

Tawnie looked down at the gymnasium door and saw the masked soldier staring in her direction. She reached for her assistant's shoulder and squeezed it tight.

"Ladies and gentlemen, I apologize, but I have bad news!" She said. "Outside right now are soldiers who appear to be here to slaughter us all!"

The crowd began to mock her. Fortunately, there were individuals in attendance who recognized her. They attempted to share her ideologies but couldn't seem to sway the scared citizens.

"Hey, listen!" Tawnie tried to yell over them, but it was no use. As the crowd grew rowdy, the gymnasium doors swung open. Her mouth opened, and she felt her body numb as she stared.

"Dr. Simms, we have to go!" Abbie yelled as she pulled her down from the bench seat. Men entered the room with their guns drawn, holding down their triggers. The sound of the guns was horrifying. The low frequency of the blast could be felt from every round shot. A streaming laser sound followed the booms. Holding Milo in her arms, Abbie pulled Tawnie along as she bolted through the crowd. Many were confused, unsure whether they should duck for cover or flee. But no matter where they went, soldiers flooded in from every angle. Down on the floor was a squad blasting flames and a second group shooting their rifles. The wave started to sweep through the bleachers, killing everyone without question.

Tawnie and Abbie found a small access hatch at the top of the bleachers that sat against the wall. Abbie opened it and saw a ladder going down to the floor. She stayed up, allowing Tawnie to start her descent. She grabbed Milo and carefully attached him to Tawnie's back. The boy cried out, fearful of the chaos.

"Milo, grab hold!" Tawnie screamed. He did as he was told, grappling her neck and wrapping his legs around her waist. Tawnie flowed down the ladder first. Abbie followed behind, closing the hatch as she descended. They reached the floor, and Tawnie ran to the side, allowing Abbie to come down. She placed Milo on the ground and looked around. She could see the massive mechanism used to control the extension of the bleachers.

"Dr. Simms, we could hide here!" Abbie suggested as she looked around as well.

"Absolutely not!" She yelled. "We're sitting ducks here, Abbie! We need to get out of here."

Meanwhile, Milo whaled as he clutched his mom's leg.

"Hey, Spud." She attempted to call him. But he would continue to scream. "Spud, snap out of it!" She yelled. Still, nothing. Finally, she slammed her fist into the boy's head, forcing him to stop and look up.

"Milo!" she screamed again, causing him to flinch. He looked up at her, realizing she was angry as she kneeled to speak with him.

"Alright, love, you need to be strong for Momma, okay?" She asked him. Instinctively, he nodded. "I need you to be a big boy and stop crying, got it!" She asked. Again, he nodded. The crowd continued to stampede above as the tortured screams caused them pain in the ears. There was so much fire that they could see the flames coming through the slats of the bleachers. The wood began to catch fire before them. Tawnie noticed the weakening structural integrity. She saw a door behind the bleachers that looked like an exit and pointed her friend to it. Abbie reached for the door knob. She opened it, and Tawnie noticed a hallway on the opposite side. It was the main hall. She poked her head out and checked for soldiers but saw none.

"The coast seems clear," Tawnie said. "I'll go first." She said as she ran out into the hall.

"Mommy!" Milo screamed. Abbie put her hand over his mouth to muzzle him. Tawnie looked back at him with horror in her face. Suddenly, someone shot another round at her. A blueish ball of energy blazed as it flew past.

"Whoa!" She screamed as she ran back into the room and closed the door. She looked at Abbie wide-eyed as she leaned against the metal entryway.

"This is not going to end well."

Chapter IX

The bleachers set ablaze behind them as they tried to make space between themselves and the door. The screams of the civilians had started to die down as Tawnie could only assume they were all dead. Soldiers slammed against the metal door, attempting to break inside the storage room. In addition, the room started to fill with smoke, and breathing became difficult.

"What do we do now?" Abbie asked. "We're trapped!"

"Abbie, stay calm!" Tawnie urged as she guided her and Milo toward the wall.

"I'm going to have to ambush this man when he comes in." She announced.

"What? Are you insane?" Abbie asked as she grabbed for her boss's arm.

Tawnie gave her a cold look. "Do you happen to have a plan, Abbie?"

The young woman paused and released Tawnie's arm. The soldier slammed against the door again, and Tawnie prepared for a fight. As she timed the subsequent impact, she opened the door before it could stop his momentum. The soldier stumbled inside. Tawnie took advantage of this and punched the man in the face, causing his mask to fall off. There was a brief hesitation as the man felt for his head and realized he was no longer protected. His eyes bulged as his fingers swept across his brown facial hair. It was as if he was introduced to air on a new planet and unsure if he could breathe. Tawnie became intrigued at his reaction. She noticed an oxygen tank on his belt and some other intriguing objects. But she didn't have time to investigate. More soldiers stood outside the door, waiting for their battle buddy to get his bearings. But Tawnie attacked while he was distracted with his mask.

"Freeze!" The soldier outside growled as he pointed his weapon at them. He placed his finger on the trigger, but it was too close of a shot to guess.

"Fuck!" He yelled as he brought his rifle down. "Get in there!" The man yelled at the other soldiers in the hallway. They pointed their barrels at the door and started to run inside. Tawnie's heart began to race as she continued roughhousing with the soldier. She caught glimpses of the others, but suddenly, a bright flash of light swept the wall. In the blink of an eye, all of them were gone. Tawnie took the opportunity to give one last strike to the man's neck with her elbow. With a fading grumble, the man went down. She looked at Abbie, whose eyes were wide with fear.

"What just happened?" She asked Tawnie. She stood up after grabbing the man's rifle, watching the door. She looked at Abbie and smirked.

"I don't like that look," Abbie commented as she observed her.

"Lydia, is that you?" Tawnie called out. There was a shuffling in the hallway as someone approached the door. The young girl popped her head into the threshold and smiled at her.

"Oh, perfect," Tawnie said as she approached Milo. She grasped his shoulder in her hand and moved him to the door. She looked back at the burning bleachers as they began to collapse. "We get the hell out of here, and you get to meet our next rising star, Abbie!"

Tawnie and Milo stepped past Lydia while the young girl stared at Abbie.

"Hi." She awkwardly said to Tawnie's assistant as she approached. With a bewildered expression, Abbie's mouth clicked.

"Uh, Dr. Simms?" Abbie called. "What the hell was that?"

Tawnie looked around, checking for an exit. After a moment of silence between them, she turned to look at her assistant.

"Abbie, meet Lydia, your next trainee," Tawnie announced.

Her eyes grew large as she stared at her boss in wonder. Lydia also held her mouth open in disbelief.

"Dr. Simms, I can't…" Abbie began to say. But Tawnie

squared her shoulders and raised her chin as she spun around to stare at the woman.

"I mean, I haven't prepared for this yet." She recoiled.

"Abbie, life is unpredictable. You'll get taken by the best if you aren't prepared for the worst," Tawnie said, relaxed and smiling.

Abbie and Lydia locked eyes. The woman introduced herself to the teen, extending her hand.

"Now, was that so hard, ladies?" Tawnie asked.

"No, but," Abbie continued. "Is she a..?"

"She is," Tawnie confirmed as she examined the rifle in her hand. Suddenly, she raised the barrel to them. Abbie could see her from the corner of her eyes. Just to confirm her fear, she turned for the sake of verification.

"No!" Abbie screamed. Tawnie took a shot directly at her assistant. A blast of light exited the barrel and went between the two women and down the hallway. A lone soldier approached, and the beam pierced his head. Blood immediately splattered on the wall behind him. Milo covered his eyes the entire time. Lydia seemed impressed by the shot. But Abbie was mortified.

"Dr. Simms?!" She screamed. But Tawnie was more impressed with the gun she just fired. "A little warning would have been nice!"

"Yeah, Abbie, hold on a sec?" Tawnie said as she approached her colleague, still examining the gun. Her inquisitive expression was cause for concern.

"What is it?" Abbie asked.

Tawnie shook her head slowly. "I'm not sure what I'm looking at here."

She handed the rifle to Abbie. The woman grabbed hold of it as Tawnie stepped back. Abbie's body dipped as she struggled to hold it up.

"Wow, you made this look easy!" She grunted. Lydia stepped in to help. Her eyes grew wide as she looked at Tawnie.

"What?" She asked them as she waved for her son to come closer. "I don't miss my workouts."

Abbie examined what she could, but her eyes grew large.

"Yeah, why does a rifle need that many electrical components?" Tawnie asked. "Or any at all?"

Abbie shook her head. "I don't really know."

"It also doesn't have bullets." Lydia pointed out as she placed her hand underneath the chassis. "There's no magazine here."

"Why do you know that? You're only seventeen." Tawnie asked.

The girl shrugged. "My father taught me many things he wished he could teach the son he never had."

Both Tawnie and Abbie stared at her, then at one another.

"Let's move on before she decides to clarify," Abbie suggested. Tawnie smiled and nodded as they looked back down at the gun.

"South wing, all clear." They heard someone say through a two-way communicator device. They all looked around at the bodies on the floor.

"North wing, all clear." Another said. Tawnie looked at Abbie in shock.

"West wing, good as dead."

Tawnie ran to a body and tugged on the shoulder to roll it over.

"Second platoon, do you copy?" A man asked. Tawnie frowned in disdain as she grabbed the radio from the man's chest.

"Copy that," She said, attempting to make her voice deeper. "East wing, all clear."

Immediately, Lydia yelped and bit her hand.

"What's your problem?" Tawnie asked her.

"All units report to the gymnasium, immediately!"

Tawnie held the radio away from her as she looked at Lydia, confused.

"This building doesn't have an east wing!" The girl squealed.

"Fuck! We gotta go!" Tawnie said as she picked up her son in one arm and carried the rifle in the other.

Abbie and Lydia stared at her in amazement as she headed for the exit. She turned and realized that nobody was behind her.

"What are you two doing?" She yelled. "Come on!"

They immediately stepped out of their stupor and jogged toward her. As they drew near, she turned to continue walking.

Suddenly, a crash in the distance sounded like someone kicking in a metal door. Tawnie turned to hand Milo off to Abbie. Her assistant grabbed the kid, looking at her boss with great discomfort. Tawnie was free to raise the rifle in the direction she heard the noise. Slowly, she made her way down the hall, looking for enemy soldiers. She walked past a set of locker rooms with a twisty hallway heading inside, no door. She briefly pointed the rifle into each threshold as she passed it by. But there was another noise behind her. She quickly turned to face the direction of the noise.

"Was that them?" Abbie asked.

"Shh!" Tawnie said as she walked toward the end of the hall. A set of double doors at the end led to another part of the school. Tawnie kept her eyes on it as she walked toward it. Light passed through the bottom of the threshold, which she used to see when someone moved in front of it. She looked back to Abbie and Lydia, holding up her fist to get them to hang back. Suddenly, there was a shadow. Tawnie prepared to squeeze the trigger and took a step backward.

The handle on the door was depressed and slowly opened. The steel hinges creaked. Tawnie stepped back into the men's locker room. Abbie and Lydia stowed away in the women's. Tawnie peaked around the corner to see a man's hand holding the door open by the fingertips. She stared at the ceiling to get her nerve as she prepared to shoot. The person entered the hallway, allowing the heavy door to shut behind him. They could all hear shallow footsteps in the quiet hall. Tawnie bit her bottom lip, anticipating the moment she needed to act.

Her body ran hot, and her muscles tensed.

"It's go time," she said to herself just before rushing out into the hallway, following the barrel of her weapon. She stepped out, blind, and put her finger on the trigger. She had no intention of seeing who it was, but something felt different.

"Hold!" A man screamed as he flailed to protect his face. "Don't shoot!"

Tawnie dropped the gun's muzzle to the floor, and her eyes sharpened.

"I'm not with them!" He said. That fact became evident when she noticed he was a cop. Instead of wearing black armor and a gas mask, he wore a black police uniform. Upon seeing that he was no longer in danger, he stopped flinching and stood straight.

"Hey, I know you!" She said as she stepped closer to him. Abbie and Lydia stepped out of the other restroom with Milo as well.

"You're that dickhead police officer that argued with me yesterday!" Tawnie snarled at the man. The officer nodded and continued to look behind him.

"What happened?" Abbie asked.

Tawnie pointed her middle finger in the man's face, "This dick threatened to arrest me because I asked him a question."

Abbie looked at him for a moment, processing what was going on. She reached for her face and rubbed her chin as she looked him in the eyes. "Yeah, you'd think he'd be more curious." She added. Tawnie tossed her hand up in relief.

"I'm glad you understand, Abbie!"

"Hey, listen!" He growled. "Those men are right behind me. We don't have time for this conversation!"

"Dammit, Dickhead, why didn't you say that before?"

"First platoon, in position." Someone said into the radio. Tawnie looked at the police officer and noticed that in addition to his police radio, he had one of theirs as well.

"Quick, answer for Second." Tawnie urged. Confused, he grabbed the radio from his chest and raised it to his mouth. He pressed the button and answered.

"Second platoon, in position."

The soldiers moved on, "Third platoon, ready to go."

"Fourth platoon, down for some action."

Tawnie held her breath, staring at the man, wondering if it worked. Things went silent for a moment. Suddenly, the radio beeped again.

"Second platoon, what is your access number?" The man asked.

"Shit!" The police officer barked. Tawnie shook off her worry and walked to another body and grabbed their gun.

"What are you doing?" The officer asked.

"You're going to need this." She said as she approached him, still staring into his cold, blue eyes.

"I don't want any dead dicks on my watch."

Chapter X

Tawnie handed the rifle to the policeman. He grabbed hold of it with the same fascination as she did earlier.

"Who the hell are these guys?" He asked as he examined the weapon.

"I would love to know that myself," she answered. "Unfortunately, we won't get the answer to that from here. We need to leave this building."

Everyone looked around the environment for a moment, planning their escape routes. Milo reached out to grab his mother's leg.

"Mommy, I'm scared." He whined. She looked down at him and placed her hand on his head.

"I know sweetie." She said as she kneeled to get at eye level with him. "But once we get out of here, I'll take you to that place you've always wanted to go."

"Really?" The kid roared.

"Absolutely, Spud!" She assured him as she stood. She looked at the police officer, noticing he was watching her interaction.

Tawnie parted her lips to introduce herself but heard the soldiers rushing into the area. They stood back to back, pointing their guns toward both ends of the halls. Men were chanting and slurring out loud as if they were hunting for wild game.

"I guess we are going to die today." The officer stated.

Tawnie sneered as she played around with the settings on the rifle. "The fuck we are!"

The light emitting from the gun transitioned from blue to white as she played with the dials and switches.

"Hey!" Lydia yelled, poking her head from the restroom. "We can escape through the window!" Tawnie looked back at the officer, and he nodded. They all ran into the bathroom. Lydia guided them to the back wall where Abbie already stood. The window was small and set higher on the wall. But Abbie thought it would be worth a shot.

"I don't know if it's big enough." The policeman said. "I'll hold these guys off while you escape. They could hear the many men outside rummaging through the halls. It was only a matter of time before they entered the restroom.

The short window sat above the counter. Lydia sprang up, attempting not to slip on the water from the sink. Once she got her arms up, she tried to push it open, looking back at the entrance. Unfortunately, the glass didn't move.

"Hurry!" Abbie screamed.

"I'm trying!" Lydia yelled back as she began to beat on the window frame. But suddenly, she stopped.

"Wait, what are you doing?" Abbie asked. "That's our only way out!"

Lydia jumped from the counter and held her arms out to her side.

"Stand back." She said as they began to glow. Everyone did as they were told and gave her some space. Lydia stared at the window and sneered as she concentrated. Each second, her hands glowed brighter. The others shielded their eyes. Tawnie, however, faced the door, pointing her rifle to the entrance.

"This one!" she heard someone yell from the hall.

"Whatever you're going to do, Lydia, now is the time," She said.

The teen threw her palms toward the window, releasing a ball of pure light energy. The beam landed against the wall, creating a sound resembling a car running through it. The floor rumbled as the wall caved in, creating a mudslide at the back of the restroom. In seconds, half the room was covered with mud and ice. Water pipes in the wall were destroyed and sprayed all over, adding a slip factor to the situation. The now crisp winter air flowed inward, moving water particles over the group.

"Oh!" Abbie chirped. She climbed into the hole and headed up, running through the water. But a soldier ran inside the restroom and let off a round. Fortunately, the shot was seen but not felt. It went through the group and hit the mound of dirt near Abbie's hand. She felt the excess heat and became frozen in fear momentarily. Tawnie pulled her trigger, and a large blast of orange light flew toward the entrance like a missile. As soon as it pierced the wall, there was another explosion. The soldiers screamed, letting Tawnie know that she hit her mark. The ceiling collapsed at the end of the room, slamming debris down on the soldiers. Abbie reached back to pull Milo up through the escape route. The boy scratched his way up the incline to free himself. Tawnie went up next. By this time, more soldiers squeezed through the debris to enter.

"Get'em!" One soldier said after breaking into the restroom.

More of them followed his lead and raised their rifles as they entered. The policeman took cover in a stall, preparing to return fire. Abbie reached back to pull Tawnie. She continued to fire back at the bathroom entrance. She caused a string of concussive blasts that rattled everyone in the small space. The commotion, accompanied by the exertion of her powers, made Lydia panic. In desperation, she followed the policeman into the stall. She sat against the wall, sliding down onto the wet tiled floor.

"Officer, come on!" Tawnie screamed over the sound of explosions and hysteria. The man took a deep breath as he stared at her. Then, he came out of the stall, returning fire to the soldiers at the end of the restroom. He made it to the hole in the wall and climbed in. Suddenly, the soldiers began to shoot back. The first round hit Abbie. She fell to her hands and knees as blood dripped from her body, causing a crimson mess on the tile underneath.

"Abbie!" Tawnie screamed as she attempted to run back in. But the officer held her back, trying to make her leave instead. Simultaneously, a bigger threat was brewing in the corner as Lydia began to glow. Her entire body emitted a bright light. Every inch of her exposed skin illuminated the room and grew brighter by the second. The girl screamed in agony, causing the officer to spring into action.

"Get out of here, now!" He screamed at Tawnie as he ran to assist Abbie. But as he picked the woman up, she smacked his hand away.

"Save yourself!" She yelled. "I'm not going to make it!"

"Abbie, get up, please!" Tawnie cried out. But the officer looked down at the wound on her body, only to find that she had been hit in the abdomen. Blood secreted through the back of her shirt and dripped from her midsection. Once she toppled over, the policeman ran to the exit.

"No!" Tawnie screamed as she stopped shooting and tried to run back down to save her friend. But the officer intervened.

"We have to go now!" He yelled at her. He managed to get Tawnie and her son out of the building. The shooting stopped as that restroom filled with so much light that nobody could see a thing. Tawnie looked back, juggling the decision to keep moving or return to help her friend. But the police officer grabbed Milo and ran away with him.

"Hey, stop!" she screamed as she ran behind him. The ground shook, causing Tawnie to stop running. She looked back at the exposed room she had come out of and saw how much light filled it. White beams cascaded out like a cluster of spotlights.

"Oh shit." She said as she turned around to look for the officer. The city seemed to get quiet all of a sudden. Tawnie looked around and saw more soldiers coming toward them from different directions. Tawnie sighed and got down to her knees. The officer stopped running as he could see soldiers approaching him as well.

"Get on the ground!" One soldier yelled at the policeman. Holding a child, he was unsure how to proceed.

"Wait, wait!" The officer screamed as they closed him in, pointing their guns. "I am not a threat!"

"Control, Control, come in." Tawnie heard someone say on the radio she was still carrying.

"Go for Control." Another man said on the radio. Tawnie looked around for the person talking and found him. He stood yards away with a group of men staring at the police officers and her son. She slowly moved to her feet but was immediately threatened by the soldiers.

"We found the boy." The man expressed over the radio. Tawnie's heart started to pound out of her chest. She immediately became overcome with nausea and covered her mouth with her hand.

"Apprehend him and bring him back to base."

"Copy." The conversation ended.

Filled with unrelenting anger, Tawnie grabbed the rifle beside her.

"She's reaching for the weapon!" One soldier yelled. The others became alert, waiting for her to make a move.

"Skill makes the big difference here, guys." She said. She sprang up from her position and ran straight ahead, gunning down the man in front of her. Before his body could hit the ground, she jumped over his shoulder. She used him as cover until she could spin around. She took down four more soldiers in the time it would take her to make a full 360-degree rotation. She kept her finger in the trigger well, shooting back at the soldiers. The rifle rested on the man's shoulder as the last bit of life left his body.

Behind her, more soldiers surrounded the police officer.

"Drop the kid!" The soldier demanded.

"Fuck off!" The officer yelled as he held the kid tighter. Another soldier slammed the butt stock of his rifle into the man's face. Blood splattered from his lips over the snow nearby. Milo screamed as he rolled across the pavement. The soldiers huddled around the kid and grabbed him.

"Mommy!" He shrieked as he attempted to break away from their clutches.

The policeman immediately jumped back to his feet as they carried him away. He took a swing at a nearby soldier. He punched his mask, breaking it and exposing the man's face underneath.

"No, no, no!" the soldier yelled as he stumbled, his hands trying to plug the holes in the mask. He took the soldier's rifle and pointed straight to the men taking Milo.

"Stop, now!" he screamed as he aimed. Unfortunately, behind him, more soldiers were closing in. Tawnie blasted her way to the vehicle where they carried Milo.

"Mommy!" The boy screamed again.

"Hang on, Milo!" She screamed back to him as she fought her way through the soldiers who, at this point, minimized all use of their weapons. Tawnie's little boy had become their primary objective. Men swarmed the two as others approached a parked vehicle.

"No!" Tawnie shrieked as she was forced to watch her son get dragged away. Suddenly, an explosion came from the restroom, knocking Tawnie and the officer to the ground. Debris scattered all over as the entire wing of the school collapsed. The concussive blast caused everyone to be thrown around by the unseen force. Tawnie's ears rang, and she could hear nothing as she got back up. The police officer managed to get up before any of the soldiers. Milo, at the time, had been knocked unconscious. The officer rolled him over his shoulder and ran back to his mother. She stared back at the building in shock.

"No!" She screamed in disbelief. She could hardly hear the man talking as he tugged on her arm. But she would turn to him, seeing her son over his shoulder, and snap out of her grief. The two of them looked back at the soldiers getting back up. Before they could, Tawnie and the officer had already disappeared.

Chapter XI

Tawnie and the police officer sprinted to escape the incident. Milo draped over his shoulder. Tawnie displayed her distraction continuing to look back at the crumbling school. In a regular occurrence of that magnitude, one would usually hear sirens. But the rising, thick, black smoke, seemed to prompt nothing. The once crowded area was now eerily quiet.

"We have to rest." The officer suggested. Tawnie saw an alleyway behind a nearby building to retreat. She gasped, attempting to catch her breath. Meanwhile, the officer kneeled to lay Milo on the ground.

"Be careful!" Tawnie sneered.

The man nodded, not seeming to pay her any mind. He continued to handle the boy roughly, and Tawnie lunged at him.

"I said, be careful!" She screamed.

"Got dammit!" The man snapped back. "I was a combat doctor in West Bengal! I know what the fuck I'm doing."

Tawnie's eyes grew wide as she stared at him. She sat aside, allowing him the opportunity to care for her son. Feeling helpless, she sighed loudly, temporarily distracting the man.

"He's fine, by the way," he said as he held a finger underneath his nose. He took quite a spill, but it looks like he just fainted."

"Wonderful news," Tawnie said as she stood back up.

"Who are these soldiers?" The officer asked as his eyes wandered behind her.

"I'm not sure yet," Tawnie answered, looking around for nearby threats.

"Come on," The officer said as he removed his coat and placed it underneath Milo's head. "Soldiers swarm the city, targeting your kid in the process, and you don't know who they are?" He grinned. "I call bullshit, lady!"

Tawnie sighed again. "I don't know who they are… yet."

The man's smile left his face as he noticed that she seemed worried. He approached slowly, looking down into her eyes. After a moment, he extended his hand. Tawnie looked down at it, eyebrow raised.

"It looks like we will need each other if we plan to leave here alive." He said. "The name is Daniel Gordon." Tawnie's head tilted.

"Daniel, nice to meet you – again," Tawnie said as she took the man's hand. "I'm Tawnie, and that's my son, Milo."

The man's eyes grew large as he stared at the woman.

"Well, I'll be damned!" He said, continuing to examine her thoroughly. "It's you!"

Tawnie smiled, tears filling her eyes, before looking down at her son.

"Fancy meeting you here, Sergeant Gordon!"

He looked at her from bottom to top, wondering how he didn't recognize her sooner.

"But, I imagined you'd look older now." He said, scratching his head. "You look exactly the same as I remember."

Tawnie shrugged her shoulders. "I have a good skin care routine."

Gordon looked back at the kid and sighed, his smile quickly disappearing. "I'm sorry I couldn't defend him better."

Tawnie chuckled as she walked around the officer to get back to Milo. She took a knee next to him and raised his head. The boy began to awaken. He sniffled as if he would cry, and Tawnie looked around again.

"It's okay, Spud." She said to him, "We're going home now."

He sat up and looked directly at the man standing before him. "Milo, this is the man who helped us escape the bad men," Tawnie announced. Milo got up from the ground and looked up at him.

"What's your name?" The little boy asked.

The man smiled. "Call me, Gordon."

Milo seemed to get spacey suddenly. "Milo, what's wrong?"

With sadness in his eyes, he looked back up at his mother.

"Where's Ms. Abbie?" He asked. Tawnie froze. She felt a pit in her belly growing as images of what she saw earlier haunted her again.

"Uh, she went back home to…" Gordon started to say, attempting to think of something on the fly. "To get her phone. She said she'll see you later."

Milo looked back at his mother, who stared at Gordon, trying not to get emotional.

"Alright, kid. Are you ready to get out of here?" he asked as he walked to Milo, touching his shoulder to turn him around. As Milo began to walk to the end of the alley, Gordon spun around to look at Tawnie. He shook his head as he whispered, "Not now."

She wiped her tears away before she gave him a nod.

"Alright, Milo," Gordon said as he ran before the boy, peeking into the street. "We have to make sure we don't get caught."

"Yeah, Spud," his mother added. Just like we practiced, "We have to get back home without these people seeing us, okay?"

Gordon shook his head. "What the hell do you mean, practice?" He asked. "This?"

Tawnie shrugged as she pulled the rifle from her back and switched it on. She stepped out onto the sidewalk.

"Mommy, wait!" Milo called out, stunning her into jumping backward. After catching herself, she spun around to look at him.

"What is it, Spud?" She asked.

"I'm scared." He muttered.

Tawnie looked to the sky and allowed her arms to fall. She took a deep breath and closed her eyes for a moment.

"You'll be fine, little man," Gordon said as he reached down to pick the boy up underneath his arms. "You are under the watchful eye of IFPD's finest, Ricochet Gordon!"

Tawnie chuckled as she watched the man in awe as he hoisted her kid like it was nothing.

"Ricochet Gordon, huh?" She asked. "Where did that name come from?"

He smiled as he tossed Milo into the air, spinning him around simultaneously.

"Woah!" The boy shrieked as Gordon caught him again, raising him over his head to place him on his shoulders.

"They called me that in the Army because I can bounce back

from any challenge." He answered with a grin and a wink. Tawnie chuckled again.

"Charming," she said. "I think I'll get him back home to his father now."

Gordon's eyes grew wide as he stared at the woman.

"Oh, you thought I was flirting." He acknowledged, shaking his head. "I wasn't kidding about that."

The man stepped out of the alley holding eye contact with her before looking around again.

"Take the lead, Tawnie." He said. "I won't be much help shooting with Milo on my shoulders." Tawnie did as she was told and stepped out front. She looked around for any threat nearby and ended up closing her eyes. Annoyed, Gordon looked at her.

"Step back in the alley," she demanded. Gordon stepped back hastily and raised one eyebrow.

"What happened?" He asked. But Tawnie threw a finger up to him. They waited silently, causing the officer to lose his patience. Just as he opened his mouth to speak, he heard something in the distance. It was men talking. He looked at Tawnie, who suddenly seemed agitated. The two stared at one another as they heard men conversing as they marched through the streets. Tawnie looked out of the alley. Her heart racing as she set her sights on the other end of the block. To her dismay, it was undoubtedly a group of soldiers.

"Fuck, they are everywhere!" She whispered as she pulled her head back. "We have to be extra careful."

"How far are we going?" Gordon asked.

"We have a few miles to walk. I'm pretty sure that driving is not an option." Tawnie answered. Once again, she stepped out of the alley and looked both ways.

"With your senses, we should be able to get there without getting spotted," Gordon said. Tawnie glared at him over her shoulder.

"My senses can't make up for your big mouth." She said,

The two of them maneuvered the streets, attempting to be as quiet as possible. They examined the environment, careful not to accidentally come across any soldiers. Eventually, they heard more commotion happening in the area. It was a few blocks from the alley, and Tawnie led Gordon into a parking lot of what looked like an office building. Along the building were tall trees and shrubbery they stepped behind. Gordon stepped into his cover and immediately put Milo down. Afterward, he pulled the rifle from his back and looked around. At the edge of the parking lot was a brick wall dividing the parking lot from the next property.

"Based on all the noise over there, I'd say we've stumbled across a base, " Tawnie said. On the other side, they could hear people talking and generators humming.

"Should we turn back?" Gordon asked. Tawnie shook her head.

"Absolutely not," she answered without even thinking. "We have to get around this base, or we'll be stuck in this spot. There's no other way to my house."

"Roger that." The officer said as he jumped out of the bushes and ran to the wall across the parking lot.

"What the hell?" Tawnie asked. He put his back against the brick and looked at her. She threw her hand forward with a curious look on her face.

"What are you doing?" She whispered, hoping he could read lips.

"Scoping," He whispered back. Silently, he crawled his way to the end of the parking lot. The wall ended, and he was able to use the shrubs to hide behind. He switched the rifle off, and the light faded as he moved around the corner. Tawnie's eyes grew large as she watched him vanish. She immediately heard an engine roaring.

"Milo, get down," she whispered as they kneeled. She could still see out to the street through the thicket before her. A black SUV slowly drove away from the camp. She waited for the vehicle to pass, hoping that Gordon would somehow be unnoticed. She started to devise a plan of her own. But before she could take action, another group of soldiers were walking down the road.

"Shit!" She whispered to herself. Suddenly, she could hear Milo's stomach growl. The boy looked up at her with puppy-dog eyes. Tawnie sighed.

"I know, Spud." She said. "I'm working on it now. We just have to make sure Officer Gordon is okay."

Tawnie looked out to the street again, seeing men marching in both directions.

"Well, that ain't good." She said to herself.

"Mommy, is he going to get caught?" Milo asked.

Tawnie shook her head. "Not on my watch."

She pointed her gun out of the bushes and looked through her sights. A small group appeared in her cross hairs. Her index finger hovered over the trigger. But she looked down at Milo again, and he watched the men closely, waiting for one to drop dead.

"Dangit, Spud." She said as she put the rifle down. "I need to find another way."

She started to look around, attempting to devise a plan on the fly. But as she waited, and watched the foot traffic on the street. Activity was picking up in the camp.

"Come on, Tawnie, think!" she said to herself. Suddenly, she pulled out her phone and fumbled with it. Milo became intrigued.

"Mommy, what are you doing?" He asked.

"Playing a little game." She responded as she looked around.

"What kind of game?" He asked. "Can I play?"

Tawnie scowled at the boy.

"After we're far away from here, Spud. I'm trying to keep Gordon safe."

Milo walked around to look over her shoulder. He watched the screen momentarily. She scrolled through various blueprints, graphs, and machine scripts. Milo's eyes seemed to ignite with excitement as she continued.

"Oooh!" He cheered as he pointed at the phone.

"What?" Tawnie asked as she moved the phone closer to him. The kid placed his index finger on the screen and pulled it down, revealing more information. Tawnie gasped as she took the phone back.

"How did I miss that?" Tawnie asked with a smile. "Milo, you are definitely growing into a little genius!"

The boy giggled as he placed his hands behind his back and twisted from one side to the other. Tawnie giggled as she started to manipulate the information. On the street, a group of men were walking away from the base. They suddenly stopped to look down at their rifles. Tawnie started to laugh as she watched them examine the now inoperable artillery. The light had turned off, and the buttons were dead, nor could a switch be flipped to get it back on.

"That oughta do it," she said as she put the phone back in her pocket and stood.

"Milo, we're going," Tawnie said as she reached for the kid's hand. They stepped out of the bushes. The men saw them and stopped what they were doing. Tawnie watched as they stared at her and her son.

"I guess we have to do this the old-fashioned way." One soldier said as he placed the rifle on his back and stepped into the parking lot.

"Milo, stand back if you don't mind," Tawnie said as she let go of his hand. Milo walked a few paces away and turned back around. Tawnie grabbed her thick, curly hair and put it in the hair tie she wore on her wrist.

"Fellas, I don't want to do this," she said as she approached them. I just want to get my kid home."

"Freeze!" One soldier said, pointing his rifle at her.

"Really?" She asked as she threw her hands up. The three men all stepped forward. Tawnie took a deep breath, shaking her head in annoyance.

"Fields, get the kid!" The man out front commanded.

"Roger that!" The man said as he attempted to run past Tawnie.

"I wouldn't do that if I were you," she warned him. The man stopped before passing her. She could not see his eyes through the mask but could feel him staring at her. The soldier looked back to his superior.

"What the hell are you waiting for?" The leader asked. The soldier took another step toward Milo. The boy started to tense up where he stood. He wanted to run, but he was too afraid to move. Suddenly, Tawnie swung her fist to hit the man in the jaw, knocking his mask off.

"No!" He screamed as he scrambled to fix it back to his face. Tawnie watched him in shock.

"What the hell is the big deal?" She asked. The man ran back to his counterparts. After pleading for help, one of them grabbed him by the collar and jammed a knife into the base of his neck. The man began to gargle as he reached for the wound. Tawnie only watched, following him with her eyes as he went down.

The soldier ripped the blade out of his neck and stepped over him. He kneeled to wipe his knife on the uniform of his dying comrade.

"I'm not going to lie. This makes things a little easier," Tawnie said. The man in front of her prepared for a fight, but the sheer look of disinterest in Tawnie's demeanor worried him. He looked back at the other soldiers and nodded. They also pulled out knives, and the two of them began to circle Tawnie. Milo, still trembling, stepped back even further to avoid the men.

"Mommy!" He cried out.

"It's okay, Milo." I'll be there in a second. The first man attempted to approach from behind. His goal was to shank her in the kidney. However, Tawnie spun to avoid the blade. Her absence caused the other man to stumble. Tawnie then grabbed the exposed strap of his mask. As he fell forward, it slipped off. He scrambled to get his mask back on as the woman watched with raised eyebrows.

"I'm sorry. I thought this was a fight," Tawnie said as the last man approached, reaching behind him.

"Smart." He growled as he pulled a pistol from behind him and quickly shot his comrades in the head.

"What the fuck!?" She asked. "You're going to wish you didn't do that!"

Finally, the man stepped in front of her and pointed the gun at her forehead. Her eyes crossed as she looked at the barrel.

"Am I?" He asked. Tawnie grabbed his hand quickly and forced it into the air. The gun went off next to her head as she spun around him, twisting his arm. The gun fired twice, hitting him in the back of the leg. He roared in pain as he fell to his knees.

"Who are you?" Tawnie asked as she grabbed the gun from his hand. "Why are your people invading this city?"

Through the pain, the man began to chuckle.

"I won't tell you shit, Oracle." He snarled. Tawnie took a deep breath before stomping on his leg wounds. Again, he howled as she jammed the barrel of the pistol into the back of his head.

"I'm flattered that you know who I am," she said. "But let's consider the consequences of disobedience here."

The man squirmed. "Even if you knew, it wouldn't make a difference!"

"I guess we'll have to test that theory," Tawnie said as she stepped around him. The gun still pointing at his head the entire time.

"Never have I ever seen grown men whine like your men did when unmasked," Tawnie explained. "It was almost as if you people are afraid of a little Idaho breeze."

It had become quiet momentarily as the woman looked down at him again.

"You are foolish to believe that I'll tell you anything." He chuckled. "You are better off killing me now!"

Tawnie shook her head. "I can't promise you'll die today. I can only promise that I won't do it."

The man was confused, grunting as he attempted to piece together her motive. Suddenly, Tawnie thrust her hip backward and sent her foot flying toward the man's face. He screamed as he buckled, trying to block the attack. But he wasn't fast enough. His mask succumbed to the kick, entirely breaking the hard, plastic armor. His face was exposed, and his worried eyes stared at her. Tawnie smiled at him and threw the gun down to the pavement in front of him. "I'm the Oracle. Nice to meet you." She said before stepping away to grab Milo.

After fumbling with his mask in disbelief, the soldier allowed the pieces to fall to the ground. He looked up at Tawnie, then down at the gun before him. Tawnie took a knee to talk to her kid while the man behind her grabbed the pistol from the ground. All the while, the soldier's eyes were locked to the woman's back. He raised the gun, hand trembling as he pointed it at her. A moment of silence swept over them as she hugged her son. Tawnie covered him from the visual until she heard the sound of the gun firing. The boy trembled at the sound. Tawnie was frozen and he let out a soft whimper as if he was only seconds away from sobbing.

Tawnie slowly released him. Her eyes met his, "You okay, Spud?"

The boy nodded and reached up to his face to wipe tears from his eyes. Tawnie pat his head. "Eyes closed." She commanded before standing. The boy did as he was told and closed his eyes. Tawnie turned to find the mercenary lying on his back, the pistol in his hand. Smoke exited the barrel as his body twitched. His eyes were left open and the crimson liquid spread across the pavement underneath him. His mouth was wide and an unnatural fleshy mess peeked between his lips.

"Milo, keep your eyes closed for me, sweetie." She said as she picked him up and walked back to the bush. In the distance, the woman spotted Officer Gordon staring at her in disbelief.

When she stepped back into her hiding place, she put Milo onto the ground and turned her eyes to the sky. She proceeded to place her hands on top of her head and pace. Eventually, Gordon followed her into the hideaway.

"Tawnie, what the fuck?" He asked. The woman looked at him with worry in her eyes. Gordon immediately realized that something was wrong.

Tawnie shrugged as she let her arms fall. "I think I know why these soldiers are here," she said. "If I'm right, we're in more trouble than we could imagine."

Chapter XII

Tawnie, Gordon, and Milo escaped the city's catacombs and made it to the outskirts of town. They trekked across the plains covered with high grass and many mud pits. Tawnie looked back at the city, the sun setting over it. The smoke rising from all over barely let the setting sun through.

"I can't believe this is happening," Gordon said as he looked up to ensure Milo was comfortable.

"Can't you?" Tawnie asked him. "You're a police officer in a small city. Cops get bored here and start trouble for citizens all the time."

Gordon shook his head. "Of course, the conspiracy theorist believes that every government-funded organization is corrupt."

Tawnie nodded. "That's because they are."

The two stopped walking and turned to one another.

"Speaking of," She started. "What are the chances I'll get booked for something after this is all over?"

Gordon grunted as he stepped away.

"All I'm saying is that our good ole' U.S.A has some checkered methods for problem-solving."

Again, Gordon stopped. Milo jerked forward on the back of his head and pressed his thighs into the officer to keep from falling off.

"Look, I'd rather not have this conversation with you right now." He said. Tawnie stepped out in front of him. She looked up into his eyes. A devious grin appeared on her face as she stared.

"Any other time, you would be justified to ignore the

conversation and move on. But not now."

He grunted. "Look, I don't know what's happening here." He announced. "I was only out on patrol before the explosion. My only job was to get people to safety."

His head fell as he began to feel shame. The grin on Tawnie's face vanished.

"It's not your fault, Daniel," she assured. "It's only, but so much you could've done to…" She paused for a moment as her head fell as well.

"Trust me," Gordon added. "I know the feeling."

"Mommy, everything is going to be okay," Milo told her.

Tawnie cracked a smile.

"Good job, kid!" Gordon said as he held his arm up to fist-bump the boy.

Then, her eyes tore away from them and headed to the distance. She became intense in a way that worried the officer.

"What is it?" Gordon asked. "Are they here?"

Tawnie held up a finger to him as she backtracked away from the neighborhood. She stepped slowly through the grass as if she were hunting. A shrub sat nearby, and she approached it with caution. Her first instinct was it was probably nothing. But the last time she ignored her instincts, it caused a lot of trouble. She reached for it, grabbing a handful of the shrubs. Gordon stepped closer to see what was happening. Tawnie pulled back a branch, and something sprung at her. She swung her fist without grasping the situation, and the object shrieked as it flipped into the air. Eventually, it landed a few feet away from them, furry and disoriented. It paused momentarily and shook its small body before running off into the grass.

"Just a coyote." Gordon sighed.

Annoyed, Tawnie raised her arms to her side and took a deep breath. "We have to leave this field before the exterminator finds us."

"That statement I can agree with," Gordon responded. "How far are we going?" Tawnie took a moment to peer into the distance.

"We don't have far," she answered. "The neighborhood is just over there. I can see it from here."

She pointed to a neighborhood with large homes that appeared gated. A stone fence surrounded it.

"The fancy neighborhood, huh?" Gordon asked. Tawnie snapped her attention to him.

"Don't patronize me, officer." She said to him before starting to walk. "I work hard for everything that I have."

"Hmm." The officer responded. "I thought you said you were married."

Tawnie shook her head. "I didn't. What are you getting at?"

"You just sound like a single mother to me. I'm not sure where a man fits into your attitude."

Tawnie stopped walking. Gordon stopped behind her. She turned to look at him with a smile on her face.

"Is this the attitude you want me to have, Mr. Officer, Sir?" She asked, still holding her expression.

"Hmph." He responded, "There is no need for sarcasm. I was just curious why you hadn't shown any concern for your so-called significant other."

Tawnie's eyes squinted, her smile still big. She approached the man slowly. He raised an eyebrow and took a half-step backward. They stood before one another in silence, staring into each other's eyes. That is until Tawnie grabbed him by the shoulders and raised her knee to his abdomen.

Gordon howled in pain as he doubled over. Tawnie reached to grab her son under his arms and pull him off. She stood him on the ground beside her and then pushed the officer off his feet.

Tawnie grabbed Milo's hand and left the man doubled over in the field.

"Hey!" He yelled for her. "Don't you know it's illegal to attack an officer of the law!"

"I don't think that law applies to Idaho right now," Tawnie responded without turning around. "Good luck, Officer."

The man was confused, watching the woman walk away in shock. He scraped himself up from the ground and stood up. But in the distance, he could see something to the right and the left of where she walked. He tried to regain his composure as he looked into the distance where the same mysterious object sat on both sides. A red light began to pulse at the top of the cylindrical object, going faster the closer they approached.

"Wait!" He yelled as he ran toward them. Tawnie stopped and

looked behind her.

"What the hell is your problem?" she asked before taking another step. Gordon caught up to her, pulled them both by the waist, and ran in the direction they had just come from.

"What are you doing? Put me down!" Tawnie screamed. But the man ignored her and kept running.

"Mommy!" Milo screamed in fear, causing Tawnie to shift her weight forward. Her heel slammed into the ground, causing them to stop short. Gordon flipped over her petite body, and Tawnie could grab Milo again. The officer slammed down to the ground by himself in the tall grass.

"What's your deal?" she yelled. The man grunted as he got up from the ground. "Those drums over there," he grunted. "I don't like them."

Tawnie looked back into the field, bewildered. "What are you talking about?" She asked. As she looked, her eyes popped upon seeing the objects. A lot of them.

"What the…" She began to say.

"I have a plan." Gordon cut her off. "We need to detonate one."

Tawnie looked back at him with squinted eyes. "What, no!" she responded. "What if they're in series with one another?"

The man paused as he placed his hand on his chin to think.

The woman turned to him. "Besides, there's no telling how many goons will come running when they hear that."

Gordon nodded. "Agreed. But there is no doubt that those things are proximity-based. The lights on them interacted with your movements just now."

Tawnie looked down at Milo momentarily, then back at the officer. "Yeah, that's a bit problematic."

Gordon scanned the field, searching through the tall grass that surrounded them. Tawnie watched him with some confusion.

"What are you doing?" She asked.

"Trying to find something to help us get through the trip sensor."

"What if they all blow up?" Tawnie asked.

Gordon paused as he found a broken brick in the grass.

"There's no other way. So, we'll have to take a risk," he responded.

Tawnie grabbed her son to pick him up. Gordon watched her

walk away with her child until she was at a reasonable distance. She turned around and nodded to the officer. He nodded and then spun counterclockwise, holding the brick up with his right hand. After about seven turns, he released the brick. Tawnie watched the stone fly through the air, skeptical that it would cause any reaction. But she noticed the lights on top of one unit as the brick got closer. The closer it came, the faster it flashed. The woman stepped back and kneeled to cover her son. Gordon dived into the grass away from the alleged bomb. The brick against the unit and echoed through the field. The lights atop began to strobe.

Just as Gordon suspected, the object exploded. Milo screamed, and Tawnie started to caudle him. Gordon looked back to see the flames coming straight toward them. They were far enough away from the blast but not the affected area. In mere milliseconds, Gordon knew they would be consumed. He sighed and put his head down, accepting his fate. But the fire passed right over them. Once he realized that he hardly felt any heat from the flames, he raised his head again. He noticed Tawnie, still upright and rocking her panicking son.

The woman's eyes were wide and her mouth closed. She stared into the distance while her son walked. Gordon got up from the ground, noticing something appalling, but couldn't stop to look. He ran to Milo and covered his mouth with his hand.

"Tawnie!" The officer called out to her. But she didn't do as much as blink. "Tawnie, snap out of it!" He growled. This time, shoving her shoulder. Finally, she began to blink and breathe. She found Officer Gordon staring at her from close proximity as he held his hand over Milo's mouth.

"You good?" he asked, staring directly into her eyes. She stammered as she tried to respond but eventually pushed the man away.

"Yup, I'm good," she said as she got up. "But, we made a fuss here and gotta go."

As soon as she said that, she snapped her attention into the distance. Her head jerked, and her eyes closed.

"What... what's wrong?" Gordon asked. But she didn't answer. Tawnie only held a finger up to him as she took a deep breath. While she was doing that, Gordon noticed light underneath his feet.

"What the..?" he grumbled as he moved aside, staring at the ground. Small cracks appeared underneath him, and a red glow emitted from them with a lot of heat. The grass around it was singed, and Gordon followed the line with his eyes only to find more charred grass lines.

"There's a helicopter coming," Tawnie said. Gordon snapped out of his stupor and looked around for somewhere to hide.

"What now?" He asked.

"To the neighborhood, quick!" Tawnie responded as she grabbed Milo's hand and dashed through the meadow.

Chapter XIII

Tawnie bolted through the grass with Milo draped underneath her arm. Officer Gordon was just a few steps ahead of her. They began to see the helicopter's light in the distant skies. It appeared to be headed straight toward them. A spotlight shined down to the ground underneath it.

"Almost there!" Tawnie yelled as they approached the fence surrounding the neighborhood. The fancy brick and stone wall was about 10 feet high and had no footholds to climb.

"Help!" she cried out as she raised Milo. Gordon kneeled and buried his head between Tawnie's knees, hoisting her into the air. Sitting about eight feet up, she was able to pass the boy to the top of the wall. Once he got up, he looked down to the other side. His body tensed, causing him to almost tumble back toward his mother.

"Milo, focus!" She yelled at him.

"Tawnie, go!" Gordon commanded. She worked her way to her feet, standing on top of his shoulders to reach the top of the wall. With one final push, Gordon got her to the to top. Tawnie looked for the helicopter, "We're running out of time!" She yelled. She draped her torso over the wall and reached for the officer. But he waved her on. Her eyes grew wide as she stared at him. The whirring of the helicopter propellers getting louder behind them.

"Go!" He yelled. "Save yourself!"

Tawnie froze momentarily, wondering if the man had lost his mind. But again, he insisted. Tawnie planted her hands on the structure as if doing a push-up and propelled herself away from it.

"Mommy!" Milo screamed as she fell to the ground. Upon impact, she rolled backward and jumped back to her feet. She approached the wall again, opened her arms wide, and looked up at her son.

"Milo, come on, baby!" She said to him.

Milo peered down at her, fear filling his tiny body.

"You have to jump, Spud!" She yelled. Tawnie glanced back at the helicopter and seemed to get antsy.

"Milo, jump, dammit!" She yelled one final time. The boy closed his eyes and leaped. Tawnie caught him out of the air. Without a second thought, she dashed across the yard she found herself in. The grass was still green and lush. The area was adorned with various outdoor furniture she had to navigate through. She considered going into the house. But she somehow knew it would be a bad idea. However, an elevated wooden deck on the back of the house was lined with a decorative lattice. As she approached, Tawnie saw the helicopter peaking over the house's roof. Tawnie reached for the lattice and tugged on a few pieces to find a loose board. Just as the spotlight started to land on the deck, she saw a board with a loose nail. She gently pulled it away from the deck and pushed Milo inside. She went in after him and pulled the lattice back into place.

Tawnie looked through the openings of the lattice to see if Officer Gordon had made it into the yard. The spotlight passed over the deck and into the grass. That's when she saw the police officer flipping over the wall and crossing the space. Thinking on his toes, he recognized a picnic bench. Briskly, he ran to slide underneath it. The spotlight beamed onto the table, and Gordon braced himself against the underside. He looked toward the house to find Tawnie, but he couldn't see her behind the lattice boards. The spotlight locked onto the table. Even in the cold, Gordon began to sweat profusely. Sure that he was discovered, he prepared to run for it. But he looked ahead to see Tawnie's hand hanging out of the lattice. A single finger held up, signaling him to remain calm. The man took a hard swallow and a deep breath, hoping they would move along. Suddenly, the light moved and scanned the yard toward the stone wall at the end of the property.

"Daniel!" He heard Tawnie yell. Without a second thought, he jumped from his cover and ran toward her. The lattice opened as he ran across the yard at full speed. At the same time, the spotlight doubled back. As he approached the house, he could see Tawnie waving to him. He jumped head-first into the opening, and she closed it behind him as the spotlight passed over the deck. She could see his face through the light that shone through the deck boards. He held a finger up to them as they began to hear thumping around them.

They began to hear glass breaking and crashing inside the house as a group of men thrashed their way into the yard.

"Under the table!" They could hear a man yell. The soldiers tore through the yard, flipping furniture as they checked for prey. "Are you sure you saw something, Blackhawk?"

The radio chirped as he finished his question. Tawnie checked the radio screen hanging from her lapel, ensuring it was off.

"As sure as the devil is real." A man responded to the communicator.

"Area clear!" A soldier yelled to the commanding officer.

Tawnie tried to look out into the yard at the men, but Gordon held her collar from behind. She looked back at him; this time, he held his finger up to her.

"Perimeter clear!" Someone else said into the comms. There was a brief silence as the helicopter returned to the yard.

"What the hell set off that damned proximity bomb?" The leader asked.

"Must have been another coyote, Sir." A soldier answered him quickly. "Squad seven reported a lot of them in the last few hours."

"Hmph!" the man growled as he headed for the yard's entrance. " Is the house clear?"

"Hoah, sir!" Someone answered.

The man looked back at his men, then up at the helicopter above. "You all better hope you're right and nobody is here!"

"Hoah!" His unit all roared.

The man pointed to the front of the house, and the soldiers began to exit the yard. They could hear hundreds of footsteps as the helicopter skated above the neighborhood. Just as Gordon believed the coast was clear, he prepared to leave his cover. But Tawnie grabbed his arm, keeping him from moving. When he looked at her, she only shook her head. Again, she held up her index finger. Gordon and Milo stayed as still as possible, watching Tawnie for confirmation.

A few seconds passed, and the footsteps and helicopter sounds faded into the distance. However, Tawnie still extended her finger.

"Clear." they heard someone say just outside. Gordon's eyes widened as he stared at Tawnie in amazement. As they listened to the man leave, Tawnie finally lowered her finger.

"Now we can go," she said as she moved past Gordon and pushed the lattice outward. Milo crawled out of the hole behind his mother as Gordon watched. After Milo stepped out of the opening, Tawnie bent at the waist to look in at Gordon.

"You coming?" She asked. The officer shook off his confusion and began to crawl outside. Once they were all out, Tawnie quietly reinstalled the lattice to the deck. Gordon looked at her with an eyebrow raised. She held a finger to her pink lips and walked slowly to the gate separating the backyard. The wooden opening was closed, and the woman neglected to push on it, fearing that the hinges would creak. Instead, she pulled Gordon to the opening and pushed his shoulder down.

"Wait, what?" He whispered. Again, Tawnie urged him to stay quiet. As he sat on one knee, the woman took his hands and extended them for him. She rotated his wrists so that his palms were faced skyward. Then she stepped into them. She placed her soft hands on the side of his neck and tapped him. Immediately, he began to lift. She swung her opposite leg over his shoulder as he slowly raised her. Her shirt began to rise as she came closer to him, and he could see straight up her surprisingly tight abdomen. He quickly glimpsed her belly button piercing and her black lace bra. In addition, the woman's legs were open, with her pubic region sat in his face. He took a deep breath to calm down, but that only worsened the situation. As he came to his feet, Tawnie planted her hands onto his shoulders to assist in mounting his shoulders. As the blood rushed to his head, he was tempted to throw her off. Suddenly, Tawnie smacked the side of his head.

Appalled, the man looked up at her.

"Focus!" She commanded. The officer clenched his jaw and planted his feet as she lifted herself to look over the wooden fence. She gasped as she took sight of what was out there. Concerned, Gordon looked up again.

"What?" He whispered. But Tawnie didn't answer. She simply dismounted Officer Gordon and shook her arms as she sighed.

"What is it?" He asked again.

"The good news is, they have moved on from this yard," Tawnie answered as she walked to the gate and nudged it slightly. Gordon stepped up and took a look for himself, but what he saw was inconceivable to him as well.

His mouth opened slightly, and his eyes widened, "Shit!"

Chapter XIV

Gordon pulled the gate closed.

"This neighborhood was much more peaceful before the hooligans moved in." Tawnie smiled. Through the dark, he recognized her teeth.

"How can you joke at a time like this?" Gordon asked. The woman grabbed her son by his shoulders and moved him before her. She then proceeded to cover his ears with her hands. Calmly, he looked up at the officer, not even attempting to break free.

"If we die tonight, I figured we could at least be in a good mood before we depart!"

Gordon shook his head, "Where is your house?" Tawnie let go of Milo and pointed a finger toward the back of the neighborhood.

"Straight up this road, to the right." She answered him. The officer nodded and mouthed something to himself as he turned toward the gate. He opened it slightly to look out again.

"Why are there so many of them?" He asked. "We won't be able to move an inch through this mess!"

Tawnie shook her head as she pulled the rifle from her back. "My guess is they are looking for something in particular. We may want to be careful."

The officer nodded. "Yeah, they'll probably shoot on sight."

Tawnie approached the gate again to look out.

"Unfortunately, killing us is not the final nail in the coffin here," Tawnie announced.

The officer was perplexed by her statement. "What do you mean?" he asked. But she only shrugged and proceeded through the gate.

"Wait," Gordon said as he reached for her arm. "You can't just walk into the lion's den like you own the place!"

Tawnie nodded. "I do own a place here." She said as she broke away from him. Gordon looked down at Milo, who was now staring at him with intrigue.

"What now, kid?" he asked. But Milo didn't answer. Without saying a word, he followed behind Tawnie.

She got low and ran behind a bush at the yard's edge. It grew along the fence line bordering the next yard over. It had gotten so dark that Gordon could hardly see them at all. He could make out her hand, gesturing to him to follow. Believing in what he had seen from her thus far, the man followed the instruction. The officer ducked and hurried across the yard to get to them. Once he got there, he leaned against the vinyl fence and looked at Tawnie. She held a finger up to him again.

"Wait," she whispered to him. The man started to object, but as soon as he did, he could hear men talking as they approached their location. They all sat completely still so as not to make any noise as five soldiers marched past the bush. They shined flashlights toward the gate to the backyard. But neither of them checked the surroundings as they made it to their destination.

"Where are we going, Battle?" One soldier asked the man leading the charge.

"I want to check one last spot." The leading soldier admitted. "Something didn't feel right just now."

"Maybe that paranoia is spreading these days," another interjected. The group laughed as they headed into the backyard again, their guns pointed ahead.

"What the?" Gordon whispered. Not even five seconds passed before the goons began to demolish the wooden deck. Gordon's eyes nearly popped from his skull.

"How do you keep doing that?" he asked the woman. She gave him a soft grin as she got up from the bush. Milo jumped with her, and the two ran out onto the sidewalk. Gordon hurried behind them, attempting to keep up and fearing getting caught. A group of soldiers waved flashlights from across the road, looking for more victims.

"What was that?" he asked as the three of them ran into the yard next door. They found another bush to hide behind, and the soldier across the way became fixated on that spot. He and his people crossed the road, attempting to find the suspicious activity but found nothing. That's when they heard the other group ransacking the house next door.

"Hey, Mason, Whimbush, that you guys?" One soldier yelled.

"Yeah, it's us!" Said another soldier.

The second group became distracted and joined their colleagues behind the house. Tawnie tapped Gordon, and the three of them got up to their feet.

"Yeah, I thought I saw something." The first soldier said.

"Yeah, me too." Said the second. "But I guess it was just one of your guys."

Tawnie looked over at Gordon and smiled as she tried not to laugh. But the two groups were distracted and made a clearing to allow Tawnie to get closer to home. They ran up the dark, unsupervised street and took cover in the yard of the last house. From the corner of the main road and her street, she could see her front door. To neither of their surprise, soldiers were filling her street as well.

"You have a plan?" Gordon asked.

Tawnie shook her head. "Not yet." She whispered as she looked around for an opening. The men on her street seemed focused on protecting the area from intruders. There was an armed lineup on either side of her home that appeared to be ready to shoot on sight. They had lantern-looking objects attached to their rifle barrels, illuminating the entire area. So they could see everything as they hid away from the men. There were piles of what looked like trash in the streets and lawns. All houses had been broken into and raided at the front door. Tawnie's mouth dried out as she watched the scene in silence.

"What are they defending here?" Gordon whispered.

Tawnie shrugged her shoulders before pointing just past the lineup. A few men stood on the lawn of Tawnie's house. They appeared to be engaged in a conversation.

"Is it safe to assume that I'm in trouble?" she asked. Gordon could only shake his head out of frustration. During the conversation, when one of the four men seemed to be doing all the talking, he kept pointing at her house. Finally, their conversation broke, and the men separated into two groups. Each of the two groups joined the soldiers on guard.

"Platoon, attention!" a man yelled. The guards all stood straight, their rifles standing on the butt stocks next to their left foot.

"Alright, men, change of plans." The leader said. "The target is not here! Neither is the asset."

Gordon and Tawnie glanced at one another, both seeming perplexed. "On my next command, we return to HQ to regroup."

"You know what he means by that?" The officer asked. But Tawnie didn't answer. Instead, she looked at Milo in silence. The boy's big, brown eyes stared at her, full of innocence. Quickly, she turned forward.

"No idea." She answered.

"Platoon, fall out!" The man called. All of the men began to march away from Tawnie's house. Down the road, the other group walked away as well.

"They're leaving, now's our chance." Tawnie excitedly said. The men departed, taking their light with them as they traveled the street. Tawnie and Milo ran out of the bush and headed across.

"Wait!" Gordon said as he hopped out behind them. Before entering her house, Gordon noticed Tawnie had stopped at one of the trash piles left by the road. He approached her and recognized the problem. Tawnie turned to him. Even through the dark, he could see the tears in her eyes sparkle.

"Hey, kid," Gordon said to Milo as he stepped around Tawnie. "Why don't you go sit on the front porch for a minute? Let me talk to your mom in private."

Milo looked past the man and stared at his mother. She nodded, and the boy left for the porch. The two stood alone in shock before one of many chest-high piles. The smell was putrid, and everything was charred. Smoke still rose from it even though the flames that burned it had recently extinguished. Deep inside, a faint smolder accompanied the sound of crackling. Ironically, the sight sent shivers down the woman's spine. Tawnie reached up and palmed her head, pressing her hands into her eye sockets. She groaned as if she was experiencing pain. The officer watched, wondering how to help her through this. All he could do was touch her back, giving a gentle rub to console her.

"Why would they do this?" She asked.

Gordon sighed as he looked into the smoldering pile. He could see the silhouettes of various body parts in front of the flame that burned inside. He reached for his chest as he felt bile build up inside his throat. The man then cleared his pallet and gently pushed Tawnie toward the house. He looked over at Milo and saw that the boy seemed uncomfortable.

"She's fine, kid," Gordon said. "She just needs a minute."

Tawnie approached the house and sat down on the step next to her son. He laid his head on her and began to rub her leg. But the woman acted as if he wasn't there. She curled up and put her head in between her legs as she began to hyperventilate. Gordon stepped forward, prepared to console her again. But the woman's body began to shake.

"No." She muttered. "Not now!"

Milo ran away from her and hid behind Gordon's legs. The officer looked down at the kid with widened eyes.

"What?" He asked. "Tawnie, who are you talking to?"

But she didn't answer. She continued to shake and mutter things that seemed inaudible. It was as if she was speaking a language he couldn't recognize. Then, after seconds of gibberish, she would start speaking English again.

"Now is not the time." She said as she got back up from the step. She stood still for a moment as her hair covered her face.

"Tawnie?" Gordon called out to her.

"Mommy?" Milo called. "Are you okay?" After an awkward silence, she finally shook her head.

"I'm okay." She said as she turned around and stumbled up the stairs. Gordon watched as she entered the open front door and vanished into the dark house. He looked down at Milo, who was now looking up at him.

"It's all good, kid," Gordon said as he looked back into the house's front door. "I think."

102

Mankind will be lost to division and deception. This will be the sin that reignites the Arcanin Flame. Once that fire is ablaze, no pocket of matter nor point in time is safe from the Rapture.

-Excerpt of the Arcanin Prophecy; Translated by the Oracle

Chapter XV

Gordon walked into the house with little Milo beside him. The boy seemed eager to find his mother, but the officer held him back as he tried to run behind her.

"Tawnie?" he called out, but he got no answer. Again, he called her name as he walked deeper into the house's foyer.

"Mommy?" the boy yelled. Still, she did not respond. Gordon remembered a time when he had witnessed this kind of behavior before. As a police officer, he had encountered it more than he would have liked. He began to sweat as the pit in his stomach grew with each step. They heard a noise coming from the back of the house. Gordon's attention snapped to the dark hallway in front of him. Immediately, Milo ran inside.

"Milo!" Gordon yelled as he tried to grab his coat. But, he slipped away, vanishing into the darkness. He looked behind him at the world outside to ensure he was not in anyone's line of sight. He pulled a flashlight from his belt and shined it before him. The noise stopped, and the environment became eerie and uncomfortable.

"Tawnie, Milo?" The officer called out. Again, he got no answer. He approached an intersection in the hall where there were three doorways. The one to his left led to a living room area. On his right was a dining room, and in front of him was the kitchen. In the dining room, he saw something moving in his peripheral. He flinched as he spun the flashlight into the room to see what was coming at him. But nothing was there when he finally got the nerve to open his eyes.

"What the hell?" He asked. He shined the light around the room. He saw an average dining room with a glass dining table seating eight. He stepped closer to the threshold to get a better look around. He noticed that the room was minimally furnished. It still seemed undisturbed, considering that the house had already been invaded. Using his flashlight, the man had scanned the entire room. Suddenly, he heard a crackling behind him. He spun around to see what it was. Again, nothing was there, at eye level, at least. He looked down and saw Milo standing in front of him. He shined the light on the boy to see a concerned look on his face.

"Milo, it's just you." The officer said. "Did you find your mom, buddy?"

The young boy nodded as he pointed behind him. Again, the officer slowly raised his flashlight across the floor and into the next room. He scanned across the carpeted floor until his light shined on a pair of feet. It was her. He moved the light up her curvy body and stopped once he got up to her face. The void-like look in her eyes made the man feel sick. She seemed emotionless. Gordon didn't know how to proceed, so he waited momentarily to see if she would say anything.

"Tawnie, are you okay?" He finally asked. But the woman didn't answer him. Instead, she pivoted toward the kitchen and slowly walked away.

"What the?" He asked as he grabbed Milo's hand and followed behind her.

"Hey!" he yelled for her. He entered the kitchen and saw her leaning on the island, her hands covering her face. "Why are you not answering me?"

"Sorry." She finally responded. "I didn't mean to scare you."

Gordon stepped to the island and found a few bar stools. He picked up little Milo, sat him on one, and converted his flashlight to a lantern. He turned the brightness down and sat it on the counter.

"You didn't scare me," Gordon said to her as he stood across from her. But I am concerned about you now."

Tawnie shook her head. "Your only concern should be the

people whose bodies are burned out in my front yard."

"Maybe. But I don't have any of those people grieving in front of me right now."

She stared at him momentarily, her eyes gleaming in the soft light. Milo also watched her, and his concern for his mother was evident.

"I'm okay," she tried to assure the officer. The man nodded as he stepped around the kitchen island. He wrapped his arms around her. She tried to nudge him away, but it only caused him to hold tighter.

"It's okay, Tawnie." He said. The woman began to hit him.

"No, get off!" She yelled. But the man rested his cheek on her neck and his hands on her lower back. Finally, the woman submitted to him and began to sob.

"It's a fucked up situation. I understand your pain." He said to her. "But we must keep fighting through whatever the hell this is."

Tawnie continued for a few minutes and then started to calm down. The man held on to her the entire time, but when she pulled away, she still appeared sad.

"I just hope that Abbie wasn't in that explosion." She muttered. Gordon's expression changed to a frown, an obvious indicator that he had no faith in that being a true statement.

"One could only hope." He responded as he slowly walked around the island.

The woman sighed and stepped away from the kitchen.

"Where are you going?" The officer asked. Tawnie unconsciously turned around and reentered the room.

"Sorry, come with us. We are headed to the bunker." She answered. Gordon shook his head with disbelief. "You have a bunker?"

Tawnie turned to look at him before leaving the room. "You don't?"

The two of them stared at one another for a moment in silence. Then, she and her son stepped out of the room.

"You just about to throw that out there without an explanation?" He asked. But she ignored him as she vanished into the dark again. Quickly, he followed with the lantern to keep from getting left behind. He found them standing in the back of the house's living room in front of a plain wall. Only a small decorative mirror and a family portrait hung on it. Gordon walked around behind the two of them, eyes locked onto the portrait of the happy family. Tawnie held onto her son with a smile that warmed him. Milo made a funny face in front of her and behind her was her husband. Slender, chiseled jaw, and a pompadour haircut and glasses.

"You have a beautiful family, Miss," Gordon said.

Tawnie chuckled. "I've been meaning to take that picture down, actually."

His eyebrows furrowed, "You guys look so happy."

She looked away from the mirror at the photo. Gordon could see a green laser in the center of it.

"Yeah, I guess we did," Tawnie said as they all heard a loud click. Startled, the officer began to look around for the sound.

"What the hell was that?" He asked.

Suddenly, a doorway-sized section of the wall indented itself.

"Access granted." A synthesized voice said. "Welcome, Agent 0."

Gordon's mouth fell open as he watched the cutout slide to the side, revealing a secret passage.

Tawnie seemed to have become tense as she closed her eyes and sighed.

"Who?" The man asked.

Tawnie looked back at him, shaking her head before entering the secret chamber. He followed the two of them into the doorway. Inside was a set of stairs that descended into the ground. But the more he descended, he noticed the space was not attached to the main house structure. The steps were enclosed by walls made of metal and featured small light fixtures on both sides. The door behind them closed, causing him to spook.

"What the hell is happening here?" He asked her.

"It's okay, Daniel," Tawnie said to him as the light fixtures began to turn on, slowly filling the small space with light. The bottom of the stairs opened up to a large room that seemed to be the size of the house. Gordon looked around in awe as he took in all the cool things that she had. In the center of the room was a large desk that looked like a lab. She had various glass tubes and vials in stands with all sorts of lab equipment. Against the walls were large computer monitors and control panels that seemed important. On the other side of the room, there was a large camera setup facing a set that resembled a cozy office space. There was a small desk covered with papers and a cork board on the wall behind it that was full of papers as well. They all seemed to have something written on them that seemed like a different language. He couldn't read them, but he knew he had seen the symbols before.

"What the hell?" Gordon asked. As his eyes followed her across the room, he noticed a giant metal door in the back.

"Milo, you know what to do when you come down here." Tawnie said to her son.

"Yes, Ma'am." He said as he left her side. Confused, Gordon watched Milo instead. The kid found a chair at the desk in the middle of the room, pulled it out, and sat down.

"Who has their kid trained like that?" Gordon asked. Tawnie turned to him, arms folded over her chest. "He has been so quiet and serene during all of this. How?"

Tawnie shrugged as she walked to her desk.

"It's probably because he's scared." She answered as she opened the drawer, looking for something.

"Despite almost dying three times now, he's not as scared as he should be," Gordon said as he looked back at her. Suddenly, the woman gasped as she cleared the drawer. She pulled out a device that looked like a tablet. Gordon could see a familiar emblem on the back of the device. He approached the desk and leaned

forward to get a closer look. It was a silhouetted bird with open wings and a large ring around the body. He looked for any visual significance of the logo, but she was moving too fast.

Tawnie put the device down with the screen facing up. The interface was unlike any system that Gordon had ever seen before. He looked at it in awe, trying to figure out what was on it. It appeared to be a bunch of graphs and profile pictures of people. But one man at the top of the list seemed familiar to the officer.

"Okay, Tawnie, years ago, when we met, we were on a mission where details about your past were irrelevant. But now, people are killing entire cities searching for you. So who the fuck are you?" He asked her as he stood tall. However, Tawnie stood silently, staring at him. "I'm serious. Who are you?"

The woman's already annoyed look transitioned into anger. Her stance went from relaxed to defensive as she removed her hands from her hips. Slowly, she emerged from behind the desk, causing the officer to step backward, his eyes still fixed on her.

"What do you want me to tell you, Officer Gordon?" she asked. The man shook his head, his eyes full of impatience, and responded, "The truth."

Tawnie slowly shook her head. "I can't do that," she said to him. "That violates a lot of laws on my end."

The man chuckled as he aggressively turned away, breaking eye contact with her. He walked over to her set and stepped into the fake office. He stood behind the desk, staring down at the paperwork, trying to decipher the strange text on every page. Tawnie rolled her eyes and walked toward the vault in the back of the room. She passed Milo on the way and ran her hand through his hair.

"Interesting," he responded. "This is one of the spots where you record your show?"

Tawnie passed him a look of intrigue. "So you are familiar with my work?"

The man nodded. "I am familiar with you, but not your content." He explained, "I was shown a video once and paid no attention to it because I'm not fond of the tin-hat lifestyle."

Tawnie chuckled at the statement and began to punch keys into the keypad.

"I do, however, remember this set…" He said as he approached her at the vault. "And one could never forget that face."

Tawnie stopped what she was doing to look at him. Her face was blank, but he could tell she was trying not to smile.

"You are just a mysterious face with some secrets I want to uncover," he continued.

"Why?" Tawnie asked. "Are you going to arrest me for keeping secrets, Officer?"

He chuckled as he shook his head. "No, but if it turns out that you are somehow connected with what's happening here, that would be problematic. Wouldn't it?"

The smile on Tawnie's face vanished, and her eyes sharpened. Her face twitched as she finished with her code. There was a loud beep, followed by the door opening to the vault. Tawnie pulled the giant door open and stepped inside. Officer Gordon followed her into the room, and the lights turned on. The contents of the room were enough to take his breath away. It was like a walk-in closet, with multiple displays and carrying weapons. The arsenal included various guns and hand-held weapons such as grenades and swords. The man didn't know how to respond.

"Pick your poison. We're definitely going to need it." Tawnie said as she headed to a section of the wall that held a rifle resembling the one she took from the soldier. She compared the two guns. She took a hard swallow, and her eyes widened during the examination, as wide as Gordon's during his.

"Shit!" She barked as she threw the rifle aside.

"Why do you have so many guns?" The man howled.

"Not now, Gordon." She calmly said as she began to pace the floor.

"You have more guns here than the army outside! Are you a terrorist?" He yelled as he approached her. "Are these guns registered? Do you illegally own this artillery?"

Tawnie grabbed the man and drove her knee into his abdomen. After the air was forced from his body, she shoved him down onto the floor. He squirmed as he groaned, trying to catch his breath. But when he rolled over, he could see Tawnie hyperventilating and crying. Her hands were on her head again as she began to panic.

"Mommy!" Milo yelled as he ran into the vault. The boy grabbed her leg and pushed her toward the nearest bench.

"Breathe, mommy." He said, jumping into action as if he's had to do this often. The officer watched the interaction as he got up from the floor.

"What the hell?" He asked as he looked at Milo, covering his mom as if protecting her from him.

"Leave my mommy alone!" He screamed. Officer Gordon threw his hands up and stepped back. The boy turned around to tend to his mother. Gordon nodded and left the two of them in the vault. He shook his head as he walked back to her desk. While waiting for her to calm down, he moved the papers around until he found something in English. Other papers had some sort of decryption that he could hardly understand. There were diagrams and math equations drawn out on many of them to his surprise. Gordon's throat bobbed as he noticed the aggressive lines crossing out most of it that nearly tore through the pages. The text was there and Tawnie attempted to translate it, but couldn't. She had the phrase noted at the bottom of the page, somehow knowing the answer to the equation but struggling to connect the start to the finish. He looked at the vault opening wanting to rush back in there to question her, but she was still having an episode. Gordon read the final message and halted in fear.

Chapter XVI

Officer Gordon sat at the set desk reading through Tawnie's memorandum. His heart raced as he finished, and the sweat on his brow became thick. The last sentence, '*The Obliterator will end it all.*'

The noise inside the vault had died down, Tawnie was somewhat calm again. Other than small shuffles and the occasional sniffle, the silence was deafening. Gordon wanted to check on her but couldn't bring himself to do so after being attacked earlier. Eventually, he could hear Tawnie moving inside the bunker again. He stood from the desk and slowly walked to the vault door with his hands in his pockets. Tawnie was inside, grabbing various weapons and throwing them into a large duffle bag.

The woman looked into the lab, seeing the man standing there watching her. She made eye contact for a moment before continuing to stockpile weapons.

"Need some help there?" Gordon asked.

Slowly, she shook her head. "I don't think so," she softly said. A few seconds passed. He approached the vault's threshold, finding Milo on the bench inside, watching him.

"You know, I need to apologize to you," Gordon announced. "I really thought you were some sort of criminal mastermind or something. I thought that you may have really been behind all of this."

Tawnie chuckled. "In a way, I am behind this." She said as she looked at her son.

"Yeah, I now know what you mean by that," Gordon assured her. "I should have trusted you."

Tawnie stood from the floor, staring down at the duffle. "Don't mention it."

She started to look around the room for anything else she wanted to take.

"Let me ask." Gordon interrupted. "What made you quit being a psychologist, Doctor Simms?"

Tawnie stopped what she was doing and glared at him.

"I'm just curious. How does a psychologist go from analyzing the humans to analyzing ancient languages? How'd you go from from the therapy couch to making online conspiracy videos?"

Tawnie sighed. "I wanted to make a real difference."

"You were one of the most trusted advisers of the U.S. Government. Your position was geared toward making 'the' difference."

"My position was geared toward finding fault in innocent people!" She yelled at him. "I was a criminal psychologist. I was only employed to make people guilty based on the perceived nature of their behavior. Tell me, which part of that should I be proud of?"

Gordon looked away, clearing his throat and hoping to ease the tension in the room.

"I served as a tool to put good people behind bars. You couldn't even comprehend the burden that comes with that!"

Gordon nodded. "Help me understand then."

Tawnie's head fell as she sighed. The man could see tears falling from her eyes again. "This is all my fault." She muttered.

Gordon raised his hand and tapped her arm. "Don't say that."

Silently, she raised her head to look at him. Her eyes were blood-red, and her face was drenched in tears.

"Unfortunately, good people fall victim to their circumstances." Gordon continued. "It happens to all of us."

The woman wiped her face with her forearm. "If that's true, Daniel, I managed to be the predator and the prey all at once."

Gordon nodded again as he walked away from her. He stopped and raised his eyes to the ceiling.

"You obviously know something I don't about what's happening outside." He said as he turned around to face her.. "Also, we seem to be sitting ducks in this house, why did we come here?"

Tawnie shook her head in shame. "I came back hoping that I could reach out for help."

"Help?" Gordon asked. "The police are probably all dead, and we don't know if these guys are government or foreigners of some sort."

Tawnie placed her hands behind her backside and kicked one foot back as she stared at the floor. "Fair point." She said. "But these guys are exterminators and they are not government agents of any sort."

The man crossed his arms. "Then who are they and why the fuck are they doing this?"

Tawnie went silent for a moment as she thought of an answer. "They're on a mission to kill all of us."

"Why?" The man barked. "What purpose do they have?"

"I want to know the same thing." Tawnie answered as she looked back at Milo who was still sitting in the vault fidgeting with his fingers. "I need more information because right now, I even have more questions than answers."

Gordon nodded as he stepped closer to her. "What's the plan now?"

Tawnie looked as if she had spaced out of the conversation. She walked toward the computer station in the center of the room. She logged into one of the units but quickly realized that there was no connection.

"Dammit!" She growled. "They took out the power and the network. How convenient."

Gordon looked around. "How exactly does this place have power?"

"Ion generator." Tawnie answered as she got back up and walked to her set desk. She shuffled through the papers on the surface, attempting to find something.

"Care to explain that?" Gordon asked.

"Just technology that's ready to be stolen at this point." Tawnie sarcastically responded.

Gordon threw his arms up in frustration.

"These guys are copycat assassins. They're using stolen tech to exterminate innocent people." Tawnie explained before pausing. She stared down at a paper on the desk with her mouth slightly opened.

"What is it?" The officer asked.

"Innocent people." She repeated. "What if the people aren't so innocent at all?"

Gordon stared at her in silence. "I'm not following." He said as he approached the desk.

"The men had on masks. They are protecting themselves…" She explained.

"Yeah, but what do they need protection from? The harsh potatoes in the air?"

Tawnie stood from the desk. "Man will gain control of power they cannot control." She whispered.

Gordon's head tilted as he stared in wonder.

"What was that?" He asked.

The woman shook her head as she pulled open a drawer and pulled out a black device.

"What is that thing?" Gordon asked.

"Evidence." Tawnie quickly answered. "I assume those guys were looking for this, among other things."

"What makes you so sure?" He asked as his eyes followed her to the bag she had left at the computer.

"They tried to take my son at the school earlier," Tawnie said as she paused. The man stood still as he recalled the situation. He looked back into the vault at the boy, who was now just watching the two of them.

"What do they want with a five-year-old?" He asked.

"I'm thinking leverage," Tawnie answered as she continued to pack her bag.

Gordon sighed and let his head fall.

"Tawnie, if we are going to be side by side through all of this, I need a reason to trust you." He said to the woman. The small wrinkles on her forehead became prominent as she glared at him.

"All I'm saying is I need to know what you are not telling me." He continued.

Tawnie shook her head and continued her packing.

"I won't be responsible for bursting that bubble. You'll have to figure it out without me," she said.

Gordon sneered and walked into the vault. Milo observed him. The man stood at the entrance and looked around for a weapon. He went straight to the back wall where a rifle hung that caught his attention. He expected the kid to run. But Milo sat silently on the bench, still kicking his feet and fidgeting with his fingers.

Gordon noticed his resolve and stared at the kid in awe as he walked back into the lab.

"Just watching your kid, I know it's something suspicious about you." He announced.

Tawnie slammed the bag on the floor and crossed her arms as she stared at the officer.

"You have something you'd like to get off your chest, Officer Gordon?" Tawnie asked.

The man stood the rifle against the wall and sighed. "You got some secrets that make me uncomfortable."

Tawnie chuckled. "They're my secrets and my life. Let me live it on my terms.

"It's only your life if your secrets only get you killed," Gordon added. Tawnie dropped her arms and stared at him from across the room. She approached him slowly and engaged in eye contact the entire walk.

"Why are you grilling me so much? I'm just trying to figure this out, too!" Tawnie exploded.

"I'm saying when nut-jobs go wild, there's usually a certain way to deal with that." He said. Tawnie stepped away momentarily, biting her bottom lip to remain calm.

"I can't believe this right now," she grumbled.

"Look, It's obvious that you get off on making enemies because all you do is spread rumors and speculation."

It got quiet. Even inside the vault, Milo could see the gears losing teeth inside his mom's mind. She stepped away from the man, clenching her fist tight as she chanted something under her breath.

"Listen." She responded as she faced him and clasped her hands together in front of her. "This country is plenty corrupt on its own. It doesn't need me to point it out for it to be obvious."

"This country is the lifeblood of freedom!" Gordon yelled, disagreeing with her statement.

"This country is the destroyer of liberties outside of what they allow you to have. That is the reason those men are outside now." Tawnie stepped even closer to him. "Even if I'm the one they're after, what liberties give them the freedom to exterminate humans."

Gordon dropped his head. His eyes scanned the floor as she stared at him.

"I know guys like you," Tawnie grunted as she returned for her bag. She signaled for Milo to approach her as she kneeled on the floor. "You serve your so-called country and swear to protect some bull shit oath. You defend everything they do like they can't do any wrong."

The officer glanced at the department crest on his shoulder. His blood began to boil as he clenched his fists.

"Oh yeah!?" He roared. "I'll have you know that I served this country faithfully. I protected people like you so that you could be free to have an opinion in the first place!"

Tawnie took a deep breath as she slowly came to her feet. She turned around to find the man seething. Veins protruded his neck and forehead, and his face became red as a beet as he stared at her. Tawnie placed her hands behind her back and slowly headed toward him. He took a hard swallow, almost afraid of what she would do.

"You know, Mr. Gordon." She smiled. "I'm famous for my opinion, and now we'll all die for the truth."

He sighed as he looked her in the eyes. A single tear fell down her face as she looked at him. His features softened, empathizing with her for a moment.

"I have to survive so that all these people won't lose their lives. They can't suffer over these manufactured truths!" She explained. "So, if you don't mind keeping your patriotism in check until we make it to safety, that would be great!"

The man didn't know how to respond. He could only stand silently, waiting for her to carry on. Suddenly, the lights went out, and the room became completely dark. Gordon looked around, hoping to see something. But he couldn't. He pulled out his lantern again and turned it on. He noticed the look of defeat on Tawnie's face as she stared distantly.

"What did you say was powering this room again?" Gordon asked her.

"Something that they just knocked out." She answered as she looked at him. "They know we're here."

Chapter XVII

"Milo, you know what to do." Tawnie said to her son. "Get in the vault."

"You guys practiced for this?" Gordon asked. Tawnie ignored him and reached into the duffle bag to grab two rifles. She handed one to the officer and faced the entrance. Gordon used his forearm to wipe his the sweat from his brow.

"It's getting real hot, real fast." He said.

"Uh, yeah," Tawnie responded. "The power's out, so there's no ventilation."

She looked at the vault. The door was slightly open, and Milo was inside.

She turned forward and raised her rifle, pointing it up the stairs.

"Daniel, press the button next to the rear sight picture and kill that light," Tawnie ordered. He switched the lantern off first and began to feel for the button she mentioned. His fingers slowly probed the cold steel. After hearing movement in the stairwell, he found it. As he clicked it on, The sight picture began to show the targets through the dark. Intrigued, he pointed the rifle in the dark room only to find that the soldiers could be seen perfectly as if they were walking through the light. His heart began to race, and his finger quickly covered the trigger. Then, he moved behind the table in the center of the room.

He pulled his eye away from the sight, looking for Tawnie. But still, he couldn't see a thing. Suddenly, he felt a gentle touch on his knee.

Tawnie tapped him repeatedly as the soldiers filled the space before them. She transitioned to rhythmic double taps, and

Gordon prepared for an ambush. During the last tap, Tawnie dragged the tip of her finger up Gordon's thigh. She got up and stepped backward while shooting into the crowd. Gordon caught on and jumped back with her. Gunfire filled the room. Gordon and Tawnie went to the vault and pulled the door with them. The woman took the lantern from him and turned it on. Gordon continued to shoot to maintain their cover. Tawnie went for the wall again, grabbing a few more materials.

She ran back to the vault and stood in front of Gordon.

"We're sitting ducks!" He yelled across the room.

"Exactly," Tawnie said as she tended to some parts in her hand.

Gordon stopped shooting for a moment. "What's the plan?"

"Pick a religion and pray," she answered as she pushed the vault door open. Gordon yelled at her, "What the hell are you doing?"

But Tawnie ignored him and threw three items out.

"Close it!" She roared. Gordon grabbed the handle and pulled the steel door until he heard the lock click. The room had gotten quiet despite the commotion on the opposite side of the blast door. Suddenly, there was an ear-shattering explosion. The concussive blast caused the two of them temporary hearing loss. Frustrated with the pain, Tawnie punched the floor and shook her head vigorously.

Gordon watched her ready the rifle she was holding and stood to her feet. Without hesitation, she rammed the vault door with her shoulder and pushed it open. She slipped out of it and started to shoot into the room. In the meantime, the surviving men recovered from the explosion. Gordon ran out as well, looking toward the stairs. Soldiers continued to enter after the explosion, and the officer shot them on sight. Bodies barreled down the stairs as their blood stained the walls of the incline. Eventually, the men stopped entering, allowing Gordon to rest.

"We have an opening, Tawnie!" He said. The woman stepped around him, holding her son's hand as she stepped over the bodies of the fallen. The duffle bag draped from her back as she proceeded.

"Hey, let me go first." The man requested. "If there are others, we'll have a better chance of keeping them at bay if I'm up front."

"Good point." Tawnie agreed. The three climbed the bodies on the stairs to reach the main floor. Gordon reached the doorway at the top of the stairs and looked into the house. When he didn't see anyone, he flickered the lantern to signal Tawnie to come up. The woman ran up the stairs with her son in tow. As she exited the threshold, there was a shot into the house. The three of them ducked into the stairwell for cover. The single shot transitioned into a stream of rounds ricocheting through the structure. Gordon stood steady, waiting for a break in the gunfire. The house began to chip away around them.

"Aaand," he said as he waited patiently and readied his rifle. The second he heard the silence and took the step, Tawnie had already stepped out to shoot down the soldiers.

"Woah!" Gordon yelled as he threw a hand up.

"We have to get out of here!" Tawnie said as she walked to the window to look outside. All over, she could see the laser emitters from the dozens of soldiers lurking outside. Each of them approaching the house like hyenas on the hunt. A suspicious wave of heat filled the house. Gordon gulped in fear that he was about to be slain the moment the soldiers broke past Tawnie.

"Daniel, stay here and cover me!" She asked as she bolted up the stairs.

"Wait, what are you doing?" The man asked as he started to hear her stomping up to the third level of the house and leaving him to defend Milo. He began to see the lasers around them. He reached for Tawnie's duffle bag and threw it on his shoulder. He held his rifle pointed to the door until he saw another laser on the threshold. He pulled the trigger of his rifle and took down another soldier.

"Kid, stay on the stairs!" Gordon screamed. Milo did as he was told and hid within the destroyed secret door. The officer stepped forward, shooting at each red laser shining into the living room.

"Tawnie!" the officer screamed. "It's way too many of them! I can't do this for long!"

"MOMMY!" Milo screamed. Gordon could hear rumbling in the ceiling as the woman seemed to be wrecking her own home. Suddenly, they heard glass breaking in the distance. He hoped that it wasn't someone breaking in but saw a second series of rounds coming from above. Tawnie's shooting skills were impressive, as she hit 90% of her targets. A quick glance outside and he could see body after body fall to the ground.

"Woohoo!" Officer Gordon cheered. After her frenzy Tawnie rushed downstairs and retrieved Milo from the basement entrance. The two rushed to the kitchen, and the man heard keys jingle.

"We got a plan?" He asked. "This victory won't last long."

Tawnie had opened the door to the garage and looked inside. It was dark, so she fumbled with the keys she grabbed from the hook by the garage door. She found a car keyfob remote and tapped the unlock button. A car's lights flashed out of the abysmal space and illuminated the garage and part of the kitchen. Gordon saw the glow in his peripheral vision and began to move toward it.

"Tawnie!" He called to her.

"Back here!" She yelled as she buckled Milo into the car seat. Gordon reached the garage entrance and saw the dome lights inside the car. He stepped inside the garage and closed the door behind him. The man reached for his lantern and switched it back on. He could see that the home's garage was clean and nearly empty. The car inside was a small, silver hybrid hatchback.

"We just about to pull out and drive through all of them?" The officer asked.

"Maybe," Tawnie answered as she closed Milo's door. "But we have to open the door somehow without electricity."

Gordon nodded. "I got that."

The man got on top of the car and reached for the locking pin that attached the electric opener to the door. He got down and headed to the opening. He looked at the woman as she approached the driver's door. He grinned, "How long do I have before you leave me here?"

"I'll do what I need to keep you alive," Tawnie answered. "No man left behind."

He smiled as he looked down at his hands. "On your mark." He said to her. Tawnie took a deep breath as she prepared to make the call.

"Mommy?" Milo called.

"Yeah, Spud?" Tawnie answered, looking back at him. The boy seemed hesitant to ask his question, making his mother nervous.

"You okay, Miles? Do you have to pee?" She asked.

Milo shook his head.

"Then what is it, Spud?" She asked as she became impatient.

"Are we going to die?"

Tawnie's body stopped as she heard the men outside breaking into the house. Her skin became flushed, and her eyes were spacey as she pondered his words. His question had stolen all of her confidence.

"Go!" Gordon yelled, forcing the door over his head.

The hybrid's wheels spun in place as the vehicle reversed. There were individuals outside walking along the front of the house. She hit three with the car, knocking them down and causing them to slow down. Gordon raised his rifle and began to shoot at the remaining soldiers. In the distance, more soldiers laid fire. Gordon did his best to hold the men off and keep them from getting any closer. As he walked to the car, he saw one of the men sticking out from underneath the vehicle. Gordon quickly shot the man. As the life slowly faded from the man's body, his arms and neck slowly went limp. Gordon knocked on the window, and Tawnie hit the switch to roll it down. As he continued to fire, he swung his legs into the window. Sitting on the car door's edge, he yelled for Tawnie to drive.

"Heading out to the right!" Tawnie warned. Before she cleared the driveway, Gordon shot down a good number of men. He slid down into his seat to readjust and began to shoot at the soldiers to the right. The car stopped upon clearing the driveway, and Tawnie spun the wheel. Meanwhile, Gordon did what he could to clear the road. The laser-like artillery pelted the front of the vehicle as Tawnie headed toward them. The small car bounced over the fallen bodies while still being hit consistently on one side. Tawnie mashed the gas to the floor. She sped through the neighborhood, leaving the firing squad in the dust. She turned out all the lights and reached for the eyeglass compartment. She pulled out a pair of dark-tinted glasses that started to glow green at the edge. Gordon fell back into the car and sighed as Tawnie checked the mirror to see if the soldiers were following.

"I think we're good," She said.

Gordon looked back himself, noticing the light fading where

the outpost was.

"Holy shit!" He said as he checked the back seat. "Milo, you good back there?" Gordon asked.

"Yeah." The kid nervously responded.

"Good job back there, Spud," Tawnie added. "We wouldn't have made it out of there without you."

Gordon looked into the back seat, finding the boy grinning.

"Did I miss something?" The officer asked.

"Obviously," Tawnie said as she examined the rear view mirrors. "Let's just say he has more tricks than the average."

Gordon began to look around himself, suspicious of her wandering eyes. He noticed the bright light ascending into the sky from the opposite end of the neighborhood.

"Were we not going to discuss the helicopter coming for us now?" Gordon asked.

"Oh yeah, I was gonna tell you as soon as we got away from it."

The officer's head fell as he sighed again.

"What's the plan?" He asked.

Tawnie smirked, "We get away, or we die."

Chapter XVIII

Tawnie looked forward. The car went silent as the two checked for the helicopter behind them. Tawnie hoped that as she drove in the dark, they wouldn't be found during their escape. Gordon's heart raced as he watched the vehicle maneuver above the horizon. It hovered in one spot for only a moment as if the pilot was unsure where to go. He felt relief as the car rushed along, creating space between them.

"As long as you don't have to hit brakes anytime soon, we'll be okay, I think," Gordon announced as he sat back in his seat.

"I pulled the fuses for the lights," Tawnie responded. The man looked at her with squinted eyes. "Who the fuck are you?"

Tawnie turned her attention to him momentarily. "That's not important."

Angrily, the man shook his head. "The hell it is!" He snarled. "You claim to know that all of this was going to happen! You have a secret armory under your house. You own classified documents as a conspiracy theorist who hasn't been assassinated!"

Tawnie looked forward. "Look, now is not the time to get into that. We need to focus on surviving." She calmly said to him.

The man went silent as he stared at her. Again, he shook his head as he looked forward.

"Fucking night vision and weird gadgets and shit." The man grumbled. "Where are we going, Tawnie? Do we even have a plan?"

"Can you stop bitching?" She exploded. "I'm trying to think! It's not like we're on the verge of being exterminated or anything!"

The man grunted. "Maybe you should give them what they came for."

"Ha!" Tawnie said. "Humanity doesn't deserve that."

Gordon immediately looked at her with suspicion. Suddenly, the helicopter started flying toward them.

"Shit!" Tawnie growled.

"Is it coming this way?" Gordon asked.

The woman nodded as she drove faster through the darkness. They left the neighborhood and entered some desolate back roads. Gordon looked at the scenery. The empty fields on both sides of the road concerned him.

"This isn't good." He said.

Again, Tawnie nodded. "Yup, we're out of luck here, and our only hope is to fight back."

Gordon reached into the floor of the back seat until he felt Tawnie's duffle bag. "I hope you packed something powerful in here," he said with a smile. Tawnie also smiled.

"Alright, Spud. This ride is about to get bumpy," She told her kid. "So I need you to remain calm and keep breathing deep, okay?"

"But Mommy, I'm scared." The little boy said as he clutched the straps of his car seat.

"I know Milo," she responded. "We're all scared. But we're in this together, and we'll make it through."

There was a brief silence as Gordon looked over at Tawnie in admiration.

"You promise?" The boy asked.

"Super promise!" Tawnie laughed.

Gordon pulled a large rifle from the bag and examined it the best he could in the dark.

"You wouldn't happen to have another one of those goggles, would you?" The officer asked.

"I may have a pair in that bag." She answered. "However, it may be best that you didn't put them on."

Gordon paused. He looked at the road before them and couldn't see a thing. His body trembled as he became unnerved. The only light around were from the dim buttons on the dashboard and the helicopter behind them. Gordon was forced to trust Tawnie to drive the route.

"Gordon, snap out of it!" She yelled. "We don't have much room for error here."

"Yeah, got it!" He said. "What do you need me to do?"

Tawnie sighed. "As soon as that spotlight hits us, I need you to open the sunroof and start shooting."

"Hmm." The man nodded. "Sounds easy enough."

Tawnie continued into the night, hoping the vehicle would make a U-turn at some point.

"If it came out this far, I assume we're caught," Gordon said as he reached for the sunroof button.

"Wait!" Tawnie yelled, smacking his hand down. "I have a plan."

The man looked at her as if she was insane. "A plan other than shooting them out of the sky?" He asked. "I hope the new plan can top that."

"Tawnie shrugged. "I'm not sure, but we must try something before we ultimately get killed."

"What's up?" Gordon asked. "Because we're about one minute from getting descended on by the world's most efficient killers."

"There's a patch of forest coming up that we can take cover in, maybe we could–"

"Maybe?" The man interrupted. "Are you going to take a chance like that?"

Tawnie went silent, continuing to formulate her plan.

"That chopper is likely clad with artillery. I don't plan to go to war with it." Tawnie explained. "We can't be sure that those bullets will take it down if we're exposed."

Gordon growled. "If this doesn't work–"

"I know." Tawnie quickly cut him off. "But we don't have a choice. If we keep driving, we're just a moving target."

Again, Gordon growled. "Fine, I'll keep my finger on the trigger."

Tawnie approached the wooded area that she mentioned and slowed the car. She pulled into the ditch and looked at him. She could see the discomfort in his eyes as he stared ahead. They waited quietly for the vehicle to pass. Tawnie stared out the sunroof. Her heart raced as she hung their survival on a theory. As the sound of the propellers got louder and could be felt throughout the car. Suddenly, she saw the light reflecting from the treetops as the helicopter approached. The woman held her breath as she watched it pass them by and hover in the distance.

Moments later, after everything had gotten dark again, Gordon let out a sigh of relief."

"Holy shit!" He said. "I can't believe that worked."

Tawnie giggled, "Me either."

The man slowly turned to her with his eyes wide in shock, causing her to laugh harder.

"Milo, you okay, Love?" She asked her son.

"Yeah." He answered.

"Good, you need anything?"

The boy hummed momentarily before answering, "I need to pee."

Tawnie looked at the officer, and he appeared to be thinking.

"It looks like both of you guys need to go," Tawnie said as she unbuckled herself. "Can you?" she asked as she gently touched Gordon's arm.

"Oh yeah, I got it." He said as he opened the door and got out of the car. He opened the back door and helped Milo out. Tawnie pulled out the communicator radio she had taken earlier. Officer Gordon held the lantern to give Milo enough light to see. Gordon looked around, hoping to not find any danger. He noticed that Tawnie got out of the car as well. She turned a knob on the radio that made an obnoxious click, followed by a quick succession of beeps. The woman walked to the wood line and began to unbuckle her pants with one hand as she held the radio up to examine it.

"Woah!" Gordon yelled as he turned his head, thinking that she would stop. But with another glance, he recognized her bare legs and clean-shaven pelvis as she began to squat.

"Oh!" He yelled again as he turned around completely. "Why the hell would you just undress without warning?" He asked. Tawnie only smiled as she continued to switch through the radio channels.

"Relax!" She yelled. "Have you never seen a woman before? I couldn't hold my pee any longer either."

Gordon grunted as he shook his head, clear of any lingering images of her body.

"Good to know I'm too hideous to look at." She joked.

"Dammit!" Gordon growled. "Just put your pants back on."

Quietly, Tawnie finished up, standing after to wipe and dress herself.

"Let's hope they warn us here before they make their next move." The woman said, still examining the unit. She approached Gordon and noticed the red on his face as she walked around him.

"Wow, I did a number on you just now, huh?" Tawnie asked, trying to press her elbow into the man's sternum for a gentle nudge. In the process, Tawnie would unintentionally feel a hard bulge in his pants.

"Oh no, I'm so sorry!" She said as she jumped backward. The woman burst into laughter, only furthering the man's embarrassment. Gordon began to seeth. He went for Milo and directed the boy back to the car.

"What's so funny?" He asked as he subconsciously buckled his trousers during the short walk.

"Nothing," Gordon quickly answered. "Your mom is just being a crazy person right now."

He helped Milo back into his car seat and stared over the car at Tawnie. She was walking back with a grin on her face. The man shook his head and got inside. Upon getting into the car herself, Tawnie noticed the scowl on his face and began to laugh again.

"Aww!" She said as she grabbed the man's arm. "It isn't that bad, is it?"

"Drive the damn car, Tawnie." Gordon snarled.

"Okay, okay!" She giggled as she put the car into gear and began to drive. They sped through the night in silence. But Tawnie continued to snicker to herself.

"What the hell is your problem, Tawnie?" Gordon asked. But the lantern's light still shined on her face, and the man could see her wiping tears. He gasped.

"What's happening?"

Tawnie shook her head and smiled. "It's just…" she stopped short of answering.

Gordon took a deep breath and stopped staring so intensely. This allowed her to calm down. She sighed and laughed again.

"I still got it." She muttered. "Thank you for showing me that."

Gordon grunted as he looked over at her left hand on the

steering wheel. Her ring finger was empty. Officer Gordon was about to respond but thought against his statement.

"I don't recall," he said. Tawnie looked over at him and noticed the grin on his face.

"You alright back there, Spud?" The woman asked her kid.

"Yeah," Milo answered.

Tawnie put her shades back on. "Alright, this will probably be a long road trip."

She looked back at Gordon and noticed that his smile had vanished, and he folded his arms across his chest.

"You okay?" She asked him.

He only nodded as he turned off the lantern. As it got dark and Tawnie's glasses activated, she could see him shake his head in shame. But instead of meddling, she chose to drive.

Chapter XIX

Hours later, Tawnie stopped to devise a plan outside of Idaho Falls. She parked in a crowded car dealership where their presence wouldn't be so obvious. At this point, she could see the sunlight coming over the horizon. She looked into the back seat to check on Milo. He was sleeping. On the passenger side, Officer Gordon still folded his arms, looking forward. He had not said a word since their pit stop.

"What happened?" Tawnie asked.

He cut a look at her, hardly turning toward her. "What are you referring to?"

"You," Tawnie said. "One minute, we could have a conversation, and you're ice cold the next. Did I do something wrong?"

The man shook his head. "No." He answered. "I did."

"What, Daniel, I've had an accidental nip-slip on camera in front of millions. I'm not bothered by you seeing my vagina."

"Oh yeah!?" He asked as he turned to her. "And what would your husband think of me looking at your vagina or your flirtatious nature?"

Tawnie cleared her throat and looked ahead.

"Just as I suspected." He grumbled. "And you don't even have the decency to wear your wedding ring."

Tawnie looked back at Milo to ensure that he was still asleep. The bead of drool from his mouth was all the evidence she needed. She turned forward and peeled the glasses off, shaking her head.

"I was married before, and my ex-wife had the nerve to sleep with my best friend and think we could reconcile. So I detest a cheater." Gordon explained. "I respected you up until what you did last night."

Tawnie didn't mutter a word. The man looked at her and saw the focus in her eyes.

"You don't look like you have a bit of remorse." He continued. She sighed as she looked at him with angry eyes.

"Why do I need to be remorseful over being left by my husband?" She asked. The officer's heart stopped as he stared at her. He opened his mouth to say something, but the words could not formulate in his thoughts.

"Look, you've been assuming the worst of me since we met, and you threatened to shoot me." She said as she placed the shades in the eyeglass compartment in the overhead console. "I think we need to go our separate ways."

"Shit." He said. "Tawnie, I'm sorry."

"No, it's okay." She smiled. "I'm used to it when it comes to people like you."

Gordon shook his head and stared at her with anger in his expression.

"You think that I'm racist?" He asked, pointing at himself. "I am not at all racist!"

Tawnie chuckled. "No, I was talking about cops. But I find it interesting that you said it first."

"I... I–" He started to say. But Tawnie simply touched his arm to get him to stop talking.

"It's aye-okay," she said with a smile. "I can leave you here and we can go our separate ways like you want."

"Tawnie, wait. I didn't mean to–"

"Well, what did you mean, Officer?" She asked. "If I had known that peeing in front of you was going to offend you so much, I would have done it in this seat. At least I would have avoided this conversation with you!"

Suddenly, a gleam of light in the distance caught Gordon's attention.

"Wait, Tawnie–" He attempted to interrupt. But the woman only continued to ramble.

"Who do you think you are anyway?" She asked. Gordon didn't answer. He looked around the environment for possible changes, completely ignoring her.

"Are you listening?" She asked.

"No!" He growled, causing her to flinch. "We are surrounded."

Tawnie stopped talking and stared at him. Her eyes slowly looked away to the outside of the car.

"What did I miss?" She asked.

"I saw a gleam of light over there." He said as he pointed behind her. "Then…"

Tawnie nodded as her eyes slowly scanned the area.

"Yeah, I see it now," she said as she reached between the seat and the center console to pull out a large handgun. "Of course, I was too distracted to notice the imminent danger all around." Gordon watched as she frantically gathered materials for a fight, and then he looked back at Milo. He was still asleep.

"What's the plan here?" He asked.

"We run for it on foot while attempting to suppress their fire," Tawnie answered as she looked into the back seat. "Feel free to leave once we are out of hot water."

"Where exactly would I go, Tawnie?" The man growled. "I'm pretty sure they've already cleaned this town dry too!"

Tawnie leaned back and stared at him for a moment. While maintaining eye contact, she reached into the back seat and tapped Milo's foot.

"Milo, wake up, sweetie," Tawnie called. The boy snorted as he snapped out of his slumber, appalled and confused.

"Okay, Spud, something came up, and now we need to get out of here," Tawnie explained. The kid rubbed his tired, weary eyes with his hands. She waited for a response, periodically looking around the environment.

"Milo!" she yelled as she shook his leg, startling him. The boy became alert as he unbuckled himself from the car seat.

"Look, personally, I don't care what you do. I just need you to get away from me."Tawnie said to him.

The man sighed. "Tawnie, I believe we need to stick together to get through this. We need each other."

Her eyes grew large at his statement. "Another man telling a woman what she needs in her life." She snarled. "I don't need you, Daniel Gordon. You need me!"

The man nodded. "I'm not disagreeing. I do." He said, causing her rage to subside momentarily.

"Tawnie, you're obviously a lot bigger than some social media conspiracy theorist." He assured her. "I like to win, and this is a game of survival. So I want to join your team because I think you know how to. We may disagree on something big, but we're on the same page there."

Tawnie smiled before thinking about their previous conversation. He could see the worry in her eyes.

"Also, I'm sorry if I offended you," he said as he readied his rifle. "I allowed my personal situation to cause me to lash out at you."

Tawnie looked away and sighed. She reached into her pocket and pulled the electronic device from her vault. The screen illuminated, revealing a map. She cycled back to what appeared to be the home screen and scrolled into another part of the interface. Gordon attempted to see what she was doing but couldn't figure it out.

Suddenly, the woman picked up the radio and began to switch through the channels. Simultaneously, she watched the screen on her device and the radio.

"Gotcha." She said as she stopped on one channel in particular and looked around again. The radio began to broadcast a conversation about their whereabouts.

"Subjects are parked at the car dealership. All units engage!"

"Time to go!" She screamed as she jumped from the vehicle and pointed her rifle down the road. She began to see shadows lurking in the distance. She placed one eye behind the sight picture.

"There she is!" They heard someone yell over the radio. But Tawnie began to shoot. Gordon fumbled out of the car and followed behind her. The man was fascinated with her skill as she fired round after round into what appeared to be darkness. While the return fire was in burst, Tawnie sent single shots on her own in different directions. It looked like she was doing target practice to the police officer. Suddenly, the radio was activated, and screams were heard through it. Tawnie just kept shooting.

"All troops engage now!" A man screamed with fear in his voice. "We have encountered Agent 0, and she is extremely lethal!"

"That's our queue, Gordon!" Tawnie yelled back to him. The officer hurried to open the rear door of the car. Milo jumped out and fell to the ground. Gordon reached into the back seat and grabbed the duffle bag.

"Tawnie!" Gordon yelled for her. "We're good!"

The woman continued to shoot downrange as she moved to the right. They found themselves in the middle of a parking lot and approached a line of parked cars.

"Get behind the cars!" She yelled. She hid behind one car while Milo and Gordon hid behind another. Nervously, the man looked around to see if anyone was there. Suddenly, his heart dropped as he saw Tawnie standing next to her hybrid car again, still shooting.

"Tawnie!" he screamed as he prepared to run. But immediately, he felt a tug on his jacket. He held his breath, thinking it may be a soldier who had snuck up on him while he wasn't looking. He only knew it was too heavy of a pull to be Milo. He clenched his fists and prepared for war until he heard a soft-spoken voice call his name.

"Daniel, wait!" She yelled. Stunned, the man squeezed his eyes shut and opened them to ensure he saw Tawnie returning fire. Quickly, he turned around to see her there as well.

"Tawnie..." He muttered as he glanced back at the person shooting.

Tawnie moved first, staying as low as possible. Gordon and Milo did the same. They moved around the side of the dealership building, passing open garage doors. Tawnie took a look inside and noticed blood all over the shop floor. There were no bodies, and everything looked unkempt, as if it was all abandoned in the middle of a shift. A car on a lift hung halfway down from its back wheel. Toolboxes were left open, and tools were on the floor, soaking in the pooling blood. Unable to react, Tawnie ran inside the shop. Gordon and Milo followed. Almost instantly, a vehicle drove past the bay doors. Gordon looked down at the woman with suspicion. She shook her head as she pulled out the radio.

Someone announced, "Subject and her accomplice are back in the car! All units engage with extreme caution!"

Tawnie pulled out the tablet-looking device and cycled

through some unknown screens. The function she arrived at was a map on one half of the screen and a view from the front of the car.

"Let's have some fun, boys," Tawnie grinned. She clipped the radio to her waistline and slid her finger across the tablet screen.

"The car is on the move!" Someone screamed. The soldiers all turned their attention to the moving vehicle as the woman watched it on the screen. Gordon watched as red dots appeared on the map, swarming the vehicle fast as it escaped.

Vehicles rushed to the car, using all their artillery. However, Tawnie seemed excited about the chase, worrying the officer. The car traveled away from their location, allowing Gordon to sigh with relief

"Now, it's time for the finale," Tawnie said as she swooped her finger on the screen.

"Wait, what?" The man asked. "What the hell is happening?"

"Hologram in the car and a remote," Tawnie answered.

Tawnie looked at him and continued to grin. She stepped outside the garage and took a deep breath. She walked toward the main road as the flood of black SUVs approached.

"Stay here with Milo!" she yelled back to Gordon, putting the rifle down to her side and holding a tablet in her other hand.

"You don't need help?" He asked.

"Nah," She yelled. "I got this."

Seemingly, with no fear in her body, Tawnie stepped out onto the road and stood directly in the center. Gordon watched in horror as the hybrid and all of its following closed in on her at about eighty miles per hour.

"What the hell is your mom doing, Kid?" Gordon asked as he clenched, eyes locked onto the car.

Tawnie tapped the screen and a wave of distorted energy emitted from the car in a ring-like wave. It was colorless but had the appearance of a heatwave. Gordon watched as the energy came near.

"Oh shit!" He yelled as he cringed, bracing himself from impact. He opened his eyes seconds later, noticing it didn't cause any harm to him or Milo. The lights flickered throughout the garage warehouse and finally switched off. Other electronic humming in the background stopped, causing it to become eerily silent. All of the SUVs crashed into the back of the car as it stopped in the middle of the road, causing a pileup behind it.

"Egress, egress, egress!" Someone yelled over the radio.

Once, Tawnie picked up the tablet and stood her rifle before her. She could see the men in the front cars looking at her. She felt their eyes on her despite their masks, making their faces impossible to see.

"There she is!" The man said from the front vehicle into the radio. "Get her!"

Men began to reach for their window switches and try to open their doors. But their vehicles were dead. Tawnie shook her head and reached for the tablet screen to press one final button, and the car exploded. The blast went in the direction of the dozens of vehicles behind it. Flames and shrapnel tore through the entire fleet. Tawnie somehow watched the explosion with a calm demeanor. She placed the tablet in her coat pocket and threw the rifle over her shoulder as she stepped forward.

Gordon was shocked at her actions, wondering how far she would go. Tawnie walked through the center of the road with burning SUVs piled up on both sides. One particular vehicle sat at the end of the line. Stalled out, it couldn't move, but it was fortunate not to be affected by the blast too much. When the woman approached the vehicle, passengers were already stumbling out. The soldier who sat behind the driver ran around the vehicle, pointed his rifle, and pulled the trigger once he saw Tawnie. However, nothing happened. The woman glared at him.

"Guys," He screamed to his comrades, "My gun isn't working!"

"You idiot, she blasted us with an EMP!" The driver yelled.

"RUN!" The other rear passenger screamed. They all attempted to escape. Tawnie just watched them in silence as she stood against the open driver door of the vehicle. The driver was still inside, fearful and seemingly unable to move. When it seemed like the men would escape, she pushed away from the truck as the rifle fell from her shoulder. She pointed it just like she had earlier, and with three trigger squeezes, the three men hit the ground.

Tawnie approached the vehicle again and examined the lone survivor in silence.

"Please," He begged. "I need help."

She smiled before looking around the environment.

"So did the people of Rigby," she replied. "Did you not assume they were humans who simply needed help?"

The man began to snivel. Tawnie reached up and undid his mask, revealing an older white male, approximately 45. He was balding at the top of his head. His facial hair was shaved close but maintained a five o'clock shadow. He continued to hyperventilate as Tawnie watched, unbothered by his struggle.

"Sir, you appear to have been affected by the EMP," Tawnie said as she approached him. "You must have a bad heart… probably a pacemaker in there keeping you going?"

The man nodded, tears falling from his eyes. "Aren't you at all bothered by the air?" she asked. The man shook his head, and Tawnie grabbed his collar.

"Well, I am." She snarled. "What's with the masks?"

"It's… It's in the air!" He muttered.

Growing impatient, Tawnie placed her other hand flat on the man's chest. She pressed into his sternum, and he began to scream in agony.

"What the hell are you talking about?" She yelled.

"The virus!" He roared. "The virus is in the air, and everyone is affected by contact!"

The woman's eyes widened as she released his uniform. Thinking about what he said, she took a step backward.

"What virus is strong enough to cause you guys to kill innocent people on this scale?" She asked.

As he maintained a little space from her, the man hurried to grab something from his pocket. Tawnie rushed to stop him, thinking she was about to be attacked. Instead, the man pulled out a knife and placed the blade on his own neck. His arm swiped across him, and his crimson insides splashed all over the ground.

"Dammit!" She growled as his body fell out of the vehicle.

Back at the garage, Gordon looked out into the distance, attempting to find Tawnie.

"Mommy!" Milo called out as he saw her emerging from the flames. "She's okay! Mommy, over here!"

Officer Gordon looked down at the child and smiled at his innocent cheer. But when he looked up to see his mother approaching, his heart raced with fear.

Chapter XX

The officer took a hard swallow as his eyes followed the woman over.

"Mommy!" The kid yelled with glee. "You beat the bad guys!"

"Hey, Spud!" she greeted him with excitement. "Were you good for Mr. Gordon?" She asked. The kid nodded his head as he put one finger to his lips. Tawnie turned to Gordon after picking Milo up from the ground. But the officer stepped backward. His eyes widened, and his nose flared.

"Daniel," She called. "What's the matter?"

"You just killed dozens of men and did it with a smile." He responded. "I think the term bad guy may be used in the wrong context here."

Tawnie smiled again and nodded. "I found us a car," she said. "Shall we hit the road again?"

"Yes!" Milo sang as he threw one hand up. Tawnie put the little boy down, and he skipped away. Meanwhile, his mother continued to glare at the officer.

"It seems like you have something to get off your chest, Daniel," Tawnie said.

Softly, the man nodded. She took a deep breath and looked away.

"I never want to have to be like that." She muttered. "I just couldn't let them kill me and take my son."

Gordon sighed as he watched her appear to unravel. A brief smile of understanding graced his lips, and his eyes softened. He stepped away from her to follow the boy. Then, he would follow Milo as he skipped toward the main road. Tawnie sighed and followed behind them, stepping out front. She led them toward one of the SUVs that survived the explosion.

"Here it is." She said, pointing to it. She stopped walking. Officer Gordon stepped around her and proceeded to the truck. He opened the driver's door and peeked inside.

"What are you looking for?" Tawnie asked.

But he was too focused and missed the question. She pulled her son along by his hand. "Come on, Milo."

She escorted the boy to the back seat and allowed him inside. Once the boy was seated, she helped him buckle up.

"Mommy?" Milo called as his mother prepared to close his door. She stopped and looked inside at him once more.

"Yeah, Spud?" She asked.

With a huge smile, the boy said to her, "Good job, mommy."

She smiled and gave the boy a nod just before closing the door. Tawnie turned away from the vehicle and put her hands on her hips. Gordon watched her closely, realizing that something was wrong. Milo, however, had no clue. The officer watched as she looked to the sky and took a deep breath before wiping her face with her arm. She discreetly turned around and got into the truck. Her face dried, and it appeared as if she was okay. Officer Gordon reached for the ignition and pressed the button to start the engine. To his surprise, it started. He looked around the vehicle to examine the interior as he searched for the key fob. He looked at the instrument cluster, and his eyes gravitated toward the odometer.

"Woah!" He said to himself. Tawnie looked at him but didn't say anything.

"This truck is brand new," he continued. "It only has a few hundred miles on the engine."

Tawnie nodded and looked back out the windshield "Meaning that someone fronted a lot of money for this." Gordon put his hands around the steering wheel and prepared to drive away.

"Where to?" He asked.

But Tawnie shook her head. "I don't know," She said. "I don't have anywhere to be except for online."

Gordon winced at her statement. "You don't have any family you want to check on?" He asked. "Because, you know, the next option is to get the hell out of the state."

Tawnie sighed. "The only person I have is my mother-in-law,

and I'm not sure I'm good enough to want her to survive this."

"Now is not the time for jokes," Gordon told her.

Tawnie turned in her seat toward him, "What about you?" She yelled. "I'm trying to think, so I need you to get off my case!"

Things went silent between them. Tawnie spent a long moment staring at the man so that he could see the pain in her eyes.

"I'm sorry." She whispered. "I don't know what to do."

Gordon sighed and let go of the wheel, allowing his back to crash on the lumbar of the seat.

"No, I don't have any family either," he said. A long-lost sister somewhere is all I know. Sometimes it gets to me, too."

"I'm not bothered by that," Tawnie responded. "I've gone what seems to be a few lifetimes on my own. What's bothering me is that the guy I cornered a minute ago said that a virus was in the air."

"A virus?" Gordon questioned. "So these guys are here to quarantine us by force?"

Tawnie shrugged her shoulders. She continued to look forward as she calculated possible outcomes. A simple prediction prompted her to pull out the tablet she had used earlier.

"What the hell is that?" Gordon asked.

"Something I had to use on my last job." She said as she started to work.

The officer watched the screen from the driver's side. She logged in, and the interface looked like a government control system. Tawnie started typing code and command scripts with no hesitation. Gordon swallowed hard as he watched as if she was putting on a show.

"You're a doctor, right?" He asked.

"Yeah, a psychiatrist," Tawnie answered.

Gordon nodded, squinting his eyes. "Right, so how does a woman at your age have the time to go to school for psychology, learn to fight the way you do, and hack like you're doing now?"

Tawnie paused and raised her head. "It's just some skills I acquired over the years." She answered.

"Bullshit!" The man yelled. "If you want me to trust you, I need a reason, Agent 0."

Tawnie stopped talking and stared at him. Then, seeming to ignore his request, she continued to type on the tablet. She punched in a code, and her body became tense, anticipating an inevitable result. But unfortunately, the tablet began to beep.

"Shit," She growled as she sat back in her seat. "I was a part of an organization that works outside the government. We resolve supernatural issues before the public finds out."

Gordon stared at her, stunned. "Get out of here!" He laughed, looking away for a moment. But when he looked back at Tawnie, he realized she was not smiling.

"Wow, you're serious." He said. Tawnie nodded and looked forward again.

"I've been attempting to contact my former associates for guidance and back up. But these goons, or whoever they work for, have locked this area down. There's no communication in or out."

"That's unsettling." Gordon nodded, "Are we able to find the source of the block?"

Tawnie leaned against the door with her hand on her head. "I tried. But whoever is managing this system, has it wound pretty tight."

Suddenly, Tawnie's tablet began to beep.

"Woah!" Gordon said. "What's happening to it?"

She flipped the tablet over. Milo Senior displayed on the screen. "It's my husband," she said.

"Daddy?" Milo interrupted.

Tawnie took a deep breath and closed her eyes before tapping the screen, "Milo?"

"Yeah, it's me." Her husband said.

"Daddy!" Little Milo yelled again.

"Hey there, Spud!" The man said.

"Milo, listen. We don't have time for pleasantries," Tawnie interjected. "Are you okay?"

"Yeah, I'm fine." He answered. "What's going on?"

Tawnie spent a moment explaining what happened.

"Holy shit! That's not good at all!" He responded. "I'll leave here and come back home now!"

"That's not possible right now," Tawnie warned. She continued her investigation on the tablet.

"Why not? How bad is it?" He asked. "Well, our neighborhood has become a lay station for hundreds of soldiers. In addition, all my neighbors are dead."

Milo went silent. The sound of him moving around his office rustled through the speakers.

"Are there any other survivors?" He finally spoke.

"Yeah. I'm with a police officer who helped us when they locked us in the school," Tawnie answered, looking over at Gordon. "I did find Abbie, but…"

"What about her?" He obliviously asked. "Did she…?"

The man waited for an answer, but Tawnie stopped to hold back her tears.

"Did you reach out to… you know who? Maybe they can combat this." He added. Tawnie growled again and looked away as the tears began to pour again. She spent a moment wiping her face before giving him a response. She looked at Gordon again, then back to her son in the back seat.

"Milo, remember that worst-case scenario I told you about?" She asked.

"Yeah." He answered briefly, "You're not saying that—"

Tawnie nodded. "I am Milo. I don't believe we will make it out of this one."

Milo Jr. began to cry. Officer Gordon watched as the woman he was so afraid of earlier started to sob in the passenger seat.

"No, I refuse to give up like that!" he interjected.

"Wait, who was that?" Milo Sr. asked.

"Hey, Mr. Simms, I'm Officer Daniel Gordon with the IFPD. Your wife got us out of a few sticky situations here in the city." He announced.

"Yeah, Officer, thank you for accompanying her." Her husband replied. "Sorry, we had to meet in these conditions."

"Sir, I'm vowing to reunite you with your family despite the current landscape here."

Tawnie glanced at the officer and held her palm up to him.

"Wait," Tawnie said. "I briefly recall that Primotech was researching in Idaho Falls a few weeks ago. What was that all about?"

"Uh," Milo said, attempting to concoct an answer. "Uh, I'm not sure. I was given an assignment and only did my job. I'm not sure what the research was for."

Tawnie nodded. "Shortly after this big job, Primotech has an emergency mission in Yellowstone. Is that to watch this chaos from the high ground?"

Her husband scoffed, and Gordon squirmed in his seat with discomfort.

"Are you insinuating that my company is responsible for this quarantine?" He asked.

"I'm insinuating that as one of the lead researchers, it's suspicious that you have no clue why you're doing your job. You either suck at it or something fishy is happening."

"Wait, wait, wait!" Gordon interrupted. "There has to be a way to get to a resolution without bloodshed."

"In a perfect world where Tawnie isn't the self-righteous conspiracy guru," Milo said.

"Or Milo didn't work for the devil himself!" Tawnie responded.

Gordon looked at the woman with squinted eyes.

"Do what?" He asked. "Jacob Maxwell? The philanthropist?"

Tawnie nodded. "I know a front when I see one. And a front that big is hiding something even bigger!"

Gordon sighed as the couple continued to argue. He watched the rage in Tawnie grow as she continued. Milo was still crying in the back seat. He watched the kid, wondering what damage could be happening to him psychologically. The officer began to sweat again as it started to feel warm. This time, he looked around, wondering about the temperature. The truck was running, but the heat was off.

"Hold up!" He yelled, causing the two of them to quiet down. "Mr. Simms, with all due respect, we are in the middle of a war zone right now, so we don't have time to unpack all of that."

Gordon looked over at Tawnie's tablet for guidance and then at her. She shrugged her shoulders in defeat.

Gordon shook his head. "Look, from what I'm hearing, Mr. Simms, your company is–"

"Look, Officer!" Simms cut him off. The two of them looked at one another. Gordon was appalled, but Tawnie had an eyebrow raised and a smirk as if she saw it coming.

"I don't know who you are, so discussions about my business are out of the question." He warned the officer.

Gordon looked in the passenger seat at Tawnie, who was taking a deep breath to calm herself.

"Look, Mister–"

"Doctor!" Simms cut him off.

Frustrated, Gordon leaned back in his seat and relaxed himself.

"Alright, Doctor," He sarcastically said. "I can see that this conversation is regressing far from being productive. Your wife and kid are in danger. Why do you seem like you're not concerned?"

The doctor went silent again. Despite trying to remain calm, Tawnie still had tears streaming down her face. Gordon looked into the back seat and saw Milo close his ears with his hands.

"I will head back as soon as I can. Where are you located?" He changed his tune.

Gordon nodded, "Yeah, we're in Rigby right now."

"Right," Dr. Simms said. "Primotech has a developing facility in Rexburg. Hopefully, you guys can make it up there?"

Tawnie flinched as she heard the news. Gordon looked at her again with suspicion. She just shook her head upon looking at the man."

"Yeah, we should be able to make that," Tawnie said as she looked at the map again.

"That works out," Gordon said. "I have friends in Rexburg. We can visit them, provided they aren't dead yet."

"Alright," Dr. Simms added. "Stay safe, and I'll see you soon, Tawnie."

Tawnie remained quiet for a moment, thinking of how to respond.

"See ya." She replied. But to their surprise, Milo Sr. had already hung up.

Tawnie looked at Officer Gordon. The man recognized the look on her face but neglected to say anything. He started the vehicle and immediately reached for her hand to comfort her.

"I'm sorry." She whispered. But the officer squeezed the back of her hand as he drove off into the sunrise.

Chapter XXI

It was dawn. The winter sun shone brightly over the flat lands of the Gem State. Gordon squeezed the steering wheel with frustration as he searched for signs of life. The roads were empty and desolate, just like the barren winter. There were nothing more than golden fields as far as the eye could see. There were a few tiny houses here and there, but overall, the area was empty. Tawnie hoped she would see people outside warming their cars or recently coming home. But despite vehicles being present at many, there was a sense of abandonment. An unexplained quiet that felt wrong. Milo sat silently. His mother and the officer stared out the windshield. The radio would be on, but somehow, every station was nothing but static. In addition, Tawnie held the communicator she stole closely. She hoped for some clue as to where the exterminating soldiers would strike next.

"You're driving like you have a destination," Tawnie said.

The man nodded. "Yeah, I have a friend in Rexburg that could help us." He answered. "If we are going to fight an army, we will certainly need them."

Tawnie looked at him. "Cop buddy?"

Gordon shook his head. "No, military." He answered. "None of my cop friends had what it took to survive."

Tawnie raised an eyebrow. "What makes you think your military buddy survived?"

The man shrugged. "I don't know." He answered. "My military buddy is just that special, I guess."

"Proximity sensor tripped." A voice came over the radio. Both of their eyes bulged with concern. "Unidentified vehicle approaching from state route twenty."

"Shit!" Tawnie growled as she grabbed the cold rifle from between her legs.

"What do we do?" Gordon asked, tapping his index finger on the steering wheel as he focused intently on the road.

"I don't know," Tawnie answered, "If we turn around, they'll only follow us."

The man nodded as he rubbed the stubble on his chin. "Yeah, that's a good point," he answered.

"Mommy, you can do the thing!" Milo blurted. Gordon glanced over his shoulder at the kid, then at Tawnie.

"Spud, mommy doesn't have a thing." She assured him. "I'm still not sure what you're talking about."

"What is he talking about?" Gordon asked.

The woman pursed her lips and shook her head softly while rolling her eyes. "Kids and their overactive imaginations." She said, becoming giggly and suspicious. Gordon squinted his eyes.

"Do we fight our way out again?" he asked. Tawnie heard the question and suddenly became somber. She leaned back in the seat and took a deep breath. Her eyes looked forward, and her jaw clenched as she stared down the open road.

"I can't promise you guys' safety if I do that." She explained. "Besides, we can't be sure what we'll see up here. I can't say how many soldiers we are up against now."

"Good point," Gordon answered. Can we avoid the onslaught while driving one of their vehicles?"

Tawnie shook her head, "I can't say for certain."

Gordon nodded and began driving the speed limit. They stayed on guard for a few miles until they noticed something damning crossing the South Yellowstone Highway. There was a giant, dark metallic wall that stood around twenty-five feet high. Black SUVs sat near the closed opening on the southbound side. Traffic going northbound was funneled into a tunnel. A raised platform constructed in the median served as a lookout. Soldiers filled the building above the road and stood in formations on the ground. Gordon's heart plunged out of his chest. He thought of slamming on the brakes but thought against it in an effort not to be suspicious.

"I suppose if I turned around, they'll be onto us." He said as he looked around the cabin.

"What are you looking for?" Tawnie asked.

"I thought I saw…" He said, eyeing a pile of black linen inside a black helmet in the back seat beside Milo. At that moment, the kid grabbed it and chucked it over his mom's seat, landing on her head.

The helmet fell but left the clothes on Tawnie's head. She shook her head to get it off. "What the hell?" she asked, eventually grabbing it. "What the hell is this? It smells like used gym shoes!"

"Milo, my man!" Gordon shouted as he unrolled the article with his right hand. "This is a diversion strategy!"

Tawnie fixated on the black shirt belonging to the soldier they stole the truck from. She grabbed the wheel quickly, allowing the man to unbuckle himself and put it on.

"Hurry up!" She sneered with her eyes locked onto the roadblock.

"Got it!" He said. "Any spare masks lying around?"

Tawnie looked behind her. Then she turned forward, eying the glove compartment. She quickly opened it.

"Ha!" She shouted. "There's actually one in here!"

The clock was ticking, and their vehicle was less than a half-mile from the blockade. Soldiers stepped out and stood in the middle of the two-lane road, guns ready to shoot.

"Tawnie, can't you just…" Gordon began to ask, gesturing a gun with his hands.

She shook her head. "It would be wise for them to believe Agent Zero is still in Rigby. Gordon nodded and slipped the mask over his face like a hood. He pulled the straps under the ears tight to secure it to his face. He grabbed the helmet and slammed it on top of his head. Upon finishing, he looked into the passenger seat to discover that Tawnie was gone.

"What the hell?" He asked as he attempted to look back.

"I'm in the back," Tawnie answered. "Act natural and make up something." Tawnie and her son tucked away on the floor in front of the back seat. She rummaged through her bag and found a large handgun that she wrapped her tiny hands around.

"Stay quiet, Spud." She said to him. The boy nodded and closed his eyes.

Gordon took a deep breath and slowed the vehicle down as he

approached the gate. He looked up at the building spanning the entire highway and noticed the number of soldiers in the window, watching them closely. The platform supporting the building stood approximately seven feet high. From up close, the wall spanned as far as the eye could see. In front of them, he could see a chain link gate blocking the tunnel. The armed soldiers still stood before them, staring at the vehicle as it slowed to a halt. A few men also stood on the ground and approached the vehicle's driver's side. Gordon pushed the window switch. The soldier paused, facing him, until the window was rolled down completely. The man outside gave him a nod.

"Heading back to base, battle?" The soldier asked him.

"Yeah, I need to report the incident in Rigby this morning to Top," he said. 'Top' refers to a military unit's first sergeant or officer in charge. In this scenario, Gordon hoped it would also work for this group.

The soldier nodded. "What is there to report?"

Gordon looked ahead, then bowed his head as to seem remorseful. "We encountered Agent Zero." He said. "She killed everyone. I was able to get away unnoticed and get back here."

"Shit, man!" The soldier said. "What happened to her?"

"I know I should have stayed to find out, but I…" Gordon paused.

The man nodded again. "No worries, battle." He said. "As long as the mission is not compromised, the boss won't have to know about it."

"Yeah, it's not like that bitch is getting through our gates." The other soldier added.

Gordon nodded. "I hope so, Battle." He said to them in a low tone. "If you saw what I saw, you'd also be questioning your judgment." One of the men standing beside the vehicle raised his hand. Signaling another standing atop the steel platform. The man stepped to a pedestal-style switch panel at the platform's edge. He pressed a button that opened the gate.

"Go ahead through, soldier." The man said. Gordon raised the window and watched the gate part. Bright white lights shined throughout, resembling sunlight, but they were artificial. Gordon didn't know what to make of what he was seeing. The men on the ground waved him on, and he eased forward through the gate.

"What the hell?" He asked.

"What?" Tawnie asked. "What is it?"

The SUV pulled through the gate, and Gordon could see through to the other side of the highway. A line of vehicles sat at the southbound gate. But armed soldiers prevented them from proceeding.

"We're about to go through that tunnel," Gordon told her. "But something doesn't look right about it." He said as he stared into the long corridor, unable to see the other end.

Men walked alongside the vehicle as Gordon took it into the pavilion-styled structure. As he got closer, he could see the panel lights on the ceiling covering almost every square inch. The semi-circle tunnel was constructed of a metallic alloy connecting twenty-foot sections. Light panels on the ceiling spanned the entire length. They looked like fluorescent tubes with red LEDs between them. Tawnie looked up front, seeing the fixtures through the windshield.

"You have got to be kidding me!" She sneered. As soon as Gordon's body passed into the tunnel, he felt something unusual. He continued and looked down at his hands, wondering why they felt heavy. The soldiers outside watched him through the window. He became happy that he was wearing the mask because his face would show a grimace as full-body pain set in.

"Gordon, what's wrong?" Tawnie asked. "You good?"

The man grunted. "You don't feel that? My entire body is in pain."

"Shit!" Tawnie said as she sneakily crawled to the center armrest between the two front seats. She raised her head over the base of the window and saw the soldier who walked beside the car. He looked back, and Tawnie went back to the floor before he could see her.

"Gordon, hang on!" She whispered. But the man was fading. He could feel his heart racing, and his entire body felt like he was sitting in flames.

"Is it just me?" He asked again. "Why do I–"

The man outside tapped on the door, motioning Gordon to roll down his window again.

Tawnie felt like she was going to be sick. "Fuck." She whispered to herself as she gripped the handle of her gun.

"Hey, Battle, you're good," the man outside said. "Tell that loser, Davis. I'm at forty-two Caster kills so far."

Gordon managed a nod before the man turned around to walk to the gate. Tawnie crawled over the center console to grab the wheel just as Gordon's body went limp. Luckily, the soldier had walked away. His foot stiffened on the accelerator, sending the SUV speeding down the corridor. Tawnie squeezed into his lap and kicked his foot off the gas.

"Mommy, can I come up now?" Milo asked.

"No, it's not safe yet, Spud." She said. Her eyes focused on the end of the makeshift structure. The bright light from the sun flowed into the end of the tunnel, almost blinding her. But as she reached the exit, she could see another group of soldiers waiting for the vehicle to approach.

"Shit." She muttered. She had to think on her toes to execute a plan that didn't get them caught. She slammed her elbow into Gordon's waist.

"Daniel, wake up!" she yelled, hoping he would respond. But he didn't. The tunnel was still affecting him.

"Dammit!"

"Mommy, what's wrong?" Milo interrupted.

"Nothing, Sweetie." She smiled, "Mommy just has a little situation to get us out of."

Approaching the end fast, Tawnie closed her eyes. Her fingers gripped the steering wheel tightly. Her nose flared as she rode past the soldiers. A group of eight men stood just outside the tunnel. One man nodded as Tawnie drove through. Her eyes widened as she looked into the side mirror. The men didn't move from their spots.

"Holy shit." She said to herself. "That worked!"

She looked into the rear view mirror to ensure their safety. The men remained in their positions.

"Alright, Milo. You can come up now." She told him, "We're safe."

Chapter XXII

Gordon woke up in a cold sweat, hardly able to breathe. He gasped for air and choked on his saliva as he opened his eyes to see the dark gray linen on the ceiling of the SUV. His hands gripped the handle on the driver door and the center armrest as he hoisted himself up. It was as if he was awakening from a bad dream. He hurried to pull the mask off that he still wore—unbuckling the straps at his cheeks and slipping it off. His eyes closed as he breathed a satisfying breath of air not ridden with carbon dioxide from his lungs. He looked into the passenger seat and noticed Tawnie sleeping peacefully. Her chair was leaned back, and her body curled like a cat. In front of her was her son, being her little spoon while trying to stay warm.

The officer looked around. The vehicle was off. He could see his breath in front of him with every exhale. The windows were lined with condensation on the inside and a thin layer of permafrost on the outside. He opened the door of the vehicle and stepped out. He found himself standing in the parking lot of a supermarket. People moved in and out of the store and parking lot as if all was normal.

Somehow, it was back to business as usual. His lower lip curled in as he looked down at the ground, wondering what was happening. He raised his arm and looked at his wristwatch at 8:14 AM. He grunted as he looked at the people all around. He opened the door again and got back inside. Before closing it, he began to raise his seat. The sound of the electronic motor, coupled with the door closing, caused Tawnie to awaken. Her eyes squinted to adjust to the light as she raised her head. Gordon looked at her as she began to yawn.

"I'm guessing that everything went well." He said as he looked forward.

Tawnie grunted. "No thanks to you." She joked as she slowly sat up in her seat.

Gordon smiled and nodded. "It all felt like a bad dream." He said as his eyes got spacey. "I've never experienced that kind of pain before."

Tawnie looked down at Milo and smiled at him. A hint of worry underlined her expression.

"What the hell was that thing?" he asked her. "Why the hell was I the only one affected by it?"

Tawnie's lips rolled into her mouth as she ignored his question.

"Tawnie, you knew exactly what that thing was when you saw it." He added. "What the hell is the reason for all of this?"

The space became quiet, and Gordon stared at her, waiting for an answer.

He cleared his throat. "Tawnie, that soldier back there said something about a Caster. I'm assuming he wasn't talking about furniture wheels."

The woman sighed and leaned her head against her hand.

"Tawnie." He called her again. "Why did that tunnel do that to me?"

The woman raised her hands and brushed her fingers through her hair. She held her hands at the back of her head as she looked at the windshield in wonder.

"Tawnie!" He barked, startling her.

"Caster." She muttered. "A word that I was hoping never to hear again."

"What does it mean?" Gordon asked.

Tawnie looked down at her son to ensure that he was still asleep. She touched him softly, and the boy let out a soft groan.

"Things are happening here that society should have never been exposed to." She explained. "I'm afraid that Idaho Falls was the site of a mess that those soldiers were responsible for cleaning up."

"So what is the mess?" Gordon asked. "The Casters?"

Tawnie leaned forward. She placed her elbows on her knees and interlocking her fingers underneath her chin. "I believe so.

Casters were supposed to be a closed case."

Gordon stared at her, his face folded as he awaited more words.

"That last mission was all for nothing." She finished.

Gordon shook his head. "What mission? Riyadh"

Tawnie opened her mouth to speak but hesitated as she glanced at him with glossy eyes.

He leaned toward her, "What is it?" He asked.

"Daniel, I have something to tell you," she said. "And you're gonna need to brace yourself for this."

Gordon leaned back in his seat, one eyebrow raised as he stared at her.

"Mommy," Milo interrupted. Tawnie looked down with haste as she reached for him, her body tensing. Gordon could see her becoming anxious as she looked down at him.

"Oh, Spud, you're awake!" She said, trying to be as cheerful as possible.

"Mommy, I'm cold." The boy said.

Tawnie grinned as she stared at him.

"Brake?" She said to Gordon. Baffled, he stared at her as the woman's eyes locked onto the start button.

"Oh," Gordon said as he started the vehicle. "There you go, buddy. We'll get it warm for you in a sec."

Tawnie took a deep breath and pushed her hair behind her ears.

"I'm going to run into the store really quick to use the bathroom," she said. "Is anybody else?"

She looked at Milo first. The poor boy made eye contact and shivered a bit. She smiled. "Stay here and get some heat, Spud." She looked at Gordon. The man shook his head.

"I'm good," He said. "I'll stay here with Milo and let him get warm."

Tawnie smiled at him as she closed her coat. "Thank you," she whispered as she opened the door and stepped outside. She looked around the parking lot for anything suspicious and headed into the store. Gordon could see her walking away through visible clearings in the windshield's frost.

Milo took the opportunity to sit up and raise the car seat. Surprised, Gordon looked at him with wide eyes. The boy stared at him as well. Gordon sat back in his chair and sighed in silence.

"Do you like my mommy?" the kid asked. Gordon turned his

focus to the boy again, his heart beating fast as he considered his question. He grunted, attempting to bide for an answer.

"What made you ask that?" Gordon asked.

The boy partially hid his face with his forearm as he watched the man. "Because you look at her like I look at Phiona from school." He said.

Gordon was appalled. "What did this boy just say?" He thought to himself.

"Milo, your mom is happily married," Gordon told the boy as he looked away. The man felt his face burning as he focused on the store's entrance. He watched Tawnie disappear into the sliding door.

"It's wrong to come between people meant for someone else."

Milo stared at the man, making him nervous about what he could be thinking.

"My daddy doesn't look at her like you."

Gordon stared at the kid for a brief moment, clenching his jaw and shaking his head.

"Look, I understand how you feel, kid," Gordon said. Milo looked up at him. "Really?" He asked.

The officer nodded, "I was a bit older than you when my parents went through it."

Milo looked forward, tears welling in his eyes as he sat silently. Gordon placed his hand on top of the boy's head.

"Simply remember that your parents are only human." Gordon continued, getting a nod from the boy. "Everything will work out in its own way."

Across the country, in Washington DC, the United States President sat in a conference room at the White House. With him, Vice President McTierman and Chief of Staff, Allan Waddell. The Secretary of Defense and the Director of Homeland Security were present. They were barely at the tail-end of a lengthy discussion about what was happening in Idaho. They had somehow reached nothing but pinned-up frustration and silence. Everyone in attendance had their heads down, ignoring each other's presence. The president still studied the files handed over to him by the Department of Defense. As frustration caused his blood to boil, he flipped the book closed and looked at the door. A secret serviceman entered with a cell phone in his hands. The president's eyebrows furrowed as he looked at the man with wonder.

"President Wesley, you have a phone call!" The man announced.

The president shook his head as the frustration began to turn into anger.

"I'm a little busy at the moment! The call can wait!" He said.

"Excuse my breach of protocol, sir." The young man added. "I don't think so, Sir. I'm told this particular call can't."

President Wesley looked around the room. Everyone in attendance shifted their eyes between him and the serviceman.

"Alright, "he said as he stood from his seat and headed for the phone. He looked at the device and realized nothing was on the caller ID, not even a phone number. The call was answered, and the timer already initiated at the top of the screen warned. He took a deep breath and stared at the ceiling, biting his bottom lip as he put the device to his ear.

"This is P.O.T.U.S." The man said into the phone, looking back to ensure he was out of range of the others.

"Remember that scripture I told you?" A woman said to him. His chest began to flutter. His eyes widened, and he could feel his body itching as the sweat started.

He cleared his throat. "Agent Zero?" He muttered. "It's been a long time."

Tawnie grunted. "Not long enough, I'm afraid."

Again, he looked back at the table. This time, everyone looked in his direction. President Wesley opened the door to exit the room. Two men stood outside on each side of the door. Both men were taller than the towering president, who stood at approximately six-foot-two. They were both dressed in pressed, black suits with white shirts underneath. The president looked at them with frustration before angrily signaling them to leave.

"I'm a busy man. Why are you contacting me, Tawnie?" He asked.

"I thought you may want to know that the tin-hat woman won our little bet," she laughed. "Which means that the world is about to lose."

"Now look here–" He said. "I warned all of you what would happen." Tawnie cut him off. President Wesley nodded as he leaned one arm against the wall and stared at the floor.

"Look, I don't know what you want from me." President Wesley said. "But I told you I didn't want anything to do with this."

Tawnie smiled. "It's not that simple, Wesley," she said. "You were there just like I was. Nothing but a clone trooper military general quote-unquote doing his job. Isn't that right?"

The president punched the wall out of anger. "I have far too much going on right now to deal with the unsolicited riddles of some social media influencer!"

"Like the crisis in Idaho, Mr. President?" She growled. Her audacity startled him into silence. He stared down the hall at his security detail and waited for her to continue.

"Do I have your attention now, Nate?" She asked. "I'm sitting in Idaho right now. Swimming in the middle of soldiers who I can only assume mean the destruction of humanity. Or maybe a loose end here needs to be dealt with."

The man chuckled. "Sounds like all this will be over when that knot is tied, huh?"

Tawnie shook her head as she briefly exited the corridor to the restroom in the back of the store. She looked around for anything suspicious and returned to the hall.

"The problem is, I'm not the only rope dangling in the wind, am I?" She asked.

The service members approached the president, but he held his index finger to them.

"What exactly are we dealing with here?" He asked, clenching his jaw.

"Would you happen to know who hired us in Riyadh?" Tawnie asked.

The president grunted softly, stopping himself as he began to speak. "I have no idea." He said. "It was above my pay grade, and I was just–"

"Following orders." Tawnie interrupted. "Unfortunately, it was a dark assignment for us as well."

The president cleared his throat and wiped his forehead. "You were also following orders, Agent Zero? Are you saying that whoever sent you has no idea who hired any of us?"

"I don't know." She answered as she pulled the high-tech computer out of her pocket. She flipped it over to examine the insignia on the back. "I tried to separate myself from this life and its associates long ago."

The president chuckled. "Let me be the first to inform you that you've done a horrible job at that. You post a video talking about this shit every Thursday."

Tawnie smiled and looked out into the store again. "I won't argue with that," she said. "But so that you know, all of Idaho Falls have been locked down by this unknown group. If you didn't send them, we're in trouble. I'm trapped here."

Wesley looked around to see if anyone was standing within earshot. The service members stood too close for comfort, so he stepped down the empty hallway.

"What the hell did you just say?" The man asked.

"Yeah, I couldn't believe it either." She said. "But these guys rolled into the city in a convoy of hundreds of trucks and slaughtered everyone on sight."

"An operation that big?" Wesley asked as he ran his hand over the top of his head. "Who has the power to conduct something so grand?" There was a brief silence as he waited for her to answer.

"The president of the United States." She said. "You.

The president shook his head with disbelief. "Do you think I'm capable of doing something that vile to my own people?"

Tawnie went silent, letting the man wrap his mind around the problem.

"Another thing to note is that every single one of them wears air filtration masks as part of their uniform." She added.

The man cleared his throat again. "Who are they?" He asked.

"Not sure," Tawnie answered. "But if I'm being honest, they look like the U.S. military."

"That's impossible!" The man growled.

Tawnie chuckled. "After Riyadh, you still know that word, Nathan?"

Frustrated, the man sneered as he turned to head back to the conference room. "I'll figure out what's happening and fill you in as soon as I know something. I have to go."

"Mr. President, you know I'm more effective without you," Tawnie said. "I don't have to deal with the bureaucracy of the American government. That's not why I called."

The man shook his head in disbelief. "Well, why did you call

Agent Zero to gloat about your bet?"

Tawnie chuckled. "No, I called you to warn you," she said before pausing. "They are targeting our team. I'd be foolish to believe they only came to Idaho for vacation. They have made it clear that I am one of their targets and won't stop until we're all gone."

The president stopped walking. His mind was so preoccupied that his eyes almost stopped working.

"Uh…" He began to say. "How many of you are there?"

"Not many," she answered him. "But despite the danger that we're all in, their new target is the real problem."

The man placed his hand in his pocket and took a deep breath, trying not to freak out.

"Who's their new target?" He asked.

Tawnie parted her lips to answer him but suddenly chose to keep quiet.

"Watch your back, Nathaniel." She said as she started moving toward the front of the building. "If they are willing to go this far to prove a point, I doubt that you are safe."

Chapter XXIII

Riyadh, Saudi Arabia, 2073. A young Tawnie was on a cargo transport plane, waiting to depart. She kept looking out the window, seeing the desert sands stretching to the ends of the Earth. The harsh Middle Eastern sun created heat waves, making the view appear ruffled. In the plane with her was a group of U.S. Army soldiers, all geared up with armor and holding large rifles. She felt under-dressed, only wearing a light jacket with a T-shirt underneath. Looking outside, she realized she would also have to come out of the coat. She wore a pair of jeans that were ripped at the knees. Her entire outfit was a bad idea. She could have been more prepared if she knew where the day would take her.

One of the soldiers, a large man, stared at her from his seat on the opposite plane wall. He was intimidating, but Tawnie was too distracted to acknowledge him. He had his hands raised, clutching the collar of his bulletproof vest.

"Are you alright, Sergeant?" one woman asked him, noticing his uneasiness.

"Not at all," he said, still staring at Tawnie. After hearing him, she looked in his direction. "I'm not sure why we have to babysit some civilian on this mission," he said. "I can't wrap my mind around why she's here."

Tawnie gave all of her attention to him. Her body heat matched the temperature outside for only a moment before she took a breath and leaned back. After the day she had, she visualized all the ways she could shut him up, including the rifle he was holding. He was a platoon sergeant. The other soldiers looked at the two, waiting for the next word to be exchanged. Suddenly, the rear hatch of the plane opened, and the harsh desert heat rushed into the vehicle. The heat wave and sand caused everyone to flinch except for Tawnie. Even when the soldier retreated due to the environment, Tawnie only stared, emotionless.

"Alright, team, let's go!" The man said as he got up from his seat. Tawnie's eyes followed him as he walked off the vessel. However, she did not bother to move. She crossed her arms and closed her eyes.

"Hey, kid." One of the women called out to Tawnie before leaving. The young woman opened her eyes and looked at her without turning away. This intimidated the soldier.

"Are.. Are you co-coming?" She stuttered.

"I'll stay here until I speak with General Wesley."

The woman nodded and stepped off the plane. Her squad leader looked at her suspiciously as she walked down the ramp.

"Bartell." He called out to her. "Where is the asset?"

"Sergeant, I don't think she's much inclined to cooperate if she's treated like a child." The woman argued.

The man angrily shook his head, "That's exactly what she is! She's barely out of high school!"

Shamefully, the woman let her head fall. "Well, she's not moving until she talks with General Wesley."

"Who do she think she is?" He roared. "She's not going to give us commands like she's running this!"

The rest of the squad tried to calm him, but he marched back into the plane with an iron fist. He vanished into the shadows of the cargo bay. Master Sergeant Victoria Bartell exited the plane, leaving her unit behind.

"Master Sergeant, where are you going?" One soldier asked as he followed.

"I'm going to get the general." She said.

The plane was situated on a small private airfield that was riddled with U.S. soldiers from all branches. A small building sat at the end of the airstrip that served as the airport. Not far from that were the command center and General's Quarters, where Victoria headed. The giant chain link fence that stood in the distance was one of many containing the base. Towers with armed guards surrounded the settlement, and a single road entered a gate. Nearby was a parking lot filled with military vehicles and large conexes.

Victoria walked into the small building and was met by a two-star general who sat at a desk against the wall. Aside from that desk, there were a few chairs, large file cabinets, and shelving lined the walls. On the back wall were two doors. One door was labeled restroom, while the other was labeled office.

"May I help you, soldier?" The general asked as she stood from her desk.

Repeatedly looking at the office, Sergeant Bartell began to answer.

"Yes, the restroom is right there. Feel free to use it, but make it quick." The general interrupted.

The sergeant shook her head, "Ma'am, I need to speak with General Wesley about an important issue." She explained.

"Not going to happen, Sergeant." The two-start general retorted. "General Wesley is on important business calls at the moment. The room went silent as Sergeant Bartell stared on. The general sat back down and continued working. Feeling disrespected, Victoria ignored the woman's response and headed to the office. Before the general could reach her, Bartell pushed the door open and stepped inside. Inside was a mirror image of the other room, just smaller. General Wesley sat behind his desk, writing something, and looked up at Victoria as she stormed in. The two-star general followed her.

"Soldier, I said you can't be in here!" She yelled at Bartell. The sergeant stood at attention and looked at the wall before her. "This is punishable by UCMJ action! Do you know the trouble you just made for yourself?"

General Wesley grinned. Bartell glanced at him, still not finding her situation as amusing as he did.

"Is it obvious how new she is to this operation?" Wesley asked. The two-star looked at him and smiled.

"Is that so?" She asked him. "Where you coming from, Sergeant Bartell?"

Upon hearing the question, she smiled, trying to keep herself from laughing.

"Ma'am, the 316th Ordnance Battalion," Bartell answered. The woman raised an eyebrow and looked back at her boss.

"General Warren, excuse my trying to add light to the

situation," Wesley said. "But can I get a moment with my soldier, please?"

The two-star general was confused. She looked at both of them with wide eyes.

"You just let anyone walk into your office without an appointment?" She asked him. Wesley could see Bartell's hand form a tight fist at her thigh.

"Warren, we are all human here, not military ranks. The people conducting the operation deserve as much, if not more, respect than the people leading it." He explained. Defeated, Warren left the office quietly and closed the door behind her.

Sergeant Bartell released the grip on her fists, took a deep breath, and looked at General Wesley.

"You know, I do talk to you more than your First Sergeant, Victoria." The man announced. The woman shook her head in frustration.

"He's intimidated by you, Sir." She responded.

"Yeah." He nodded as he looked away momentarily. "What can I do for you today?"

"Speaking of First Sergeant, you may want to come with me." She advised.

Seconds later, Sergeant Bartell escorted General Wesley out of the office building. The two of them made their way to the plane that just landed.

"Group attention!" Sergeant Bartell yelled to the platoon as the general approached.

"At ease, make way!" yelled another, causing the others to move out of his way. He marched up the ramp with Sergeant Bartell closely behind. They saw the first sergeant bent at the waist, screaming at Tawnie.

"First Sergeant, what the hell are you doing?" General Wesley asked. Startled, the First Sergeant looked to the back of the plane.

"I... I... I was just–" "You were just what?" The general cut him off. "I told you to be an escort to this young lady, not treat her like an inmate."

The man stepped away from Tawnie. Unbothered, her eyes nonchalantly followed him. General Wesley approached her after. His eyes locked onto his soldier as well. The man sighed softly and stood in parade rest.

"You know what, Tyler? We are going to have a discussion about this later." The general said. "We will have to make accommodations for your biases. Prepare yourself because you are not going to like them."

The man let his head fall and began staring at the floor. "Yes, sir." He responded.

"Get out of my sight!" Wesley said with a smile as he pointed toward the rear of the ship. The man transitioned out of parade rest and allowed his arms to fall to his side. He headed to the back of the plane, passing Bartell on the way. The two made eye contact as he passed the woman, glaring the entire way. Her eyes followed his, waiting for him to make the wrong move. The general looked at her, and she was already shaking her head.

"I believe that guy was a great choice for Platoon Sergeant, don't you, General?" She asked.

"Master Sergeant," Wesley called to her as Tawnie stood before the man.

"Ms. Everwood, I can imagine you feel the same as us about the area, so I'll skip the welcoming for now," Wesley said as he extended his hand to the girl. Compared to him, he felt like he was reaching down for her. She reciprocated the motion and grabbed his hand to shake it. The two of them shook in silence as they locked eyes. The man found himself feeling anxious.

"Thank you for that, sir." She said to him.

"You're our guest, Ms. Everwood. You came highly recommended by the Pentagon to be the one person capable of this mission." Sergeant Bartell explained.

The young woman smiled. "Call me Tawnie.

The General nodded as he stepped back. I'm Lieutenant General Nathaniel Wesley, and this is Master Sergeant Victoria Bartell." The man said.

Tawnie nodded again, looking between the two of them as if she were taking a mental image of their faces.

"Nice to meet the two of you." She said as she reached into a satchel that hung from her hip. She raised the flap at the top to pull out a laptop. "Show me where I can set up to work, and let's do this."

General Wesley crossed his arms and leaned back on his heels as he looked down at the woman.

"What exactly are you here to do for us again?" He asked her. "I can't say I understand why we needed a civilian contract for this."

"I am here to point your team in the right direction." She answered. "Once we get down into that temple, you will need me to help get to the Treasure of the Arcanin."

The general shook his head in disapproval. "I don't buy all of this stuff." He said.

Tawnie looked at him and shook her head as well. "Unlike finding success, Mr. Wesley, just because you don't believe in this war doesn't make it any less real."

The three of them stood silently for a moment before Bartell stepped in. She gestured for the two of them to leave the plane. Tawnie stepped out first. Wesley and Bartell followed closely behind. A man ran to the back of the plane and looked inside. He wore a green flight suit and a helmet with a headset attached.

"You guys good, General?" He asked. Wesley gave the man a thumbs up. He nodded and stepped inside. Seconds later, the rear hatch was closing, and Victoria led everyone away from the vehicle. The loud engines of the jet fired up, and Tawnie looked back at it.

"Now's your last chance, Tawnie." The general yelled over the loud roar. "You sure you want to do this?"

She stopped walking. Wesley stopped next to her. "I never had a choice, Mr. Wesley."

Chapter XXIV

Tawnie headed to the front of the store. Her eyes wandering the floor, looking for any suspicious activity. On high alert, everything seemed out of the ordinary. The man grabbing a candy bar at the checkout counter caught her eye, as did the greeter at the door, who stared at her. Suddenly, someone tapped her arm. Tawnie spun around, her fist clenched and ready to fight. But it was only a small, elderly woman pointing to the top shelf next to her.

"Excuse me, dear." She said, her voice gravely and wet. "You're a bit taller than me, can you?"

Tawnie looked up at the top shelf to see fully stocked rows of black beans.

"Yeah, sure." She said as she grabbed it for the woman. She handed it over, and she thanked her. Tawnie sighed and watched the woman scoot away with her basket. She continued to the front door and saw Gordon standing by with Milo. His face twisted, and his eyes squinted. She approached briskly and reached for Milo's hand. She looked at the man with a smile, but he was suspicious.

"You look like you either stole a Snicker or one of those guys are in here, too," he said.

Tawnie looked behind her once more. "I'm…" The man's head was now tilted, and an eyebrow was raised.

"You can never be too cautious, you know?" She said as she walked out the door. Tawnie and Milo stepped out into the parking lot. Gordon picked up his pace to catch up to her. They approached the vehicle, and he ran around to get in front of them as the woman headed for the rear door. Tawnie stopped as Gordon almost shoved her out of the way. She was about to scream at him until he opened both doors and stepped aside, almost as if he was presenting their chariot to them..

She stared at him for a moment in almost a state of confusion. The man gestured toward the car with his eyes, urging her to get inside. But she was stunned. Her body paused where she was, and her jaw fell open.

"You okay?" he asked. "It's a bit cold out here, so get inside before you freeze."

She stepped forward and handed her son off to him.

"Yeah, I'm fine. It's just—" She stopped again and simply stared at him. Gordon turned his head to the side, peering at her from the corner of his eyes.

"You know what, never mind." She said as she got inside the vehicle and closed the door. Milo climbed inside, and Gordon shut the door behind him.

Gordon walked around the front of the vehicle, noticing that Tawnie's eyes followed him until he got inside the truck. The man quieted, waiting for her to say something, but she only stared. Finally, he turned his head. He found that her mouth was open as if she was preparing to speak.

"What's up?" He asked. Tawnie gasped as her head jerked backward.

"Nothing!"

Suddenly, Tawnie's eyes widened, and her mouth opened again.

"Mommy!" Milo called out to her. "Oh no!"

Gordon looked into the back seat at the kid and he suddenly looked afraid.

"What the hell is happening?" He asked the boy.

"Tawnie, are you okay?" But Tawnie didn't respond. He looked at her, examining her chest, there was no rise or a fall. She wasn't breathing. Her eyes rolled back slightly, revealing more white in her eyes.

"Tawnie, are you okay? Do I need to find medical attention?" He continued. There was a silence as Gordon waited for her to snap out of it. Suddenly, she let out a gasp of life-sucking air.

"Yeah, you can never be too careful, you know?" Tawnie blurted. Gordon attempted to shake off some of his confusion.

"Huh?"

"You were talking about how I was being cautious just now." She said with a grin. "If we see the soldiers, I want to be ready." His eyes shifted away from her for a moment. Then, he squinted, transitioning into a soft nod.

"Right on." He said to her before putting the vehicle into gear.

"I can't explain this, but I've never been to Rexburg." She said, Gordon's eyes remained squinted, and he balled his mouth inward.

"Not that hard to explain," he muttered. "You never drove up Route 20 to Rexburg."

Tawnie shook her head. "Gordon, I have a memory of tomorrow!"

The man paused. He could feel pressure in his head rising as he processed what she said.

"Tomorrow…" He said again. "As in, the day that hasn't happened yet?"

Tawnie gave him a distressed look. The man waited for her to say it was a joke, but she didn't. His eyebrow twitched as he reached up to rub his forehead, trying to keep a smile on his face.

"Bullshit!" He exclaimed. "If you have a memory of tomorrow, then why couldn't we get a warning about the day before yesterday?"

"Daniel, I don't know!" She yelled at him. "I'm freaking out over here because–" She paused.

"Because what?" He asked as he started to drive. Tawnie glanced over her shoulder at Milo. "Oh my God!"

Gordon became wide-eyed as he watched her closely. She began to breathe short, heavy breaths, and tears welled in her eyes as she began to fan herself with her hands.

"Oh shit." He said as he rolled the window down slightly to let air in. "Tawnie, what's up?" He asked again.

She shook her head, Covering her mouth with her clasped hands. Milo grew concerned, leaning to his left to look around his mother's seat.

"Maybe you just need rest. I have some friends that live in Rexburg, not far from here." Gordon said. "We have to find somewhere to lay low and get rid of this truck!"

Tawnie lowered her head and wrapped her fingers around the back of her neck. Tears dripped down her coat as she began to sniffle.

"We can't go there," she responded. "I don't want to get anyone else involved."

"I understand." He said, offering her a genuine smile. "But we are running out of options."

They rode in silence for a while. Tawnie seemed as if she was still out of her mind, staring out the windshield and hardly blinking. Eventually, Gordon found a parking garage and pulled up to the gate.

"Are we leaving the truck here?" Tawnie asked.

Gordon nodded as he reached out the window to grab a ticket from the kiosk. The liftgate ascended, and he rolled inside slowly.

"There is a motel nearby that we can go to and lay low until we devise a plan." He explained to her.

"Good idea." She nodded. The officer parked the large SUV and hopped out with haste. Tawnie got out and quickly opened Milo's door. The kid jumped down to the floor and took his mom's hand.

"I'll get the bags," Gordon said as he jumped for the luggage. They closed the doors and proceeded to leave the parking structure. They walked for a mile or two until they reached a local motel. It wasn't the worst Tawnie had ever seen. However, paints were chipping away, there was trash all over, and a foul stench that almost turned her away. In the front office, Tawnie and Gordon approached the front desk. A man stood behind it, staring as they approached.

"Can I help you?" He asked them.

Suddenly, Tawnie began to get nervous as she glanced at Gordon.

"Yeah." She started. "We need a room for a few nights. The man began to click around on the computer.

"ID, please." He requested. Tawnie pulled out her wallet, grabbed an Idaho State driver's license, and placed it on the counter. Gordon got a glance at the name on the card. It wasn't hers, but it was her photo. Tawnie looked up at him, noticing the card got his attention.

Chapter XXV

In Washington, DC, the president sat back down in his meeting to discuss the situation in Idaho. After his conversation with Tawnie, he didn't know if he should proceed. He looked around the faces in attendance, attempting to determine who was trustworthy.

"So how much do we know again?" Wesley asked.

The people at the table began to look nervous. The Chief of Staff loosened his necktie, and his face began to turn red.

"What the fuck do we know?!" He yelled again.

"Uh… Mr. President, Sir." The Secretary of Defense chimed in as he shuffled through pages of a beige folder he held. On a white label were the words 'top secret' in bold, red font. "We are informed that this situation was due to biochemical weapons research at an Idaho black site."

The president leaned over the table and allowed his head to fall. He grunted loudly, hoping it would help him deflate his stress.

"I want to remind you all that we have been in this room for nearly twenty-four hours. We have been deliberating on something that is not supposed to happen in the first place!" He roared as he jumped up from his seat. The chair he sat in slammed against the wall behind the head of the table.

"Someone explain to me who these men are that have an entire state on lockdown! How is it that nobody can enter the state on land or in the air?"

Everyone went silent as if they had taken a moment to think about the question. But they were afraid to answer. All except Vice-President McTierman, who stared at the Commander and

171

Chief.

"Nate, don't we want to keep a calm, leveled head on our shoulders for this particular problem?" The man asked. President Wesley turned his attention to him. The look on his face struck fear in everyone. "I'm only saying we must be rational, even when our enemies are not."

"Agreed, Mr. President." The FBI Director added. Wesley turned his attention to the man, and his intense stare made him shrink.

"We understand, Sir." McTierman continued. "You were on the front lines, I get that. You would love to lead a unit onto the battlefield just as President Washington once did. But you have nothing to prove here."

As he finished, President Wesley's eye twitched. It was as if that last word was the flick of the hand that lit a match. The man nodded and turned around to head back to his chair. Sporadically, he looked around the room as he faced the wall. Everyone looked at one another in discomfort as they waited for his inevitable break. He finally turned to face the table. His hand raised, and his mouth opened as if he was about to speak, but he stopped again.

His head lowered, and his fist knocked against the table's surface repeatedly. The taps started light but increased in force the more he punched. The others looked at one another, almost wondering how much more he would do to blow off steam. His fists went right through the solid wood table as he reached punch number seven. Everyone jumped from their seats and moved away from him. The fear in their eyes only seemed to make the man angrier. His security detail rushed into the room, ready to react. Immediately, he turned to the door and pointed at the men.

"I didn't call for you!" He yelled at them. "Get the fuck out of here!"

McTierman stepped forward and tried to hold the man back.

"Nate! Let's not cause a scene!" he yelled at him. The man snapped out of his rage and looked at McTierman with wide eyes. It was as if he didn't know where he was momentarily. But after taking a few deep breaths, he finally came to his senses. Wesley patted the man on the shoulder, and the Vice President returned to his seat.

"I want to be perfectly clear here, folks," Wesley said. "This situation is nothing to underestimate. Mishandling this has some long-term repercussions.”

“Well, obviously, Mr. President Sir!” Senator Diane Greasly spoke up. “But–”

The president raised his hand to cut her off and cleared his throat as he uncuffed the end of his sleeves. “The Republican party's approval rating is in the toilet because of this scandal,” he said. “If we don't stop this and give the American people a good explanation, they'll have my head.”

Everyone nodded in silence.

“Someone better have answers for me by end of day.” He said as he headed out of the room. As soon as he stepped into the hallway, he saw someone standing in the distance. He was talking with a few members of the security detail. He had on a long trench coat and shiny, black dress shoes. His coat was peeled back, his hands in his pant pockets, opening up to his pressed, navy blue suit.

“Director Grant!” President Wesley called out. The man turned around, his eyes showing no change as he looked at the Commander and Chief.

“I know that look.” The man continued. “You have bad news.”

As he approached the president, the man looked down at the baseboards on the wall to avoid eye contact. “Mr. President,” he said, sounding like he had to get something off his chest.

“What is it, Holland?” Wesley asked. “I'm sure that as the Director of Homeland Security, you are not visiting the capital just to say hello.”

Grant stopped in front of him and looked around. The security guards were walking away, and nobody was within earshot.

“Mr. President, how much do you really know about this situation in Idaho?” Grant asked, staring at the president like a common criminal.

“Look, Holland–”

“Nate, don't get me wrong, man.” Grant cut him off. “I respect your position, but I have a job to do.”

The president paused and cleared his throat. He relaxed his body, letting his shoulders fall to seem less aggressive. Somehow, he understood the magnitude of the situation just by looking into the man's eyes.

"I understand." He said as he looked down. "Why do you ask?"

Again, Grant looked up and down the hall, then back at the door to the conference room. His eyes squinted as he walked into the president, clutching him by the arm as he pulled him away.

"Wait, hold on now," Wesley said to him.

"Yeah, yeah," Grant replied. "I don't want this to go any further than it needs to. But I have it on good authority that you are connected to this mess in Idaho."

Wesley looked at him with widened eyes. His heart began to beat out of his chest, and his mouth dried.

"Wha-what did you just say?" The president asked.

"Yeah, I'm just as concerned as you." The man said as he started to walk away. But he turned to look at Wesley again. "I suggest you hide whatever skeletons in your closet a little deeper, Nate."

The two men looked into each other's eyes for a long, uncomfortable moment.

"I'm not going to press play on this particular case yet because I have faith that you are an innocent man." He explained. "I just need you to know that whatever good faith I have in you won't matter if you are guilty. I still have a job to do."

The president nodded. "I understand." He said. "I'll fix it."

"Great!" Grant replied. "Anyone else would be underneath the Pentagon right now, so don't screw this up."

Wesley watched as Grant walked away. He wondered how he, of all people, became a suspect. Or, better yet, what evidence did Holland Grant have that incriminated him? As Grant disappeared from the hallway, more security members entered. They approached him like they were already in action.

"What's going on?" He asked.

"Mr. President, sir, we have direct orders to place you on lockdown," the officer said. Wesley's head jerked backward like he was punched in the nose. His eyes grew wide as he stared at the man. His arms flexed backward, and his fists clenched. The six men in front of him cautiously stepped backward, remembering his background.

"On whose authority?" He growled.

The man in front of him took a hard gulp before answering. "Sir, Director Grant has placed the entire capital on protective lockdown protocol."

Wesley's eyebrow raised.

"Sir, with everything happening in this country, we are taking some extra precautions." the officer said as he stepped forward. "But your life may be in danger."

Chapter XXVI

Tawnie and Gordon got their key from the receptionist and headed to their assigned room. On the way to the back of the facility, the woman looked around, cautious that an ambush was coming. Gordon watched her as she walked a few paces ahead, wondering how he could help her relax. He wondered if she'd look suspicious and draw attention to them somehow. She got to room 148 and fumbled with the card key momentarily before opening the door. Before he got there, she and Milo had already headed inside. By the time he did, Tawnie was already clearing the room, ensuring nobody else was inside. The room was small and had one queen-sized bed. The walls were covered with gray shiplap material, and the carpet was a light brown. There were numerous stains in various places on the floor. Gordon wondered if a few of them may have been blood. There was a small 32-inch TV, a microwave plugged in but didn't work, and a small refrigerator.

"Hmm," Gordon grumbled. "I've definitely stayed in worse."

"All clear," Tawnie said as she walked to the front of the room to close the curtain over the large window.

"Yeah, Tawnie, this is a pretty small room," Gordon said as he turned his attention to her. "We could see it was clear from Idaho Falls."

The woman turned to him, her loose hair flying into her eyes. She reached up and moved it aside. Her eye locked onto him, and her lips pursed as if she was about to say something. She ignored him and checked on Milo, who was now sitting on the edge of the bed.

"Milo, are you doing okay?" She asked as she kneeled in front of him.

"Yes," he muttered. But shortly after answering, his stomach began to growl. The two of them heard it. Tawnie stared at the boy, tears pooling in her eyes.

"Hey, Milo," Gordon called. "Whadda ya' say I go and get something to eat? What are you feeling?"

The boy smiled. "Cheeseburgers!" He roared.

Gordon chuckled. "You got it, kiddo."

Tawnie stood up and walked to the bathroom in the back. A giant mirror sat on the back wall, and Gordon saw the woman unraveling. Instinctively, he wanted to check on her. But he got within inches of her, contemplating touching her back to comfort her. But thought against it and headed for the door.

"Alright, Milo, I'll be right back."

He said before taking the spare key card and heading out the door. Tawnie watched him through the mirror as he closed the door behind him. Gordon checked his phone as he left the room behind. He remembered that he didn't have a vehicle to go to as he walked through the parking lot. Luckily, there was a fast food spot within walking distance. He looked at their room's window, ensuring nobody was watching him. Then he dialed out on his phone. The contact on it read, 'Francie.' He placed the phone to his ear as he continued his journey to get food.

"Hey," He said. "Yeah, I know it's been a while. But I'm in Rexburg and…"

The person on the other end cut him off.

"I know," he responded. "But I need your help, and I don't trust anyone else with this."

Meanwhile, back in Washington, D.C., President Wesley retreated to his chambers deep inside the White House. His wife, Madeline, was on the bed reading a book. Their eyes met as he closed the door behind him. Madeline closed the book around her thumb with a look of concern. She looked out the window, smirking at the daylight she could still see.

"This is unusual." She announced. "It's midday."

Slowly, her husband nodded. "I know," he muttered, "But today is an unusual day."

He unbuttoned the top of his shirt and sulked toward the bed.

"You look like shit." The first lady said to him. He stopped and allowed his head to fall as he smiled. He looked back at her. Her smile was radiant enough to put him back into a good mood. He stopped to admire her momentarily, and she swung her legs over the side of the bed to stand. She wore a moderate navy blue skirt, a white blouse, and a powder pink collared shawl. Her brown hair was straight and flowed down her back. Some pinned up to the sides of her head to keep it out of her face.

"Who are you right now?" She asked him as he approached her. She dug her index finger into his chest as she pointed. He laughed as he looked into her eyes, but her expression was solemn.

"What do you mean?' He asked.

"You are coming for advice, or you need to be talked off a ledge," she explained. "You wouldn't be here at this time of day otherwise. But I need to know who you are so I know which character will answer your question."

The woman dropped her hand and took a step backward. "Who are you right now, the president, the superhero?"

The man's head fell again. Frustrated, he threw his tie to the nightstand beside the bed.

"Right now, I wish the only thing I was was your husband," he admitted. "I don't feel very super right now, and I'm failing as president."

The man vented without ever having the courage to look at his wife. She waited for him to pick his head up, but she could see the shame in his expression. Her arms opened and wrapped around him. Despite their size difference, he leaned forward to lay his head on her shoulder. Her heart sank as she began to feel moisture on her cheek. The president's tears.

"I haven't been your husband in so long, Madz." He called her by her nickname. She inhaled deep to keep herself calm, attempting to keep her tears to herself. But her exhale was choppy, causing the emotional dam to break.

"It's okay," she said as she wiped her eyes. I knew what I got myself into the moment you became a politician. I knew I would someday have to share you with billions of people."

He chuckled. "Thank you for believing in me."

Madeline smiled. "I love you." She whispered into his ear. He repeated it, and she pulled away from him slightly. She looked into his eyes, and they stared for a long, sensual moment. His eyes were still full of fear and worry. She could still feel the love. She reached up and wiped his eyes with her fingers. She pulled on his arms toward the bed and sat down, patting the spot next to her as an invitation. He sat beside his wife and stared into the distance momentarily.

"Now, tell me what's wrong." She requested. "Is this about the siege again?"

The man shook his head. "I'm not sure," he answered. It's hard to tell anything now."

Madeline sighed as she took his hand in hers. "What do you mean?"

The man's throat bobbed as he took a hard swallow. "I just talked with Holland Grant, and he put us on lockdown."

Madeline nodded, "Yeah, I talked to him too."

"Madz, he said he has evidence that I may be involved in this mess somehow." He told her.

"WHAT?" She yelled. "How?"

Nate shrugged. "He said that something I did in the past could have been linked to this situation.

Madeline opened her mouth to speak, but she was breathless. She stared at her husband, attempting to figure out how to respond.

"I have absolutely no idea what he could be referring to." Nate continued. "But he said I need to reevaluate any skeletons I may have in my closet."

Madeline shook her head and stood from the bed. One arm crossed her abdomen, and the other touched her chest as she began to pace.

"That explains why he questioned me earlier." She said.

Nate became angry. "He what?"

"I didn't tell him anything or incriminate you in any way." She said.

"I know love," He grumbled. "But that crosses the line."

Madeline looked at her husband and smiled. "To be fair, it sounded like he wanted to help you. Holland is not the one to sleep on a lead."

Nate stood from the bed, continuing to stare at the woman in front of him. She grew concerned as the look on his face became more intimidating.

"What is it?" She questioned.

"That's not all, Madz." He said.

Impatiently, the woman threw her hands, urging him to proceed.

"I got a call from… her… today." He said.

Madeline's eyes widened as if she were in a horror movie and had just seen the killer. She began to shake her head. "No! Are you serious right now?" she asked.

The man nodded, and his eyes went to the floor. "She's in Idaho right now."

A tear fell from Madeline's eye as she stared at him. "This can't be a coincidence."

The woman stepped to the window and stared out into the courtyard. Her mind wandered a mile a minute as she stood in silence.

"Madz." The man called as he approached the window as well.

"You know her better than anyone," he said. "Do you think her theories have any weight to them? Are we in over our heads here?" Madeline looked up at him. She turned to face him and then lowered her head.

"If she's reaching out, Nate, it means that everything she told us was correct."

The man took a deep breath, raising his chin and staring at the ceiling.

"Now," she continued "We should prepare for the worst."

Chapter XXVII

Riyadh, Saudi Arabia, 2073, the sun had set over the arid lands, and the heat had turned into a frigid chill. The gates of Base 287 were now locked, with a few more visitors inside who arrived just hours before sunset. General Wesley assembled an exceptional team consisting of the unit's finest non-commissioned officers. He and Tawnie sat in a small meeting room inside a second trailer. It was quiet, except for the sound of Tawnie's keyboard as she typed.

"General, it's time." The young woman said.

The large man raised an eyebrow. "They're coming," he assured her. Tawnie finished up whatever she was doing and leaned back in her seat, crossing her arms. The impatience on her face made the man uneasy. Wesley pulled the blinds over the window and cuffed his free hand around his eyes to see into the dark.

"They're here." He said as he walked to the door and opened it. Tawnie raised her wrist and looked down at her watch to confirm the time. Suddenly, soldiers began to file into the door, one by one.

"Thank you all for joining us," Wesley said as he saw Sergeant Bartell take a seat near Tawnie. "You're late," he added.

Bartell stood again. "Sir, it requires more recon than it should to keep classified information classified."

The other soldiers nodded and groaned in agreement.

"At ease, soldiers," Wesley said as he turned on the monitor on the wall behind him. A collage of photos of an ancient temple appeared.

Tawnie looked around the table at the soldiers. There were only three she'd met before then. She met Sergeant Bartell and a few men from her team on the plane. Periodically, she would catch their eye as they stared at her.

"As you guys have already deduced, the people on this base are a bunch of gossip queens," Wesley announced, making everyone laugh, except for Tawnie. "We are here and have been here reconning and planning for the mission we are about to embark on right now."

"Wait, this is that mission, General?" A man asked. The general gave him a slight nod and stood in parade rest.

"Folks, here today are the strongest, toughest, and smartest personnel in this battalion. That is why you are all here this evening."

Everyone was lost. The six men and women all looked around at one another to see if he was joking. But the general nodded with a serious look on his face. They opened up a sidebar conversation, but he shut it down.

"Alright, we are running out of time!" he roared. "If you guys can see back there at the head of the table, is a woman you all need to familiarize yourselves with."

Everyone turned their attention to Tawnie. She unfolded her arms and leaned forward.

"Tawnie is a government-hired hacker and information specialist." He went stiff for a moment and grunted, changing the energy in the room. " She will lead this mission."

The soldiers began to groan again.

"Before we have any tears, can I have you all introduce yourselves at least?" Wesley said as he sat at the other end of the table. Everyone paused and looked around at one another.

"Sure, I'll be an adult here." Bartell, the pretty, blond woman announced. "We've already met Tawnie, but I'm Victoria Bartell."

The man next to her was skinny and fidgety. His butt danced in his seat like he just wanted to get up to move. "I'm Sergeant Miles Myopovic." He said with what sounded like a German accent.

"I'm Sergeant First Class Avonna Maison." The dark-haired woman said from the opposite end of the table. Another man sat across from her on the other side of General Wesley. This one with reddish-colored hair. "I'm Sergeant First Class Shane Scott."

Next to him, a black man sat and tilted his head back to Tawnie in salutation. She mimicked him.

"I'm Master Sergeant Victor Parker."

The next man beside him, across from Sergeant Bartell, was the last to introduce himself. He sat straight up in his chair. His eyes seemed focused as if they were telling a story of relentless passion for his duty as a soldier. "I'm First Sergeant Daniel Gordon." Tawnie nodded at him as well and stood from her seat.

"Right." She said as she looked down at the table for a moment. Her eyes raised, and met with First Sergeant Gordon. She stared momentarily and almost forgot what she needed to say. "Good to meet you all. My name is Agent Everwood. Like everyone in this room, I exhibited phenomenal talent and became the authority in my field. I recognize you all for your reputation as the Army's Seal Team Six. I commend you for that despite how young you all are. Here's the thing: I won't let your ages cloud my judgment, and I suggest you follow suit."

Gordon's eyes grew large as he looked at his best friend, Bartell, for confirmation. They made eye contact, then looked back at General Wesley, who smiled and leaned back in his chair.

"I am the leading weapon specialist and system control analyst for a group whose name is classified. I am here to represent them." She continued, "This mission is dangerous and should not be taken lightly. Do I make myself clear?"

"Yes, Ma'am." They all responded.

"Alright, soldiers, listen up," Wesley interjected. "This is the ancient Al-Faw temple south of here. Sources indicate an ancient energy emanating from the site. Our mission is to get there, extract, and contain the source of that energy. We must do this while remaining conflict-free with the locals."

"Sounds like one hell of a job." Sergeant Myopovic stated.

"Sir, we have searched those ruins before." Said Sergeant Maison. "Was something there this entire time that we missed?"

"Likely," Tawnie answered. "This temple was built almost a million years ago. So the architects likely didn't want commoners to get inside easily."

"Do we have any clue as to what we are going in there for?" Sergeant Gordon asked.

"Yeah, Top," Sergeant Scott interjected. "It sounds like we just stumbled into some kind of Area 51, ol' sci-fi foolishness."

Wesley shook his head.

"I assure you, the energy we seek is real and cannot be explained now," Tawnie interjected.

"Go figure," Scott said. Tawnie stared at him silently, then reached down to her keyboard and tapped a key. A video began to play. It was a man running through an alley. The camera that followed appeared to sway unnaturally like a drone. He reached the end of the corridor and looked back to see if he was still being followed. As he saw the drone, he got spooked again and kept running. He looked at the camera again as he passed an innocent bystander on the sidewalk—a faint light burned in his eyes.

"Wait, what the hell?" Sergeant Parker asked as he leaned in. The bystander suddenly displayed signs of dysphoria and confusion. The camera stopped, paying attention to him instead. The suspect continued running through a crowd of innocent people, seemingly afraid for his life. The man in front of the camera swiped at the drone. It moved out of the way to avoid. He seemed to be losing energy, or his bones were turning into dust. Blood began to pour from his mouth, ears, eyes, and nose as he fell to the ground.

"Oh my god!" Sergeant Bartell said. The camera turned to follow the suspect again, and the people he ran past fell to the ground in a wave. Tawnie turned the video off and leaned over the table.

"This video was taken about a month ago in Massachusetts." She explained. "The suspect's name was Ahmed Al-Salir. His victims include 193 citizens of Springfield. This including all the family he migrated with to America."

Scott shook his head in disbelief. "He killed his family, too?"

"He didn't kill anyone." Tawnie corrected him. "193 people died as a result of energy that we or Ahmed couldn't comprehend."

"It has been discovered that Ahmed and his family migrated from Saudi Arabia," Wesley added. "He was an employee at the Al-Faw temple. Agent Tawnie's organization believes that he may have absorbed the energy somehow. And this caused him to…"

Everyone turned their attention to General Wesley.

"To what?" Bartell asked.

"It seems ridiculous, and I didn't want to say it." He

announced.

"He developed powers due to his exposure to the energy in that temple." Tawnie cut in.

Sergeant Scott stood, his eyes displaying frustration as he stared at Tawnie. "You want me to believe that somebody got powers?" He asked. "Like a goddamn supervillain?"

"Alright, Scott, shut the hell up and let them finish!" Gordon stepped in. The man got quiet and looked around the room. He now had everyone's attention.

"SIT DOWN!" Wesley roared at the man. Sergeant Scott flopped back down in his seat. After the room settled again, Wesley nodded to Tawnie to continue.

"As we see in the video, this power is nothing to take lightly. We need to extract it before anyone else is affected," Tawnie announced.

Sergeant Bartell raised her hand. "Are we not worried about being affected by the energy?" She asked. "What's stopping us from being infected?"

"As this energy is radiation-based, it is harmless in short-term exposure," Tawnie answered. We have a containment case that will isolate it upon retrieval."

Gordon raised his hand. Tawnie nodded at him. "What is the worst-case scenario here?"

She slowly took her seat. "We go in and never come out."

Chapter XXVIII

Gordon headed back to his hotel room. As the day continued, the sun was blocked by a cloud system that ominously rolled in without warning. In addition to the darkness, snow began to fall. It had gotten so cold that he lost feeling in his limbs. He clutched the food like a football, hoping it would still be warm when he returned to the room. He looked around as he stepped into the motel parking lot, feeling like he was being watched. He stopped walking when he heard a car door slam but didn't see anyone. Gordon clenched his fists and prepared to fight. The deeper he walked into the lot, the more his head swiveled.

"Hey!" Someone yelled. Gordon's eyes darted from side to side, scanning the area. Then, he saw him. A slender man darted out of the space between two vehicles with a hand up.

"Hey there, battle!" the man yelled. He was wearing a large puff coat that he had zipped over his chin and a winter hat with faux fur around the ears and forehead. Gordon could only see his eyes, nose, and lips. His chin down was covered in a scarf.

"Daniel Gordon, long time no see my brother!" The man said.

"Lester France," Gordon called out as he approached the man. The two men connected with one hand and pulled each other close to hug.

"What's up, man?" Lester asked.

"I wish I had a good answer to that question," Gordon said as they let go of one another. "Where's Vickie?" Gordon asked as he continued to look around. "She said she'd be in momentarily."

Gordon nodded. "Alright, I gotta get out of this cold."

Gordon walked to his room and fumbled with the card key. He knocked on the door first before swiping the card at the lock.

"Tawnie, it's me!" He said. The man swiped the card, and the light on the lock beeped and flashed green. He put his hand on the knob and pushed it open. He stepped in, holding the door open for Lester. The room was dark. The only light inside was from outside, but considering the weather, it wasn't enough to see.

"Tawnie?" Gordon called out as he looked around. But he didn't see her. Suddenly, he saw Milo pop up from the side of the bed against the wall.

"Milo?" He called out. "Are you okay?"

The boy nodded and stepped out of the small space. Gordon walked over to greet him. He handed the boy a burger from the bag and saw his mother curled up, leaning on the wall beside the bed.

"Alright, Milo. Let's bring you over to this table so you can eat," Gordon said, pushing the boy toward the chair.

"Is she good, DG?" Lester asked, calling Gordon by an old nickname.

"She started screaming," the boy casually said. The two men looked at him and then at one another.

"It's okay, kid. Eat," Gordon said as he patted him on the head. Everything will be fine."

Gordon stepped into the restroom area and switched the lights on.

"Ahh!" Tawnie howled.

"Hey, hey, hey!" Gordon said as he rushed to her and put his hands on her shoulders.

"What's the matter?" He asked. But the woman sobbed instead of answering.

"What's going on?" Lester asked as he stepped in to assist.

"Alright, Ma'am, I'm Officer Lester France of the Rexburg Police Department." He said as he took out a badge to flash.

"No cops!" She muttered. "Why'd you call the cops?"

Gordon shrugged. "I didn't call anyone but my friend."

"Oh, my bad." He responded as he attempted to help Tawnie up onto the bed. Still, she groaned in pain, trying to hold her head with her hands. Milo had lost focus on his food and watched as they handled his mother.

"Tawnie, what do you feel?" Lester asked. "Where is the pain?"

Again, Tawnie grabbed her head with both hands. Lester looked at Daniel. "We have to get her to a hospital." He suggested.

Tawnie shook her head. "No, they'll find us there!" She growled. Lester looked at his friend again. "Who–?"

"That's what I wanted to talk to you guys about." Gordon interrupted as he guided her head back to the pillow.

"What's the plan, man?" Lester asked.

"I'll get into that in a second." Gordon said as he stepped into the water closet. He grabbed a hand towel and put it into the sink, soaking it in room-temperature water.

"We make her comfortable, and hopefully, it passes like the last time." He said as he rang the excess water from the rag.

"How often does this happen?" Lester asked. Gordon shrugged. "I'm not sure. I met her a couple of days ago."

Tawnie began to speak. It sounded like gibberish, causing the two men to look at one another in shock.

"You know what language that is, fam?" Lester asked.

Gordon shook his head. "No idea."

"Man, what the fuck did you drag me into this time, Dan?"

Suddenly, Milo jumped down onto the floor and hid underneath the table. Tawnie continued to scream and shout in the mysterious language.

"I don't know what to do, man," Lester said as he brushed his hands together. "I think I'm just going to head out! I can't be involved with no drugs!" he announced.

"Man, what?" Gordon questioned. "You will just leave in the middle of all this mess?"

Lester smiled as he headed back to the door.

"Good to see you again, Daniel," the man said as he grabbed the handle of the open door. "Let me know when you're back in town with a lot less going on."

Suddenly, a heat wave rushed through the room, almost knocking the men over. Lester looked back at his friend with widened eyes.

"What the hell?" he asked. He looked back outside, trying to find something out of the ordinary, but he saw nothing. He walked back into the room and looked at Tawnie, then at her son in the corner.

"What kind of freaky-deeky bull shit is this?" He asked.

"Dude, I don't know!" Gordon answered. "All I want to do is survive and get the hell out of this state!"

Tawnie began to speak again. "No, you can't!" She screamed. The two men looked at her, waiting for the climax of her screams.

"I can't, fam," Lester said as he headed for the door again.

"Little Man," he called out to Milo. "Enjoy your burger; it's nice to meet you."

Tawnie howled in agony, her torso lifting simultaneously.

"Nice to meet you too, miss." He said as he finally crossed the threshold of the room. Suddenly, Lester saw his wife in the distance. Even though the snow billowed into his eyes, he could tell her walk. She was curvy but slim and fit. Her blond hair flowed in the wind, and snowflakes gathered in her hair as she approached the room.

"Honey, good news," Lester said. "I found Daniel, and he's good. He finally found somebody, but she got a kid, and she crazy."

Lester's wife stopped in front of him. She looked as if she had already lost patience for his banter.

"Are you leaving?" She asked.

"I was, but I feel like you are about to veto that decision." The man said.

His gorgeous wife smiled at him and raised her hand to wipe her hair behind her ear. "Daniel is in town, and I haven't seen him in ages. He called in distress, and that seems normal to you?"

Lester paused for a moment and nodded as he looked past her. "I see your point," he answered. "I'm just not sure about the kind of trouble he's in this time."

Lester's wife scoffed. The man leaned in a bit closer and found her ear. "I think he kidnapped this poor girl and her son."

The woman laughed and gently punched Lester in the shoulder. He moved aside, allowing him access to the room. She saw the open door and stepped inside. The man was looming over the bed. Tawnie had a knee up and her palms flat on the sheet. She began to lift herself.

"I got you." He said to her.

"First Sergeant?" the woman called him. Gordon looked over his shoulder at her. He smiled as he helped Tawnie up to the edge of the bed. Victoria laid eyes on her, and rage captured her face the instant she realized who she was.

"Victoria," Gordon called out after turning around to face her. But she completely ignored him as she stared at the woman sitting at the edge of the queen-sized bed.

Her eyes sharpened, and her head lowered as she growled. "Tawnie!"

Victoria stepped into the room, her eyes locked on Tawnie as she sauntered. Lester attempted to make a joke, something he usually does. But Gordon held a finger up, hoping he didn't make matters worse.

"Victoria." I need you to keep calm." Gordon said. "There is no need for any added hostility."

Tawnie stood from the bed and watched the woman pace beside her. Gordon placed his shoulder in front of the small woman to block her.

"Daniel, what the fuck?" Victoria asked. "Have you lost your mind hanging with this one?"

" Wait?" Lester interjected. "You know this chick, Vic?"

"Yeah," She answered. "She's the reason Riyadh went down the way it did," Victoria said as she approached Tawnie. Gordon attempted to hold her back. No matter how close Victoria came, Tawnie didn't move.

"A little help here, Lester?" Gordon requested.

The man shook his head. "Nah, man, Vickie can handle her own." He said as he crossed his arms. "I know better than to get involved with her affairs."

Gordon grunted. "Man, it's not Vickie I'm worried about here."

Finally, Victoria moved. The leverage allowed Gordon to slide her across the room. He pushed her back into the bathroom counter at the back of the room. Gordon spun around to look at Lester again.

"Get in here and close the damn door." He yelled. Lester shrugged his shoulders and stepped in.

From behind, Victoria pushed Gordon. He stumbled into the half wall dividing the two sections of the rooms.

"Vickie, stop!" Gordon said as he spun around to confront her. She walked toward him.

"I'll deal with you after her," She yelled, pointing her finger in the man's face. She approached Tawnie and grabbed her by the collar. Victoria pushed the woman onto the table in the front corner of the room and pulled her fist back to strike her. The entire time, Tawnie's face remained unchanged. There was nothing but uncomfortable eye contact and a lack of emotion. As Victoria's fist finally began to travel to her target, she heard someone scream, "Mommy!"

Chapter XXIX

Her bare knuckles slammed against the table surface. The room got quiet, and the men waited for the situation to blow over. For a moment, Victoria stood over Tawnie, looking down at her with a rage that her husband had never seen before. He caught goosebumps as he waited for her fury to conclude.

"Vickie?" He called out to her. Snapping out of her funk, she looked at him. But he wasn't looking at her. He nodded toward the wall behind her. Victoria looked beside her and found Milo trembling in fear as he looked up at the woman. His face was riddled with tears, and his bottom lip quivered as he stared at her.

"Oh no," Victoria said. "Oh my god!"

She pulled Tawnie up by the jacket collar and stood her upright.

"Tawnie, are you good?" Gordon asked. She nodded slowly, her eyes still locked onto Victoria.

"Well, it appears you two don't need any introductions," Gordon said.

"Yeah, but I do!" Lester chimed in.

"Right," Gordon said. "Lester, this is Tawnie Simms."

Lester looked at the woman briefly, and his eyes grew wide again. Her name alone had blown his mind.

"Holy hell!" He shouted as he approached her. "The Oracle!"

Victoria shook her head and turned away.

"I didn't even recognize you, Madame Oracle!" he continued. "I watch your stuff all the time. I never knew my wife hated you, though."

After saying that, the man turned to face Victoria.

"You know the Oracle?" He asked, full of excitement. "Both of you?"

"Lester, I need you to keep it down, man!" Gordon said. "I didn't call the two of you to make more trouble for ourselves. We have enough of that right now."

Gordon turned toward Tawnie. Cautious, he approached her, looking into her eyes.

"Tawnie?" He called. "Are you okay? Do you need anything?"

Victoria looked at her husband, her face red as he approached her. She looked away from him out of embarrassment.

"I'm fine," she said to Gordon. "In fact, I'm a bit... divine." She paused.

Gordon needed clarification. "Wait." He said. "You were literally crying bloody murder just now. What was that?"

Tawnie shrugged. "I get migraines." She answered just before turning away to look at Milo. The boy looked up at her and fell back down into the corner. Gordon squinted, watching the interaction from across the room. He looked at Lester, who had the same expression. It was the look of a child who had been abused. But Gordon had spent almost forty-eight hours with the pair. Surely, there would have been more evidence if that were the case.

"Tawnie, what the hell is happening?" Gordon asked.

The woman took a deep breath. She turned to look at him and shrugged again.

"Well, I thought I was hallucinating." She said. "But we're going to get into that another time."

Gordon looked back at his friends, each of them lost.

"Daniel, how did you end up finding this crazy bitch?" Victoria asked.

Gordon turned to her and slumped his shoulders. "I just kinda ran into her back in Idaho Falls."

Victoria shook her head in disapproval. "Okay, better question. Tawnie, how did you run into Daniel after all these years?"

Tawnie turned away from her kid and looked at Victoria. "Honestly, it was a coincidence." She said. She approached Victoria, looking her square in the eyes. The former Master Sergeant was still taller than her. She stared at her over the tip of her nose, waiting for her to do something.

"Since I met you two, I've gotten married, started a family, and dedicated my career to destroying the systems that keep us blind," Tawnie explained. "I followed my husband here and settled in Idaho Falls seven years ago. Victoria, how long have you and your husband lived in Rexburg?"

Victoria looked away, seemingly doing the math in her head.

"I just wanted everything to go back to normal." Tawnie continued. "But the two of you coincidentally found one another in the same state as me!"

Lester stepped into the conversation, raising his index finger high. He pursed his lips to ask a question.

"It's classified," Gordon announced. "We're not allowed to talk about it."

"Rules, rules, laws, rules!" Tawnie screamed as she threw her hands into the air. "Everyone wants me to follow the rules that they make up to keep me from destroying their wall of lies! Meanwhile, all I want to do is live in peace!"

Victoria's eyebrows furrowed as she grew confused.

"You two couldn't have known why they sent us on that mission! Why would any of us?" Tawnie yelled. "All I did was follow orders! Now I must deal with you idiots blaming me for your problems!"

Gordon sighed and let his head fall. "We lost a lot of good people that day."

"Yeah," Tawnie said. "We lost ourselves that day too, didn't we?"

Tawnie stepped into the corner where her son sat and bent over to grab him. The boy whined as soon as she touched him. Victoria moved past her husband and went to stand in front of the door. Milo cried as Tawnie picked him up, and another wave of heat filled the room momentarily. Tawnie turned around and saw Victoria blocking her exit. The blond folded her arms over her torso and stared into her eyes again.

Tawnie shook her head. "You want to play hardball, Victoria?" she asked as she raised her arm, pointing her palm toward the door. Gordon approached her and grabbed her hand.

"We are going to try being civil," he said as he pushed her hand down. "And we will try being understanding."

Gordon reached for Milo and took him from her clutches. She suddenly appeared submissive. She stood idle, watching Gordon as he pulled her son away.

"I just want the truth." She said to them. "All I want is to take back that day."

The room got quiet, and everyone looked at one another.

"Yeah, me too," Victoria said. "But turning back the hands on the clock is impossible, so we may as well move forward."

Tawnie's eyes popped as if she'd made a revelation. "Actually, it may be more achievable than you think."

"Okay, so we have a new problem now," Gordon said. "Riyadh has nothing to do with what's going on here today, so let's focus on what's in front of us."

"Yeah," Victoria added. "Now that we're on the subject, what the hell is going on?"

Gordon was lost. He looked at his old friend with thin eyes and a raised eyebrow. "You mean to tell me you haven't heard about what happened in Idaho Falls?" He asked.

Victoria looked at Lester. He shrugged his shoulders, unsure what any of them were talking about.

"Did something happen there that we should know about?" He asked. Tawnie looked at Gordon. Both of them lost.

"How is that even possible?" Gordon asked her. She shook her head and looked to the floor. "The explosion, the killings, the quarantine? What the hell is happening around here, and how could people in the next town over not know about it?"

Tawnie folded her arms. She took a moment to think, putting all of her evidence together in her mind.

"I hate to be the bearer of bad news, love," Lester said. "But none of this seems like a coincidence."

"Lester, it's top secret. We can't tell you anything about the mission." Victoria said. "Besides, that was seven years ago. What does that have to do with the here and now?"

Tawnie shook her head. Each of them turned their attention to her.

"What if I told you that our mission seven years ago may have everything to do with this mess?" She asked.

Victoria stopped for a moment to think. Then she shook her head. "I can't revisit that now."

"You may not want to revisit the past, Master Sergeant Bartell. But I'm going to need you to grab your passport. We're telling your husband about this mission."

Gordon and Victoria were both stunned as they stared at her in shock. "I need to tell you exactly what we took from those ruins and why we're in this predicament now."

At the point in human history when the eleven Servines of the Universal Order are found, the beginning will meet its end.

-Excerpt of the Arcanin Prophecy; Translated by the Oracle

Chapter XXX

Riyadh, Saudi Arabia, 2073, at the Al-Faw temple. The time was approximately 9:45 PM, and the heat of the desert had dissipated completely. Tawnie stood outside a tourist entrance, staring up at the dilapidated stone structure. The people of Saudi Arabia did their best to upkeep the temple, but it was truly in bad shape. Holes and cracks filled the structure, and loose gravel and dirt fell from every point overhead. But there was only so much that could hide the fact the building was almost a million years old. The majority of it appeared like a hill of dirt. A mound that served as the outer structure of the world inside. The temple was set up as a minor tourist attraction but closed for the night.

"You scared, kid?" Sergeant Scott asked as he approached Tawnie from behind.

Tawnie shook her head. "More annoyed than anything."

The man smiled and looked at her. "Has that got something to do with you being an obvious I.T. girl who's being treated like an archeologist?"

"No," She said. "It has something to do with me not wanting to talk to you."

Tawnie stepped closer to the ruins and looked around. The moon brightened the sky, partially illuminating the grounds below. The others joined the conversation as Tawnie walked off. She could hear them all joking with the man.

"That's what you get for messing with a minor," Bartell stated.

"What?" He blurted. "I was just trying to be friendly."

General Wesley joined the group. Everyone was dressed in full protective battle gear.

"Alright, soldiers!" Wesley announced. "Toe the line, and let's get this show on the road!"

Everyone in the group crowded around their leader for a mission briefing. Everyone except Tawnie.

"Alright, soldiers. We are about to have a long night," Wesley announced. We recently discovered that this temple has a lot more underneath the surface. Our mission is to find out what that is exactly and isolate it."

Scott looked down at his rifle and threw his arms up. "Sir, I thought I'd be shooting something on this mission. What targets did we get in that dirt pile?"

"The general stared at him with resentment in his eyes.

"There is an aspect to this mission that remains classified. We can neither confirm nor deny there will be any hostiles in there." Scott nodded.

"In addition, soldiers, we will have multiple civilian units joining us. We need to be extra vigilant in our pursuit."

Everyone looked around the group at one another.

"Okay, now I'm concerned." Sergeant Maison said. "We are going into some ruins built almost a million years ago and expect to see a threat inside?"

Wesley's eyes thinned as he looked at his group.

"We are following orders from Washington." The man stated. "Our personal grievances with this mission are irrelevant."

The general walked away from his group.

"Boots up in five minutes!" He grunted at them as he marched to the civilians. This group consisted of scientists and archeologists. The general pulled them into a huddle to speak with them, presumably telling them the plan. Victoria filtered the noise and found Gordon in the crowd. He seemed distant, carrying this faraway expression as he looked on at Tawnie.

"You pining for jail bait over there?" She asked him, half-way expecting him to chuckle or at least smile.

"No, I'm just having some trouble digesting this feeling I got." He answered.

Victoria looked around, seeing if they had anyone's attention.

"What are you thinking?" She asked. "Because it seems like an easy grave-robbing mission."

Gordon nodded. "We are risking a war with the Emirates all because we want to deface sacred grounds and take their treasure. We are stomping on their entire religion, for what?"

The woman looked at him and nodded. "It seems like you are asking questions that are not at liberty of being answered again. Do you want to disappear?"

Gordon sighed. "I'm not joking here, Vickie."

"Me either!" she cut him off. "These are the questions that make alive people not alive anymore! Be smart about how you are doing this, First Sergeant!"

Gordon turned away and grunted as he looked up at the starry sky.

"If an entire army invades this land while we're down there, at least we'll have our M16s."

Gordon stepped forward and called the platoon to fall into formation. The six elites stood at the end of their squads. Their lower enlisted soldiers standing beside them.

"At ease!" He commanded. "The time is now for our mission to take place. Many more questions have been revolving around this mission. In reality, we have been preparing for this day since the beginning." He announced. Tawnie stood next to General Wesley as First Sergeant Gordon made his speech.

"I have a question for you," Wesley asked Tawnie. But the girl remained quiet and simply nodded. "How does a teenage girl become a subject matter expert in an operation like this?"

Tawnie looked up at him with a smirk on her lips. "I was just the first to figure all of this out," she answered. "I tried not to be, but in my organization, I'm the best at everything I do, including war."

The First Sergeant allowed two of the five platoons to step ahead. They walked in a staggered pattern in two lines. Between the two groups, the civilians marched. Tawnie ran ahead and stepped out front.

"On my lead!" The young woman roared to the back. After the first two platoons left, another group stepped forward with similar configuration. After that, the last group tailed in a triangle pattern.

This group included the remaining archaeological and research teams. Group one consisted of Victoria and Sergeant Maison. Group two had Sergeants Parker and Myopovic, and the tail gunners of the unit were led by Sergeant Scott. Cautiously, Tawnie led the company into the catacombs of the ruins. There was a large space in the center of the ruins that had nothing but sand there. Ancient dilapidated slabs stood high on both sides of them, crumbling and full of holes. Tawnie stopped in the very center of the ruins and looked around. Everyone behind her stopped.

"Hey, is everything okay?" General Wesley asked. Tawnie didn't answer him. Instead, she turned around to face the dozens of people.

"Yeah." She finally answered with a grin on her face. "This is where things get weird."

Sergeant Gordon nodded. "Alright, let's get moving so we can get what we came for."

Feeling rushed, Tawnie locked eyes with the man and began to pace while looking at the ground.

"What the hell is she doing?" Gordon asked.

Victoria shook her head. "Hey, are you looking for something?" Tawnie kept moving in small circles, growing bigger in size the more she kicked through the sand.

"This structure was once the gate that led to the place we seek." Tawnie explained as she walked back to the center of the architectural intersection. She pulled a small device from her hip and pressed a button before throwing it to her feet.

"What the hell was that?" Victoria asked.

Tawnie hopped away from the device and kneeled in the sand nearby.

"Take cover!" She screamed to the unit behind her. A red light shone from the device, and it blinked rapidly. In a panic, everyone ran from the intersection, and an explosion blasted the entire area. A wave of sand was pushed away from the site, crashing through the crowd of soldiers and civilians. Gordon could see everyone around him running in the opposite direction. But what the wave of sand revealed underneath caused him to freeze in a rush of emotions. The entire topography shifted underneath their feet. People started to sink into the sand, losing traction as they slid toward the impact zone. Gordon tried reaching for objects to keep himself from being swallowed by the vortex. He saw people being sucked in around him and began to feel helpless. After a few moments, it had finally gotten quiet. Everyone began to pop up from the sand like groundhogs, looking around for the others in their group.

"What the hell was that?" Sergeant Scott asked as he rose from the dirt in the back. He made it to his feet and walked to the front of the unit. He found Gordon standing next to a crater, looking down into it.

"Yo, Top, what's up?" Scott asked as he approached his First Sergeant. His eyes naturally gravitated toward the newly formed crater in the sand.

"Holy, God damn!" He said. "I don't think that was part of the tourist attraction."

The soldiers and civilians all made their way back to the crater.

"I don't believe this," Victoria said as she looked to the bottom of the crater. "First Sergeant?"

Gordon shook his head. "I'm just as amazed as you are."

"Tawnie!" General Wesley called out to her from the top of the dune. "What the hell was that?"

The young girl remained standing where she was. But she was now about thirty feet below the others. The only difference was the elevation. She found herself standing on another stone surface marked with ancient carvings. The civilians all took out large spotlights to shine inside the crater. The audible sound of roars and cheers filled the area. The platform, in its entirety, was round. Stone steps led down into the cavity, but the sand covered most of it.

"First Sergeant, are we clear to enter?' One of the civilians asked Gordon. He became flustered, unsure what to say.

"For the moment, stand back and allow us to assess the situation." He answered as he waved to his soldiers. "Platoon sergeant, squad leaders, let's move in!"

As Everyone headed into the crater. Bartell and the other leaders could hear the assistant platoon sergeants calling orders. As Gordon traversed into the pit, he noticed strange markings on the sides of the walls. Outside the four flights of steps on each side of the intersection, larger blocks sat in rows. Each block was approximately eight feet tall and layered like a flight of steps.

Every layer was lined with strange carvings from top to bottom. Each of them looked around in awe as they descended. Once they reached the bottom, they headed to Tawnie, standing in the center.

"What the hell is all of this?" Wesley asked.

Tawnie shrugged. "I'm not sure yet."

"There's no way we are about to go to war over some hieroglyphics, right?" Gordon asked. "With that explosion, you probably raised a lot of attention, so the discovery had better be worth it."

Tawnie nodded as she looked around the crater.

"We are standing in history, folks!" She blurted. "Look around!"

As they were told, the group examined the area around them.

"Once upon a lifetime ago, an ancient civilization wrote our destiny in the stone of this pit!" she explained as she walked to the center of a large symbol carved into the floor. "This is the first Arcanin Tomb of five. Each tomb tells not only history but the fate of humanity."

Sergeant Parker examined the lines on the platform underneath them. Following with his eyes and mapping the intersections.

"Is this a pentagram of some sort?" He asked.

"A decagram," Tawnie answered. "Representing the ten core elements of universal balance."

They looked around at the decagram's symbols, beginning to see the elements in the stone. Gordon identified the fire symbol, water, earth, wind, life, time, space, and magic. But then realized that one symbol was duplicated on both sides of the carving.

"I only see nine elements." He said. The girl moved aside and revealed a tenth symbol underneath her feet.

"Alright," Tawnie called out to get everyone's attention. She pointed at the two triangular, light symbols that pointed back to the center of the decagram. "Aside from these two, everyone finds a symbol to stand on."

Confused, everyone looked at one another as they

unconsciously walked to one circle containing an element. The soldiers all found a spot, leaving the flame symbol uncovered. Everyone looked at the girl in anticipation. She looked up and pointed to a random soldier at the top of the stairs.

"Hey!" Tawnie called out. The soldier looked. "We need your help! Get down here!"

Slowly, the man made his way to a flight of stairs and descended into the pit. When he got to the bottom, Tawnie pointed to the symbol, and he made his way to it. He stood on top of it and looked at the woman for approval.

Tawnie smiled at her accomplishment thus far and rubbed her hands together.

"Is everybody ready?" she asked. But nobody responded. They simply looked around at one another, still confused about what was happening.

"Sure," Wesley answered. "Let's get this over with."

Tawnie kneeled and placed her palm on the symbol in the center of the decagram. She watched in amazement as the symbol began to glow. The light filled the cell that held the symbol and traveled throughout the decagram. The soldier's eyes gaped as the illumination spread through the veins like a slow liquid. There was a flash once every part of the carving was completely filled with light. The light transitioned into two of the ten cells. The leaf in the Earth cell and the flame in the fire cell were the only two points illuminated. Tawnie stood with a menacing grin on her face. The light completely faded, and the ground began to rumble. Concerned, the soldiers began to look around.

"What's happening?" Victoria asked Tawnie. The girl smiled and walked around the decagram, locking her eyes on the symbol in the center. "Ladies and gentlemen, you've just unlocked your first Arcanin Vault." Tawnie announced as parts of the crater's floor began to fall. The team watched the stones sink into the Earth. The more stones moved aside, the more visible the prize underneath became. A large set of stairs opened up, leading into a dark cavern underneath.

"Folks, I want to make it clear that this is a horrible idea! There will be unfathomable dangers in this temple, so stay on high alert!" Tawnie said. General Wesley approached and looked inside the chasm.

"Well shit," He said. "Here's to following orders."

Chapter XXXI

"The discovery of this temple is the easy part of the mission," Tawnie told everyone. "Everything from here on out becomes tricky. Be cautious of your emotions and keep a clear mind as you navigate this space."

Wesley glared at the tiny woman. "First of all, you took my speech," He said to her, pretentiously pointing at himself. "Second, what the hell are you talking about, a clear mind?"

Tawnie held a finger up to the man.

"Arc-Team spread out and record all of these symbols. Army, take the lead!"

She winked at the general and headed for the entrance to the cavern. The soldiers gathered around Wesley. They noticed the man's concern as he watched Tawnie walk away.

"Does anyone else have a sinking feeling about this?" Parker asked, his voice echoing in the cavern.

"Hmph," Wesley grunted. "My optimism flew out the window when I realized that she knows exactly what we're looking for, and we don't."

"Maybe we can corner her and question her," Myopovic suggested. "We can squeeze the truth out of the little girl."

Gordon shook his head. "Bad idea," he added. "We may not know where she's from or who her superiors are, but I can say for sure that she's a specialist of some sort. I've heard of people from Dark Ops and what they can do. If she's one of them, confronting her is a horrible idea."

Scott laughed. "What's wrong, Top? The little girl got you scared or something?"

The man looked away at the temple entrance. "I'm playing it

smart."

"We don't know who she is or what she's capable of," Victoria said. "All we can do now is follow our orders and hope for the best."

"What's our worst-case scenario here?" Myopovic asked. Everyone looked around, waiting for an answer. They all seemed to pause, imagining something horrible taking place. They turned to their General and waited for him to answer.

"Realistically, we follow her lead. Whether it's a dangerous cave or not, we don't have any options here. We got orders."

Everyone began to descend into the chasm. The civilians brought more light into the opening. Eagerly climbing into the trenches to begin recording the symbols. Groups of their people started to pull out cameras and notebooks to investigate. More soldiers escorted the remainder of the archeology team to the bottom of the ravine. They used the stairs to make their descent all the way to the entrance of the temple.

"Alright, people!" Tawnie blurted as she exited the ruins entrance to receive the civilians. The soldiers looked at her sideways as she elbowed through the group.

"The objective is just below!" she yelled. "Archeologists leave no stone unturned. If it can be used as research, record it."

Tawnie walked into the temple entrance. She shined a flashlight forward that seemed to illuminate absolutely nothing inside. The opening had stairs where mounds of sand lie at the bottom. The steps ended when the lights above couldn't reach into the cavern. The cave consisted of a downward grade that was mostly degraded and loose. Every step seemed like it would cause a rock slide. On the left side of the path was a large, gaping opening that seemed to go on forever.

"Oh, hell no!" Scott squealed. "Where the hell does this hole go? How deep is this thing?"

Sergeant Parker looked at him with one side of his mouth twisted.

"Are you actually afraid of heights, Scott?" He asked. "You're literally the most reckless of all of us."

Some of the others chuckled in apparent agreement.

"Look alive!" Gordon roared, making them all stop. "We don't know what the hell to expect here, so be on guard."

The air inside the cabin was wet, and the temperature dropped fast. They walked silently down the seemingly windy slope with a rocky wall on one side. Occasionally, they would see a written message carved into the stone. Tawnie looked at all of them, focusing on them with her flashlight. General Wesley walked closely behind, seeing her read the script.

"What language is this?" he asked. "It doesn't look like Arabic."

"It's not," Tawnie answered. "It's the first human language ever written. It was created millions of years ago when humanity learned to communicate on Earth."

The general grunted at her answer.

"Is there a way to decipher it?" he asked. "This could be cataloged human history."

Tawnie stopped walking and looked back at him. The man shined his flashlight at her chest, careful not to put the beam directly in her eyes. He could see her face in the ambient light with a smirk.

"We passed history at the surface. These are warnings." The man swallowed the lump in his throat, and Tawnie continued into the cave.

"General, you good?" Gordon asked from behind.

"He's absolutely fine!" Tawnie yelled loudly to cover the distance she made in front of them.

"What the hell?" Gordon asked as he looked around with his flashlight.

"What is it now, First Sergeant?" Victoria asked as she nudged his back with the back of her hand.

"Did anyone hear an echo when she yelled just now?" He asked. Everyone thought in silence as they continued down into the cave.

"Wow," Maison said. "I guess I didn't."

"What's the big deal?" Scott asked.

"It means that there is a very big space ahead," Wesley answered.

"Nowhere for the sound to reflect." Gordon continued.

The unit descended into the cave for approximately an hour. About thirty-nine minutes into their trek, the spirals stopped. The grade continued straight like they were on a ramp. There were no walls or ceilings. The cavern was eerily silent. Gordon tapped his finger against his M16 to create extra sound to avoid going insane. Even the sound of people walking around him wasn't enough.

"How much longer ?" Wesley asked.

Tawnie looked back over her shoulder. "How should I know?" She asked. "I've never been here before."

Suddenly, a red light ignited behind them. They all looked back to find Scott igniting a signal flare.

"What the hell do you think you're doing?" Wesley asked.

"I was curious if we could see anything in here," Scott said as he threw the flare into the darkness.

"Scott, you idiot!" Gordon yelled as his eyes followed the flare into space.

Tawnie shook her head. "Get your man, General." She said as she turned and continued walking. Their eyes followed the flare as it reached its apex and proceeded to the chasm below. On its way down, everyone anticipated that it would hit something. But the stick flipped as it barreled its way to the ground. As it got smaller, it finally landed about two hundred feet below. The area the flame shined on was jagged and looked like a wall made of giant gray jewels and blades surrounding it.

"Found the ground finally." Scott joked.

"Don't fuck with me, Scott!" The general growled. He approached the non-commissioned officer, pointing his entire, straightened hand into his face. "I will Court Marshall your ass for going off books if you do something like that again!"

Scott stood at attention and looked past his superior.

"Do I make myself clear, soldier?" He asked Scott.

"Sir, yes, sir!" The man shouted. Everyone focused on the walk again. They shined their lights on Tawnie, who stood at the end of the incline. The grade ended, and a platform made of stone blocks sat just beyond the craggy cave floor. The group shined their flashlights around. In front of them was a giant opening. It was an imposing sight, with colossal stone pillars towering around thirty feet high, creating the impression of a grand entrance.

"Who the hell is this big ass door for?" Scott asked.

"Finally, a question from Sergeant Scott that isn't stupid," Maison said. The other soldiers laughed. Gordon, Wesley, and Victoria stepped forth, looking at the giant temple entrance. The closer they got, the more ancient text they saw.

"Is this it?" Wesley asked Tawnie.

"It is." The woman said as she slipped out of the backpack she was wearing. She unzipped the bag on the ground, reaching in to find something.

"It's been a long journey down, folks," Tawnie said as she pulled out two tubes, handing one to Gordon and one to Wesley. The tubes were made of a glass-like material that seemed as hard as a diamond. The center of the tubes had an electronic device that appeared to be recessed to fit a sphere. The components inside carried wires, lenses, gears, and motors.

"But the real challenge will be inside this temple."

"What the hell are these?" Gordon asked.

"They appear to be some specialized containers," Maison answered.

"Correct, Sergeant Maison," Tawnie answered as she placed the backpack on her back. Without warning, she stepped forward. The others followed, cautious of their surroundings and not knowing what to expect. Gordon looked up at the threshold of the chamber before him. The entire thing had a script of Arcanin text wrapped around it. He looked down before them and watched Tawnie pass through the two pillars. The text around the threshold began to glow.

"What the hell?" Scott said as he noticed the light, filling the vein-like openings in the floor. The civilians in attendance seemed to spring to life. The giant, circular room they were in was slowly illuminated. The same decagram was carved into the floor and illuminated like the one on the surface. The various symbols flashed in sequence, illuminating then slowly fading as another glowed. The floor rumbled underneath them, causing Tawnie to look back toward the door. The green Earth and red fire symbols and the entire back wall were illuminated. The soldiers all became spooked and pointed their guns. Tawnie stopped on top of the symbol in the center of the decagram and stared to the back of the room.

The entire room was fully illuminated, and they could finally see. A loud screeching sound came from behind them. Everyone looked back, but there was no light outside to see anything.

"What the hell is happening?" Gordon asked. Victoria was in

awe of the dome-shaped stadium-sized room.

The rumbling stopped suddenly, and Tawnie looked at the floor with concern. The deafening silence returned, and all the soldiers looked around at one another.

"What the hell?" Gordon asked.

"Tawnie, what's happening?" Wesley asked as he approached the woman.

She sighed and clenched her fists, staring at the lights before her.

"Something is not right," she said. "You folks may want to brace yourselves."

The soldiers all stared at her with inquisitive looks. Suddenly, Victoria collapsed to a knee.

"Bartell!" The others called as they huddled around her for support.

"Give her space!" Wesley yelled to them.

"What's wrong, Bartell?" Maison asked her. The woman grunted.

"I just started to feel faint out of nowhere," she answered.

"A good sign," Tawnie said. They all looked at her again.

"Everyone here is supposed to feel faint," she added as she turned to face them with wide eyes. "They told me that you all would."

"What the hell are you saying?" Parker asked. "What do you mean-"

The man said as he started to stumble. Wesley raised his hands to his head, pain beginning to hit him. Even Gordon cleared his throat As his body began to shut down.

"Tawnie, you want to explain why we are getting sick?" He asked.

Tawnie sighed again and turned around. "You are transforming," she said. "That means the rest of you are going to die."

Sergeant Scott snapped. "What the heck did you just say?"

Suddenly, there was another scream from outside.

Wesley glared at Tawnie. "This was a trap!"

Chapter XXXII

Tawnie took a step back, still watching the soldiers. Gordon, Wesley, Parker, and Bartell were all taken to the ground. Their groans and screams gave her chills. They could see a reasonable tone of fear in the girl's expression for the first time since meeting her.

"Tawnie, what's happening?" Wesley screamed at her. But she ignored his question as she became fixated on the remaining soldiers. Tawnie looked at each of them, her eyes full of remorse, and bit her bottom lip in frustration.

"What the hell do we do?" Scott asked.

"I'm so sorry." She said to them. "But it's too late."

Tawnie ran toward the light sources at the back of the chamber.

"Where the hell are you going?" Myopovic asked. But she ignored them, leaving them to tend to their fallen comrades. They heard more screaming outside the chamber and saw a mysterious light as they looked out the door. It flashed a brilliant silver color that seemed to have filled the entire cavern, and in a split second, it was gone. Scott bent at the knees, prepared to hoist the large General Wesley to his feet.

"Come on, General. We have to go!" He said to the man, who could barely hold himself up. He writhed in pain as the soldier attempted to move him. The others weren't doing any better.

"Grab a person, let's go!" He yelled to the other two. "Hey, kid, can we get a hand here?"

Tawnie looked back at them and started to shake her head as she continued to the light source. She stood in front of two giant pillars that protruded from the wall. At eye level were openings in the columns, almost resembling a shrine. There were intricate designs around it. Inside, the opening was embossed with ancient text everywhere.

"This is it." She said to herself as she opened the tubes she held.

The bright red and green light faded. The only light remaining was the dim white light that burned in the lines of the floor. It got eerily silent. The soldiers moved toward the door. Scott and Maison gave their fallen comrades a pep talk as they made their way.

"We can't leave Tawnie behind." The General said to Sergeant Scott. The man looked over his shoulder to find her. But the room had gotten dark, and he couldn't see her. He could only see a nearly extinguished flicker of red and green.

"Tawnie, come on!" He yelled. "We have to go now!"

They continued to the door, and Victoria fell. Myopovic and Maison tried to hold on to her while also trying not to lose Sergeant Parker.

"Bartell!" Maison yelled as she tried picking her up. But the moment she touched her, the woman stopped. In that moment, Victoria felt the sharp edges of her pain gradually dulling. As she looked up at Maison, she observed that the woman had come to a sudden stop, her expression filled with concern.

"Maison?" She called. But the woman said nothing. "Maison!" She yelled again. She realized that Scott and Myopovic were in the same vegetative state.

Suddenly, there was a gunshot outside the chamber.

"What the hell?" Wesley asked. "Scott, what's your problem?" But Sergeant Scott had no answer to give. Gordon looked at the three of them in suspicion.

"Myopovic, Maison?" He called out. But they didn't respond either. The two men were facing forward, their eyes wide and lifeless. Maison loomed over Victoria. She could see something strange about the situation and began to get nervous. Suddenly, the light from the decagram faded, and the room was shrouded in darkness. The deafening silence returned. The three soldiers waited, anticipating what could be wrong with their battle buddies. Gordon pulled out a flashlight and shined it around. He didn't bother asking for anyone's status; he just shined his light on Scott. Victoria could see the darkness of Maison's eyes in the residual light. There appeared to be nothing left to her.

"Top, what's happening?" Victoria asked as her body began to shake.

"I don't know." He said, still looking at Scott from his profile.

"Hey Scott, now is not the time for jokes," he said as he touched him. Scott's reflexes caused him to catch Gordon's hand almost without being seen. He squeezed the man's wrist, and Gordon grew concerned.

"Scott, what the hell, Soldier?" He screamed, but the man still didn't answer him. He only turned his head slowly and proceeded to stare at Gordon. The look on his face was emotionless, thoughtless, even soulless. His eyes were void of any character at all. It was as if Gordon was looking at a mannequin. His grip became painful on Gordon's wrist, and another gunshot was heard outside. Suddenly, Maison began to strangle Victoria, and Myopovic targeted General Wesley.

As the men fought, Victoria found herself lying on her back with Maison's thumbs lodged into her neck. She clawed and kicked at the woman to get her off, though nothing seemed to be working at all. Gordon pulled Scott toward him and sent his opposite elbow soaring to the man's mouth. Scott spun away from him and fell to the ground. Wesley jabbed Myopovic, and the small man seemed to flip away from him. They could hear Victoria gagging, attempting to catch her breath. The moment they shined the light on her, Tawnie had already run past, delivering a knee to Sergeant Maison.

All of their seemingly lifeless battle buddies were grounded.

"What the hell is happening here?" Gordon yelled as he approached Tawnie. Gordon shined his flashlight at her hand and noticed something intriguing.

"That's what we came down here for?" He asked as he pointed at the tube she prepared to push into her backpack. Tawnie paused. Gordon approached and snatched it out of her hand. He raised it to his face, examining it in full. He shined a light and saw what looked like a glass ball approximately four inches in diameter. It appeared to be nothing on the surface. It was transparent with no gloss, yet it had a reflection inside. Though

Gordon was unsure, he thought he saw a green glow inside, but nothing was there.

"Is this what we came here for?" He questioned. "Some damned Arabian glass?"

"Could that have something to do with this attack?"

Tawnie took the tube back and stuffed it into her backpack. "We don't have time for these questions!" She yelled at them as she looked around. "We have to get out of here, now!"

The three zombie soldiers stood back up. Their body language seemed unorthodox to their battle buddies.

"Maison, Scott, Myopovic, snap out of it!" Victoria yelled. However, their movement did not elicit a visual response.

"No use. Tawnie said. "They've been destroyed by the energy in this room."

Wesley's eyes sharpened, and he shook his head. "What the hell does that even mean?" He asked. "They are our friends! What are you saying?"

Suddenly, there was a shuffle behind them. Daniel looked back, seeing the soldiers and archaeologist from outside. They were walking into the chamber.

"The energy in this room is meant only for those with a certain genetic type. Congratulations, you're all special." Tawnie said. "But your friends signed their death warrants the moment we stepped into this temple."

Gordon turned around and faced the group. His light revealed a dozen people, many holding weapons. Their faces were emotionless and cold in their stares.

"What exactly does any of that mean?" He asked.

Tawnie sighed. "It means that your dead friends will have to die a second time so that we can live. Or we are going to die in here with them.

"Guys?" Gordon called out. The group turned around and saw the people behind them.

"Dammit!" Tawnie growled. "This situation just went from bad to worse."

"There has to be a better way than killing them!" Wesley said.

"General, I don't think you understand," Tawnie argued. "These people are already dead."

The moment she said that one of the soldiers from outside

raised his rifle and shot a round in their direction. The archeologists all fell to the floor and began to crawl like spiders toward them. The soldiers all raised their rifles. Realizing they had no cover, Tawnie threw out a smoke bomb and guided the living away from the zombified. Bullets started to fly across the room as the five of them ran to flank them from the side. The soldiers prepared their weapons as well and aimed to shoot at their attackers. Unfortunately, the crawling people got to them first. Their arms were twisted backward, and their hands still facing forward. They were quick. One hopped up like a cricket and attacked Gordon, clotheslining him from his feet. A group of them swarmed the man and began to attack him in more ways than one. They clawed, bit, and punched the man into submission. All he could do was curl up, hoping his gear would protect him. Parker stepped back and moved away from his group, sending rounds back into the cloud of smoke. He popped a few attackers but took a round in the shoulder. Victoria saw him go down and approached him while covering the others.

Wesley grabbed and punched at the spider-acting people as he assisted Gordon. The attackers attempted to take him down, but he was too big and too strong to be subdued. The general plowed through the competition while shooting at men in his own uniform. At first, he was hesitant to take a shot. But through the fading smoke, he could see one of the men pointing his rifle straight at him. Quicker with his draw, Wesley shot him first. The living regrouped as Tawnie made her way to the exit.

"Come on!" She screamed. Wesley got Gordon up, and he limped toward the door. Parker did the same with the support of Victoria. They moved around the staggered unit and made their way out of the temple. Once they got outside, they saw many bodies lying on the floor. Both soldiers and civilians alike, bleeding and full of holes. One man even had his chest cavity completely ripped open. They all looked back and heard the people approaching from the darkness behind them. So, in unison, they proceeded to the incline ahead. In the distance, Wesley noticed the signal flare in the cave that Scott had thrown earlier. They saw that the ground around it had been disturbed. It was flattened, and the diamond-like structures disappeared.

"What the hell?" He asked himself as they ran up the incline.

Suddenly, in front of them, more soldiers appeared.

"Dammit!" Tawnie roared as she pulled a pistol from her hip. Gordon looked back at the temple entrance, and the remainder of the dead were approaching.

"I'm not giving up now," he said, pointing his rifle down the incline. Everyone else pointed forward.

"Hooah."The other three soldiers chanted their Army battle cry.

Chapter XXXIII

The motel room was dead silent. Lester France squinted his eyes as he attempted to digest the story he just heard. Milo sat at the table eating his burger, and the group heard questionable noises from the unit next door. Gordon and Victoria seemed distant, almost seeming consumed by their past.

"That's how it went down?" Lester asked his wife. The woman couldn't bear to look at him, so she stared at the floor in front of her. Her husband struggled to get her attention.

"Lester," Gordon called out. But he held a finger up to him as he still stared a hole into his wife's face.

"Thirty-seven." She said. Tears ran down her face as she attempted to suck it up.

"What?" He asked.

"Thirty-seven people died in that tomb." She continued. "And for what?"

Gordon shook his head, forcing his way back into the conversation.

"Tawnie, I really don't see how digging into that mission is relevant here," Gordon said.

Tawnie shrugged. "Me neither, but now I think it would be a good time to tell you what we stole from down there."

"Wait," Victoria interrupted. You said back then that we walked into a trap. What was that all about?"

Tawnie sat in silence. She crossed her arms and placed a fist to her chin as she contemplated an answer.

"Right." Tawnie stood. "We all knew what happens to people in the presence of that chamber and any others like it. Human DNA occasionally has a genetic marker that allows metaphysical modification. This modification allows one to become… special.”

“Special?” Lester asked.

“Yes,” Tawnie replied as she walked to the window and peeked out the curtain. “Everyone in your unit was supposed to be tested for the Omega Chromosome before that mission. I told them what would happen if they didn’t.”

The room got quiet for a moment.

“Can’t believe you thought some jewels were more important than this.” Gordon patronized.

“I…” Tawnie stammered.

Victoria cut her off, “So, walk us through the ideal mission in Riyadh that night. Humor us.”

Tawnie growled, frustrated That the veterans wouldn’t allow her to finish. “We were supposed to go down there. Everyone was supposed to get only a headache. Maybe scrape themselves up, get the artifacts, and then leave.”

“Like us,” Victoria said as she crossed her arms. “Interesting.”

“I guess that would have made the entire situation more tolerable,” Gordon added. “But, Tawnie, what does any of that have to do with what happened in Idaho Falls?”

“Yeah, I was getting there before being interrupted,” Tawnie said as she checked on her kid.

“It’s all theory right now, but you know the idiom about the right equipment falling into the wrong hands?” She asked. “I believe we may be dealing with this now.”

“Who, exactly?” Lester asked.

“That is who we are tasked to figure out,” Tawnie answered.

“What exactly do they have?” Said Gordon.

Tawnie paused, staring distantly at the door.

“The artifacts we took from the Al-Faw Temple were the Pyro Stone and the Tetra Sphere.” She finally answered. “The energy that caused the explosion in Idaho Falls was the same that drew us to that Temple.”

Gordon shook his head. “The investigation then,” he said. “I’m assuming it was never closed.”

He gave Victoria a look of realization that assumed the world was about to end.

Victoria looked at Tawnie. “This is your fault.” She murmured.

Tawnie sighed deeply. “Sergeant, just like you, I was following orders. She said. "However, I will take responsibility for my part in this. I should have never been in that desert."

"So, let me get this right," Lester interjected. "You just said that some glass balls out there can decimate an entire city?"

Tawnie's eyes grew wide. "No, Mr. France, I am saying that, if used to do so, there is a ball of energy out there that can be used to destroy the entire galaxy."

Gordon, Victoria, and Lester looked around at one another. The disbelief was evident on their faces.

"Okay," Victoria said, waving her hands and shaking her head as if she were wiping the slate clean. "There are far more questions than answers here," she said. "But my biggest question is, who the hell are you working for?"

Caught off guard, Tawnie sighed. "It doesn't matter now."

"Bullshit!" Victoria snapped. "Ever since you showed up, I've been on edge, looking over my shoulder and sick to my stomach! You owe us that answer!"

Tawnie gasped as she looked at Gordon. It was apparent that he felt the same. Tawnie sat at the table and leaned her elbows on the surface. Her eyes darted back and forth for a moment as she seemed to come up with an answer.

"I was an agent for hire," she said as she sat up straight. I was a subject matter expert on Arcanin Lore, so the government hired me to investigate the issue."

"The United States Government hired a kid to save the world?" Victoria asked.

Tawnie growled and took a deep breath. "I'm older than I look," she said. "But please, if you guys are going to keep asking questions, ask the right ones! I just told you that the world is about to burn!"

Victoria stared at her for a moment, then looked at Gordon. "Yeah, I think I'll excuse myself of this." She announced as she headed for the door. "I'm not enlisted anymore, and I've dealt with a lot of chaos that I'm not willing to allow back into my life."

Victoria opened the door. The cold swept into the room again as the woman looked back to call her husband. Tawnie jumped from the chair.

"Wait! You don't understand!" She said.

"No, you don't understand!" Victoria snapped. "I spent ten

long years in the service and have seen things no man should ever see! I put a fucking bullet in the forehead of my best friend in that temple. If there is anyone who understands, it's me! So now it's your time to understand that you should leave me out of it!"

Victoria turned to look outside. Just as she took a step forward, she felt something unusual. It was as if there was a force keeping her from walking and invisible ropes tied around her ankles, neck, and wrists.

"They are going to kill us," Tawnie said. "Something happened to all of us that night that has bled over into what's happening in Idaho today."

Victoria took a step back and closed the door before turning to stare at Tawnie.

"What the hell was that?" She asked. Tawnie approached her slowly.

"Something that connects us all in ways I can hardly explain." She answered. "But we are not the only ones attempting to understand it."

Tawnie looked back at Gordon and then down at her son. The boy had finished his food and looked around the room at the adults.

"Tawnie," Gordon called her. "I saw something about all of this on the desk at your house. With all your preparations and the escape plans, the stockpile of weapons, the bunker. Did you know this was coming?"

The woman's head fell. "I've had my suspicions but didn't know for sure until the other day."

"How could you possibly know the state would be invaded?" Victoria asked. "What clues pointed to mass genocide?"

Tawnie reached into her pocket and pulled out the computer. "I've been collecting data on the aftermath of our mission since before we went on it." She explained as she activated the device and began to scroll. "I've hacked government databases and followed data to keep up with the artifacts we stole from the ruins."

Gordon took a deep breath and sat on the edge of the bed. "Wow." He said. Lester raised an eyebrow and walked to the nightstand to grab the TV remote. He turned it on and immediately switched to the news.

"I've been getting hell for that mission ever since," Gordon said. "You mean to tell me that we're still on it?"

Tawnie nodded. "Yeah. I guess we are."

"Of all the wild things I've done, that mission is the one that pushed me to an early retirement," Victoria admitted.

Tawnie's face went sour. Her eyes and lips showed pain that could only symbolize remorse for the woman. "I'll fix this," she said. "I don't know how yet, but I'll fix this."

"I'd say that is a tall order there, little lady," Lester said, grabbing everyone's attention. He pointed at the television with the remote and raised the volume. They all looked to see a news broadcast. Tawnie's heart dropped when she saw it. The headline read, 'Biochemical Attack Sieges Idaho.'. The image on the screen was an aerial view of a decimated city. Buildings were destroyed, and streets burned. The drone flew through clouds of black smoke to closely examine the wreckage. A location banner at the top left of the screen read Idaho Falls, ID. Tawnie felt herself getting sick. Her hands raised to her mouth, and she watched with tears in her eyes. Victoria stepped to her son and did what she could to distract him from the screen.

"Government officials are calling the Gem State Siege a threat to global security. The alleged biochemical threat has caused a 100% fatality rate in Idaho Falls and is spreading throughout the state," The news reporter said. "A special operations unit has been deployed into the state to assist with a quarantine to prevent the deadly, airborne virus caused by the biochemical from spreading."

Tawnie stood, and her fists clenched at her side. She began to grind her jaw as she became fixated on the screen.

"Tawnie, stay calm," Gordon said.

"Sources at Homeland Security say the Codex biochemical was unveiled during a secret mission in Riyadh, Saudi Arabia, seven years ago during an unauthorized military operation."

"You may remember this notorious mission," the other anchor added. "This mission was led by the current United States President, Nathaniel Wesley, who landed our Commander in Chief and his surviving subordinates in hot water."

"This is getting worse by the second," Gordon said. Then, pictures of them all appeared on-screen.

"Along with the president, others to blame include First

Sergeant Daniel Gordon, Master Sergeant Victoria Bartell-France, Master Sergeant Victor Parker, and social media conspiracy theorist Tawnie Simms."

Everyone looked at the TV. Each of them was shocked in their own right.

"Holy shit!" Victoria screamed.

"Vickie!" her husband called. She looked at him with quarter-sized eyes and opened her mouth. The man pointed at Milo, and the boy looked up at her.

"President Wesley?" She said. "They're pinning this on him too?"

Gordon shook his head. "Seems that way." He said. "Poor guy can't even hide."

"He should be out of sight by now. I already warned him." Tawnie said as she started to grab all of their belongings. She grabbed the radio she stole from the Siege Soldier and turned it on. Tawnie looked down at it, waiting for it to boot up. The others watched her as the news broadcast in the background transitioned into a different report.

Suddenly, a raspy voice said on the radio, "We lost sight of them."

There was a brief pause, followed by static, before the next man responded.

"Alright, if the others are taken care of, expand the siege."

"Roger that." The first man said. Tawnie reached for the knob to turn it off.

"If you see any readings of the boy again, inform us immediately." The superior continued.

Gordon shook his head. "I don't think you ever answered this question, but why do they want Milo?" Tawnie sighed as she grabbed her son to ruffle his ears.

"One tragedy at a time, please." She deflected.

"How long do you think it'll take for them to finish expanding," Lester asked Tawnie.

The woman shook her head and looked away. "We're talking about hours," she answered. And that time decreases every minute they go unopposed."

Chapter XXXIV

The group all left the room and headed into the snow-covered parking lot.

"I'm parked over here," Lester announced as he led the group to the front of the parking lot. Gordon walked in front of Tawnie, holding Milo's hand. His mother fell back, using her secret computer device to make a call. She looked away from her path, frustrated due to the lack of answers. They approached a dark blue luxury SUV, similar to the unknown soldier's vehicle. The vehicle was already running, started by a remote in Lester's pocket. The Frances got into the car, and Gordon opened the back door for Milo. He began to climb into the back seat, but Gordon lifted him in to save time. He looked back to see Tawnie with the device to her ear.

The man called her name. But she looked at him in silence. He could see the desperation in her eyes as she hoped her call would connect. Her body scrunched with every ring until she finally exploded from frustration.

"God dammit!" She yelled as she walked to the rear passenger door. Gordon watched her jump inside and got in himself.

"I'm assuming you didn't get the answer you needed?" Victoria asked from up front. Tawnie shook her head, slamming her fist against her knee.

"I'm trying to get in touch with my husband." She admitted. "He was in Yellowstone doing a job, but I can't get a hold of him for some reason."

"Don't worry, we'll get you and Milo back to your husband soon," Lester said.

Tawnie shook her head. "I'm not concerned about my safety." She said. "I'm worried about him. I think he's in trouble."

"What does your husband do?" Victoria asked. "If you don't mind me asking."

Tawnie sighed and put her device on her knee. Gordon stared at the bird logo on the back of it with curious eyes.

"Uh… He's an engineer." She answered.

"Oh," Lester exclaimed as he spun in his seat. " I heard a lot is happening in Yellowstone right now."

"Why the hell would a group of engineers be in Yellowstone, of all places?"

"All I know is that he and his team are researching there," Tawnie replied. "But he's been almost impossible to get a hold of, even before all of this started."

"I'm more curious about that logo there," Gordon said as he pointed at the device on her knee. "I've seen you do some wild stuff with that thing."

Tawnie reached for the device and clasped her hand around it.

"You mind explaining what it is?"

Tawnie picked up the tablet and flipped it over, staring at the blank screen.

"I've had this since Riyadh." She answered. "I'm not even sure I'm supposed to have it. But the organization that hired me to assist with the mission gave it to me and never retrieved it when it was over."

Victoria's head flicked to one side. Her eyebrow raised out of curiosity. "I wonder why that is." She said.

"I guess it's because none of us were supposed to survive that mission," Tawnie answered.

Gordon and Victoria both looked at her.

"What's the name of this organization?" Victoria asked.

Tawnie shook her head and flipped it over to look at the emblem. Her fingertips passed over the image, feeling its pits, grooves, and scratches all over.

"This is going to sound wild," Tawnie explained. "But I have no idea who they are."

Gordon scrunched his nose, and his eyes lowered as he looked at her.

"I know, I know," the woman said before the officer lectured her. "I showed interest in figuring out what the Ancient Arcanins were trying to tell us. The next thing I knew, I was in a coffee shop, deciphering this text because I thought it was cool. Then I was offered a job by a woman who only introduced herself as Fixer. Apparently, the public was never supposed to get their hands on it."

"Why did this Fixer person know to find you?" Lester asked.

"I stole the files and, as of now, the only one able to decipher the language."

Victoria shook her head and rolled her eyes. "Nope, don't sound suspicious in the slightest."

Tawnie growled, her eyes sharpened as she stared at the back of her blond head.

"I was too focused on my personal agenda to ask the right questions," Tawnie continued. "Maybe if I had, I wouldn't have dragged you folks into this mess."

The car went silent momentarily.

"You know, this extermination doesn't sound like it had anything to do with that," Lester added.

Tawnie chuckled. "Fat chance," she said as she activated the device. "I've been trying to use this device to connect with Fixer or whoever is associated with this emblem. Because I know it does."

"Oooh!" Lester excitedly said. His fists clenched at his shoulders as he realized something extraordinary. "I saw this hacking technique online that kinda borders reverse engineering. But have you tried–"

"Using the system's NIC to reverse the location to find out which satellite the system belongs to?" Tawnie asked. "Yeah, I tried that. The MAC and IP addresses are locked behind some kind of firewall that is encrypted to the teeth."

Lester stared for a moment, his mouth opening in shock.

"No… I was going to say to look at the system settings." The man finished. His wife looked at him with a look of sheer disappointment.

"What?" He asked as he slowly turned in his seat.

"Okay, now that we know the origin of Warcore Barbie, are we using that to proceed?" Victoria asked.

"Vicki, you don't need to be rude," Gordon said. Victoria

turned around and looked at Tawnie. Their eyes met and locked onto one another without blinking.

"I just want to make it clear that I don't trust you," Victoria told her.

"I understand," Tawnie said as she slid forward in her seat. "Whether you trust me or not, chaos always catches up to us. You're going to need me!"

"To get rid of some crooked Army soldiers?" She smirked as she turned forward.

"Actually, these guys are not Army," Gordon said. Victoria's eyes squinted as she spun around once more. "You're kidding," she said. "Not government?"

Gordon shrugged and looked at Tawnie, but she sat back in her seat and looked out the window. Milo looked up at his mother and innocently mashed the palm of his hand against her elbow. Tawnie's arm contorted across her body momentarily. She began to laugh, roughhouse, and completely forget about the matter at hand as she handled her son.

The others welcomed their playful sides to unfold. Their giggles offering a welcomed calm during the hostile time. Milo began to test his strength with her. His hands clasped against hers, palm to palm. His little arms trembled as he pushed against her.

"I'm gonna win, mommy!" The kid roared. Tawnie released her grip and allowed him to push through and get close. The space between them closed, and Tawnie let go of his hands to wrap her arms around him. Her eyes closed as she hugged him deeply.

"You've already won, Spud," she whispered to him just before pulling away to kiss his nose.

The young mother sat her son down again and noticed she was being watched. She looked at Gordon, who seemed curious.

"To attest to the previous statement, those guys aren't United States military. They're hired guns." Tawnie answered.

Gordon's eyes opened wide. "There were hundreds of them, though. They have to be military."

"I'm not saying they're not military," she said as she began rocking her son from side to side. "I'm just saying they're not United States Military, any branch."

"What? Nobody has pockets that deep to hire that many guns." Gordon added.

"Maybe not ours. Don't underestimate the competition." Tawnie said. She called Lester, and he turned halfway around in his seat, giving her his attention.

"I need you to swap plates with one of these cars here."

"What the fuck?" They all gazed at her.

"Only because I know you want to retreat to your house, and that's not a good idea." She explained. Lester and Victoria looked at one another, confused.

"Also," She continued. "By now, they may actually have scouters in the city looking out for your license plates."

At that moment, Lester and Victoria's phones both started to chime.

"What the hell?" Lester asked as he pulled out his phone. "Who's at our door?"

He logged into the app that monitors the video doorbell at their home. Immediately, Lester saw two men standing on his front porch wearing respirator masks.

"I'm assuming these were the guys you were talking about?" Lester showed the phone to Gordon and Tawnie.

She nodded. "Two of many. Also, they're in Rexburg wearing masks now."

"What does that mean?" Lester asked.

"It means that it's only a matter of time before Rexburg looks like Idaho Falls," Gordon answered. The couple continued to gaze at the men on their doorstep through the phone app.

"Lester, still need that license plate swap." Tawnie requested.

"Roger that." He responded as he hopped out of the car.

"What do I do?" Victoria asked as she looked back at Tawnie.

Tawnie sighed. "I don't know exactly, but we'll need to incorporate a miracle somewhere in there."

232

Chapter XXXV

Meanwhile, in Los Angeles, California, a young man, presumably in his mid-twenties, wearing a really expensive suit, sat in his penthouse-styled office with windows lining three of the four walls. The room was large, and from his desk, he couldn't even see the motivational mantra he had hung on the back of the door. 12 feet into the room's entrance was dedicated to floor-to-ceiling, solid wood bookshelves. The man sat in a throne-like leather chair at a glass table in the center. There was hardly any furniture besides the two basic chairs on the other side of the table. A sofa against the window to his left and the wooden desk holding tower-styled shelves behind him. Each contained bottles of alcohol, appearing to be from different countries and eras.

In front of him lay a cluster of papers, all with information pertaining to his business. He thumbed through a stack but continued eyeing the papers on the desk as if they were more important. There was a knock on the door. He put the papers down and shuffled everything into one neat stack.

He reached underneath the glass table. Just beside the leg sat a small control panel with a few buttons, switches, and knobs. He tapped one, and there was a faint click at the door. It opened, and the man stood from his seat. A slender man with the most eccentric pinup hairstyle walked in. It was dyed in multiple colors: greens, reds, and whites. A residual decoration from the previous Christmas season.

"Ah, Fabio." The man behind the desk called with a surprisingly deep and raspy voice. "Nice of you to join us today."

"Mmmhmmm." Fabio hummed as he strutted to the table. His flamboyant features making him chuckle.

"You have an appointment with Michaela Perazi of the DC Post at 9," he announced. What do you want to do?"

The man stood upright and tilted his head. His arms were folded across his chest as he stared distantly.

"Should I cancel, Sir?" Fabio asked. "I think the world would understand if you decided to stay quiet. You know, considering what you've been through."

He shook his head and leaned over the desk.

"That won't be necessary, Fabio." He answered. "When she arrives, let her up."

Fabio waited silently, looking into his boss's eyes.

"I'm serious." He continued.

"I know," Fabio said as he stepped around the table. "But I also see the struggle behind your smile."

Fabio placed his hand on the man's bicep. "You're still only human."

"That's exactly the problem," the suited man said. Up close, he noticed just how sparkly Fabio's attire was. His shirt had some kind of sequins on it. He wore bell-bottom pants that flared so much at the cuff that they looked like lace. His face was smooth, with not a razor bump or pore in sight. He almost looked like a porcelain doll.

"You are pushing your luck here." He said.

"Hmph!" Fabio mumbled as he strutted away from him. "I have to keep you on your toes!"

He pulled out his phone and looked at it while his boss retook his seat.

"Looks like she's here," Fabio announced. He nodded as if to ask if he was sure.

"Yeah, let's get this over with, shall we?"

Fabio headed to the exit, opened the door, and stepped out into the chaotic halls of the building.

Moments later, a woman entered the room. She was short but had heels on that looked cheap. She wore a black skirt suit and had her voluminous, brown hair draped over her shoulders and one side of her face. The man momentarily leaned back in his chair, watching her strut across his office. As she reached the chairs in front of him, he stood.

"Good morning." He nodded.

"Yes, good morning, Sir." She addressed him. "Thank you for allowing me to do this interview today. We know you're a busy man."

"Yeah, don't mention it." The man replied. "I do believe we both stand to gain something here. Am I right?"

The woman stared as he extended his arm to shake her hand over the table. She reached for him, and he took her hand in his. Their eyes met. . Her cheeks reddened, and her body trembled as she pulled her arm back.

"Alright, I'll just need a moment to open my recorder, and we can get started."

The man nodded and put his hands behind him as he watched her fumble with her leather handbag. She pulled out a small, silver voice recorder and placed it on the table.

"Is here okay?" She asked him.

The man nodded, never taking his eyes off of her.

"Can I offer you anything, Ms…"

"I'm okay." She answered abruptly. "I just want to finish this so I can step out of your way."

"There's no trouble, I assure you." He said. The man turned to face the desk behind him and grabbed a handle underneath the surface. He yanked on it, pulling open a drawer that emitted a white frost. He bent down and pulled up an unopened water bottle. He twisted the cap off as he gestured for her to follow him to the oversized couch. Behind it was a phenomenal view of the city that caught her eye. She ensured that she grabbed her belongings and followed him to the sofa. He sat to the left of the large seat, and the woman sat to the opposite side, leaving a seat between them. He took another sip of his water, and the room was uncomfortably quiet. She held the recorder out in her palm. A tiny red light flashed, letting them know it was in progress.

"This is Michaela Perazi. I am here with billionaire, tech wiz, and CEO of Primotech Industries, Jacob Maxwell." She introduced. The two of them exchanged pleasantries before getting into a serious conversation. Jacob sensed how nervous she was. He could see the slight tremble in her hands. Despite the earlier show of adoration, she was now uninterested in being in his presence.

"Alright, Mr. Maxwell." She said, signaling they would be

transitioning to a more serious conversation. "I can surely say that the world appreciates your dedication to innovation. Primotech has decimated any competition in its space with your most recent invention. Now that you've made such strides, what's next for the tech giant?"

Maxwell took a second to think. His eyes were still locked on hers as he crossed his arms and leaned back in the corner of his seat.

"Thank you for that," he said. "But my mission has always been to make my own way while highlighting my father's legacy."

The man momentarily threw his index finger up as he leaned forward and rested his elbows on his knees. "I believe that Primotech is the company that would take the world by storm. My next move, Michaela, is the one where I triple the momentum while doing good on my father's name."

"Absolutely," Michaela responded. "I'm sure the company has great things in the works."

She began to write something on a small notepad. Maxwell raised an eyebrow in suspicion.

"Michaela," The man called. Immediately, she looked away from the book and back at him.

"Primotech and everything it has been involved with has already been mentioned. We both know that you're not here to discuss that."

The woman's eyes lowered again, and she closed the notepad. She nervously looked at him, her throat bobbed.

"Mr. Maxwell, I apologize for the misunderstanding." She said. Her eyes locked onto the recorder on the couch to avoid eye contact. "The Post genuinely wanted to know how a philanthropist gains insight on something so grand."

He watched as her eyes widened. It was as if a smoldered flame inside her had been reignited.

"Mr. Maxwell, how do you keep making these spectacular feats?"

His mouth opened, and his head tilted back, staring at the woman down his nose.

"Ahhh, what department did you say you write for again?" He asked.

"Tech and Science column, Sir!"

He clapped from excitement and stood up. "A fellow techie, huh?"

The woman nodded with a huge smile.

"Ah, Michaela, Michaela, I knew I liked you!" the man announced as he rubbed his hands together. "It's about time someone appreciated what's going on here!"

"I would just say there are plenty of us, don't worry." She laughed.

Jacob and Michaela briefly discussed his most recent achievement and how the creation of the kaitron detector would revolutionize science. As they finished their conversation, he persuaded the young woman to have a glass of whiskey.

"Mr. Maxwell, thank you again for sharing the secrets of your success with us," Michaela said.

"Of course, Michaela!" he replied, "I'm honored to have the opportunity to share."

"One more thing." She said as Maxwell stood from the sofa again.

"People are curious about your thoughts on Idaho Falls. Do you have a theory about what could be going on there?" she asked him. Maxwell's hands went to his hips, and he stared at the floor momentarily.

"I don't have a theory, Michaela," he admitted. "I even attempted to make logical sense of the matter. But this epidemic is nothing like the world has ever seen!"

"Yes, Sir. The CDC has labeled the virus that plagues the state of Idaho the Codex Virus. Based on your views of COVID-19 years ago, how do you feel about this situation?"

Maxwell looked down at her, feeling like he had been set up. His high from boasting about his accomplishments had faded, and his good mood was gone.

"Uh yeah." He said as he sat back down on the sofa. He was slumped forward, resting his elbows on his legs. The glass of ice in his hand was leaning from the fingers he used to hold it.

"I never truly believed the COVID virus was as big of a global threat as it was when it happened. And years after it had been resolved, we found evidence of..." He stopped his sentence short and turned to the woman with narrowed eyes. "You know, Michaela, I've seen the video of the man in Massachusetts, and I was in awe of the chaos. This Codex Virus is attacking the building blocks of human existence. In my opinion, that's terrifying."

Michaela cleared her throat and leaned toward him. "This, coming from a man labeled as the most fearless entrepreneur of all time."

He nodded, staring down at the floor. "Yeah," he said. The latest update is that the virus can be transmitted through the air, blood, sweat, and saliva. Side effects may include loss of humanity or transformation into a disease-spreading organism, as observed in Massachusetts.

"Yeah, pretty much!" Michaela nodded.

"My company has donated millions in disaster relief to assist with this epidemic. I'm hoping we can find a solution to stop the spread."

Again, Michaela nodded. "And Mr. Maxwell, would you care to respond to a statement made by Tawnie Simms in her recent video?"

Maxwell quickly cut his eyes at the woman. His fists clenched, and his jaw tightened, becoming visible just behind his broad chin. He looked away as he took a deep breath. Then, a large smile showed on his face. It was as if he flipped a switch, causing Michaela to question his sanity silently.

The man chuckled as he looked down at the reporter. "Tawnie, who?" he asked, pretending to be too large to know who she was. Michaela took a mental note of the jab but waited for him to continue.

"Enlighten me, Michaela." He said as he stepped back to his desk and placed the drinking glass against the glass table. The audible crash seemed loud enough to justify the entire table breaking. Michaela flinched. But as she opened her eyes, she saw the man staring at her with his hands pocketed and chin upward.

"Oh!" The woman chirped before grabbing her notepad again and flipping through it.

"And I quote," Michaela started. 'The government has shadow operations with big corporations like Atlas and Primotech, who secretly fund projects that will inevitably be our undoing as mankind. People think Jacob Maxwell is this pretty boy philanthropist. But there is a saying about the nicely dressed wolf in the sheep's den."

Maxwell lowered his head and began to pace in front of his desk. He watched his feet as he clicked his shoes on the marble-tiled floors. Michaela watched, wondering if she should have skipped this part of the interview. She grabbed all of her things and stood in front of the sofa. At that point, the man approached her. She watched him cautiously as the distance between them closed.

"You know, I've been up here on this mountaintop for a while," he responded. "With many, slander is the only way to make it in the same conversation with someone like me. So, Ms. Perazi, if you don't mind, I will not dignify that with a response."

Michaela nodded, turned off the recorder, and slipped it into her jacket pocket.

"Well, Mr. Maxwell, thank you again." She finished as she headed toward the door.

Maxwell watched the woman walk away, noticing her curves just before she left the room. He lifted his arm and rubbed the hair on the back of his neck as he walked after her.

"Hey, Michaela!" He yelled. She turned around with wide eyes as if she had done something wrong.

"Yes, Mr. Maxwell?" She asked.

He approached her and stood close. His calming demeanor pulled the nerves out of her as she looked into his hazel-colored eyes. She found herself on the verge of whimpering as her body became tense.

"You can call me Jacob," he said to her, reaching into his pants pocket. He pulled out a black leather wallet and opened it. Michaela instinctively looked down at his hands, only to see the thick wad of cash he had. He reached in and grabbed something with his index finger and thumb. He pulled out a glossy black card.

"Here." He said, handing her the cards.

She glanced at it, realizing it was a business card, and grinned.

"I encourage you to use that if you need anything from me," he casually reminded her. He watched for a moment as her eyes lowered to inspect it. But he walked away before she flipped it over. Upon flipping the card, Michaela noticed a magnet strip. He had also given her a card with a mag-strip on it.

"Uh, Jacob?" She called. The gentleman turned and looked at her halfway over his shoulder.

"I think you accidentally gave me–"

"The key to my penthouse." He cut her off.

The two continued to talk for a while, but this time, off the record. She left his office smiling and passed Fabio, who was standing outside the door. The man stared at the woman, attempting not to say anything with his facial expression. When she left, Fabio went into the office to speak with his boss again.

"The reporter was your type," he said as he approached the desk Maxwell was now sitting at. "I should have known you would indulge a little."

"I don't want to have this conversation right now," Maxwell responded.

"I just didn't trust her, that's all." Fabio finished. "Something about her didn't sit well with me."

Maxwell grinned as he shook his head. "You're the jealous admirer. There's nobody that sits well with you."

Fabio made a noise that sounded like a breathy cry for help as he placed the back of one hand on his forehead.

"One day, I'll get you to try a little dark meat."

Maxwell's eyes grew large. "Fabio!" He yelled as his face turned red.

"Yaaas! Say my name, King!" Fabio continued. He danced and snapped his fingers over his head, momentarily toying with the man.

Maxwell buried his head in his hands. "Why are you here? Don't you have work to do?"

His assistant stopped playing and approached the table.

"Dr. Simms left me a message to give you," Fabio announced. The smile was swept off of Maxwell's face as well.

Chapter XXXVI

Victoria gripped her hands around the steering wheel as she looked forward. Anger filled her eyes despite her husband's attempts to calm her from the passenger seat. Gordon and Tawnie observed from the back seat while Milo entertained himself.

'What are they doing now?" Tawnie asked.

"Nothing," Lester answered as he looked down at his phone. He flipped through various cameras in their home, seeing nothing but carnage. They put holes in the walls and destroyed furniture. Tables were flipped, dishes were shattered, and windows were broken. Snow infiltrated the couple's home and accumulated underneath the windows.

"Why the hell are they here, of all places?" Victoria asked as she hit the steering wheel.

"I told you, we weren't supposed to survive that mission," Tawnie said. "If something is happening here that needs cleaning up, they wouldn't want liabilities out in the world blowing the cover on their plans."

"Are you really doing your Oracle thing right now?" Gordon asked, a tone suggesting that he was annoyed. "Maybe we get more information before blindly heading down a rabbit hole?"

Tawnie sighed. Her jaw clenched tightly as she stared at the man.

"Do you know why I became the Oracle?" She asked. The man swallowed his pride and waited for her to continue.

"We all know that there are secret forces at work out there and powerful organizations keeping the public from knowing the truth." She explained as she leaned forward in her seat. "I am just the person who asks the questions that many are afraid to. Check my track record if you need to. I'm hardly wrong."

"She's right about that, y'know," Lester interjected. "She once predicted the very moment a riot would break out after a police brutality situation."

Victoria scoffed. "Not hard to do that if a cop kills someone unlawfully."

Lester nodded. "Even if the killing hasn't happened yet, and someone predicts the exact date of the fallout and that a white officer would murder a woman of color?"

The woman's eyes narrowed as she looked at her husband.

"You say what now?" She asked. But Lester threw his nod to the back seat. Victoria turned to look at Tawnie, one eyebrow raised as she made eye contact.

"How would someone even be able to do that?" Gordon asked her.

"Guys, what's happening in front of us is far more important than any of that," Tawnie said as she stared at the group of men raiding the house.

"What do you think they're looking for?" Lester asked.

Tawnie chuckled. "They're looking for you two."

The four of them went silent, and Tawnie used the opportunity to turn on the communicator she stole. The beep it made as it turned on caused Victoria to jump in her seat. She looked into the back seat again as she held her chest.

"You always spazz like that, Bartell?" Tawnie asked as she turned the dial at the top of the device.

"What the hell?" She asked Tawnie.

"Now is a better time than any to listen in for their next move." She closed her eyes for a moment as if she were thinking. Victoria looked at her husband, confusion written all over her face. He shrugged his shoulders. Lester looked forward, seeing one of the soldiers standing in front of the house, talking into a communicator.

"Top, what's she doing?" Victoria asked. The man smirked as he closed his eyes.

"Wait for it," he said. Lester tapped his wife on the thigh. She looked to see him pointing at their yard.

She squinted, and her mouth clicked. "There's no way."

Everyone was calm as they waited for something to happen. Victoria sighed silently. Suddenly, Tawnie took an audible, deep breath as her eyes popped open. She grabbed the tuning knob of the radio and found the exact channel the soldier was speaking on.

"Hey, G," Victoria called. "How many channels on that thing?"

"Uh, 42, I believe." He answered.

Victoria sighed as she shook her head.

Tawnie turned up the volume and immediately tuned into the conversation.

"Yeah, they're not here." A grungy voice emitted from the radio. "So far, no intel on Operation Codex was found in their home."

Suddenly, there was a knock on the driver's side window. Victoria yelped and placed her hand on her chest. They all looked, only to find an older gentleman, maybe in his fifties, standing outside the window. His shoulders were hunched forward underneath his puffy coat. His arms were wrapped around him as he struggled to stay warm. He stared down at Victoria before bending at the waist to look inside. Tawnie growled in annoyance. She bounced from her seat and crawled over Milo and Gordon. The officer looked down at her as she rested her hand on his thigh for leverage.

"Hey, you!" She yelled, "Get out of here. Are you trying to die?"

The man looked at Tawnie through the back window, hardly hearing her screaming. He could see Victoria through the front, but she was frozen with uncertainty. She looked at the soldier, but still, he hadn't noticed.

"Mr. Gentry, get back inside, man!" Lester yelled.

"Hey, are you guys alright?" Gentry asked, yelling at the vehicle. "I saw those men at your house, and they looked like they were up to no good! Why are you all the way down here?"

Victoria aggressively tried to shoo him off. Meanwhile, Tawnie still leaned across Gordon's lap, yelling for the man to do the same. But he was screaming too and couldn't hear her.

Suddenly, the soldier's head snapped in their direction.

"Oh shit!" Lester said, seeing the man turn his body to face them. Undoubtedly, he saw the nosey neighbor standing outside their vehicle. Tawnie looked at the soldier, noticing his trajectory as well.

"Run!" she screamed at him, but the man persisted in finding out what was happening. He stepped away from the vehicle and began walking toward their house. The soldier held his weapon low and ready as he closed the gap between them.

"Hey, what are you guys doing at my friend's house?" He asked.

"Everyone quiet!" Tawnie roared as she sat upright and braced herself to the door and the seat in front of her. The soldier raised his weapon at their neighbor.

"There's no way," Lester grumbled and shook his head, doubting the soldier's intentions. "He won't."

Lester reached for the door handle to his right and the pistol on his left hip.

"Lester, don't!" Tawnie persisted as she gripped both seats with her soul in her fingertips. Lester looked at his wife, concerned for their friend's safety. But Victoria shook her head and reached for the start button.

"Please, stop moving!" Tawnie said again.

As the civilian approached him, the soldier pointed his rifle and shot the man directly in his face. His remains splattered on the windshield of Lester's SUV as his body fell toward the house.

"Holy shit!" Lester yelled.

"Quiet!" Tawnie barked as she closed her eyes and took a deep breath.

The soldier brushed past the falling body and immediately approached the vehicle. No matter how he turned, his rifle muzzle still pointed at the cabin. The first thing he noticed was the license plate, but he didn't stop investigating. Milo grabbed the radio from his mom's lap and turned the volume down.

"Shhh," Tawnie said again as she sat with her eyes closed. The man walked along the vehicle and looked inside. He cuffed a hand around his eyes to look into the driver's window. Victoria hyperventilated after seeing the inside of her neighbor on her windshield. But right beside her was the dark figure of the soldier, looming in her peripheral. The soldier walked around the vehicle again, inspecting it before walking back to the house. He stepped over Gentry's body as he reached for his radio.

"This is Stormfire requesting authorization to siege Sector

042," he said into the radio as he walked back to France's house.

"Authorization granted, Agent Stormfire." A woman responded on the radio. "Have you encountered the subjects?" The woman asked.

"Closing in," He answered as he ran into the house. "We suspect that we have her on the ropes. Updates soon to come."

"Hooah." She replied to end the conversation. Tawnie slumped in her seat, and her eyes closed.

"Victoria," She muttered. The woman looked back at her from the driver's seat, seeing how lethargic she had become.

"What the hell happened?" She asked.

"Yeah, Tawnie, are you okay?" Gordon asked.

But she threw her hand away to interrupt.

"Get us out of here." She muttered just before collapsing toward her son and Gordon.

"Mommy!" Milo screamed.

"Get us out of here!" Gordon yelled at Victoria as he took hold of Tawnie.

Victoria started the vehicle and exploded into an immediate U-turn. She drove away from her home, looking at it through the vehicle mirrors. She sighed as she sped through the suburban area to get away. Suddenly, Tawnie's weird tablet began to ring. The sound was akin to a siren and was low in tone.

"Milo, hand me that," Gordon commanded the boy. As he was told, he reached for the tablet and handed it to the officer.

"Is she getting a call?" Lester asked.

"Yeah, I think so," Gordon answered as he flipped the device over. "Holy shit!" He said as he recognized the name on the screen.

"Who is it?" Victoria asked. But Gordon was so stunned that he paused.

"Gordon!" She screamed again. He shook his head to snap out of his trance.

"Uh… It says President Wesley." He answered. Victoria's eyes peeled open wide in disbelief.

"What do I do?" Gordon asked. There was a silence in the vehicle as the two of them began to think.

"Just answer it," Lester interjected.

Without even giving it another thought, he answered it. The

screen changed, and a call timer began.

"Hello?" Gordon said.

There was a silence for a brief moment.

"Hello?" The president said. "This is an encrypted line. Who is this?" He asked.

"Officer Daniel Gordon," he announced. The man on the other end of the call was shocked into silence as he stood from his seat.

"Daniel Gordon." President Wesley said. "Well, I'll be damned."

"General," Gordon called. "It's good to hear from you again."

On the other hand, the president stood in his chambers in the White House, staring out onto the front lawn.

"I see you have reconnected with our mutual friend," he said. "With that said, this must be worse than I thought."

"It most certainly is, Mr. President," Victoria answered.

"We hope you can help shine a light on our current situation, sir," Gordon said.

Wesley sighed deeply as his jaw clenched. "Ironically, that's why I dialed this number." He responded. "I don't think anyone could shine a brighter light on this situation than Tawnie herself."

Chapter XXXVII

Riyadh, Saudi Arabia. The mission was over. Of everyone that walked into that underground temple, only five exited. The surviving soldiers escorted Tawnie out of the cavern and back to the parked vehicles. Each of them is covered with blood, cuts, and bruises. Upon arrival at their campsite, Wesley stumbled into a Humvee. He opened the rear passenger door to take a seat. He exhaled what seemed to be a sigh of relief, but it was choppy and slow. His soldiers gathered around him, staring and waiting for him to give an order. Tawnie walked past them, looking down at her phone and tending to her affairs.

"What the fuck did I just witness, General?" Victoria asked.

The man shook his head with wide eyes and stared into the distance. Gordon leaned against the vehicle and hunched over, placing his palms on his knees. He tried deep breathing as he could feel his blood pressure elevated to the point that he could hear his pulse. He reached to his head with one hand and wiped his sharp, dark eyebrow. He could feel the moisture in his hair that he had hoped would be sweat. His hand fell only to find crimson liquids all over it. He felt sick as he looked at his battle buddies, who were just as drenched. Even Victoria's golden-white hair looked as if she dyed it red and purple.

"How?" Victoria asked. "What the fuck was that?" She waited for someone to answer, but the men were all shocked. The impatient woman gnashed her teeth and walked away from the group. Wesley caught a glimpse of her marching toward Tawnie in an enraged state.

"Hey, kid!" She yelled. Tawnie turned around and received a

tightly clenched fist to the jaw.

"Ghah!" She screamed as she fell to the ground, dropping her device as well.

"Victoria!" Gordon yelled as he ran after her.

"Get off of her!"

Parker ran to the scuffle when he saw his battle buddy mount the civilian.

"Vickie, get off of her!" He yelled. But it was too late. Gordon pulled one of her arms and jacked it behind her back. His other arm wrapped around her neck. She screamed in pain as he clutched her tightly. Parker kneeled to tend to the civilian woman. She whimpered as she curled her body on the desert sand, covering her face.

"Tawnie, I got you." The man said as he helped her up.

"Aah, get off of me!" Victoria roared as she tried breaking away from Gordon's grip. Parker realized the pummeling left a laceration under her ear, a broken nose, and bruised eyes.

"Victoria, what the fuck?" Gordon screamed.

"All of our friends are dead, and it's because of her!"

"I didn't do it!" Tawnie cried out, her face now unrecognizable. "This wasn't supposed to happen like this!"

The young girl sobbed as she fell to her knees, and despite her blind rage, Victoria shed tears of grief as well. Gordon let go of her, and she immediately placed her clenched fists on her lips.

"We're responsible for all those people!" Victoria cried. "And we broke protocol so that we can fail the mission in return!"

"We didn't fail!" Wesley finally stepped in. Gordon stood aside, allowing the man to approach Victoria. "Our mission was to retrieve two artifacts, and we did that." He announced as he picked up Tawnie's bag from the cold sand. "We lost good men and women today but did not fail our mission."

He pulled out the glass cylinders, revealing the orbs inside. This time, they looked like ordinary Crystal balls.

"General," Gordon called as he unbuckled the clasp on his helmet. "Bartell is right. Someone will have to answer for everything that went wrong on this mission."

Wesley slid the tubes back into the backpack and looked at Gordon. Gordon felt he knew what Wesley was thinking as they made eye contact.

"I've known you for too long, General." He said to the man. "I can't allow you to take all the blame for this."

Parker stepped into the conversation and pointed his finger at Wesley. The man pointed at himself and jokingly looked over his shoulder.

"General, we won't be able to take full blame for anything if we blame the dead." The giant man's eyebrows furrowed as he stared at his subordinate. The sergeant folded his arms as he waited for a response. Even he could tell that he somehow pissed the man off.

"Parker, what you are suggesting is unethical. Does that sound like something a Knight Rider would do?"

"Fuck the Knight Riders!" He exploded. Gordon and Bartell both looked at him in horror. "General, with all the bodies we left down there, it's safe to say that the Knight Riders are finished. We won't get out of this with more than a nickel once I.A. sinks their teeth into us!"

General Wesley nodded. "You're right, Parker." He said. "That's why fixing this mess is up to me."

Gordon's eyes narrowed, and he shook his head in resentment. "I can't let you do that, General."

Wesley clenched his jaw so tight that it caused his cheeks to rise. "Excuse me?" He asked.

"I'm just saying, it's not all on you." Gordon attempted to explain.

"Who's it on, Gordon?" He exploded as he approached him. The First Sergeant immediately snapped into the position of attention. His head held high and his eyes forward. Wesley stood almost toe to toe with him, almost in shock. The anger on his face dulled, and he looked at the other two soldiers. Victoria, who was still sobbing, made eye contact with him and began to stand. The tears from her eyes create perfect paths down her blood-stained cheeks. Sergeant Parker also stood at attention as well, Wesley was humbled.

"After all that, you are still professional and poised." He smirked. "I'm actually impressed."

By this time, Tawnie slowly peeled herself up from the ground. Sand stuck to her face, arms, and clothing in the areas of damp blood all over her body. Still, she softly whimpered in pain as she tried crawling away.

"Tawnie!" Wesley yelled as he dismissed his soldiers. The man went to help her up. He reached for her dirty hand and pulled. She stumbled upon getting to her feet and stared at Victoria with pure anger in her eyes. Victoria approached her, prepared to help. But in an instant, Tawnie unexpectedly jabbed the woman in the jaw. Victoria's helmet flew from her head as she fell to the ground. Her feet were seemingly still planted where she stood.

"Ooh!" Sergeant Parker yelled as he tried to assist his battle buddy.

"It wasn't my fucking mission!" She yelled again as she shrugged Wesley away. The young woman left the four of them and proceeded toward the vast desert. The men looked at one another, unsure of what they just saw. They looked down at Victoria and realized that she was out of it. Her eyes were spacey and non-focusing, and blood dribbled from her sputtering lips. It was as if she had a concussion.

"Tawnie, you can't walk the desert alone." Wesley reminded her. This caused her to turn around to look at him over her shoulder. She held onto her backpack straps and placed one foot forward. Her black, curly hair blew out of her face and to the back of her.

"Look, you guys have served your purpose." She said. "I actually have to go deliver what we found. I want to get back to my life and put this all behind me."

"Where are you going, exactly?" Gordon asked.

Tawnie sighed and looked away as if she was attempting to make up an answer. "I'm getting away from you idiots so I can think." She answered. Tawnie began to walk away. Her body faded into darkness as she moved away from the lights set up at the camp.

"Tawnie!" Wesley called out. "Why did you even agree to do this mission if you didn't want to do it?"

She stopped walking suddenly. An eerie silence passed over them as they waited for her to respond. Wesley held his hand out to his men, signaling them to stay behind him.

"Why are you even on this mission?" He asked again.

Tawnie turned around to look at him. Her chin and eyes raised, climbing the general with an entire foot and a half height over her.

"This was dangerous." He said. "This mission was not a guaranteed success and you knew that coming in. You are not Army, yet some organization has used your intellect to end up here. Why?"

Tawnie frowned as she stared at him. She rolled her eyes in discomfort and pursed her lips, ultimately refusing to answer.

"Tawnie?" He called again, this time a little louder.

"I have…" She started to say. Her eyes shifted away from him, and her chin fell, allowing her to stare at the ground as she caressed herself. "My mother is sick… and I was promised the money to help make her better if I did this." She answered. Wesley cringed at her confession, kneeling to close the gap between their height.

"When it was discovered that I could read this ancient language, they stalked me and made it impossible to say no."

She pulled out the tablet and showed him its back. The bird emblem gleamed against the light from the camp.

"I don't know their name. The logo is all I have."

Wesley sighed as he took the device from her. "I've never seen it." He said as he turned to look at his men. "Fellas? Does this emblem look familiar to you at all?"

Both men approached him to examine the case. They shook their heads and stepped away.

"At this point, I wish I had more intel on that," Wesley said as he turned back to face Tawnie.

The girl shook her head. "It's alright." She said as she took it from him and placed it back into her bag. "The mission is over, and that's all that matters now."

Wesley nodded as they began to hear a roaring noise in the distance. They both turned to look at the dark dunes and saw a faint light behind them.

"The Saudis are on their way here," Wesley said. "We'll take care of the politics."

Tawnie's attention snapped to him. "What?" She yelped. "We all have to get out of here! You could compromise the mission!"

General Wesley shook his head as he pointed to a vehicle at the edge of the campsite.

"You get in that Humvee over there and finish what you started!" He commanded. "Our mission is done!"

Tawnie looked at the Humvee he had mentioned and then back at him. "What will happen to you guys?"

Wesley sighed again and wiped down his face with his palm. "These guys will be fine." He said as he looked at his team. "Even Victoria." At that moment, she was being helped up by the two men and trying to snap out of her stupor.

"I have to deal with the government." He added as his tone went low, and he turned to look out into the dunes of the dark desert. "Someone has to take responsibility for what just happened here."

Tawnie shook her head. "Then I'll stay here."

She walked in the opposite direction toward the other soldiers. Before going too far, she was caught by the shoulder. It was Wesley, yanking her back.

"What the hell?" She snarled.

"Listen, kid, there are two important things I learned on the way to where I am today." He said as he stepped in front of her. "When the Army sends you on a mission, you don't question the objective. You do it and get back to hear the next one. Second, if someone says a mission is top secret, you better not say shit."

Tawnie stepped back, looking up at him with saddened eyes. Wesley nodded at her again, assuring her that leaving was okay.

"Get out of here before the Saudis capture you, too."

Tawnie turned away and ran to the brown vehicle with paint patches that matched the sand. She reached for the door to get inside. It was heavy and brutal for her to move, but she was able to get inside and find the loose knob that activated the engine. She looked around at the interior, realizing there was not much to look at. It seemed industrial and very uninviting. There was no radio nor climate control to warm her. Despite attempting to leave earlier, she had no idea where she was going. She looked at the light behind the dune. It had gotten brighter since she last looked. Something was coming. Her feet slammed on the accelerator, and she whipped the wheel to the right, starting her escape. She turned the vehicle's lights off before the Saudi Arabian Army emerged over the sands.

General Wesley looked at his surviving unit and smiled.

"General Wesley, what do we do?" Gordon asked as a dozen armed sand riders came zipping down the dune. They began to circle around the area as if they were stalking prey. The vehicles had three-wheeled drive trains and a long body. The front was constructed with two wheels, and they sported aggressive styling on the grill and hood. The headlights were full LED and bright enough to make the soldiers grimace like the sun was out. The cockpit had four seats, and the roof was held up with a trellis-tube cage, which was presumably removable. Guns mounted to the vehicle to be controlled by the person seated in the passenger seat.

Wesley approached his crew and put his hands up. "We're going to surrender." He said to them.

"I'll be damned!" Gordon said as he followed the order. Parker put his arms up as well. Victoria looked around as if she was looking for a way out. She made eye contact with Gordon. He silently shook his head.

"Don't make this harder than it needs to be." He told her. Her jaw clenched, and her eyes sharpened as she joined the men, raising her arms. Before long, the soldiers jumped out of their vehicles and approached them. Their weapons were at the ready position. Soldiers began to speak in a different language, likely Arabic. Wesley and his soldiers casually looked at one another but were all clueless. Finally, one soldier approached the group from the swarm and addressed General Wesley. His eyebrows furrowed, and his hands slowly fell as they locked eyes.

"Nathaniel Wesley." The Arabic man announced. Wesley nodded, "That's me."

The man clenched his sharp jawline a few times as he looked at the general from bottom to top. Almost as if he was sizing the man up.

"You need to come with us." He said.

Wesley nodded with a slight grin. "Yeah, I figured as much."

Wesley noticed that his uniform was different from the others. It was similar in style but different in color—it was all black. He had never seen it before.

"I am Special Agent Karaan with Interpol." He said, causing Wesley's eyes to get large. "We have it on good authority that you and your battalion have defiled sacred grounds."

Wesley looked back at his team. His grin was gone, and he now looked troubled. With a nod, he agreed to go, and the Interpol agent spoke in Arabic to the soldiers he arrived with. As they were being escorted to the vehicles, Gordon looked at Victoria. She was already staring at the side of his face. Her expression said that she was suspicious of something.

"I don't like this one bit." She said.

"We'll be fine," Gordon replied.

"On the contrary, Sergeant Bartell, Gordon, Parker." Agent Karaan said. "Everything will be fine, but maybe not for you."

Chapter XXXVIII

Present day, far away from Rexburg, Idaho. Victor Parker walked to his office building located in downtown Manhattan. He wore a suit that seemed a bit worn but also sharp enough to present that he cared for his appearance. He had just emerged from the subway and headed down the sidewalk, thinking about the day ahead. As usual, he passed a crowd standing in line for his favorite morning indulgence. A food truck that He believed to be the finest croughnuts and coffee he had ever tasted.

"Oh, Victor, hi!" A man said from the middle of the line. Victor recognized the man, and the ends of his mouth curled for a smile.

"Grayson, what's up, man?" He asked as he approached the line. He noticed the menacing stares of everyone behind Him. Ignoring them, he held his fist forward for a bump and stepped back.

"You're usually at the front by now, man," Grayson said. "What's going on?"

Victor looked around momentarily, his eyebrows angling down at his nose.

"Something happened that made the train late this morning." He answered. "I won't have time to get anything today."

"Bummer." Said Grayson. "Hey, I could get your usual for you and bring it to the thirty-seventh floor."

Victor's eyes thinned as a huge grin appeared on his face.

"Grayson, you don't have to do that!" He said.

The man shook his head with closed eyes. "I insist." He replied. "The least I could do for you helping me land that account last month."

Victor thought about it for a moment. "Fine, it doesn't look like you're leaving me much room to say no."

Grayson pointed at him with a half-witted wink. "Smart man." He continued. "Besides, you are usually on your way to your office now. It'll be fifteen minutes before I get up there from here. If you had to go to the back of the line now, you may as well go home and forget work altogether."

The two men broke eye contact and looked to the back of the line. Victor nodded. "Good point."

His eyes narrowed as he looked at his friend. "You sure about this?"

Grayson twisted his mouth as his eyes narrowed with attitude. There was a brief silence before Victor began to laugh uncomfortably.

"Alright, I'll take it." He said as he placed his hand on the man's shoulder for the breath of a second.

Grayson shook his head. "Not a problem, friend." He replied. "You go ahead. I'll catch up in a bit."

Victor nodded. He clutched the strap of the leather satchel draped over his shoulder. Then he walked away and continued to his office building. He made it a few blocks down the sidewalk with a crowd of individuals all going in the same direction. It was unconscious. He had made this trip more often than his brain would allow him to stand. But on this day, his intuition screamed for him to pay attention. He didn't know what was happening, but something about the air in the city seemed different.

The average pace he was accustomed to was now a lot slower. The crowd blocked his path ahead like a crowded highway. He stood on his toes, attempting to see what the holdup was. He looked up for an obstacle. The road may be blocked by another crane that was doing construction nearby. There was nothing there but the sight of his building, not even a football field away.

"Great." He said to himself. "Guess I was destined to be late today."

He noticed a construction area surrounded by plastic sheeting. Large scaffolding stood in front of him along the building. He forced his way through the crowd, attempting not to step on any toes. Once he reached the breezeway, he saw caution tape. He glanced at his watch and decided to ignore it. He headed into the tunnel underneath the scaffolding, wondering about the roadblock. The further he traveled, the more noise he heard from the street. The roar of diesel engines filled his ears. It sounded as if there was an army of giant quarry rigs on the opposite side of the plastic. He found a hole in the drapes and placed his face to it, wondering what he would see. But all he saw were police officers blocking the road. Orange barriers and cones were used to control the traffic. Victor manipulated the plastic sheet to look further down the road. But there was still no apparent reason for the blockage or the noise.

"Odd," he said. The blockade spanned past his office building. Traffic at the opposite end of the block was stopped as well. The sound of vehicle horns filled the air, and people began to shout at the police officers.

Victor reached into his pants pocket and pulled out his phone. As he approached the building, he logged in and made a call.

Someone answered. "Go for Madsen." A raspy male voice said.

"Mr. Madsen, this is Parker," Victor announced.

"Parker, you're calling me with your ass in your office chair, I hope!" He growled.

Victor sighed. "Actually, sir, I'm outside, and NYPD is blocking the building." He answered as he looked out into the road again. That's when he noticed an FBI transport truck parked in front of a police car.

"Yeah, the FBI is here too." He added.

Madsen made a guttural cry, almost sounding like a roar. Victor rolled his eyes, waiting for him to finish. "I don't give a fuck if the president himself is out there!" He sneered. "We have our meeting in two minutes! Get your ass here now!"

Victor sighed. "Yes, sir. On my way."

He slipped the phone into his pocket and grabbed the strap of his bag as he walked toward the entrance. He stepped out of the scaffolding tunnel and onto the open sidewalk, where nobody else was. The police on the road all looked in his direction.

"Sir!" One officer screamed over the roar of the city. He was a seasoned veteran. The rank of Sergeant was sewn into his coat sleeve, and his hair was as silver as a new quarter. He approached Victor alone with his left hand hovering over his hip. He confirmed with one glance that he was reaching for his gun. Immediately, Victor dumped his bag from his shoulder and put his hands on his head.

"Sir, what are you doing behind the line?" The officer said. As he approached, Victor could see the embroidered name on his chest.

"Officer Staunton, I am just trying to make it to work." He told the officer.

"Which building?" He asked. Victor threw a nod toward the skyscraper behind him. Victor noticed all the officers and FBI agents looking in his direction. Officer Staunton looked back into the group of officers behind him. One man sent him a nod, and he turned around to face Victor. He stepped forward, grabbed his bag from the ground, and flipped the cover to expose the contents. The officer reached into the case without permission and combed through his paperwork. Soon after, the man grunted and closed the bag. He turned halfway away from Victor and slammed the case onto his chest, mouth side down. Victor hardly had time to pull his hands down to grab it before it fell. The laptop he contained inside nearly slipped out and fell to the concrete below. His eyes narrowed as the officer stepped away from him, not even with as much as an apology. Victor headed to the entrance of his office building. He looked over his shoulder as the sergeant nonchalantly joined his team again.

As he walked into the lobby through the carousel doors, a group of FBI agents exited the other side. His heart sank as he entered the building. A receptionist behind a large wooden desk stared in his direction. His eyebrows hiked as they made eye contact as if Victor startled him. He approached the desk, looking behind him at the many officers outside.

"What was that all about, James?" Victor asked. The receptionist shook his head. "I don't know. But they say they're looking for some rogue soldier. Supposedly, it's someone who works here and is involved in a terrorist operation."

A woman exited the elevator at the opposite end of the counter. She ceremoniously did what all employees do upon exiting. A computer sat at the end of the station, facing outside for foot traffic access. She stopped before it, digging into her jacket. She pulled a badge from a retractable lanyard cable on her collar and tapped it to the reader next to the PC.

"You gone for the day, Mrs. Pike?" James asked. The woman nodded. "Yeah, I am."

James laughed as he walked to the end of the station. "You're usually here until the evening. I hope everything is alright."

"No, everything is fine!" She waved as she answered. "I came in early to research a case."

Victor walked to the computer to use it when she was finished. He tapped his badge as she stepped away from the desk.

"James, Mrs. Pike, you guys have a good one." He said as he walked backward toward the elevators. "If I don't get upstairs about five minutes ago, Madsen will throw me from the twenty-fifth floor."

"Yeah, you don't want to piss him off." Pike chuckled. "A little advice, though, Parker."

The woman stepped into the elevator with him. "Elliot Madsen may seem tough. But like a bear, he backs down if he thinks you're bigger."

Victor's eyebrows hiked in surprise. He awkwardly chuckled. The advice seemed suspicious as it came from a direct colleague of his boss. "Alright, thanks, Mrs. Pike."

The woman saluted and headed toward the exit. Her expensive designer shoes clicked on the marble floors of the the lobby.

"Dammit!" Victor grunted, remembering that he didn't call for the elevator. He pressed it, then looked at the sign for the stairs hanging from the ceiling. Twenty-five stories, his next thought was inconceivable.

He looked out the door as he waited. Mrs. Pike was approached by soldiers wearing all-black gear. They were armed giants compared to the small woman. Victor noticed something strange about them. They were in gas masks. One soldier appeared to be pointing the woman back into the building. The other clutched her bicep and attempted to force her back. The elevator door opened before Victor, but he was too focused on the scuffle outside. It wasn't until the elevator's chime broke his trance that he realized everyone in the lobby saw the same. Victor stepped forward and blocked the elevator from closing. However, couldn't take his eyes away from Pike and the two soldiers. The woman broke away from the soldier who held her and screamed at them. Her finger pointed at them as her hand trembled in anger. One soldier, again, threw his finger back at the building as if it were her last warning. Instead of abiding, Mrs. Pike walked right between the two men, and one raised his gun. With one loud gasp filling the lobby, Mrs. Pike was executed in cold blood.

Victor's heart sank as he stepped inside the elevator. The door closed, and he leaned forward on his knees as he felt ill. He whipped out his cell phone and immediately dialed a number that wasn't saved to his phone. Once he arrived on his floor, he stepped out to see the hallway had what looked like light panels fixed to them. Immediately, he screamed in pain as he fell to a knee. It seemed as if his insides were on fire or his blood had become acidic. He looked for help but noticed other bodies lying on the floor of the hall. Suddenly, two soldiers, just like the two outside, came around the corner at the end of the hall. The man reached for his shoulder and grabbed a radio attached to a strap. A beep echoed as he pressed the button on the unit.

"Dispatch, we found him." The soldier said. "Patient Zero is in our sights."

"Copy that." A woman responded. "Apprehend the victim. Dead or alive, he must be captured."

"Roger that." The soldier finished as he and his battle buddy approached Victor's body. In a final effort to fight for his survival, Victor lunged to his feet. A flash of light emitted from his hand as he tried to swing at one soldier. But his arm was caught, and the man sidestepped, yanking his arm behind him. As Victor screamed at the compounding pain, his body completely stopped working. The soldier behind him pointed a pistol downward behind Victor's collarbone. He pulled the trigger, and the relentless struggle of the former soldier had come to a halt. He fell to his knees and stared into the doorway straight ahead. It was the office of his boss, Mr. Madsen. In one of his last thoughts, he wondered if Madsen had suffered the same fate, hoping it was equally or more brutal. He began to aspirate on his blood, and he could feel himself fading as he struggled to intake air.

"What do you think is the likelihood that he passed this disease to everyone in the building?" One of the soldiers asked the other.

"A disease like this, airborne as it is, has been spread to everyone here." He answered his battle buddy.

"That means Mr. Madsen as well," he finished. As they continued their conversation, Victor Parker's world went dark.

262

Chapter XXXIX

Downtown Rexburg was business as usual. The snowfall did not stop the city from living. Victoria had driven to a bar in town, hoping to get refuge. The environment was familiar. Occasionally, someone would pass the booth they sat at and speak to the France's. They were regulars there. The four sat in a booth, drowning their thoughts in the loud country music playing throughout the bar. However, some patrons gave them strange looks, many talking amongst one another and staring.

A waitress approached, covered in a dusting of various powders and sauce stains. She shook her head to whip the straight, black hair from her face. Then she dug into the pockets at the front of her apron and pulled out a receipt book and a pen.

"Are you folks ready to order?" She asked.

Everyone paused and looked at one another as if they had hoped for anyone to answer but themselves. Tawnie stared into the distance, resting her elbows on the table and holding her cheeks in her hands. Gordon sat next to her, his head tilted in defeat. Across from him was Victoria, who looked around the group, expecting someone to order.

"I'm not really in the mood to eat," Tawnie replied, still offering a blank stare across the room.

Lester shook his head, silently waving the woman away from the table.

"Alright, folks." She said, placing her receipt book and pen back into her apron. "If you need me, just give me a holler."

Gordon watched as she stepped away from the table. He then looked around to make sure nobody could hear them.

"Guys, I think we should warn the townspeople about this!" He suggested before looking around once more for good measure. "This is exactly how it started in Idaho Falls!"

Tawnie sprang to life, looking at the man with furrowed brows. "What are you saying?" She asked with her voice elevating toward the end of the sentence.

Gordon shook like a child in trouble and had their entire name called.

"Uh, we got a call last week to IFPD." He stammered. "Some supposed domestic dispute involving men with rifles and some with suits."

Tawnie shook her fists at the man and growled. This raises the attention at nearby tables.

"You didn't think that information was relevant before now?" She asked him. The officer looked across the table at his friends before answering.

"No. Actually, I didn't."

Tawnie shook her head in protest. "You didn't, huh?" She asked. "So these goons come to Rexburg to make a house call? That's everything but random. I suspect that domestic disturbance was a precursor to what happened on the I-15."

Victoria crossed her arms with saddened eyes and shook her head. "It's so strange that nobody is actually talking about that here."

"Yeah, they want to keep it under wraps," Tawnie replied. "God forbid they make people believe it's the end of the world."

Suddenly, she caught a glimpse of the television that hung behind the bar. Her eyes gravitated toward it, and her ears tuned out the rest of the conversation. Milo, who sat between his mother and Gordon, saw Tawnie's focus redirect.

"So, who lived at the place in Idaho Falls?" Lester asked.

Gordon shrugged his shoulders. "All usable property details were scrubbed from almost all databases. Even the city assessors had no record of this house's existence."

Lester shook his head. "Not sketchy at all." He muttered.

Tawnie tuned into the conversation for an iota of a second. "Do you think you can remember the address?" She asked.

Gordon paused momentarily, eyes wandering as he tapped into his memories.

“Yeah, I think I do.” He responded. “It’s 6171 Redwood St.”

Mr. and Mrs. France paused momentarily and looked at one another for confirmation.

“Yeah, I feel like I know that one,” Victoria said. “Not directly. But, like, I had to write it at some point and just held on to it.”

Tawnie pulled out the tablet, clicked through various screens while focusing on the TV. She typed the address in and handed the tablet to Gordon. He looked at her, puzzled. But she avoided any eye contact. He grabbed the device and looked at what she tried to show him.

“Arthur McCade, forty-seven, moved into the house on Redwood about two years ago.” Gordon read. “Home was raided on February 2nd due to a biochemical quarantine concern.”

Just before Lester and Victoria could react, Tawnie snapped to get their attention.

“Guys, look!” She yelled. Each of them turned their attention to the television.

A news broadcast showed random footage of President Nathaniel Wesley performing presidential tasks. From volunteer work in the soup kitchens of Washington to the cliché, kissing of babies. It displayed many positive qualities of the man the group once called The General.

“President Wesley’s secret, dark past could be linked with the massacre in Idaho.” Victoria read the headline displayed at the bottom third of the screen. Her lips smacked as the words even tasted vile to her lips.

“What the hell?” Gordon asked. “Wes would never do something like this!”

Tawnie looked around after noticing some other patrons reacting to the news. She remembered that most Idahoans are conservative. That wouldn’t go well for Wesley’s defense.

“Alright, it’s about to get really politicky in here, guys,” Tawnie said to the former soldiers. “I’m going to need you two to keep your cool.”

Victoria and Gordon looked at one another with sharp brows and squinted eyes.

Upon hearing the first patron slander the president’s name, Lester nodded with a grin.

“Right, gotcha.” He said.

"I knew something like this was going to happen?" A man on the other side of the bar yelled, talking to another customer.

The former soldiers cringed as the two men incited an uproar. This caught the attention of almost everyone around. Gordon's fists clenched on top of the table. He gritted his teeth as he looked around. But Tawnie's hand suddenly landed on his. She offered a gentle squeeze that momentarily calmed him. He turned to look at her, and the look on her face gave him comfort. Meanwhile, Victoria's face drooped, and her head fell. The corners of her lips angled downward momentarily as if she had lost hope.

"Baby, are you okay?" Lester asked. The woman silently shook her head.

"I guess that means we caused this." She stated.

"Bitch!" Tawnie screamed across the table, her attention snapping to the sad blonde.

"This is not supposed to be happening right now." Tawnie continued. "Somewhere out there is a fortune five-hundred about to implode because they got their hands on something big and screwed the pooch hard."

Lester cut his eyes to Gordon. "What does that even mean?"

Tawnie cleared her throat as she tended to her tablet.

"If we can find the company that's ball deep in bull shit, we can pass this blame back to its original owner."

"Shouldn't we be hiding our faces right now?" Gordon asked.

Tawnie raised her head, and her jaw hollowed as her lips puckered. Her eyes were wide at the realization. She looked back at the TV and realized their faces were being shown again. As her vision pulled back, she noticed that many of the bargoers were looking at their table.

"Dammit!" She barked as she focused on her tablet again. "Arthur McCade, does anyone know this dude?"

Suddenly, the sound of chairs and tables sliding across the tile floors filled the room. Silently, Gordon reached to nudge Tawnie's shoulder. When Tawnie looked back up, the same people who had been sitting and staring were now standing.

"We may want to deal with that some other time," Gordon suggested.

A man came from behind the bar at the other end of the room, eyes locked onto their table. He was short and round, with a receding hairline and deep forehead wrinkles that showed his age. He held his hand out to everyone as he approached the booth.

"Hey, France, Misses." He announced, now standing at the head of their table.

"Hi, Moe." Victoria addressed him with a wide grin, assuming things were about to get awkward. "Have you met Tawnie?"

The man took his eyes away from Victoria and threw them across the table at Tawnie. His jaw clenched, and his expression went blank. They stared at one another for a moment, and little Milo scooted against his mom for comfort. She wrapped an arm around the boy and pulled him close without looking away from the bar owner.

"I know exactly who she is." Moe sneered.

"Oh, so you're a fan then." Tawnie poked.

"I came over here for one reason, France." He continued. Tawnie shrugged and lowered her attention to the tablet again.

"We don't accept people like her here. And she's gotten your bunch in a bit of trouble. I'll give you a head start to get out of my bar and never return."

Victoria looked at her husband with shock on her face.

"Moe, wait." Lester said, "Man, we've been your loyal customers for years! I even proposed to Vickie right over there." He pointed at a spot on the long wall of the building that resembled a stage. "You really gonna treat us like that?"

Moe clenched his jaw again, his teeth showing behind his lips.

"As I said before, Your time here is done,"

Behind him, every male of every size stared at the table. In one section of the bar was a group of people wearing black vests, chains, and spikes. They were another motorcycle gang. Tawnie thought it might be the people she had met a few days prior. One of their guys, a giant, muscular man, stepped forth. Despite how cold it was, he was covered in tattoos and wore clothing proudly displaying as much skin as a man could. Tawnie saw the patches on his vest, and chills ran through her body. The man came and stood next to Moe. The height difference was astonishing to all of them. All except for Tawnie. She smirked as she stared into his eyes.

"I think the man told you folk to get gone." He said.

"He and what army are going to make us?" Tawnie questioned.

The brawny man raised an eyebrow and looked back at his crew as if to verify he wasn't alone. Tawnie stared at him with pure conviction as he turned to look back at her. Victoria and Lester's eyes widened as Gordon palmed his face and shook his head.

"Tawnie." He called out to her. But the brute slammed his fist on the table, causing it to buck. The condiments at the other end, against the wall, flew into the air, causing Lester to flinch. The table's salt and ketchup reached their apex above Tawnie and descended toward the top of her head. Before they could land in her curly hair, she reached up with one hand, grabbed both items and slid them across the table without taking her eyes away from him.

"Tawnie, please," Gordon said again. But Tawnie reached out to touch his shoulder with the opposite hand.

"Why don't you folks step out into the snow with us." The goon said.

"Keiran Shaw..." Tawnie announced. "Also known as K-Rock, right?"

Everyone snapped their attention to her. All eyes were wide and perplexed. The look on the gang member's face almost showed concern as he twisted one end of his lip upward.

"You think you're a problem, huh Kiki? Do you realize you approached the table of three police officers and your worst nightmare?"

"I'm assuming you will try to take me down and pin something on us?" K-Rock growled. "My gang? we've been running these parts for years!" He leaned over the table, placing his palms flat. "In fact, I've had police officers make problems for me before. But strange things tend to happen to them if you get my drift."

Tawnie grinned and shook her head. "It won't be the police officers that you have to worry about, Kiki."

The man's face turned beet red, and he moved aside, simultaneously pushing Moe out of the way. He grabbed their booth table with two fingers and flung it out of its spot. Everyone flinched, but Tawnie jumped from her seat and stood between the two benches. The large man approached her. Without any sign of fear, she looked up at him with a grin on her face. The France's both jumped to their feet as well. Gordon assured that Milo was pushed back to the wall to stand out of the way.

"We've called the authorities!" Moe yelled. "They know you're here!"

Finally, Tawnie turned her head with distress in her expression. "You what?" She asked.

"You people are criminals, known terrorists!" He ranted. "I will do my part to make sure you're locked behind bars."

Tawnie smiled again. "Alright, I guess I'm fighting my way out of here,"

"You can fight all you want." K-Rock said to her as he grabbed his belt buckle, "But I love little bitches like you, and the reward money they're offering looks mighty nice."

"Tawnie?" Victoria called. "What the hell do you think you're doing?"

"Vickie," Gordon called. "You may want to let her handle this."

The room went silent. Everyone anticipated the large man taking the small woman down at any moment. But they all knew that something seemed a bit off about her.

"Hey, Kiki," Tawnie said as she began to walk around him. "I'll see you out in the snow."

Chapter XL

"She's going to get us slaughtered!" Victoria exploded at Gordon as Tawnie stared up at K-Rock. The man clenched his jaw, contemplating his next move.

"Yo, Rock!" His buddies called for him from their table as they all stood. "You really about to fight a woman a third your size?"

The gang members all crowded the tableless booth where they sat.

"Ain't no shame in me." He answered, looking over his shoulder at him. "She said she would be my worst nightmare. I just want to know which one of these bitches will try to put me to sleep."

The gang members laughed and closed in on the table like a pack of hyenas.

"Fuckin' Oracle!" Another member yelled as he approached. This man was the same height but skinny in stature. However, he appeared to be made of nothing but muscle. Still, Tawnie stared at K-Rock.

"I've always dreamed of getting my hands on this lying, cracked-pot bitch!" He continued.

"Fellas, are you really gonna hit a woman in front of her kid?" Tawnie asked.

"You ain't no ordinary woman, you dumb slut!" The skinny man objected. "You're the one who hit the panic button on our organization, and we don't take kindly to that."

Tawnie snickered, holding her forearm over the lower half of her face.

"What the hell are we doing here?" Victoria asked Gordon.

"Last we seen this woman, she was a cowering young buck that almost got us killed in Riyadh. What is she doing?"

Gordon shook his head. His eyes shifted to a look of fear.

"Vick, I don't know what happened to this woman since Riyadh. But based on what I've seen since reconnecting with her, the best we can do is stay out of her way and let her handle this."

Victoria raised an eyebrow, looking at Gordon as if he had lost his mind.

She looked back to the parting crowd, giving Tawnie and the gang space to move outside. The rest of the patrons uproared, instigating the brutes on their way to the cold, open threshold at the front of the building. Suddenly, the people that crowded around Gordon and the France's pulled out guns and pointed at them. The three cops pulled out their weapons and aimed as well. Gordon's heart stopped as he made eye contact with one of the men.

"Alright, folks, let's not do anything we'll regret here." He announced. A few men laughed at his words.

"WE won't regret a thing, Traveler!" A man answered. "The Government is offering five mil' a piece for your heads.

"I see we found the value of your life, Shane," Lester said. The man was a bit stocky. He wore a button-up shirt and jeans. His weapon of choice was a shining, chrome revolver. The hammer was pulled back already, and the dim light gleamed off his glasses, making it hard to see his eyes.

"So much for that extended family speech you gave me a while ago, huh, Shane?" Lester asked. "What happened to all of that?"

The man chuckled. "That was before we knew you people were terrorists!" He growled, waving his gun at him. Gordon listened to the crowd momentarily and heard chatter about zip ties. He looked toward the exit and saw that Tawnie was headed outside with a group of gang members.

"Take these jackasses outside too!" Moe screamed. As suspected, someone came through the crowd with their arm raised and a pack of zip ties clenched in their hand.

"Yeah, I'm not in the mood for accessorizing right now," Victoria stated.

"Vickie!" Gordon growled to get her attention. She glanced at him and noticed his hands were up. His gun pointed at the ceiling, and his finger was out of the trigger. Victoria was appalled.

"Gordon, what the hell?" She asked.

"I told you, stay out of Tawnie's way," Gordon responded as a group of patrons surrounded him. They took his gun, giving it to one of the unarmed men nearby. He looked at the pistol with fascination as he stepped away.

"Fuck!" Victoria snarled as she raised her arms. With much regret, Lester followed their lead.

"Hey!" He screamed as the men took hold of his wife. Victoria tried to break away from their grasp out of instinct. But a female gang member stepped in and threw a single hay-maker that landed at the corner of her mouth, rocking her jaw. The three of them were tied up and forced outside as well.

With all the commotion, Gordon realized that he lost track of Tawnie's son.

"Milo!" He screamed. He attempted to look behind him, but the crowd had become too thick. He begged the men to let him go so that he could find the boy, but the only thing he received was a punch to the face, then the gut. Hunched over, someone pushed him through the door, and he fell into the slushy snow on the sidewalk. Hands bound behind him, he struggled to get back to his feet. Another punch landed on his cheek as he inched up to his knees. This one seemed harder. He fell to the ground again, spitting his blood out onto the snow. The contrast between the white and red somehow made him understand just how critical the situation was. He looked up and saw Tawnie standing on the side of the road with her hands behind her back. She looked at the men with her chin raised and eyes narrowed, scoping the competition before her. The two men cracked their knuckles, arguing about who would be the first to rip her to shreds. Tawnie, however, was not affected at all by their banter. She grew impatient as she waited for them to finish.

"I have an idea, fellas," Tawnie said as she approached the two brutes.

"How about I take you both?" The two men went silent, staring at her in apparent shock. Then they turned to one another and proceeded into gut-busting laughter.

"You, against the two of us?" K-Rock howled.

"Yeah, what the hell are you thinking?" The other man asked.

Tawnie smiled. "I'll even sweeten the pot for you. I'll give myself to you in any way you want if you win. But if I win, you people let us all go."

The two men stopped laughing immediately and looked at one another. Their curiosity took the best of them, and Tawnie could see they were tempted to accept the offer.

"Alright. Let's do this." The skinny man growled.

"This is your moment, Tim!" K-Rock said. "She's exactly the type of meat you hunt for!"

"I know how you guys are motivated by pussy." Tawnie announced as she let her hands fall by her side. "Figured if I give you the illusion of choice, then we could speed this process up."

The two men began to circle around her. But Tawnie continued to look forward.

"You want to change your mind before we get this underway, Sweetheart?" Tim asked with a low, seductive voice.

Tawnie finally looked at him without turning her head. Her cold eyes followed him like prey.

"Funny, I was about to ask you the same thing." She said. As she watched him, K-Rock caught her off guard. The man punched her in the side of the face, causing her to stumble toward Tim. As she approached, the man grabbed the back of her head and planted the bulk of his knee square into her face. Tawnie's body was thrown across the road and rolled into the curb.

"Fucking easy kill!" Tim howled.

"Tawnie!" Victoria yelled as she tried again to escape the goons holding her. But they yanked her back by her zip tie cuffs and began to beat her again. Lester attempted to get to his wife again but received the same treatment. A group of men turned to Gordon, bucking and sneering at him. But the man didn't bother to react, not even a flinch.

"You want some too pretty boy?" One man asked him. But still, Gordon refused to respond. He cut his eyes to Tawnie, still curled up against the curb.

"More like overkill, Tim!" K-Rock laughed. "Dead pussy ain't as fun!"

The two of them loomed over her lifeless body. K-Rock reached down and grabbed her by the back of her neck. Shockingly, with one hand, he hoisted her into the air like a puppy.

Once she was on her feet, he handed her off to Tim. He bear-hugged the small woman, gripping underneath her arms and holding her close. Blood dripped from her nose and mouth as she looked at him with a calm grin.

"You give up yet, Sweetheart?" Tim snarled at her. Tawnie shook her head. "Aww, you poor delusional soul!" He yelled as he squeezed her ribs. He expected her to scream, but instead got a response he wasn't expecting. He looked at her again and saw the devious smile on her face. Suddenly, she straightened her hand and jabbed at Tim's shoulders. Her index and middle fingers penetrated his skin on both sides. He screamed as he was forced to release his grip.

"You stupid bitch!" He growled as he took a step back. But Tawnie turned her head to the side and cracked her neck. Again. K-Rock went for a sneak attack. A meticulous punch aimed at the side of her face was dodged by a simple rotation of the head to the opposite side. As she watched his giant fist fly by her head, she threw her shoulder up and pulled his wrist down with her opposite hand. He cried out in pain as his elbow cracked over her shoulder. Then, Tawnie sent an elbow flying back into K-Rock's diaphragm. The large man made a sound like a plane flying across the sky. As he went down to one knee, attempting to catch his breath, she kicked him in the side of his neck. The crowd went silent as they watched his body pop up as if he were trying to endure the blow. Despite their anticipation, they knew he was done. As he attempted to stand up straight, his body seized before falling over as if one side stopped working. He hit the ground and began to shake violently before stopping suddenly.

Tawnie glanced at his collapsed body, seemingly proud to be victorious. Then she smiled at Tim. She turned her head slightly to spit out a glob of blood but never took her eyes away from her adversary.

"You give up yet, Sweetheart?" She asked him.

With wide eyes, Tim looked at his buddy, who lay in the snow with one arm sticking into the air. His body was still, and his eyes were still open, but there was no way to tell if he was alive. He then looked around to his goons, who were all in just as much shock.

"Get her!" Tim yelled. Tawnie's smile grew more prominent as the gang members all attempted to close in on her. Gordon's eyes widened as he watched the gang crowd around her. But it didn't take long for her to clean the clock of anyone who stepped in to fight.

"Holy shit!" Tim said to himself. "Who the fuck is this chick?" He asked as he watched his cohorts crowd around her, continuing to swing away at her.

"I told you," a voice said behind him. His eyes grew wide, and slowly, as he turned to see Tawnie behind him. "I'm your worst nightmare."

Tim screamed but was immediately silenced as Tawnie threw an arm around his neck. She yanked him backward, pulling him off of his feet. She spun around as she descended and crouched, adding pressure to his neck. With a straight face, Tawnie stared the bar owner, Moe, in the eyes as Tim's movements grew weaker and less sporadic. Moe clenched his jaw as he looked into her eyes. Before Tim faded, Tawnie snarled, showing a demented face as she clutched him tighter. Tim's shattering bones made everyone shudder. His body immediately went limp. The scuffle suddenly stopped, and everyone looked out into the road at the two dead leaders of the gang. Tawnie stood to her feet and looked at the group of goons.

Victoria looked at her with wide eyes and an open mouth. Her surprise was evident.

"I'll take my friends, my son, and as promised, we'll go." She said to Moe. The man was too afraid to speak. He nodded at her and swiped his straightened hand across his neck to tell the others off. At that point, all zip ties were cut, and little Milo ran out of the bar to join his mother in the street. She bent down to pick him up and looked for the others. She found Gordon and smiled at him as he was released from the zip ties around his wrist.

"Does anyone else want to stop us from leaving?" Tawnie asked, looking around for anyone objecting. But nobody said a word. They were all scared. Looks of shock and horror filled their faces as they watched Tawnie closely.

Lester, Gordon, and Victoria all joined Tawnie on the road.

"Damn, Everwood," Victoria said to her as she approached.

"You may think telling the authorities our whereabouts was wise," Tawnie announced. "But when they come here, I suggest you all hide."

Chapter XLI

The gang all headed back to the motel, where Tawnie and Gordon booked a room and decided to lay low for the night. The Frances acquired a room on the opposite side of the building using fake names and identities. Shortly after getting back in, Tawnie went for a shower. The door was slightly open to the restroom where the toilet and tub were. Outside the door, the room's back wall mirror was filled with steam. She had been in there for a while. Long enough for Gordon to clean up the room of any loose debris from earlier. Milo had fallen asleep watching children's cartoons.

Gordon sat at the edge of the bed, waiting for her to emerge from the lava plume she called a shower. He heard items shifting inside occasionally. But eventually, he heard something slam into the bathtub, followed by a thud against the wall. He flinched, then stood straight, staring at the mirror at the back of the room. He grew nervous, wanting to check on her but realizing she may not be decent.

"Tawnie?" he called, but there was no answer. He looked down at Milo to see if he had accidentally woken the boy. His eyes were still shut, and his breathing was still long and steady. Gordon took a deep breath to keep calm and sauntered toward the restroom.

"Tawnie?" He called again. But still, she didn't answer. As he reached the door, he placed his hand on the knob. The hot steam wrapped around him as he stepped closer. The door's opening faced the back wall, and Gordon pushed it enough to keep from seeing inside.

"Tawnie, are you okay?" He asked. "Do you need something?"

He waited a few seconds, but she still didn't answer. He closed his eyes and took another deep breath, trying to slow his heart rate. Opening the door, he prepared his mind for what his eyes might see.

He pulled the handle toward him, allowing more steam to exit as the door opened wider. He stepped around it and into the threshold. There, he saw Tawnie sitting on the side of the tub. A diluted mess of water and blood sat on the white porcelain of the tub. Her back faced the door, and he recognized her bare, golden skin. She glistened underneath the single light above. It was the first time he saw the curves of her body, usually hidden underneath layers of winter clothing. Her hair was wet and pulled over her shoulder. Surprisingly, it was thin compared to her usual voluminous curls. He watched beads of water drip from her neck and down into the remarkably toned funnel of her lower back. He found himself following the droplets to the center of her buttocks. He looked up as something odd caught his attention. It was a tattoo of a black triangle that pointed upward. It looked about two inches across, and a smaller triangle underneath that was only an outline. Gordon cautiously approached, fully understanding how dangerous the woman before him was. But before he could reach her, he heard her sniffle. Gordon took another deep breath before reaching out to touch her shoulder. He looked down at her, expecting to see bruising, but there wasn't a blemish to be found.

"Tawnie, is there anything I could do for you?" He asked. She looked up at him. Her eyes locked onto his. He could feel his body warming inside as he recognized her vulnerability. He sat opposite her on the tub wall with his feet facing the door. Tawnie leaned back against his arm, arching her back and exposing her breast to him. Her fit body and big brown eyes took his breath away as he watched her in awe.

"What do you need?" He asked. Tawnie seemed to ignore his question and stood. He watched as the water from her hair dripped and poured off the apex of her buttocks.

"Tawnie." He groaned, shifting away.

"I'm sorry…" She whispered. "I dragged you all into my mess."

Gordon shook his head and reached for her tiny wrist. He clutched it in his hand and stroked her forearm with his thumb.

"You couldn't help what happened to us." He replied. "It was our mission, and we were the ones who had to do it."

"If only that were true."

Tawnie turned toward the shower head and stepped underneath the hot water. Gordon swallowed hard, trying to focus on the back of her head or the tattoos on her back. He wondered why he was there or why she allowed him to be. He was reminded of the photo of this woman and her family in the living room of her house. But now, she was here, allowing him to see her in a light reserved for the man she married. He realized how wrong it was for him to be there and shyly turned his head away from the sight of her. Gordon walked to the door again, preparing to leave.

"If you need anything, Tawnie, call me." He said. But as he looked back at her, she was focused on him. Leaning against the shower wall, he tried to determine what her eyes were saying. They were heavy as if she were tired, but then she bit her bottom lip.

"Danny?" She called softly. Her hands started to caress herself as she examined him from head to toe. His face became flushed.

"Tawnie, I'm not your guy. I'm sorry." He answered. Suddenly, his eyes betrayed him as they fell on her body. Eventually, he lifted his chin and took a deep breath.

"I haven't been anyone's girl for a long time, Danny." She said as she stepped over the tub wall, water splashing all over the floor. "Am I wrong to believe there is something here?"

She reached for his face and placed a hand on his cheek. He closed his eyes and leaned toward it. He took another deep breath, this time taking in the sweet scent of her body.

"What about your husband?" Gordon asked. Tawnie shook her head, disapproving of his question.

"I'm divorced, Gordon." She said as her hand gently fell down his neck and chest. She turned away from him and walked back to the shower. Slowly, she stepped in, looking back at him the entire time. Gordon felt his whole body heating up as he locked onto her eyes.

"The last time he touched me, he was hitting me in the face." She smirked. "I don't think you would treat a lady like that, would you?"

Gordon shook his head with a smile. "He must be a brave man."

"Sure, we can talk about him instead of doing what you really want to do to me!" Tawnie shrugged and closed the shower curtains. However, they were still translucent. Though cloudy, Gordon could still see her curvy figure.

"If you know I want you so bad, then why are you just telling me about your husband?" He asked as he shut the door to keep Milo from hearing them.

"Because I didn't know what to expect of you?" She said as she continued to rinse under the water. "I don't habitually tell every man my marital status."

Gordon pursed his lips, hearing the tone of annoyance in her voice. He stayed silent momentarily and witnessed her shoulders slouch, only for a second. Then she perked herself up again. The shower nozzles turned off, and the water stopped running. Tawnie reached out the back side of the tub to a towel rack hanging inches above the toilet. She grabbed one and began to dry herself. Gordon turned to open the door and stepped out of the restroom. Tawnie pulled the shower curtain open before he could close it and stepped out behind him. Wrapped in her towel, she stepped around him, locking eyes with the man as she passed. Gordon's neck bobbed as he watched her in silence.

"I'm sorry." She said to him. She turned her head to look away, and her eyes softened as she gripped the closure point of her towel with both hands. Gordon did his best not to look down.

Tawnie finally chuckled, "I thought this was mutual."

She slowly turned away, almost seeming ashamed of herself. "I guess I was wrong."

That's when Gordon pushed himself off the counter at the back wall and grabbed a handful of her bath towel. Before she could realize what happened, he had tossed it over his shoulder. With a sense of relief, as if he had been holding back the weight of the ocean. Finally, he allowed himself to look at her. He looked at the black triangles on her back, seeming to be the arrows telling him where he needed to look. Tawnie spun around, this time covering herself up with her hands. She had a look of shock on her face, which made the officer cautious about proceeding.

Gordon stepped forward, ripping his shirt over his head with one hand. His muscular body glistened under the ambient light. Tawnie looked him up and down before removing her hands from her body.

"Do I scare you?" She asked him as she approached. Her hand gently touched his chest, offering a gentle rub before dragging it down his pectoral muscle, gently swiping across his nipple. Then down to his hard abdomen, where her fingers rippled down until they passed his belly button, then onto the slanted line funneling into the top of his pants.

Gordon opened his mouth slightly and stared into her eyes. His hand lifted and fell onto her shoulder, slowly moving toward her neck. His grip pulled her closer as his fingers intertwined the hair on the back of her neck and inched upward. Her breasts pressed against his body, and a carnal hunger displayed in his eyes.

"Do I look like I'm fucking scared of you?" He grumbled. Tawnie's eyes grew large just before Gordon's left arm wrapped around her waist and grabbed a handful of her butt. He lifted her from her feet, picking her up like a child. Tawnie wrapped her legs around him as he pulled her head forward to kiss her deeply. Their tongues tied together like they were both fighting for dominance, but Tawnie moaned softly as he slammed her naked body against the wall. As he continued to kiss her passionately, Tawnie could feel his member throbbing against the bounds of her clitoris. Tawnie clung to him as he walked back into the restroom and closed the door behind him. Her lips clasped to his neck, refusing to let go. He stepped back into the bathtub and turned the water back on to drown the sound out.

"Gordon," Tawnie whispered in his ear. Gordon pinned her against the back wall of the bathtub and turned his head toward her. She gave him another soft kiss on his lips before saying, "Don't be gentle"

Gordon reached down and grabbed his belt buckle to undo it. Within seconds, his pants and boxers were around his knees. Tawnie could feel the hard cock in his hand as he slammed it against her. She maneuvered herself with a soft, innocent smile. As she opened the space between her pelvis and his, she immediately felt pressure against her clitoris. She reeled with pleasure, allowing him to play in her wetness and tease her as she bit her bottom lip. Gordon slid inside her and watched her eyes grow large before he finally reached the end. Her body trembling with ecstasy as she bit down into his shoulder to mask a moan of pure pleasure.

Gordon stopped, wondering if he had done something wrong. But she gripped the back of his head, "Don't stop!" She whispered.

Gordon kept going. The longer he shoved himself inside of her, the tighter she gripped onto him. He could feel a great deal of her strength, but he persisted. After a few minutes, she began to tremble again and buried her head into his shoulder. She bit down again, masking her moans. This bite drew blood from his shoulder.

Gordon lifted her again, detaching her and placing her on her feet. Tawnie immediately turned around and placed her palms flat against the wall. Again, Gordon slid into her. This time, he looked down to see the space between her supple cheeks wrap around him. The tone of her lower back muscles flexing as she rocked back and forth almost made his knees weak. He touched her, starting at her butt, then raising his hand along her body, seeming to make her tremble just before he felt the triangles of her back. The large, filled-in triangle began to glow when he touched it. A veil of energy filled the room. Gordon looked around in shock, then back at her.

"Oh fuck, don't stop!" She moaned out loud. So Gordon did as he was told and kept going. The energy around the room fluctuated. The closer Tawnie got to her climax, the louder she screamed. Suddenly, she collapsed. Her entire body went limp, and Gordon reached around and grabbed her breast. The other hand clutched her pelvis, ensuring she couldn't escape. Tawnie continued to scream as Gordon continued to thrust into her. Her body almost shuddering with each slam. The veil inside the room also flickered with every thrust. In the process, Gordon had reached his breaking point. His thrusts slowed as he held her body tighter. He let out a groan as he leaned forward to kiss her neck. Tawnie leaned back against him, arching her back to keep him inside. The light veil vanished, and the triangle on her back faded to black. The two of them stood in silence momentarily, breathing heavily as Gordon wrapped his arms around her for a gentle embrace.

Tawnie's body trembled as she gripped his arms. For a moment, he held her tight as the rush of climax called him near.

"Don't stop!" She yelled. To that, he increased his velocity until she whimpered. He pulled her closer as she seemed to get heavier. Her knees wobbled as she tried to keep herself up. Her screaming paused, and she stopped breathing momentarily. He could feel her entire body tightening up around him, only speeding up the process. He roared, forgetting that there was a child in the next room. As his knees weakened, he lowered Tawnie into the tub to avoid dropping her. She turned her torso toward him and pressed her lips against his. This time, the animalistic behavior had subsided. Daniel's heart began to race because he realized that this kiss said more than take me. She pulled away from him slowly, finding his eyes. She was no longer Tawnie, the assassin, Agent 0, or even another man's wife. She was simply Tawnie, vulnerable and endearing. His mouth dried as he stared at her, all of her.

"Daniel," She called him as her fingers caressed his lips. A tear fell down her eyes before she pulled away to spin around. She wrapped her arms around his neck and shoulders, pulling his head toward her. "I know you want to say it." She whispered as the aura around them dissipated. "But, please don't."

Chapter XLII

After almost an hour of enjoying one another's bodies, the two of them sat on the side of the tub. At first, it was silence. The two looked at one another with adoration, allowing the passion to subside. The restroom door was slightly open, allowing it to cool inside. The two of them got dressed and looked into each other's eyes for a longing moment. Daniel had said something witty, making her grab her face as she burst into laughter. He simply watched her in awe until she stopped.

"What?" She asked. He shook his head and looked away with a grin on his face.

"It's just… you have this energy about you that I can't explain, Tawnie." He said. "What is it about you that has me so enticed?"

Tawnie's smile faded, and she turned her head slightly. Her bottom lip fell open as if she was about to speak, but she fought internally about how to answer the question.

"I don't know if I have a suitable answer to that question.

"Of course, but you are such a polarizing and captivating being. I've never come across anyone like you before." He continued with a smile.

"I believe that." She responded. "But I am just a single mother, that's all."

"Also, leader of a society of truth and the bad-ass that took down an army of soldiers! Not to mention, a hacker that knows the ancient language of a forgotten society." He stacked her accolades. "I probably should be afraid of whatever you are, but I am more curious than anything."

Tawnie turned to him and stared into his eyes. She took a hard swallow before she pursed her lips. He could tell she had much to say, but she did not fully trust him. Daniel caressed her hand, hoping to get her to relax.

"Tawnie, can I take a shot in the dark?" He asked. Her heart sank as her upper lip became an instant victim of her teeth. She winced as she nodded in confirmation of his request.

"Alright." He said, rubbing his hands together. "One, you are much older than you look but much younger than you feel. Two, you grew up in a single-parent household with a parent who hardly interacted with you. Three, you are the youngest of your siblings. And…" He finished. Just as she opened her mouth to answer, he revealed question number four.

"You have a huge secret you feel you can't tell anyone, and it's killing you inside."

Tawnie folded her arms over her chest and stretched her shiny legs before her. She lifted a fist to her jaw and took a moment to think, smiling as she stared playfully at the man beside her.

"One, one-hundred percent correct." She said. "Two, I grew up as an orphan. Three, no siblings that I know of, and four…"

Tawnie stopped and suddenly appeared to get serious.

"That was right?" He asked. "Number four?"

Tawnie nodded. "It hasn't been any secrets. I'm just not believable yet. Unfortunately, I will be soon enough."

Daniel shook for a split second. His eyes squinted, but one eyebrow hiked as he stared at her.

"What exactly do you mean by that?" He asked.

"Tawnie leaned forward, draping her upper body over her knees and reaching to rub the back of her neck. She combed her scalp with her fingertips and threw the wild strands of hair behind her.

Her mouth clicked. "Danny, humanity's level of understanding won't comprehend what's really going on. I'm just the little harbinger of bad news. All I did was read the damn slab and find out that the end of the world is coming."

Daniel immediately shook his head with a flurry of disbelief and confusion.

"I'm sorry, come back?" He said to her. Tawnie grinned as she got up and stepped to the wall across from the toilet. Her knees were together, and her back slid down the wall as she sat on the floor.

"The Ancient Arcanin wrote about the end of the world." She continued. "The worst part is, this prophecy foretold this siege. It foretold the extermination and maybe the person responsible for it all. I didn't want to believe that part, but we'll see when this is all over."

Daniel spaced out momentarily, thinking of how unlikely the prophecy idea was.

"Maybe it's all a big coincidence." He said. "That can't be real."

"The prophecy recognized the 316th as the Noble One and their Royal Warriors." She announced. "It foretells that the Noble One becomes king over many men. But it also depicts how fate bound him to be used as a sacrifice for evil."

Daniel stared at her for a long, silent moment.

"Wait, Tawnie, does it talk about each of us individually in the prophecy?" He asked.

Tawnie closed her eyes and nodded. "Each of you has your place in history, according to the text."

Tawnie brought her knees in and hugged them. A look of stress showed on her face.

"Does it discuss every individual?" He asked.

Tawnie winced. "It doesn't work that way, Danny. If individuals are mentioned, their lives impact the final decision."

Daniel shook his head again. "Final decision? What does that mean?"

"It doesn't matter right now!" She yelled as she jumped from the floor. "We need to find a way to kill this bullshit quarantine that these unknown soldiers have us in."

Daniel jumped up as well, looking down at the woman with frustration.

"Hold up!" he said as he reached for her hands. Tawnie seemed like a child getting restless. Her body twitched as she moved toward the door. Daniel raised her hands and held them between their bodies.

"Tawnie, you can't tell me that I was mentioned in a prophecy from a million years ago and expect me not to have questions!" He yelled. "This is important to me!"

Tawnie pulled her hands back and turned away from the man. Angry, he grabbed one arm and pulled her back. Tawnie spun back around with anger in her eyes. She pushed the man away, almost hyperventilating as she tried to escape.

"Tawnie!" He yelled as he stumbled over the side of the tub. He held out his hand to push himself up from the back wall. She stepped out of the bathroom and ran to the sleeping area. Daniel ran out after her.

"What the hell is your problem?" He asked, finding her rushing to get fully clothed. He ran to her and tried to grab her again. This time, he grasped her arm, and again, she attempted to push him away. But Daniel moved aside to prevent her from knocking him down. They stood at opposite sides of the room, awaiting a move from the other. He was confused, wondering why this woman who was so sensual a while ago suddenly went off the deep end.

"Tawnie, I surrender," Daniel said as he raised his hands. "Please, tell me what you need. I can do my best to help you."

She stared at him. Her eyes seemed cold and ruthless but also afraid.

"I need this pain to stop!" She growled as she grabbed her head in distress. She clenched and fell to her knees on the floor.

Daniel approached her again with caution. But as he drew near, he saw a dim glow on the door behind her. It was as if a cell phone was illuminating the space of the room behind her.

"I'm here." He whispered. "I got you." The man proceeded to wrap his arms around Tawnie. Her body trembled as if she was cold or afraid... maybe both. Tawnie's head was tilted forward, and she allowed her arms to fall to her side. Daniel embraced her for comfort. As he caressed her again, he could see the source clearly. Then Daniel realized that this episode was just like all the others. PTSD-like outbursts and random rage, this woman is experiencing something he has never seen before. He could see the triangles on her back illuminating and getting brighter by the second. In addition, it seemed to cascade through her body. Daniel didn't react right away. He held her even tighter and rested his cheek on her head. Eventually, she calmed herself, and the light faded.

His heart raced as he knew he was responsible for asking a question he didn't want the answer to. But he swallowed his pride and pulled away. He looked into her eyes as he held her at arm's length. He could see the tears in her eyes and felt her convulse as she sniffled and took slow, deep breaths.

"Are you better now?" He asked. Silently, she nodded as she stared at him. "Good, so I can ask you a question and hope it doesn't upset you more."

Tawnie's eyes grew large. She braced for impact, not knowing if she was ready for what he said next.

"Tawnie Simms… I'm going to ask you this again," He announced. His eyes sharpened, and his head lowered, glaring at her as if she was a criminal. "Who the fuck are you?"

Chapter XLIII

There was a knock on the door of the couple's motel room. Lester, lying on the bed in boxers, looked at his wife suspiciously as she came out of the restroom in her underwear. They made eye contact as Lester reached for the TV remote to increase the volume. The knock persisted for a second round. Lester pulled a pistol from underneath his pillow. His wife grabbed one from the interior pocket of her coat that hung next to the sink. Lester sprang up from the bed and tip-toed to the door. He held the gun up and locked the slide back, preparing the chamber for a round. He gave one last look at his wife before looking out to see who it was. Another round of knocks started, this time more aggressively. Victoria hid behind the door to the restroom with her pistol ready to fire. Lester put his eye to the peephole.

The man sighed loudly before slamming his fist on the iron door.

"Love, it's just Daniel!" He announced. He palmed the door handle and twisted it with a smile. Daniel stood on the threshold, bewildered as he saw Lester in only boxers. France reluctantly waved the pistol, guiding Gordon inside. Once he got in, he looked straight to the back of the room and saw Victoria semi-nude as well. His eyes squinted with discomfort as he instinctively looked down at her body.

"Okay, it's obvious I'm interrupting something here." He said to the Frances. "I'll just take the keys and rest in the truck."

"No," Victoria replied as she bent over to pick up her pants, her butt facing him. The man blushed, realizing that the crotch of her panties were off-centered entirely. The fluids reflecting light completely distracted him.

"Yeah, you're right. I should leave." He continued. "I'm seeing far too much of Victoria right Now."

The woman hurried to get partially dressed to be considered decent.

"You're good, Daniel." She smiled. "Once a cock block, always a cock block, I guess."

Daniel threw his hands out to his side. "He was gay!" He yelled with a smirk on his face.

Victoria strutted past him with a mischievous grin. "We were just finishing up anyway."

Lester shook his head, "Speak for yourself. I was ready to tap you out!"

Victoria blushed and looked at her husband past Daniel. He pretended not to notice Lester's statement and his gyrating hip motion in his peripheral. There was an awkward silence as the couple communicated on a metaphysical level. Gordon didn't even notice.

"What brings you by, Dan," Victoria asked.

The man shook his head as he began to pace by the door.

"It's Tawnie." He said. "Something about her doesn't add up."

Victoria nodded as she and her husband sat at the end of the bed. "We are just coming to this conclusion?"

"Fuck off, Vickie! I'm serious!" He said as he went for a seat at the small table in the corner. He leaned on his elbows, staring at the table's surface in deep thought. Lester and Victoria looked at one another. Victoria nodded toward their concerned friend, sending her husband to console him.

"It's still pretty early in the evening, man. What's got you going?" Lester asked.

Daniel shook his head but never raised his eyes. He pulled a rolled stack of papers from his coat and slid them across the table. With a raised eyebrow, Victoria reached for the documents and opened them. She tried to read through what she saw but inevitably gave up.

"What are we looking at here?" She asked.

Gordon rolled his eyes while shaking his head. "This is Tawnie's research on us." He answered. "She knew where to find us at every point after Riyadh!"

Victoria skimmed through the files until she found her and

Lester's information. She could see life changes, trips, and even the most known contacts for each of them. There were even events from Victoria's life that hadn't happened yet. Things that she knew were happening soon. But there was one thing on the file that troubled her.

"Have you read Victor's bio?" She asked. "Lester took a look at the papers over her arm. The word deceased was written next to Victor Parker's profile. However, most of the pages were discolored and looked coffee-stained. Victoria's breath was cut short.

"There's no way this is real!" She exclaimed.

"Vic, the entire 316th is discussed in the Arcanin Prophecy," Daniel explained. "Wesley is called the Noble One, and we are his Royal Guard."

"Shit, all of my life is written out here. Before and after the Army!" Victoria said, still examining the papers. Then, her eyes went wide.

"What's up, Vic?" Her husband asked.

"You found February 23rd?" Daniel asked.

Lester snapped his attention to Daniel. "What happens on the 23rd?"

Daniel didn't answer. Instead, he took a deep breath, and his eyes remained locked on the papers.

"Vic?" Lester called.

"We... we die?" She asked. "What the fuck?"

"According to Tawnie, the world is about to change forever," Daniel explained. "She has been fighting for answers to this since she learned how to read Arcanin. But instead of finding answers, she's found many reasons to be suspicious."

"What the... Is she like some murder mystery expert or something?" She asked.

"It seems that way." He answered. "But it seems like her mystery is determining the fate of humanity."

"I'm sorry. Did I miss something?" Lester asked.

Victoria stood, still reading the paper. "There's a quote", she announced.

"The Pyro stone will fall into the wrong hands and risk being used for greed. Once the balance is disrupted, the war unfolds."

The room went silent for a moment. The three thought hard to decipher and process what they just heard mentally.

Victoria cleared her throat, "Why does Tawnie know all of this?" She asked. "And why are there events on this sheet that never happened?"

Daniel shook his head. "Tawnie has been having these… episodes since I reconnected with her. She'll be fine one minute, and the next, she'll be having a fit that resembles PTSD, turrets, and anxiety."

"Ol' girl got some trauma," Lester replied. "So what?"

"No." Daniel stopped him. "I think she may be connected to another dimension or something. I can't figure it out. But her episodes seem unnatural, and they always make her son spazz out. It almost looks like a dog whistle or some shit."

He stood from the chair and walked to the window. With two fingers, he peeled the curtain back and peeked outside.

"You know that thing that happened to us that we said we would never speak about, Vic?" He asked as he turned toward the couple.

Victoria turned her head and bit her bottom lip. Lester looked at her with a raised brow. She sighed and stood up as well. Before looking into his eyes, she clenched her fists.

"Tawnie knew what we became that day." He continued. "Something happened to the survivors in that tomb. Nobody was supposed to know about it. That's why we are being hunted."

"I want to believe otherwise, but I can't," Victoria responded. "That incident in Massachusetts all those years ago. It's happening here, isn't it?"

Gordon nodded slowly, confirming the worst-case scenario.

"Wait, what the hell are you two talking about?" Lester yelled as he stood.

"Honey, calm down," Victoria said.

"Lester, our mission to Riyadh directly resulted from the Massachusetts incident. It involved an individual that exhibited supernatural abilities," Daniel explained. Lester's eyes popped open as he looked at the two of them.

"It was suspected that the perpetrator infected people who he came in contact with. That would either mutate its victims or–" she stopped.

"Killed them?" Lester finished.

"Where is that bitch now?" Victoria yelled as she headed to the door. "She has some questions to answer for!"

Daniel grabbed her shoulder before she could reach the door. She looked back at him and sneered.

"We have to get her before she disappears again." She continued.

Gordon shook his head. "She needs us now." He assured her. "She won't leave us."

Victoria saw the look of sorrow in his eyes. This caused her to stop.

"Wait," She asked. "You didn't come here to vent about her, did you?"

Daniel smirked, but his eyes appeared saddened for some reason. After understanding the mood, Victoria knew she and her best friend were no longer on the same page.

"Top, I don't trust her." She said to him. "There is too much at risk here."

Daniel shrugged. "It's not like we have any idea what will happen. We need her to understand what happened to us, and she needs us to help her retrieve that stone. We owe it to the people here for exposing them to this virus."

Victoria closed her eyes and sighed. "What do we need to do?"

"We need to–" Daniel began to say but became distracted by a strange sound outside the room.

"Guessing I wasn't the only one that heard that," Lester said. Daniel shook his head and stepped toward the door. But Victoria was more vigilant and saw a blinking light through the window.

"Gordon, no!" She screamed at him. But Daniel had already grabbed the door handle and turned it. Her heart began to race. She had watched a familiar scene play out numerous times during their deployments. Victoria stepped forth and threw her hands up in front of her. A yellow glow filled the room from outside the window and through the door. Suddenly, to her, everything moved in slow motion. Victoria's hands emitted a red glow that briefly counteracted the orange light. It spread like a bubble that grew larger by the millisecond, engulfing Lester and Daniel. Once inside, the glow entered the room. The window shattered, and the door flew off the hinges. There was an explosion, and the three officers were trapped.

Chapter XLIV

The burning motel placed the town of Rexburg in an uproar. Sirens in the distance grew louder as the townspeople caught wind of the explosion. The impact was so devastating that surrounding structures were affected. Neighboring buildings crumbled, and the trickling traffic stood still nearby.

The three officers crawled through the wreckage, trapped under layers of debris. However, Victoria kept her hands steady. The red glow still maintained the shield. It somehow protected them from the heat and flames. Lester looked around at the glowing red light surrounding them, fascinated but afraid. It was something he couldn't comprehend. But when he looked at his wife and his friend, he realized it was just another evening festivity for them.

"We all good?" Victoria asked.

"Clear!" Daniel answered.

"Lester, honey?" Victoria called out.

"I'm here." He confirmed.

"Perfect," Daniel said as he looked up through the flames. "Vick, you good?"

The woman shook her head. "As good as expected, considering the circumstances."

"Alright, Les," Victoria yelled. "This bubble moves; you move with it! Okay?"

"Roger that!" He replied, still looking around in awe. "Daniel, can I get an exit here?"

"Already on it!" Daniel yelled back as he stretched into a deep lunge. His entire body emitted a blue glow, turning the light inside the bubble purple. Without warning, he shot off through the debris. Lester blinked, and he was gone. A trail of blue light outlined the path he took. The debris before them was blasted out, opening a path out of the wreckage.

"I see the sky!" Victoria called out. "Lester, stay close!"

She began to move. Lester stayed as close to her as possible. What was once their room behind them had caved in on top of Victoria's energy. As they moved, Lester could tell she struggled to maintain the shield. He looked back and realized that the entire second floor of the motel had its weight on them. His first inclination was to panic and guide his wife with a hand to her back to speed the process. But he could tell that she was already under enough stress. Her body trembled as she stepped through the flames. Every burst entered the bubble but could not be felt.

"Almost there, Vic!" Lester yelled. "You're doing great!"

He could see the atmosphere outside and almost taste the freedom. He could also hear something so damning that it made him sick to his stomach. It was the sound of someone still trapped beneath the debris. It was a muffled cry at first that seemed to turn into a gut-curdling howl the closer they got to the door. Maybe the sound was there the entire time. But once he heard one, he heard another. Then another. People were suffering, innocent people. Instinctively, he wanted to act but knew he had to make it outside first. But before they could reach the end of the debris-lined tunnel, another part of the roof caved in front of them. It slammed on top of Victoria's bubble, and she howled in pain and buckled at the knees as she attempted to hold on. Lester noticed the shield fade and felt the unbearable heat of the flames.

"Victoria!" He yelled as he touched the woman's lower back, giving her a boost of energy. She was now fighting to keep herself upright. She gritted her teeth, and every vein in her face, neck, and arms appeared visible through her skin.

"I can't hold it!" She cried out.

"Yes, you can!" Just a little longer!" Lester yelled back as he stepped before her to look at the blockage ahead. He looked for an opening in the debris but couldn't find a thing. All he saw was a fiery mess. But he didn't want to say anything that could steal her motivation.

"Daniel!" She screamed. Suddenly, a crash outside made a tremor that felt like an earthquake. Just as Victoria collapsed, her energy shot out like a stream. She flew directly into the debris, grabbing Lester as she thrashed through head-first. He soon realized Victoria's energy surrounded him, but it was now in a tube instead of a bubble. In addition, the energy quickly shifted from red to purple. Once they tore through the debris, it went blue. Suddenly, they were outside, careening through the air. Victoria used her powers to land softy, but Lester landed on the hood of a nearby parked car.

"Vic!" Daniel yelled as he found the woman lying in the snow nearby. She had collapsed and was unconscious. Daniel hurried to pick her up and quickly moved away from the burning structure. Lester stumbled off the car's hood, flopping to his knees. He panted for a moment, looking at the hood of the vehicle. He instinctively tried to figure out how bad of a limp he would have in the morning. But luckily, the snow kept him and the car safe. He stood and followed Daniel as he ran across the parking lot. The heat from the flames transitioned into bitter cold as they proceeded. He found a spot to put her down and stood back up.

"Is she alright?" Lester asked.

"Yeah," Daniel answered as he returned to the burning building.

"Hey, man!" Lester screamed at him. "Where the hell do you think you're going?"

"I have to find Tawnie and Milo!" he screamed. With his supernatural abilities, his body was again covered in a veil of blue light. He jumped into the sky in the blink of an eye. He hovered over the motel at about one-thousand feet. But, in an instant, they shot back down like a comet to the opposite side of the motel.

"What the hell?" Lester asked himself as he watched him disappear. Suddenly, Victoria began to cough, and Lester tended to her.

Meanwhile, on the opposite side of the building, Daniel saw the same devastation there. He didn't even know which direction to look for her room. The collapsed structure made everything a mess. He wondered what he could do as he bit the back of his hand in frustration. He ran to the building, prepared to do something unreasonable. That is until he heard someone call his name. He turned around and saw her standing in the parking lot. Her clothes were torn, and her face was bruised, but she was alone. Daniel looked around on his way to her but didn't see Milo anywhere.

Tawnie had her arms folded across her abdomen. Tears streamed from her eyes, cutting through the soot that settled on her cheeks.

"Tawnie!" He yelled as he approached her. "Where's Milo?" He turned around to look at the burning motel. "Is he in there?"

Tawnie shook her head. "They took him, Daniel!" She cried. "He's gone!"

Daniel's face drooped as he received the news. He felt himself getting ill, imagining how Tawnie was feeling. His mourning was cut short by the sound of police sirens.

Tawnie began to hyperventilate. Daniel looked around, attempting to make a plan to find freedom and regroup. "Tawnie, we have to go!" He said as he reached for her arm. As he tugged on her, she yanked it back.

"The authorities are on their way!" He screamed. "We need to find the France's and get away from here!"

"No!" She screamed back at him. Daniel began to feel the wind circling them. He looked up into the sky, thinking that a blizzard was coming. But the skies were clear. He could even see a full moon high above. He looked at Tawnie again and realized that light filled her coat. She clenched her jaw and exposed her teeth as she looked into the road. They could see the strobe lights of the emergency vehicles approaching.

"I won't leave you here!" Daniel said to her.

"You have to." She calmly replied. "I'm done playing games, and I want this all to end. And it will tonight."

The man went to stand in front of her. "Tawnie, I know you're upset. But please, let's play this the logical way. Nothing will come from you having a stand down with Rexburg's finest. Not like this."

Tawnie appeared to accept his philosophy, and she began to calm herself. Sadness swept over her as her light faded. Tears began to pour again, and she nodded at Daniel as he took her hand. They ran around the motel and found Lester in the parking lot next to Victoria. She was now awake and sitting up.

"Dan!" Lester yelled as they approached.

"Vic, you good to walk?" he asked, crouching beside her to help. The woman nodded, and they got her up to her feet.

"Les, you got the truck keys?" Daniel asked. Lester nodded.

They all walked to the vehicle and helped the lethargic Victoria into the back seat. Lester immediately jumped into the driver's seat. The group paused, and Daniel looked at Lester, then at Victoria.

"What's wrong?" He asked. "We have to go!"

Daniel nodded. "Yeah, we do." He said, emphasizing the word we. The silence became awkward between the group as Daniel looked out at the road.

"Yeah, one of us isn't wanted and could walk away from this." He continued, looking at Lester.

"What?" He snarled at Daniel, jumping out of the vehicle and stepping into his face. "I will not leave my wife! I am with her until the end!"

"Honorable," Daniel said to him. "Les, you saw what she's capable of. She can handle herself. But we need someone to clear our names if something goes wrong here."

Lester's anger increased, ignoring Daniel's reasoning altogether. But Victoria stood from the vehicle and faced him.

"He's right." She confirmed. "All of us don't need to fall if we don't have to."

Lester shook his head, looking his wife in the eyes. Sorrow overtook his spirit as he looked at her.

"We'll see each other once this is over," Victoria promised. "There's no way I can stay away from you."

A tear fell from the man's eyes, and she approached him, arms opened wide for a hug. The man stepped back and looked down at his wife's arms, reluctance etched in his eyes. But after looking at Daniel, Tawnie, and Victoria, he realized they were right. He gave his wife one final embrace and smiled as tears filled their faces.

"I love you so much." She whimpered into his ear.

"I love you too." He muttered. Suddenly, a strike was heard, and Lester felt a burning sensation in his lower abdomen. He stepped back and looked down, first at his blood-covered palm. Then he looked down at his shirt, which was soaked as well. He looked up at his wife and saw his gun in her hand, and the look of her face displayed a pain like he had never seen before. Tawnie stepped around Victoria and approached Daniel. She held out her hand as if she wanted to shake. He looked down at it, confused. But then, he saw a slip of paper in between her index and middle fingers.

"I can't come with you." She said. "Someone has to make sure you get out of here unnoticed."

"What the hell?" Daniel yelled. "They will kill you!"

Tawnie nodded. "They will try, yes." she agreed. "But I need you two to take this paper and follow my instructions! The fate of the world depends on it!"

Daniel sighed, took the slip, and gripped it tight. He allowed his guard to fall and stepped back toward the vehicle's driver door. But Tawnie ran back to him and embraced him. Victoria stepped back, hyperventilating as she slid the gun into her coat. She locked eyes with Lester as he dropped to a knee, struggling to stay up.

"I'll do my part. But now it's time for you two to do yours." She said. The man nodded, and she let go of him. She marched toward the front of the parking lot. Daniel drove away, leaving her and Lester behind. Tawnie waved a hand by her side, and white sparks flickered as the army of police showed up in the parking lot. Even above, helicopters scoured the skies, searching for people on the ground. Police cars and fire trucks entered one end of the parking lot while Daniel exited another. Tawnie stood her ground as they recognized her. Immediately, they poured out of their vehicles and pointed their guns. The helicopter above shined a spotlight on her and Lester. He shielded his eyes the best he could while attempting to keep his hands in plain sight.

Tawnie, however, stood there watching the men and cars as they filed in, one by one. Daniel and Victoria watched from the main road as they drove away from the scene. The two of them could see Tawnie and Lester under the bright, cool light of the helicopter above.

"Put your hands up, Tawnie Simms!" Someone said over a megaphone. "You are under arrest." She held her hands out to her side. Slowly, they began to glow, startling the officers. With that, the gunfire started. Approximately seventeen police officers were filling Tawnie with bullets.

As soon as Daniel heard the first shot, he looked away, unable to keep watching. Victoria cried out for her husband as the bullets sprayed across the parking lot. Slowly, Tawnie fell to the cold, snow-covered pavement. Gordon sped away to keep from being caught.

The line between good and evil will wash away with every challenge presented.

Humanity is full of curiosity, which will ultimately cause a collapse in perspective.
-Excerpt of the Arcanin Prophecy; Translated by the Oracle

Chapter XLV

The night was eerily quiet. Daniel parked in an inconspicuous location away from any eyes or ears. He stared at the slip of paper that Tawnie handed him, reading it with dread.

"What the hell do you think we'll find once we get there?" Victoria asked.

Daniel shook his head and shrugged. "Hell if I know." He answered before laying the paper in the center console. He leaned back in his seat and sighed.

"What the hell is all of this?" She asked him as she leaned on the door, staring out the window. "How is any of this even real?"

She reached up to her neck and wrapped her fingers around a small gold cross that dangled from a thin chain. Daniel turned to her and saw her hand caressing it.

"For as long as I've known you, you've had that necklace," Daniel announced. "Every time you run into a challenge, you fidget with it. What's the story?"

Victoria looked down at it and sighed deeply.

"My family was strong believers in the word," she said. "Every week as a child, I attended church with my family and celebrated life afterward. It reminds me of a simpler time when everything seemed so easy. Before I saw the dangers of the world." The woman had gotten quiet for a moment and adjusted in her seat.

"My father gave me this necklace at my quinceanera. He told me always to remember that Jesus struggled for us all to be here. And if I remember his struggle, I should never complain about my life."

Daniel grunted. "Didn't realize you had Hispanic roots, Bartell."

"Dad was from Spain, and mom was Italian." She said. "I used her last name when I enlisted because it sounded cooler."

"What happened to your old man?" Daniel asked.

"He died in World War III." She answered.

Daniel shook his head in regret. "Damn, you had to be young then." He guessed.

Victoria shook her head. "Yeah, I was sixteen when the war started." She confirmed. "My old man deployed to sea on an American battleship, and it never returned."

"I'm sorry to hear that. Vic." Daniel said as he tapped her thigh with the back of his **hand.**

"Sixteen years ago now." She said as she gave a blank stare ahead. "But even the results of that war keep me up at night. All those ships and planes gone missing in the middle of the ocean. So many people, gone."

When she said that, he could see that her grip on the cross had gotten tighter. Her eyebrows sharpened as if she was dealing with an internal conflict.

"It's like all the things I've learned about my faith are wavering." She stated. "People with divine powers and people playing god to Tawnie, who seems to be some sort of time traveler."

Gordon snapped his attention back to her. "Time traveler?"

Victoria released a long, choppy sigh. "Yeah, the only way to describe any of this is that she jumped through time," Victoria suggested. "She didn't find writings from an ancient civilization. The only way for this to be logical would be that she was actually there. How else could a girl we met eight years ago look like she hadn't even aged a day since Riyadh."

Gordon's eyes grew large, and he shook his head in a mixture of disagreement and disbelief.

"Look, as far as your faith is concerned, I'm pretty sure there's some fucked up, man-made reason behind all of this shit." He assured her. "Right now, it seems like we are dealing with a backhanded human error that caused a disease meant for use as a weapon."

Victoria turned to look at her former First Sergeant. "Do you think man is truly capable of doing such a thing?"

Daniel looked forward and gritted his teeth.

"Hmph." He grunted. "I came from a hard world when I enlisted all those years ago. I was trying to get away from it all and start over. Because I know that man is certainly capable of it. And that's just the darkness that we can imagine. There's far more chaos in the world we don't know about."

The car fell into a heavy silence as they both waited for the other to break it. They sat still, yearning for some comforting words to alleviate the pain. Abruptly, Victoria's grief overflowed, and she began to sob. Daniel, choosing not to pry, looked at the slip of paper again. He nodded and decided to trust Tawnie's intentions as he started the vehicle and began to drive.

On the way to the destination, the two started recognizing the signs of the siege in Rexburg. Only this time, like in Idaho Falls, the presence of the unknown soldiers was much less hostile. It appeared they were all on standby, waiting for an order. Eventually, they pulled up at an intersection where a black SUV with dark, tinted windows sat. The traffic light turned red, and the man stopped as usual. The SUV was to the leg of the street spanning to the right, and its lights were off. Something about it seemed suspicious and out of character.

Daniel stared at the vehicle the entire time, caution written in his eyes. Victoria noticed the stare and became intrigued.

"Is that one of the soldiers?" She asked. He nodded slowly, not removing his eyes from the vehicle. The two of them looked around and noticed a few other cars out.

"This could get wild," Gordon said as he turned to look into the back seat for the radio that Tawnie had. Immediately, he turned it on.

"If we're caught, then they'll speak on it." He said.

The two watched the vehicle as they waited for the light in front of them to turn green. Before it did, the SUV turned on. Its headlights shifted from side to side as they connected with the car's steering wheel.

"I'll be damned," Daniel said as the traffic light switched. He tapped on the gas lightly so as not to seem suspicious. Their vehicle rolled through the four-way intersection and onto the opposite side. Victoria turned her head to look at Gordon as they passed the other vehicle's headlights. It pulled away from its spot and headed down the road behind them.

"Shit!" Daniel growled.

"That's not good," Victoria added. "Do we try to outrun them?"

Gordon shook his head. "I'm not sure." He admitted. "Maybe."

He drove silently for a moment, watching the SUV's headlights in the rearview mirror. His hand slowly moved to the gear shifter. He put the vehicle in sport mode to drop gears and give the engine more power. Victoria lowered her head to look at the car behind them through the side mirrors.

"Does it look like he's following us?" She asked. "I can't tell."

"I'm not sure," Daniel responded as he handed off the radio to the woman. She switched through the various channels without finding any signals. But not before remembering how Tawnie had found the right one earlier.

"I'm not sure I'll be able to find the right station." She said as she dropped the radio in the door pocket. She turned around to look out the vehicle's rear window and assess how far the other vehicle was. It was approximately three car lengths behind.

"It looks like it's getting further away," she announced. Then, the vehicle activated its left turn signal.

"Oh, thank God!" Victoria sighed. "They're turning!"

Gordon shook his head and continued to pick up the speed. Moments later, they arrived in a neighborhood on the west side of town.

"This address is not far from our house," Victoria announced as they crept through the street on the paper. "This street is actually new."

"Yeah," Daniel replied. "I can tell."

The two of them looked for the address with squinted eyes. They hoped to get a glimpse of the addresses through the shadows of the night.

"There it is!" Victoria cheered. "81293 Brightstar Road."

Gordon nodded as he drove past the house first, looking around for anything out of the ordinary. The vehicles on the road looked normal, and people were hanging out a few houses down. It appeared to be a group of teens. Gordon deduced that they were high school students, at least. He drove to the next intersection and made a U-turn. He pulled up across the road from the house and looked at Victoria. She nodded, and the two of them jumped out and headed across. Both of them looked around for anything out of order. The house was a typical rancher. The lawn seemed overgrown compared to the other houses. There was no car in the driveway, and the mailbox was overstuffed. A small porch sat atop two steps, and the light was on by the door. They noticed a key box affixed to the front door.

"Shit," Gordon said in the vain of discovery as he pulled the slip of paper out again. "Here goes nothing." He said as he began to sift through the numbers on the box. Once the combination matched that on the paper, he pushed the switch. The lockbox opened, revealing a key. Assuming it was for the house's front door, Daniel took no time to insert it into the lock. To no surprise, it opened. He looked back at Victoria, and the woman pulled out her gun. He followed suit and pushed the door open. He pulled out a flashlight and shined it through the house. It was basic. The furniture setup was minimal, and one could argue that the house had squatters at some point. The living room area had a single couch and two end tables in the center. The kitchen area to the rear had almost nothing besides a stove, fridge, and island with nothing on top. The house was dead silent. The two of them split, looking around for hostiles. They were careful not to shine their flashlights at the windows. They quickly determined that the small house had been empty for quite some time.

"Clear.", they both expressed, retreating to the living room area.

"Why did she send us here?" Victoria asked as she looked around.

"I'm not sure," Daniel said as he did the same. "If I had to guess, it was just a rendezvous point after splitting up."

Victoria sighed. "Well, I doubt we'll be rendezvousing with Tawnie after that. Gordon stopped and took a hard swallow. His eyes locked on a single point as his mind drifted.

"I'm sorry," Victoria said as she walked into the living room, seeing a stack of paperwork on one of the end tables.

"I can tell you had feelings for her, Top." She continued. "I just wish I got to you in time to tell you it was a bad idea."

The man nodded as he leaned against the kitchen island. He sighed as he pictured the dozens of bullets being shot at Tawnie.

"I should have done something, Vic." He said.

The woman stopped shuffling through the papers to look back at him. A single tear fell from her eye. "A soldier must stay focused on the mission." She said.

Daniel grunted as Victoria continued to shuffle through the various papers. It was evident that someone visited to tend to things. She sorted and rearranged the mail and found something bone-chilling.

"Holy shit!" She barked as she held up a tri-folded piece of paper.

"What is it?" He asked as he walked out of the kitchen.

Victoria met him halfway, eager to hand off what she found. But when his eyes saw it, his jaw dropped. It was a funeral program—an older woman with curly hair and glasses in the photo.

"In loving memory." He read. "Our beloved, Tawnie Everwood, September 21, 2028 to December 7, 2073."

Chapter XLVI

"No." Daniel calmly said. "I can't do this right now."

He walked back into the kitchen and leaned against the island. He was cautious of applying weight due to how much it moved. Victoria followed, still examining the funeral program.

"I'm sorry, Top." She replied as she tossed the folded infographic on the counter before him. "But I don't think we could ignore this now."

The man silently shook his head. Victoria pulled back and opened the pamphlet.

"I want to know how this even makes sense." She continued.

"Maybe it's her mother," Daniel suggested. The woman stared at him, her mouth twisted and eyebrows lowered.

"I can't draw myself up to believe that…" He began to say but stopped.

"Believe what?" Victoria asked. "Believe that the woman who changed our lives in the worst way may not be who she claims?!"

"Maybe she's like a junior or something." He pressed, desperate for a logical explanation that wasn't the worst-case scenario. Victoria squinted, and her mouth opened in a fit of confusion.

"God damn Junior." She grunted before slamming the paper down on the counter again. "Gordon, the damn thing says she had no other surviving family!"

Daniel stopped momentarily, waving his hands at the relentless Victoria in defeat. He stretched his arms over the edge of the countertop and lowered his head. Victoria waited for him to conclude his episode. The light from her phone shone on the tile floor underneath their feet. Daniel took a deep, healing breath as he attempted to mourn the loss of Tawnie. He looked away and noticed something unusual about the kitchen island. The tile was scuffed along the entire length of what he could see in the dark.

"What the hell?" He asked as he popped up and activated his flashlight. He kneeled, shining the light at the toe of the cabinet where it met the floor.

"I wonder what this is all about." He said as he seemed to crab-walk the entire length around the cabinet. Victoria watched him with slanted eyes, wondering if the man had lost his mind. He stood upright, grabbed the counter's edge, and attempted to push it. Again, the island rocked but didn't move. He walked around it some more, still examining.

"Are we looking for cooking utensils?" Victoria asked.

But he ignored her as he proceeded to open every cabinet underneath.

"Alright, let's get out of here," Victoria said as she walked toward the exit.

"Wait, I found something," Daniel announced. Victoria rolled her eyes and walked back. She pointed her light into the opening. Sure enough, a control panel was tucked underneath a piece of plywood. It was designed to blend in with the floor of the space.

"I'll be damned." She said again as she stared at it. A metal box with a small LCD screen and a keypad. Above the screen were three lights—one illuminated red, signifying that the box was locked.

"It needs an access code, four digits," Daniel announced as he looked up at Victoria.

Immediately, she shook her head. "Don't look at me!"

Daniel grunted. "It would be a date that means a lot to Tawnie."

Victoria paused, ridding her mind of all the sarcasm she could apply to this moment. Then, she had an epiphany. She looked at the dates on the funeral program in her hand and called out. "1207."

Without hesitation, Daniel hit the numbers on the keypad. The light above the screen briefly switched to yellow, then to green. The floor began to vibrate, and the entire island began to slide.

Gordon and Victoria looked at one another in awe as a secret staircase was revealed. Victoria shook her head, annoyed at the impending adventure.

"How'd you guess that?" Daniel asked.

"The way the funeral program was left, to the slip of paper with the encrypted data, I'm seeing a pattern with Tawnie," Victoria answered as she stepped around the opening on the floor to shine her flashlight inside.

"I hope I'm wrong."

Daniel stood to descend the stairs. Victoria raised her hand to stop him.

"What the hell are you doing?" She asked.

He looked around momentarily, then pointed to the hole. "We have to see what's down there. If I know Tawnie, there's probably something we could use here."

"Last time I went into a hole with you, I ended up with powers I didn't want!"

Daniel nodded at the statement. "Well, whether you go down or stay up, the trouble's the same."

He casually moved her aside and descended the stairs. At the bottom was a single door. Gordon reached for the knob, hoping it was unlocked. To his surprise, it was. He stepped inside, and a light switched on automatically. It was a small room, the size of a medium storage unit. Two large foot lockers and some black utility cases were stacked in the far corner. A large steel table stood next to the cargo with a laptop on top and a scattered mess of papers. On the wall to the left hung a giant corkboard. It was filled with various clippings from newspapers, magazines, and sticky notes. In Addition, a dozen lines of red yarn connected images to different sources. But in the center, where all the string inevitably pointed to, sat a picture of Tawnie's son, Milo. One more piece of string came from his picture and traveled to another space with only a question mark.

"Damn! Combat Barbie knows how to get down and dirty for an investigation, huh?" Victoria said. But Gordon didn't respond. He approached the board and began to follow the thread.

Victoria stepped to the back of the room and activated the computer. The laptop booted and immediately opened a sign-in screen. Luckily, it didn't need a PIN or password. Victoria signed in and began clicking on the tiles and folders to see if she could find anything. Finally, after staring at the board momentarily, Daniel understood her investigation.

"Vickie, come look at this for a minute." He requested.

The woman did as she was asked and stood beside him.

Gordon nodded as he stepped forward and placed his finger on his picture.

"Back in Idaho Falls, Tawnie expressed to me that the soldiers were after her and her son." He said. "Then I wondered why armed men in high-tech gas masks would want a five-year-old."

"Yeah, in addition to the surviving members of the 316th," Victoria added. "It was obvious that they wanted to keep what they found on that mission a secret. But what does that have to do with a kid born two years after?"

Gordon took a hard swallow. "It's obvious that those of us who survived ended up with some sort of supernatural ability. What if Tawnie passed hers on?"

Victoria's eyes narrowed, and her lips pursed. "You mean, what if Milo has powers too?"

He nodded. "There would be random, unexplained moments where temperatures would rise drastically. I thought I was just standing near something hot. But I never allowed myself to see it until now."

He went silent as he stared distantly at the board again. Victoria cleared her throat.

"I only felt that heat when Milo was upset." He nodded. "Now I'm wondering how upset he must have been to cause the explosion that took out half of Idaho Falls."

Victoria shook her head, unable to believe what Daniel accused Milo of. "That doesn't seem a bit over the top to you?"

He nodded. "Yeah, but an attack on such a large scale would cause some radioactive side effects, wouldn't it?"

Victoria paused for a moment, staring at the man in disbelief.

"Yeah. It'll be like Massachusetts all over again." She added.

Gordon shook his head again. "This whole time, I figured we were looking at this calm kid." He growled. "For fuck's sake, no five-year-old is that calm."

The man stepped away from the board and walked to the back of the room where the luggage and foot lockers were. He popped the lock on the top box and flipped the cover open. Inside, he found a lot of survival supplies: canned goods, bottled water, and batteries. It was as if Tawnie had been planning for the end of the world all along. But another thing he noticed was multiple medicine bottles.

"I knew it." He said as he picked one up and read the label.

Victoria grew curious and approached him. "What is that?"

"A prescription for Tyranizine for Tawnie Simms." He said, shaking his head.

"Yeah, I think that solves the calm kid mystery," Victoria said as she returned to the board. "I keep finding reasons not to like this bitch."

Gordon's head fell. "Why didn't I see this sooner?"

Victoria turned to look at him, noticing his head was hung low. She walked back to him and placed a hand on his shoulder.

"This is not your fault, Top." She assured him. "It's hers."

Daniel exploded with rage and spun around to face her. Victoria jumped away, expecting him to strike.

"Watch your fucking tone!" He roared. Victoria's rocky demeanor faded, and she took a hard swallow as she began to worry.

"Okay, yeah." She said as she stared at him. Her hands were in the position to fight, but he seemed to be calming down. "Sorry, I didn't realize how serious this was to you."

Daniel collapsed backward and sat against the steel table. He stared at the medicine bottle for a moment, then proceeded to clamp down his fist. The bottle crackled before shattering in his palm. The top flew across the room, shooting past Victoria like a bullet. She sighed, watching a man she greatly respected as he lost his confidence and dignity. She was hurt as well. In hindsight, this momentary lapse in action would cause her to think about her husband. The man she shot in the abdomen before leaving him. She pictured the scene. He was near Tawnie's feet when the police started to gun her down. He could still be alive, she thought. But at this point, it almost felt like wishful thinking.

Victoria walked to the table as well and slowly sat next to him.

"Daniel," She called. The man looked at her. The two of them stared at one another in silence. "I don't want to die."

Daniel bit his bottom lip and turned forward, looking toward the opposite end of the room. He put his arm around the woman and pulled her tightly toward him.

"Don't forget who the fuck we are." He grumbled in her ear. His words, the bass in his voice, seemingly soothed her spirit. He stood back up and looked down at his hands. They began to glow blue.

"316th, we don't give up; we boss up," he said before walking toward the steps.

Victoria stood as well, red energy glowing around her. She looked at her hands as well. She could see the power coursing through her veins and fingertips. "Boss shit." She said as she headed for the stairs.

Chapter XLVII

In a hospital across town, multiple police officers stood in a patient's room. The man was in and out of consciousness, attempting to listen to the conversations around him. At first, it was hard to understand. His hearing would slowly become possible as the patient awakened. However, he kept his eyes closed. He attempted to move his hands and feet but immediately realized that he was shackled.

"I can't believe he made it through that." One officer exclaimed. "How many bullets and from where?"

"Two from his abdomen, one in the thigh, and one in the collar." The medical staff answered. "We were able to quell the bleeding for the moment. However, he's not out of the fire yet."

The man can hear the officers' radios periodically coming to life as dispatch calls out. There was a lot more chatter than the usual Thursday night madness.

They continued talking to one another about him, about what just happened.

"We obviously arrest him, right?" An officer asked.

"We have to be cautious there." Another officer answered. "We technically don't have anything to book him on."

The room went quiet, only the sound of heart rate monitors and CB radios.

"Alright, let's wake him up." An officer broke the silence.

"Alright, wait!" another man stopped him. This man's ghastly voice seemed whiney. "We need to get our story straight."

Another man's mouth clicked in annoyance. "Let's not waste any energy believing we did anything wrong." This man had a deep voice and a thick, southern accent. "I ain't taking the fall for no secret ranks coming through here and stirring trouble."

"We put a man in the hospital!" The whiney officer continued. "He could press charges."

"Alright." The countryman answered. Followed by another stint of silence as if he was considering his words.

"Alright, get him out of here, boys." He finally ordered the whiney officer to be escorted out.

"Come on, Finch." An officer said to the whiney man. "Let's get you some coffee, you look tired. The door opened and closed shortly afterward.

"Great," The southern man said. "Wake him up."

A hand firmly gripped the patient's shoulder.

"Hey, France, wake up, bud." One state trooper said as he shook Lester's limp body.

He didn't open his eyes right away. A few of the officers sighed loudly and shook their heads.

"France, are you with us?" The trooper asked again.

"Wait, sir!" A woman said as she entered the room. "It may be best if we allowed this patient to rest."

The nurse and the trooper proceeded to argue about Lester's well-being. Their agendas clash at the moment. Another officer placed his hand on the thick, bandaged area at Lester's collar and pressed it. With the pain jutting through his entire body, he attempted to hold his reaction. But it was far too intense for him to stay silent.

"Ma'am, this patient is a person of interest in a crime from last night." The state trooper at the door told the nurse. "He's in good hands with us now that he's all patched up."

The nurse backed away from the man. "Yeah, okay." She said as she cautiously left the room. Again, Lester attempted to move, hoping he had a better chance to do so now that he was awake. But still, it was no good. He looked around the room to get a head count. There were five other people with him. All of them stared down at him like he was a mere criminal.

"Try to relax a bit, France." The Trooper advised. "You were involved in an incident, and we just have a few questions.

Lester growled, rolling his eyes at the men. "Fellas, after the night I had, I'm not in the mood to be interrogated."

The trooper standing next to the bed smirked at another across the room. He then gave a nod that made Lester suspicious.

"I completely understand, Mr. France–"

"Cut the shit, Balvin." He interrupted the trooper. "What the hell do you need to know, man?"

Balvin seemed to get annoyed by Lester's attitude. His face turned red, and his fists clenched.

"Mr. France, as I stated before, you are a person of interest in the bombing at the Star Motel. Eyewitnesses from the scene say they saw you, your wife, and two others having a standoff in the parking lot."

Lester shrugged his shoulders.

"Considering what's going on with your wife right now. It's safe to assume that you are closely connected to what happened to that motel. Hundreds of people died there because of you."

Lester clenched his jaw and looked away. "What the hell do I have to do with that?" He asked. "I was in my room there when the explosion took place. You think I would blow myself up?"

Balvin smirked again.

Lester tried again to pull at the leather straps that bound him. "Can someone please let me out of these restraints? If I am not under arrest, I shouldn't be cuffed."

"Yeah, listen," Balvin said as he stepped away from the bed and pointed for someone to close the door. "I agree with you about the restraints. You are not under arrest yet, but we just need to ensure everyone's safety before we do that."

Lester raised his hand and snarled in protest. "What the hell do you guys want?"

Balvin cleared his throat and stepped back to the bed.

"We want you to tell us how we can find your wife and the others you were spotted with last night."

Lester allowed his head to slam onto the pillow underneath him. He had become silent and ominously calm as he stared at the ceiling. The other officers looked around the room at one another.

"Actually, I have no way of knowing where she is now," Lester answered. "I guess you guys shot me last night too. But the first to put a bullet into me was my own wife. So excuse me if I don't seem to be in a talkative mood right now."

Balvin grinned. "You're right. It's only fair that you'd get some time to recover mentally from what you saw, right?"

"I believe we can let you out of those restraints now." An older man said as he stepped out of the corner.

"Chief," Lester announced as the man stepped to his bedside. "What are you doing here?"

The older man wore a suit and had a head of white hair. His glasses slipped down his nose as they always did.

"I'm here because Officer Balvin tried convincing me that you were a part of this somehow."

Officer Balvin looked at the police chief with a grin on his face. "That won't be happening today, Chief."

The man looked at the state trooper with a grimace. "Excuse me?"

"My boss needs this man for… leverage." He said as he nodded to someone behind him. Suddenly, one of the city officers approached and grabbed the man by the throat.

"Chief!" Lester yelled as he attempted to get up again.

But the other officers held him down. "Let him go!" He screamed. But a pillowcase was balled and stuffed into his mouth to keep him from making too much noise. Lester screamed. Another officer approached the chief with a needle in hand.

"You sure?" He asked Officer Balvin.

"The boss needs what the boss needs." He answered. "And this guy is in the way."

Lester's muffled screams filled the room as the needle was jammed into the police chief's neck. The man made eye contact in his final moment. But Lester would see the life fade from his eyes. His body went limp, and the officer guarding the door knocked on it. It opened, and a man in a white lab coat casually walked in with a clipboard in hand.

"Let's make this quick, doc," Balvin told him. The doctor snapped his attention to the trooper.

"There's no need to be rude, Julio." The doctor said.

Again, Lester roared. The doctor and trooper stared at him for a moment. Their nonchalant expressions made it clear that he was in a precarious situation.

Balvin turned to the doctor. "Don't celebrate yet, my friend. This mission isn't over."

He nodded again, and the surrounding officers began to rotate around the room. One man pulled out a small tank from underneath the bed connected to a small rubber hose and an air mask. He yanked the rolled pillowcase from Lester's mouth and placed the mask on him. He tried to yell for help, but gas filled the mask, making him sleepy. Within seconds, Lester was out cold, and the officers in the room undid his restraints.

"That's it, boys. The hard part is done," Balvin said. "Let's get this man to the boss and take our payday."

The men picked Lester's body up from the bed and placed him in a wheelchair. Another officer grabbed the police chief from the floor and put him on the bed. The doctor grabbed a hospital gown, and the men undressed the chief. Lester was handcuffed to the chair. The elderly man was dressed in a hospital gown and covered as if he were the patient all along.

"Nice doing business with you, Doc," Balvin said as the policemen opened the door and headed out. The doctor nodded at him as they cleared the room. The man then walked to a computer by the door and logged into the hospital database. He pulled Lester's record and completely deleted it from the system. This erased his name as a patient on the digital patient care board on the wall. He quickly pulled up the chief's information. The name was filled in with the nurse from the previous shift.

The doctor returned to the bedside, pulled the stethoscope from his neck, and put the buds in his ear. Suddenly, there was a knock on the door. It was the night nurse.

"Hey, Doctor Hardy!" She said as she entered the room and rubbed in a glob of hand sanitizer she had acquired at the door.

"How is Mister–" She paused to look for his name on the board by the door. "Mister Keller."

The doctor shook his head slowly as he removed his stethoscope and placed it back around his neck. "I'm afraid that Mr. Keller is no longer with us."

Chapter XLVIII

The First Lady of the United States sat alone in a room in the Pentagon. It had been the first time she was out on business without the presence of her husband. Madeline Wesley, a known shark in the business world, was nobody to take lightly. As her reputation would assume, she is relentless in her methods. She was a gorgeous woman. Her eyes were sharp as knives, and her posture was as powerful as an entire army. She sat inside a meeting room in a chair at the head of a table. One leg crossed over the other, and she leaned on the arm of the chair in the opposite direction. People stood outside the office, glass lining the front wall, putting her on full display. But she stared distantly, focused on one spot in particular. Eventually, Holland Grant would arrive in the room. He approached, greeting some of the individuals standing out front.

"Mr. Grant, good morning!" One man said.

"Yeah, good morning, Trent." He replied as he looked into the office. "How long has she been here?"

"About two hours, sir." The man answered.

Holland shook his head as he walked to the door and pushed it open.

"Madame First Lady!" He said with enthusiasm as he stared at the woman upon entering. No matter how much he smiled, she was not reciprocating the sentiment.

"Sit, Holland." She commanded as she sat up straight and pointed to the chair beside her. He paused, swallowing his saliva like he had just gotten in trouble at school. The man sulked over, attempting not to show his fear and frustration. He took his seat and looked at her in silence. He waited for her to speak, but she didn't say a word to him.

"Madame First Lady, I apologize for keeping you waiting," Holland announced.

But the woman held her hand up to him.

"I am here to discuss my husband's future, not your schedule." She replied. "I am under the impression that you know something about all of this you are not telling."

The man leaned back in his seat and clenched his jaw.

"Madame First Lady, I've come across information tying President Wesley to this madness. I plan to hold off until I can give it a full investigation."

She smiled, causing the man to become uneasy. "Holland, where did this evidence come from?"

The man shook his head. "I don't know. But from the looks of it, we received it from–"

He paused, causing the First Lady to side-eye him. "From where, Mr. Grant?"

The man took a hard swallow. "The future."

The woman stood from the chair and momentarily paced around the table. She stepped to the glass at the front of the room and found a switch on the wall. She pressed it, and the glass immediately became opaque. She stood at the wall for a long breath and turned to face him again. She could see the fear in his expression.

"I need a favor, Holland." She said as she stepped back to the table. She sat back down in her chair and crossed her leg again.

"Can I ask you a question before I agree to anything?" He asked. The woman nodded.

"What is your game here?"

The woman leaned away from him and reached up to rub her chin.

"I want to protect this world from the things they could never understand." She answered quickly. "I'm doing what needs to be done to protect what's important."

"And just what is important?" He asked, leaning forward on his elbows.

The woman smiled as she stared into his gray eyes.

"Mr. Grant, trust me, you are not ready for that conversation."

Grant snarled and sat back in his seat. "You gotta work with me, Madame First Lady! Your husband was foretold in a document seemingly from the future! I am stuck between a rock and a hard place. I either indict him for what's happening or get dragged for not doing my job!"

"I know what I'm asking you to do, Mr. Grant." She responded.

Again, he leaned forward. "How could you ask me to participate in perjury to save your husband? I can have you arrested for this. Do you understand that?"

"I am not trying to save my husband, Holland!" She screamed. "I'm trying to save the world! This is bigger than the law right now! Things are happening that could change the course of humanity as we know it!"

Grant threw his hands up and sat back in the chair again.

"I can't." He said. "I won't be a pawn in wrongdoing."

The two went silent. Madeline chuckled and looked away momentarily. She sighed and reached up to flip her long hair out of her face.

"Are you familiar with Tawnie Simms, Director?" She asked.

The man nodded. "I am." He answered as his eyes perked after hearing the name. "What about her?"

"Your source wants you to believe that she and my husband are criminals. But you need to help them before it's too late!"

"What is it you expect me to do, Madeline?" He screamed. "I have men standing outside military-grade borders, trying to get into the state of Idaho as we speak!"

"If you could do your job and figure out who's behind this attack, we may succeed at breaking Idaho out of this mess. If she has to do it, we're all in trouble."

The man's head fell in defeat. He stood up from his chair and walked to the door.

"Director Grant," Madeline called him. He turned to look at her.

"The quicker you find who's truly responsible for Riyadh, the faster we can resolve the Siege. Do what you need to find who's responsible." She announced.

Holland left the room, anger breaming from his eyes.

His men stood guard, waiting for someone to come out. He looked behind him and sighed deeply.

"You alright, Sir?" Trent asked.

Holland looked at the man and nodded slowly.

"It has been brought to my attention that we are required to unveil Protocol 7," he announced. The group nearby paused. Eyebrows began to hike, and eyes grew wide as they all stared at him.

"Mr. Grant, are you sure?" Trent asked.

Grant nodded his head as his eyes shifted to the floor.

Back in Rexburg, a group of men stood in the hospital's morgue. They were engaged in a discussion about the body that was just brought in.

"How many shots did she take?" One man asked.

"Seventy-two to my count." Answered another. "I'm surprised her body isn't more ravaged."

The men walked to the freezer in question, and one doctor unlocked the drawer.

"Let's see it!" another man said as he rubbed his hands with excitement. The slide was pulled, revealing a white sheet cover over the drawer. The men stood aside to allow the tray to extend fully. A few of them were wide-eyed, and their smiles seemed to go from ear to ear. Others held their breath in anticipation. They all watched in anticipation as the cover was pulled back. Immediately, they recognized Tawnie's golden skin. Somehow, bullet casings began to fall to the floor.

The man raised an eyebrow and continued to fold the tarp toward Tawnie's bare breast.

"Did you guys leave the bullets in?" One man asked.

"It isn't our job to do anything about it!" The man closest to the body tray yelled.

"You think?" Said another man. "With everything happening right now, it may actually be our job now."

Just about everyone in the room began to laugh as they dreaded the idea of having to prepare the bodies of the dead.

"But what I called you down here for is this." The man added as he grabbed Tawnie's body by the back of her neck. He raised her until she sat up in a supine position. The markings on her back became visible to everyone in attendance. The other men squinted as they looked at the triangles.

"So what? Tattoos." An older gentleman said as he rolled his eyes.

"Dr. Perlman, I thought the same thing until I took a closer look."

"Dr. Holt, this is ridiculous!" the older man continued. Following the request, he leaned in to look closer at the markings.

"What the hell is this?" He asked.

"That is exactly what I was saying!" Dr. Holt cheered. "It's almost like some sort of implant!"

"A what?" Someone else yelled as many of them walked closer to examine for themselves. But on the front side of the body, her eyes opened. It took the men a few moments to feel the object in her skin and compliment her body. When they finished, Tawnie was laid on her back. Dr. Holt immediately noticed her eyes opening slowly. Instinctively, he ran his hand down her forehead and to the top of her cheeks, closing her eyelids. He continued to put her body back into position to close the drawer, but he was now cautious. Her eyes opened again, and the man paused. He examined her eye, wanting to believe it was just another body. Until the hazel orbs rotated and landed on him. Holt swiftly moved across the room. The other doctors looked at him with immense confusion.

"Holt, what the hell?" Dr. Perlman asked. But Holt didn't answer. While everyone watched him, Tawnie's supposed dead body swung its legs over the edge of the table. The man pointed at the woman. Her petite, tight body stood upright, and the remainder of the bullets fell off of her skin. She was perfectly unscathed. Her skin looked flawless under the glow of the fluorescent lights above.

The others looked back at the locker. Many of the men whaled in horror as they laid eyes on her.

"How?" One doctor screamed.

"I swear she was dead!" Screamed Dr. Holt. Tawnie raised her hand to wipe her hair from her face, and everyone buckled. Screams filled the room, leaving her bewildered at the sight. Tawnie walked across the cold, tile floor as they shuffled around one another to hide.

"Thank you guys for your hospitality." She said as she approached the only exit of the room."I'll be needing my clothes back."

Before reaching it, Tawnie felt that the environment had become cold and dark. She couldn't see out the door as the glass was translucent. She stopped to think about her next move as she stared at the shadow of two soldiers, a pair of silhouettes on the glass. The outline of their gear and weapons making them easy to spot. Tawnie looked back at the morgue. The screaming doctors still shifted around the room to get away from her. The shadows at the door had grown larger. The soldiers were about to enter. The markings on Tawnie's back began to illuminate. The door burst open, and two soldiers entered. They looked around the morgue. Masks still donning their faces. Tawnie had somehow gotten away.

"Where is the asset?" One soldier asked, still looking around.

"She…she…she woke up!" One doctor said.

The soldiers looked at one another and then out into the room.

"After getting hit over 70 times?" One soldier asked. "Bull shit."

The other soldier approached the man and wrapped his large hand around his neck. "You better not be lying to us!"

The man was terrified. His eyes watered, and his face turned red as he cowered underneath his grip.

"I wouldn't lie to you, sir." The doctor said. "She glowed and then vanished.

"Vanished, huh?" One of the goons looked to say to his battle buddy.

"I know, right!" He replied. "These damn Casters are making me sick!" The two men turned to face the door and walked to the threshold. One of them reached for the steel handle and pulled it closed. The doctors all stared in anticipation.

"What the hell are you doing?" Dr. Perlman asked. "We have good people here that need to get out of here!"

The soldier nodded. "Everyone will get out of here soon enough."

The other soldier raised his gun, causing an uproar in the room. As the man pulled the trigger, so did his battle buddy. Blood spilled all over the morgue, and bodies were scattered on the floor.

Chapter XLIX

Milo awakened in a dark, tight space. There was no noise, and he could only hear his breathing and whimpering. The last thing he remembered was being awakened by a loud crash in the motel room and seeing flames. He remembers his mother attempting to fight someone. But he didn't remember seeing who it was. He tried to move his arms and legs, but there was hardly any space. The space was smooth and slick, like glass or plastic. He attempted to knock on it, but his hands couldn't even get a range of motion to make complete contact.

"Mommy!" He screamed. "Help me!"

He began to squirm, hoping to loosen the grip of whatever was holding him. He screamed and howled for help as he tried rocking. There was a slight give. The more he shook, the more confident he became that he could dislodge his confinement. Suddenly, he felt something give away. The container rolled, and Milo was entangled in a gyroscope ride. He tried to roll in the opposite direction, but there was no point. The container slammed against something sturdy. The force, along with the fast-paced rotations, made him ill. He involuntarily tasted the dinner from earlier and tried to calm himself down.

Eventually, he would see the light near his feet shining through what appeared to be a tube. He tried to look down and could barely distinguish someone's silhouette due to his limited head angle. Suddenly, the container was pulled and spun. Milo was now underneath the hands of a group of masked mercenaries himself. Upon further investigation of his surroundings, it appeared he was in the trunk area of an SUV. He screamed and shook inside the tube, hoping for mercy. Or, at the least, a little pity. He could see the soldier's heads and hands moving as they conversed. Milo kept kicking, hoping that they would intervene. But the men continued their conversation.

After a few minutes of being neglected, the boy became angry. Attempting to keep himself calm was no longer working. On the opposite side of the glass, the three soldiers staring at the container were in awe. One soldier held up some sort of digital meter. He looked at it and spun the device to show it to his buddy. Milo was able to view it. The word above the screen read, 'Kaitron Meter'.

"Absolutely wild." One man said. "I can't believe this much power is coming from a child."

"Yeah." His battle buddy agreed as he began to cycle through the device's functions. "If you had told me that a five-year-old took out half of Idaho Falls, I'd call you a Caster."

The three men burst into laughter, causing Milo to get even angrier.

"Let me out!" The boy screeched, but the men continued their merry cackle. Suddenly, the scanner beeped.

"Oh shit!" The soldier breezed with excitement. "I think he's about to do it!"

"Finally!" The other soldier said as he pulled out a smaller tube, just like the one Milo was inside. He took a moment to reach for the top of the containing cylinder that held the boy and screwed the new one in.

"Please, let me out!" Milo roared again, tears filling his eyes. The men stood back, watching the meter device. The number read-out on the screen continued to increase.

"We found the source, boys!" the middle soldier gloated. In full agreement, each man gave the other a high-five in celebration. Suddenly, Milo let out a shriek as flames filled the entire tube.

"Woah!" The man on the left said as he watched the vortex of flames inside.

"So this is a Caster, huh?" The other man asked.

The middle soldier nodded. "Yeah, this kid, though! He has the same energy signature as the artifact."

The other two soldiers looked at him.

"Are there any others?" One asked.

The soldier shook his head. "Nope, just him so far."

"Well, I can see why the boss wanted him so bad then."

The soldier on the other side pulled out his radio.

"Squad 79 to Base! Come in, Base!" he said into the device. "We have the asset and are prepared for extraction.

"Copy that, Squad 79. Your location is synced," a woman replied. "Follow the rendezvous beacon on your scanner."

The man reached for the container and undid the small tube. The flames inside Milo's tube had died down and were somehow transferred into the small tube. It glowed like it was filled with lava.

"Hey, no, wait!" he screamed. But the man took the small tube out of the trunk and slammed the tailgate down. He returned to the SUV's cabin and hopped into the back seat.

"Hey, be extra careful with that!" The driver announced. "You break that tube open, and you'll kill us all!"

"What?" The man asked as he stared at the tube, waiting for an explanation. "Isn't it just fire?"

The driver peeked over his shoulder at the small cylinder. "Nope, that sample is what the boss calls Hellfire."

"Yeah," The front passenger added. "If that tube breaks now, it'll be like Idaho Falls and that motel all over again."

Somehow, Milo heard the statement, and it was then that he realized that he was the problem. The voice was muffled, but the devastating blow hit him as if he had been told directly. His eyes watered as tears welled in his ducts, but they evaporated as fast as they came.

The anger enveloped him, and the flames erupted from his body again. The men all glanced behind them into the glow of the trunk section of the vehicle. The driver repeatedly peeked into the rearview mirror at the glass coffin.

"Is this thing going to hold all of this fire?" The soldier in the back asked.

The driver shrugged and looked into the passenger seat at his battle buddy. The man nodded. "I hope so, kid."

The men went silent, listening to Milo's muffled screams in the back.

"Do you think this is all going to go as planned?" The man in the back asked.

The two men in the front groaned and clicked their mouths.

"Hayes, you ask a lot of goddam questions, man!" The driver said. "Just fucking follow orders and play along!"

The passenger shook his head and grunted loudly. As they rode silently for a moment, the man underneath his air-tight mask would be watching the sky. He knew what would happen next.

"You guys see that?" He asked. The two men looked around but couldn't recognize what he was talking about.

"The sky, straight ahead." He clarified. "Do you see it?"

The two of them looked again, the man in the back having to roll the back window down and look out. They immediately became fixated on a red aurora appearing above the horizon.

"What the hell?" The driver asked.

"Figured you had no clue what was actually happening here." The passenger looked at the driver. "The boss is working on something a lot more efficient. That is why we are here and why he had us kidnap the boy."

They approached the city's edge and neared a country road heading north. The man in the back leaned back in his seat to get comfortable.

"I don't care how he does it!" The driver added. "As long as I get what I agreed on."

"I would love to know what it's like to–"

"What!?" The other man yelled as a flash of light filled one side of the vehicle. A sharp impact pushed the SUV to the left, and all the windows shattered. Shards of glass filled the car as they spun out of control. The wrecked vehicle stopped halfway through a four-way intersection.

"What hit us?" The driver asked as he looked around.

"I don't see nothing?" The man in the back seat yelled.

"Get out, stay low!" The front passenger yelled.

"What the hell hit us?" The driver asked.

They all took cover behind the SUV, looking for anything unusual. It was late, so the majority of the city was sleeping. The roads were clear, and no cars were driving in sight.

"What the hell?" the veteran soldier asked himself as he looked around for a clue. It had become dead silent, and the men grew uncomfortable, not knowing what they were looking for.

"Clear!" The man from the back seat said.

"You idiot!" The driver yelled. "We are not clear! This damn truck ain't attack itself!"

Suddenly, a blue energy beam slammed down on the vehicle's hood. The crash was so ravaging that the rear end of the vehicle popped up and stayed elevated.

"Attack!" The veteran yelled as he began to shoot at the blue beam. His bullets penetrated the light as it returned to the sky. While they were distracted, the men were mauled by a flash of red energy from behind. They managed to turn around to see their inevitable ends. The rays of light shined on their bodies and ripped them apart on contact.

The attacker from the sky came back down and landed in front of the destroyed vehicle. The blue energy faded, leaving Daniel looking out into the distance at the burning red aura in the sky. He turned around and found Victoria standing behind the vehicle, also looking at the sky.

"This has to be the one we're looking for!" Daniel said as he walked around to the hatch of the smashed vehicle. Suddenly, he could see the dull light of a flame inside. Daniel reached for the handle and opened the door, revealing the glass tube in the trunk.

"Jackpot!" He hissed as he laid eyes on the boy in flames. He pulled the cylinder close and undid the latch at the top. Milo looked up at the officer with tear-filled eyes. His flames died down as the top was peeled from the jar, and he squirmed his way out.

"Mr. Daniel!" He exploded with excitement as he hugged the man. Daniel smiled as he looked back at Victoria, holding the communicator radio in her hand. The two nodded at one another as He embraced the kid.

"They took me away from my mommy." He mumbled.

"I know, kid." He said as he took a knee and held the boy at arm's length. "Milo, you know your mother loves you very much, right?"

The boy nodded as he held his tiny hands together.

Momentarily, the officer looked away to keep himself from crying in front of him.

"Look forward to seeing her again. No matter how long it takes or how hard it becomes." The boy grew uncomfortable and looked down at the ground.

"Milo, do you understand?" He asked. The boy nodded.

Daniel stood and peered down the road.

Victoria approached, listening to a radio call to the squad they had just killed. The squad number was 79, the same as the truck's license plate. "What now?" she asked.

"I don't know." He turned to look at the red aura swirling in the distant sky. "But something is telling me to stay away from that."

Chapter L

President Wesley stood in front of the American people in Washington, DC. The podium was bare, with no notes or a speech to read. The microphones in front of him were on. The lights burned his eyes as he attempted to look out at the hundreds of people before him. As his heart rate increased, he took long, deep breaths to relax. He was afraid that people could see how nervous he was. That would, in turn, be a submission of guilt to his current allegations. But a little quote played over in his mind. It got him through each pressing matter and stated, "No matter how good you are, most will only see the bad. When they show you their scars, show them the best support they ever had."

These were words he received from the former president during his inauguration. Wesley pondered his military service during World War III. The American people took every story about then-president Sadie Hahn and judged her. Things that were not her fault fell on her simply because of her title.

In comparison to the present day, the world is much different. People with powers had emerged and changed everything. People wanting power for themselves had changed everything. He wondered what he could say to billions of people watching. They were looking for someone to blame.

Standing on the side stage, Madeline watched the man as he held himself together. Her fingers ached from being crossed, and her knees hurt from consistent prayer. She raised her phone and turned on the screen, hoping to have a missed call. But nothing was there.

"Maddie!" she heard someone aggressively whisper behind

her. She turned around to see the White House Chief of Staff, Henry Waddell. He approached her drenched with sweat, his face so red that he looked like an apple in an expensive suit. Madeline could see the concern in his eyes and grew worried herself.

"Mr. Waddell." She greeted him with a nod.

"What the fuck is he doing?" Henry asked. "I specifically told him not to do this!"

The generous smile the woman once had disappeared.

"The president of the United States has been accused of the unlawful acts that plague the state of Idaho. You want him to stand down?"

"Madeline, I am trying to keep him safe!" Waddell yelled.

"He is on the verge of going to prison for the rest of his life, Henry!"

The man shook his head, veins protruding from his fat neck. "Madeline, with as much as that man knows, he's on the verge of losing his life!"

The two of them looked out onto the stage. The president had already begun his speech.

"Madame First Lady!" Someone else yelled. The two of them turned to see Holland Grant.

"Mr. Grant, now is not a good time!" She yelled.

"I understand," He acknowledged. "But, Ma'am, I just received terrible news about the situation in Idaho."

Madeline looked back at the stage. Her husband was still speaking.

"Why are you telling me this?" She asked.

The man went silent momentarily, staring at her with remorseful eyes. "Ma'am, as you know, Tawnie Simms was in Idaho during the Siege. Her body was just reported dead on arrival at Madison Memorial Hospital."

Madeline paused momentarily, appearing as if she was about to be sick. The man reached for her hand to console her.

"Madame First Lady, I'm so sorry," he continued.

Suddenly, Holland reached for his ear and looked away from her.

"What did you find?" He asked. Madeline looked at Waddell for confirmation. The chief of staff shrugged and shook his head at her. He sighed, let his hand fall, and inconspicuously looked around him.

"Mr. Waddell, did you order the secret service team to leave this venue?" Holland asked. Henry's eyes popped, and his lips pursed as he looked around.

"Wait, what?" He asked.

Holland approached the man and grabbed his collar, pulling him close.

"They answer to you! Who called them off?"

"I didn't give them orders to leave the American President with no defense!" Waddell yelled as he pushed the director. Holland pulled out his gun and prepared to walk out on stage until he saw Madeline already standing on the opposite side of the curtain. Wesley had given them details about his mission in Riyadh. The same mission that seemed to afford him all the negative press he was currently receiving.

"I regret to say that I have been a mere pawn in the power dynamic of the American Government. If I am to fall, then I warn you all to protect yourselves from false information."

Cautiously, Madeline approached the podium, and her husband nodded. Politically, it would be more catastrophic for him to leave in the middle of his speech. But Madeline tugged on his arm with fear written in her eyes. She felt like she could deal with the consequences some other time. She hoped he would get a hint and leave with her, but the man smiled and continued to speak. She attempted to stop him again, this time twirling her hands. He noticed it. But it was far too late to turn back now. The woman's eyes grew large as the crowd began to talk amongst themselves. She attempted to stop her husband, signaling him with her eyes. But after a few seconds, a gunshot was heard. People began to scream as they started to evacuate the building.

Wesley picked himself up from the floor and checked his body for injuries. He rejoiced for a moment after not feeling any pain, but there was blood on his suit. A second shot was heard, and Wesley ducked again. He looked around for Madeline and found her mere feet away on her back. Holland stood over her, returning fire where the gunshots came from. Waddell came out to assist and grabbed hold of the first lady, beginning to drag her by the armpits. Holland ran to the president's side and shielded him as he stumbled behind his wife. A glance at the floor made him feel ill as the maroon pool trailed off behind the curtain.

They made it backstage, and President Wesley immediately went to his wife's side.

"Maddie, no." He whimpered. She tried to speak, but she only coughed up blood.

"Please, don't speak. I'm going to get you help!"

"No need, my love." He heard her voice in his mind. "I know, it's been a while since I used my power, right?"

Madeline smiled as tears rolled down Wesley's face. He grasped her cheeks, using his thumbs to stroke the tears in blood away. He smiled at her as she shook her head, attempting to stall death as long as possible,

"Listen, my love. This is going to sound crazy." She said. "But I need you to trust me."

"Okay, what is it, my dear?" He asked.

"Don't be a hero. I need you to…"

Nate was appalled. He looked down at her with pain in his eyes. He returned to his knees, shaking his head as tears filled his face.

"You can't ask me to do that!"

"You have to let the prophecy unfold... It's the only way."

Madeline took her last breath, and her hands fell to the floor. The last thing she saw was her husband's face going blurry underneath the stage lights. Holland grabbed Nate's shoulder and tugged on him. The president looked at him with blind rage.

"Sir, I can help you with that mission," Holland assured him.

"Protocol 7 has been initiated." The president's eyes grew large, and he looked at his chief of staff as he stood.

"Protocol 7?" Waddell asked. "What is that exactly?"

"We'll fill you in if necessary, Mr. Waddell. But right now, we have to go!" Holland yelled as he tugged on the President's arm.

The three men ran through the backstage area toward the exit, and they could hear commotion from behind them.

"They're chasing us!" Grant announced. Again, he reached for his ear, "Agent Trent, meet me at the extraction point!" Wesley looked back and realized that Waddell was falling behind.

"Henry, let's go!" He demanded.

But the faster they ran, the slower Waddell moved. He turned red and wheezed with every step his fluffy body took.

"Go on without me!" He yelled. "Holland, save the President!"

The men stopped running and turned toward him, unable to carry out the request ethically.

"Henry, I'm not leaving you here!" Wesley yelled. "Come on!"

"No!" Waddell yelled back. There was a loud crash at the end of the hall. The men were getting closer.

"Get him out of here!" Waddell urged again.

Holland took the president and ran to the exit. As they turned one corner, a group of soldiers in black gear came from the auditorium. They were in gas masks and full battle gear. The same organization that had Idaho in a siege. Waddell cowered as they came closer, guns drawn as they surrounded him. A group of men ran through in pursuit of the president, leaving the others with the Chief of Staff. He watched the men with wide eyes, waiting for something to happen. As the hall went silent, he took a deep breath and relaxed. He pulled on his collar as he smirked.

"Good job, boys." He said. "I believe there will be bonuses for all of you in the future."

The back door of the building spilled into an alleyway that led to the street on both ends. But when Holland and the president ran up the alley, they were confronted by more soldiers. They stopped running and put their hands up.

"This is a bit of a problem," Holland said. But the men didn't say anything. They simply held their guns up, pointing at the president.

"What the hell do you guys want?" He roared.

The president clenched his fists and prepared to fight for his life. But her voice was trapped in his mind. "Don't be a hero. Allow the prophecy to unfold."

Wesley nodded as he put his arms down. He looked over to Holland.

"We had a good run, my friend." He said. "At least now, I finally get to spend some quality time with Madeline."

"I'm not ready, man." Holland chuckled.

A statement that made Wesley laugh. "Me neither, man. But in my position, I think I'm too close to this mess to figure out how to resolve it."

The men both sighed.

"Yeah, you'll be alright, Holland." He said as he undid his tie.

"Do what now?" The Homeland Security Director asked. "How can you be so sure?"

"The prophecy said so."

Everything went silent as Wesley stepped forward with his arms out. Without warning, the soldiers began to shoot. Holland was hit a few times and fell to the ground. Nate's body flailed as he was pelted with round after round. His blood splattered all over the alley. Finally, after seconds of gunfire, President Wesley fell backward. His vision blurred as he struggled to take his next breath. He smiled as the goons stepped over his dying body.

"Finish him!" one man growled to another. A pistol was pointed at him.

"Fucking cowards!" President Wesley said to the men before closing his eyes and allowing the final shot to end his suffering.

Chapter LI

Daniel and Victoria looked for anything unusual as they drove through Rexburg. The night was eerie, and fog blanketed the city, making it hard to see. Visibility was down to a few yards, but Daniel was determined to leave. He knew going south was not an option, so he mentally prepared to head north.

In the back seat, Milo screamed and cried like an infant. Daniel, meeting the child a few days ago, had no idea what to say. In reality, he lost his mother, and there was no telling how much he saw while being kidnapped.

"Milo!" Daniel yelled over his obnoxious screaming. To his surprise, the boy slowly ceased the noise.

"Are you aware that you can create fire?" Daniel asked.

He looked at him through the rear view mirror and noticed the painful expression on his face.

"Milo?" He called again. This time, the boy nodded. Victoria looked at Daniel with wide eyes. He gently shook his head, warding her from reacting.

"So we heard your dad is in Yellowstone. We'll head there and take you to him. The boy frowned.

"What's the matter?"

Milo groaned. "I just want my mommy."

Gordon's mouth twisted with discomfort. "Me too, buddy."

Victoria looked at him, seeing the emotional turmoil he was experiencing. His hand gripped the steering wheel so firmly that it seemed to indent where his fingers were. He slumped in the seat while his free hand fidgeted by his face.

"Gordon." She called. He looked at her with a defeated look

that almost killed her. He always knew what to do, but no amount of deployments could prepare them for this situation.

"I need to make sure that Lester is alive before we go anywhere," Victoria announced.

Daniel nodded. "Understood."

Victoria pulled out her cell phone and made a call.

Daniel pulled the car over as the line began to ring. A woman answered.

"Vickie, girl!" The woman whispered. "What the hell did you do?"

Victoria sighed as she listened to the woman scold her.

"Girl, you got my blood pressure up sky-high! These folk got pictures and video of you showing it all on the news right now."

Victoria smiled. "Now you see why I didn't just go to the precinct."

The woman grunted. "What you need, girl? It's probably illegal for me to be on the phone with you now, so hurry it up!"

"Yeah, do you have your computer in front of you?" She asked the woman. "They shot at us last night, and Lester and I got separated."

"Oh my God!" She whaled. "Do you think he's hurt!" Victoria suddenly became choked up. "God, I hope not, Pauline! I won't be able to forgive myself if he is!"

Typing was heard through the phone as the woman did as requested. "Alright, Hon', it looks like Lester was taken into custody by State Trooper Balvin. But oddly, there is no arrest or drop off, only a pickup."

Victoria immediately went into the worst-case scenario. Daniel reached to cuff her hand in his for comfort.

"Now hold on, this ain't right." Pauline continued. "There are some deleted notes in here."

The woman went silent for about ten seconds.

"Yeah, I thought so." She continued. "Vickie, what justifies deleting occurrences for perpetrators taken into police custody."

"Some dirty cop, off-the-books fuckery." Victoria answered. "It's punishable by termination or jail time."

"Mmm-Hmm! Honey, your husband was taken to Madison Memorial Hospital for seven hours before being released by... What the hell?"

Against Victoria's nature, she decided to remain quiet.

"Girl, something is not right here." She said.

"What is it?" Victoria asked.

There were a few clicks, and the woman sighed. "Your husband was taken into custody by Balvin and admitted to the hospital. Seven hours later, his info was removed from the hospital database. It was replaced with Chief Keller, who was pronounced dead this morning at 5:36 AM.

Gordon's eyes grew large as he looked at Victoria.

"Shit, Pauline. I know how close you and Keller were," she said. "I'm so sorry."

They could hear the woman begin to sob over the phone. Victoria helplessly leaned back in the seat and stared at the ceiling.

"Vickie, what the hell is going on!?" She asked.

"Alright, Pauline, I'm still trying to figure it out myself," Victoria answered. "We were accused of everything happening right now because of a mission we went on a few years ago in Saudi Arabia. I'm not complete on the details yet, so I can't give too much right now."

Pauline continued to cry into the phone.

"Hey, Pauline, thank you," Victoria said. "I'm not sure what will happen next. But I suggest you find somewhere safe and lock yourself away until all this is over. It was nice working with you, girl."

The woman went silent for a moment. "You too, Detective."

The call ended, and Victoria looked at Daniel. Her eyes thinned as she contemplated what she had been told.

"We need to go to the hospital," Daniel said.

"I think you read my mind, friend." She said. "I just…"

Daniel's eyes sharpened as well, concerned about what she was about to say."What is it?"

Victoria shook her head as the SUV began to move.

"I just wonder if any of this is related." She said.

Daniel twisted his mouth. "It's not like you to ask stupid questions.

"Daniel, what if I got my husband–" She started to ask.

"Hey!" He yelled to interrupt her. He looked to the back seat to see if Milo had caught on to what she was saying. He was still whimpering to himself. Ironically, Daniel could see the seat underneath him smoking.

"I need the two of you to be more positive!" He yelled. "You!" He addressed Milo, "We are going to find your mom! Victoria, we will find out who took Lester!"

Victoria looked like she was about to speak, but Daniel held up his index finger to interrupt. As he looked up, he saw more red aurora in the sky. At this point, the environment itself began to turn red.

After a few minutes of driving, they arrived at the hospital. Daniel was cautious as he saw dozens of police cars in the parking lot. All of their lights were on as if they were on an active crime scene.

"This isn't good." He said.

"With the Chief dying here recently, I can understand them being here," Vickie said.

"Do you think it'll be this big of a fuss if a man supposedly died after being checked into a hospital? " Daniel asked as he drove into the parking lot. He parked the car and opened the door to get out.

"Alright, guys, I'm going to check this out."

"What do you mean?" Victoria yelled at him. "I need to go in and find out what happened to my husband!"

"Yeah, I got that, Vickie." He said. "But I'm not well known here in Rexburg, especially by the police department."

Victoria bit her bottom lip with regret. She didn't want to admit he was right. So she remained silent as she leaned her elbow against the passenger door, resting her head on her fist.

"There's only a small chance I'm made and arrested." He said. "Stay here and protect Milo."

Daniel found a thick coat that belonged to Lester in the back and a skull cap. He zipped up with little free space inside, and the hat could come down far enough to cover his face. He headed across the parking lot with his hands in his pockets.

Not long after Gordon left the car, he ran into some cops on their way inside. He slowed his pace as they stepped in front of him. They paid him no mind as they rushed past to head inside.

The inside of the hospital was quite busy. People were everywhere. The emergency room was filled, and the hospital staff appeared stressed and overworked. Daniel approached the receptionist's desk and waited in a line of individuals. He took the opportunity to examine the energy in the room. It appeared hostile in a way he couldn't comprehend but also familiar.

People were screaming at one another. The news was on throughout the waiting area. It successfully added America's disasters to this impending doom. His eyes became fixated on the screen, and the longer he watched, the more disastrous it became.

Headline: "President Nathaniel Wesley Assassinated in Washington D.C."

Daniel's heart seemed to skip a beat. He took a few deep breaths, clenched his fists, and proceeded forward like General Wesley taught him long ago.

"Next!" The woman at the receptionist's desk called, snapping Daniel out of his episode. He vigorously shook his head before walking forward.

"Can I help you, Sir?" She asked.

"Yeah, I have a friend who was admitted here this morning, Lester France. Can you possibly tell me what room he's in?"

The woman looked down at the computer on her desk, clicking the mouse around. Daniel patiently waited while trying to keep calm. He looked around the room and saw a group of police officers talking down the hall with a group of hospital staff. His eyes narrowed as he wondered what the conversation was about.

"Sir, Mr. France's last visit to this hospital was years ago for the birth of his child. According to our records, he wasn't here in this hospital recently."

"Daniel's eyes twitched, caught off guard by more of that statement than she realized.

"Alright, can you tell me who the doctor on duty was for Police Chief Keller?"

The woman's eyes shifted to the side as she stared at him suspiciously.

"Uhh." She said. "Let me look into that for a moment."

Gordon continued to look around at the chaos in the room. There was another nurse behind the desk.

"What the hell happened here?" He asked her.

"Uhh. Yeah," She started. "Craziest thing, apparently someone placed in the morgue miraculously woke up!"

Gordon's eyes nearly popped from the sockets.

"What?" He calmly asked. Other people standing in line overheard and joined the conversation.

"Sir, the doctor you are looking for is Dr. Hardy."

Gordon nodded. With a smile, he asked. "Where can I find him now?"

"He's over there." The woman said as she pointed toward the group of police and hospital staff. He looked back at the woman, thanked her, then walked away.

He pulled out his phone and dialed Victoria's number. His eyes locked onto Dr. Hardy.

"Yeah, I found the doctor who had Les," he told her. "I'm going to be here for a while."

Chapter LII

Daniel hung around the hospital, tailing the suspicious doctor. The man spent a lot of time in his office. Gordon couldn't see him but scoped it out long before the doctor arrived. He verified that there were no alternative exits. There was a small seating area down the hall from his door. The former First Sergeant turned the chair to face it so he could watch for his departure. Gordon flipped his arm to view the watch he was wearing. The time was 7:39 AM. He could see a window on the opposite side of the room where he sat and hardly saw any daylight. He deduced that the windows could have been tinted to control the amount of light in the building.

Suddenly, his phone began to ring. It was Victoria. He answered it quickly.

"I was calling to make sure you didn't get caught. It's been a while." She said to him.

"Yeah. I'm waiting for this guy to leave the hospital. It's almost like he's stalling or something."

Victoria cleared her throat. "He probably is. If he's in the hospital, he keeps an alibi."

Daniel spent the next few moments relaying information that he heard over the night. This also included the dead body awakening In the morgue.

"What, wow!" She replied. "Some coincidence."

Gordon reached up and patted his head. "Yeah, tell me about it."

"Daniel, hurry up and snag this doctor," Victoria said. "I'm getting a bad feeling about all of this."

Gordon grunted and hung the phone up. He stood from his seat and headed to the office. Upon arrival, Gordon opened the door and found the man sitting at his desk. He picked his head up and looked with fear in his eyes.

"Who the fuck are you?" He asked as he popped up from his seat. "Are you here to kill me?"

Gordon shook his head. "I'm not. But the people you handed Lester France over to may have a different objective. He went silent for a moment, waiting for something to happen. Gordon stepped into the office and showed his hands before closing the door. The doctor backed himself into the corner of the room. Gordon reached up to remove his hood and reveal his face.

"You're one of the terrorists that the news has been talking about." He whimpered. "What do you want from me?"

Gordon stepped to the chairs that sat in front of his desk. He sat down and casually gestured for the man to sit in his chair, maintaining eye contact the entire time. Slowly, Dr. Hardy made his way to the chair and sat.

"Now, Dr. Hardy, I am under the impression that the RPD brought my friend here for treatment. You allowed them to remove him from the system as they took him away," Daniel said.

"What do you want me to do about it?" Hardy asked.

Gordon smiled begrudgingly. "What do I want you to do… What I want you to do is turn yourself in for aligning yourself with the real terrorists. But I'll take a confession instead."

The man grimaced. "What exactly do you want to know?"

"I couldn't give a shit less what your motives are, and time is ticking," Gordon responded. "Who did you sell Lester to?"

The doctor's eyes grew large. "I can't tell you that."

Gordon threw his hands up and rolled his eyes. "Of course you can't, man. I completely understand." He pulled out his pistol and pointed it at the doctor's face. "I hope you understand that I don't have much to lose if you don't cooperate with me. That means that if you can't give me what I need, I'll be forced to take away your life."

"You won't." He argued.

But Gordon pulled the gun toward him and pulled the slide

back.

"Explanation of your last job or last words." He said as he lowered his head, his eyes becoming sharp as he placed his finger on the trigger.

"Wait!" he yelled. "What if I told you what I knew? Could you promise me protection?" the doctor asked.

Gordon nodded and pulled his gun back. He unlocked the clip and removed the round from the chamber. From the beginning to the end, he maintained eye contact. The doctor watched his handiwork, impressed that he could break the weapon down without looking at it.

"I was approached last week about a plan that needed to take place. It involved some woman named Victoria and a man named Lester." He explained. "No definite plan was created then, but I was told they would contact me when they needed my assistance."

Gordon raised an eyebrow. "Why'd they come to you?"

"I'm not the only one, Mr. Gordon. They have individuals in professions who are able to assist in achieving the big picture. There are millions of us, everyone!"

"Interesting," Daniel added. "Who are they?"

The man went silent and almost seemed to become a vegetable on the spot. He stared blankly past Daniel as he mustered up the courage to answer.

"Based on some of the things I have seen recently, I want to say that these people are using all of you as bait."

Gordon winced. "Bait? Who exactly are they trying to catch?"

The man went silent again but stood from his seat. Uncomfortable with the situation, Gordon watched him closely.

"Mr. Gordon, I want to note that this world is full of darkness that we can't explain."

Daniel raised an eyebrow. "What exactly does that mean?" He asked. "I don't care about your philosophical beliefs right now. Tell me where you sent my friend, and maybe we can both have a good day."

The doctor turned to look at Daniel, his eyes cold and empty as if he was dead. The color of the man's skin faded. He looked past Gordon suddenly, staring at the door. His body began to tremble as if he'd seen something.

"What the fuck is your problem? Answer the damn question,

Hardy!" He yelled as he stood. The officer approached the man, and the two of them went silent. Dr. Hardy raised his hands in submission. Their eyes locked onto one another. But periodically, the man looked past the officer like something was there. Suddenly, Gordon saw a figure move in the reflection of his eyes. He spun around and pointed his gun. But to his surprise, he was still alone with the doctor in the room.

"What the fuck was that?" He asked. But the doctor began to laugh. The laugh started as a silent chuckle but eventually grew into a gut-busting cackle. Daniel looked back at the man and grabbed him by his collar. He threw him to the wall and pointed the gun at him.

"Tell me where he is!" Gordon roared. "Last chance!"

The man stared at the gun, looking down its barrel with a look that resembled fascination. He reached up and grabbed the muzzle of the gun and pulled it closer, lining it between his eyes.

"Your friend was taken so that they could capture her." He said.

Again, Gordon's eyebrow hiked. "Who is her?" He asked.

"The one whose power binds the Gods to their prison."

Gordon paused, tilting his head in pure confusion. "What the hell are you talking about, Gods? You snortin' meds or something, man?"

"I've seen the prophecy, Officer Gordon! Have you?"

Gordon released him and took a step back.

The man followed him, his body hunched like his head was heavy. Daniel watched him closely, expecting the man to hit him.

"Your friend is being held at the temple." Dr. Hardy said. "But even though you took the child from him, you still have much ground to cover before you can claim the victory!"

Gordon shook his head, impatient with the doctor's performance.

"Thank you." He casually said as he put the pistol back into the lining of his jacket. "I won't kill you today, so don't come after me."

"It doesn't matter, Officer Gordon." He snarled. "Because today, the prophecy unfolds."

He stomped toward Daniel again and stared at him, demented and loose.

"No matter how this goes, the woman you know as Tawnie

Simms will be the end of us all!"

Daniel's heart almost stopped, and his breath was cut short.

"Right," He replied before taking a hard swallow. "Do you know who Tawnie Simms really is, Dr. Hardy?"

The man seemed to become even more unhinged as he began to reach for his head as if he were experiencing a migraine.

"I do." He whined. "And because of that, I must die to protect the prophecy!"

Daniel's head snapped to the side. "What did you just say?"

But before he got an answer, Dr. Hardy exploded into a full sprint to the office window.

"No!" Daniel screamed as he ran after him. But he curled his body as he jumped toward the glass, breaking it out completely. Gordon stopped before getting to the window and looked out. Down the seven-story plummet to the ground below, Gordon's eyes gravitated to the body. He was lying in a bed of shrubs and tree branches. It appeared that he hit something on the way down that tore through him entirely. There was no chance of survival. Not many people stood around, but there were enough to see it from the main entrance. Gordon ducked out of the window and took a deep breath.

"You fucking dumbass!" He snarled before throwing his hood and hat back on.

Gordon left the hospital and returned to the SUV with Victoria and Milo. He opened the driver's door, threw himself inside, and shook his head. Victoria looked at him eagerly, hoping he had good news about her husband. He looked down at his watch again, 8:34 AM. He looked up at the sky, which was still darker than usual. The same red tint also got more profound and more vibrant. The environment around the city changed due to the red glare. People outside stared upward and took pictures with their phones. The vehicle was running. He looked at the dashboard at the temperature, 87 degrees Fahrenheit. He looked back at Milo, who had a carefree look. It was happening again, the same as what happened that day in Idaho Falls. Gordon had a bad feeling about what was going to take place.

"What's happening right now?" Victoria asked.

Daniel looked at her in defeat. "I know where Lester is." He answered.

The smile on the woman's face was bright. It had been the first time she had done so in a while. But she could tell there was something else.

"What, bad news?" She asked.

Gordon looked back at Milo again, then back up at the sky. "Someone planned for us to take Milo back and try to rescue Lester."

Victoria grimaced. "What are you saying?"

"Even though we know where Lester is, I feel we'll be walking into a trap."

Chapter LIII

Daniel received somber turn-by-turn directions from Victoria. Minutes after leaving the hospital, they arrived at the Rexburg Temple. It was a white building made of primarily concrete. A sharp steeple sat at the top, which stood higher than many other structures in the area. Daniel drove past the front entrance on the main street. The two of them scanned the building for the mercenaries.

"It's eerily quiet out here," Victoria said.

"Agreed," Gordon replied as he looked around everywhere else.

As they pulled into the parking lot, Victoria looked into the sky. The deep red was now brighter as the sun attempted to shine through an overcast. Everything around them was now shrouded in red light.

"If this is it–"

"Don't you dare!" Daniel cut her off. "With everything we've been through, I refuse to believe this is it!"

Victoria slowly shook her head. "What exactly is our plan, Top?"

He shook his head as well. "I don't know," he answered. We're going into the church; maybe we should ask for a miracle."

She looked at him with her brows slanted deep and her eyes sharp.

"My bad." He said as he turned the vehicle off. "I was trying to bring some light into this. The two of them pulled out their guns and pulled the slides back.

"What do we do with the kid?" Victoria asked.

Daniel looked at him through the rearview mirror. "If they were waiting for us to bring him here, they could be lurking inside to ambush us." He answered.

The woman nodded.

"Alright, Milo. We'll be right back," Victoria said. "Get down on the floor and hide."

The boy unbuckled himself and followed the command.

Gordon and Victoria jumped out of the car and ran to the church. Gordon led the way to the side entrance while Victoria covered the rear. Once he reached the door, he tugged slightly to see if it was unlocked. He looked at Victoria and gave her a nod. She stepped ahead of him and stood to the side with her hand on the door handle. She nodded again when she was ready, and he held his gun before him.

"Go!" Victoria barked as she opened the door. Daniel ran inside and took the left side. Victoria ran in after him and took the right. Confused, they looked at one another when they noticed the empty room.

The sanctuary was simple, with cream-white carpets and rows of folding auditorium chairs. The kind that bolts to the floor. The walls had judge's panels around the room. Four large, cylindrical light fixtures hung from the high ceilings above. This gave plenty of light to the room. The stage area in the front of the room hung a large cross from the ceiling. Gordon and Victoria both gasped when they saw it. Blood dripped down the bottom of it, pooling on the floor underneath. But it wasn't the blood of Christ that dripped to the stage below. It was Lester. He was brutalized and bound to the cross using leather straps.

"Lester!" Victoria ran to him. His eyes were closed. They hoped for the best as they closed in on him. They called his name again as they reached the stage. They looked around for a way to bring the cross down. As they looked for a switch or button, Daniel noticed a faint orange glow coming from the front of the building.

"What the hell is this?" Victoria asked. "Lester, are you okay?" But still, there was no answer. Finally, the source of the glow entered the sanctuary.

"Gordon's eyes popped as he saw a massive man wearing the same black attire as the other soldier. This man was twice Gordon's size and muscular in ways he had never seen before. However, one thing stood out about this individual in particular. He didn't carry a gun like the others. Instead, his hands and forearms were engulfed in flames.

"You have got to be kidding me!" Victoria yelled.

"Break Lester free," Daniel yelled as he kept his eyes on the giant. "I'll hold this guy off."

Daniel could see the man's fists clench tightly, flexing the muscles in his forearms. His veins glowed brighter with each second.

"You can try."

The man walked briskly to Daniel, putting his fists up to prepare for a fight. The heat he emitted was nearly unbearable. Instead of helping Lester, Victoria became distracted by the imminent danger before them. The man swung his fist at Gordon, and the officer ducked. A bright wave of fire swooped over his head. The heat was so intense that it seemed to burn all the oxygen out of the air.

Startled, Victoria continued to untie Lester. Meanwhile, the brute took another swing at Daniel. The large man stepped backward and used the same arm to slash downward at him. He jumped out of the way, the flame grazing the toe of his boots. His feet felt as if he had tried to roast them. He looked down to see the scorched leather at his toes. They were composite toes, so they may have saved his feet. The floor underneath was scorched. The carpet was so singed where he stood that it looked like embers in burning firewood.

Gordon got up and ran through the center of the sanctuary, back toward the entrance. The man held his hands out to his side, then clapped them together in front of him. A large wave of intense flames followed Daniel to the end of the aisle. He ducked behind the last row of chairs and crawled to the outer wall. The brute turned his attention to Victoria on stage. She glanced over her shoulder after releasing one of her husband's hands from the cross. He raised his foot to intervene, but Daniel popped up and shot the goon in the back. The man staggered as if he was immediately affected. But he didn't fall. He only leaned forward slightly and stopped for a moment. Victoria hurried to finish while attempting to wake Lester. The bullet that Daniel shot had fallen to the floor, leaving the giant man unharmed. It only made him angrier.

"What the fuck?" Daniel asked as he looked at the pistol in his hand. He stood from his hiding place and immediately focused on his energy. He looked at where the man was standing and calculated a path to him. The angle was tricky, but doing it wrong could result in the life of his friends. He took the shot, his body curled into a fetal position. A blue streak of energy followed him as he bounced through the sanctuary. He jumped from one side to the other until he reached the front. As he made his last bounce, he found himself on a crash course with the man. Daniel unfurled his body and held his fist forward, still shrouded with blue energy. He landed a punch right in the man's face. The giant fell, and Victoria freed Lester. Daniel headed to the cross to help. The flames on the big brute's arms were still ignited.

"Alright, we have to get out of here!" He yelled as he threw Lester's arm over his shoulder and attempted to carry him to the exit. Victoria looked at the brute lying on the ground. He was already getting up.

They made it halfway up the aisle before he returned to his feet.

"There is no escape!" They heard the man growl behind them.

They glanced over their shoulder, seeing the man get up from the floor.

"I thought that was a good attack," Victoria said.

"Yeah, same," Daniel replied.

Victoria grunted and left Daniel to carry her husband out of the building. The red energy of her powers began to shroud around her body. The brute stepped into the aisle, and Victoria extended her right palm to the seats. The man blasted fire at her. But the chairs she pointed at were ripped from the ground and blocked it. The flames melted the chairs, and Victoria returned the magma residue to him. The woman clenched her hand together, and the magma shrouded his hand. He realized what her plan was and stopped his attack. But it was already too late.

The liquid metal solidified on his hand, blocking his source of power. When he looked down at his hand, chairs hit him from behind. This assault was enough to destroy his mask and knock it off, revealing the man's face. He was a bald, evil-looking man. He had a goatee with a thick mustache and a long beard. His eyes glowed solid red inside his pupils as if flames were lit inside. Victoria spun, sending another chair flying toward his face. The strike connected, making him fall to his back. She ran toward him, holding her palm forward for the cross that Lester was strapped to. It lifted from the stage at a steady rate. But even she was surprised by how heavy it was. With a roar, she hoisted it over his head and prepared to slam the bottom of it into his skull. The man caught it with one hand. Victoria found herself in a test of strength—her powers versus his arms.

Eventually, he would outdo her power, pushing against the force of her energy.

"You think I'd be taken out so easily?" He laughed. Then he pulled the cross, causing Vickie to lose her concentration. Once he felt natural gravity pull the cross down, the man swung it at her. The massive chunk of wood came right at her. She raised her arm and ducked out of the way, but not without being grazed by the wooden block. She screamed as she went down to the floor, feeling a radiating pain in her arm and head. She opened her eyes to see the man, and he was approaching her with the wooden beam still in hand. But this time, he had it draped over his shoulder.

"This will only take a second." The giant growled as he prepared to slam the beam down on her. But Gordon couldn't allow it. Lester's body dropped to the floor as he curled into his ball and slammed into the brute's diaphragm. Out of breath, he stumbled, but Daniel fell before him. Surprisingly, the man regained his composure in under five seconds. He distracted them with a puff of flames that caused Daniel to lose his balance and fall backward. He fell to the floor next to Victoria and looked up to see the wooden beam coming down again. He rolled over and was able to kick Victoria out of the way. They rolled to either side of the aisle, and the wooden cross landed on the floor between them. As thick as the wood was, they were shocked to see it crumble as it slammed against the ground. Both of their eyes wide as they imagined being crushed by it. Daniel stood back up and grabbed Victoria. They inched away from the brute as they tried to reach the entrance. They stood side by side as they observed him. But before the tyrant could prepare another attack, a figure appeared and punched him in the abdomen. The strike seemed so strong that it physically made the air vibrate around them.

With wide eyes, Daniel and Victoria realized who had intervened on their behalf. It was Tawnie.

"What the fuck?" Victoria asked.

Gordon shook his head with disbelief. "Tawnie!?"

She looked back at them and smirked but continued the mission.

"You don't look like you're going to return to your base to deliver a message." She announced.

The man scoffed, holding his gut. "Do I look like a messenger boy?" He asked.

Tawnie shook her head. "No, but I did have a delivery for your boss. A shame he won't know what's coming for him."

Her hand began to glow bright white, and the big brute's free hand also began to glow.

"Well, maybe you should–" He began to say. Instead of finishing his statement, in a ditch effort to catch the woman off guard, he attacked. More chairs wrapped around his hand and melted, just like before. He looked down and took a step back in disbelief. The magma dripping from his arm was then redirected. Victoria sent the compound of melted metals and plastics into the man's nose and mouth. The brute went down, reaching for his face and trying to grab the magma from inside. But he couldn't. Victoria stood over his body as he struggled in his final moments. His eyes widened as he lost oxygen. The more the magma solidified, the slower his movement became. His face began to turn a blueish hue as his body ceased.

Victoria looked at Tawnie with a grin. "Perfect timing." She said.

Tawnie smiled and flipped her hair back out of her face. "You guys didn't really need me."

Daniel approached the man, watching him cool down. He thought of the irony of a volcano cooling after the eruption. He looked at Tawnie with a look of worry and disbelief. He could see a bruise on her face. He approached her and grabbed her for a hug. He squeezed her tight, and she wrapped her arms around his neck.

"How the hell are you alive?" He asked. "We saw you get

gunned down by the police."

Tawnie grinned. "I never stay dead for long. But I don't have time to get into that right now."

Victoria approached them. "Did you get burned?" She asked.

Tawnie reached for her face and rubbed the bruise on her cheek. "I guess so." She answered.

Victoria's eyebrows got sharp. "You can get gunned down and come back to life but also get a rash from a flame? I'm confused."

Tawnie shook her head, worry set in on her face as Daniel held her at arm's length. "It's the Primal Flame from the Pyro Stone. It's the only energy that can harm me." She explained. "I've come to understand that it was used recently to create soldiers who could kill me."

Victoria and Daniel's eyes met one another. They had more questions, but Tawnie broke away from Daniel's grip and walked toward the door.

"Daniel, grab your friend. We have to go," she said before turning around. "The invasion has begun, so we must find somewhere safe to hide."

They all faced the door.

"Milo, come on, sweetie!" Tawnie called. Suddenly, her kid ran from behind the stage and joined them at the door. Daniel's eyes grew wide as he watched him skip to the exit.

"Wait, what?" He said. Finally, the man's eyes met with Tawnie, and she shook her head disappointedly.

"In the car during an evil uprising." She asked.

Gordon pursed his lips as he stared at her, anticipating she would do something to punish him. Instead, Tawnie touched his head and proceeded to the door.

"To our defense, we thought all the bad guys were in here!" Victoria added.

They got outside and immediately saw the bodies of dead soldiers lying on the ground. Daniel was in shock again. The further they stepped toward the parking lot, the more bodies he saw on the ground.

"Wow." Victoria chirped with wide eyes. "We were about to be ambushed and didn't even know it."

Gordon shook his head. "No," He interrupted. "They're all facing the car."

Indeed, every soldier in the parking lot was situated as if they were being stopped from going to their vehicle. Victoria looked around at all the bloodshed and shivered as she realized how dangerous Tawnie truly was.

Tawnie stepped over the piles of bodies to reach it. It was still sitting in its parking space, completely unharmed. Victoria and Daniel looked at each other once more.

"Unbelievable." The two of them said before following them.

Chapter LIV

Daniel was forced to take one detour after another, attempting to drive away from the red aura in the sky. No matter how far or fast he went, he couldn't escape. The streets were filled with empty cars. Vehicles pointing in all different directions lined the exit route, giving a bleak reminder of what was transpiring around them. He immediately thought back on Idaho Falls, but horror swept over Victoria as this was the first time she had witnessed the soldiers' objective. There was not a body to be found. But just like Idaho Falls, stacks of smoke rose from every direction. The foul stench in the air was almost putrid.

Everyone in the vehicle was on high alert except for Lester, who rested in the back seat. Tawnie twiddled her fingers as she looked around at the crumbling order of the environment. Rage filled her eyes as she clenched her jaw, staring out the window. Milo observed his mother with uncertainty. Meanwhile, the two soldiers in the front seat watched for danger. Daniel looked down at the gas indicator and realized that the distance to empty was close. However, stopping wouldn't just remove any time they have, but it wouldn't be safe.

"I don't suppose getting gas is an option right now, huh?" He asked.

Victoria looked at the gas readout from the passenger seat and bit her bottom lip.

"I should've listened to Lester about keeping the tank full."

"It happens," Tawnie said. "There's a grocery store up ahead. Let's try our luck taking shelter there."

Daniel nodded just before seeing the store himself. He pulled into the parking lot with his hand on his pistol, looking out for any threats. He used the opportunity to switch out his half-used clip from earlier and handed it to Victoria. She then opened the glove box and found a case of bullets she used to refill it. Daniel smiled as she handed it back to him.

"Concierge bullet service." He said. "Glad to see that we're always universal."

"I learned from the best, so I meet the best halfway." She responded.

Daniel squinted with a smile. "Wesley trained you."

Her eyes grew large as she looked away, trying to recall the history correctly.

"Oh, yeah." She giggled.

Daniel parked the vehicle in the nearest parking space to the door. His head held low as he thought about what he had seen on the news just the night before. He realized he had left Victoria in the car, and she didn't know. She looked at him and saw the pain in his face.

"Daniel, what's up?" She asked.

The man shook his head, "We gotta survive this y'all!" He smashed his fist against the steering wheel in anger.

Tawnie turned her focus to him as well.

"Danny?" She called him. Suddenly, his body went numb as he let out a roaring sigh.

"Wesley and his wife were found dead last night in Washington DC."

They all went silent. Victoria stared at Daniel, her jaw dropping and tears in her eyes. Tawnie sat quietly, processing the news. But as Daniel turned to see her, the bowls of her eyes were already filled with tears. A dam about to shatter under pressure. Milo rubbed her leg in hopes of consoling his grieving mother. She looked down at him and sobbed.

"We can't allow this to go on any further!" Daniel exclaimed. "Today, we take our last stand! We will no longer be taking this kind of punishment and abuse!"

Tawnie got out of the car and looked up. The red aurora had dissipated enough to make the gray sky appear nearly normal. A dense fog rolled into the city as the heat rose.

"You alright, Tawnie?" Daniel asked as he got out of the

vehicle. She nodded.

"I don't think I realized how attached you were to Wesley." He said.

Tawnie's head fell. "It's Madeline," she replied as she looked away. It's complicated, but she's family."

Daniel tried to step forward for a hug, but she rejected him and assisted Milo out of the vehicle. He clenched his jaw, feeling a burn from her callousness. Victoria was able to awaken Lester. He opened his eyes for the first time since retrieving him. He seemed spacey and lethargic, like he was pumped with medication. His pupils roved lazily around his eyes just before he recognized the people in front of him. They exited the vehicle, grabbed some belongings, and headed for the store.

Tawnie looked around with suspicion.

"What is it?" Daniel asked.

She shook her head, "hundreds of people are inside this building." She announced as she glanced to the end of the parking lot.

"Once we get inside, I'll do my best to make it look empty." Gordon smiled as he approached and touched her back to guide her to the building.

They approached the door to the building. People came out, greeting and urging them to hurry inside. They entered the cart return area inside the main entrance and realized the store was packed. People were sitting inside just beyond the checkout lanes. It appeared they had all been there for a while. Lawn furniture and chairs had been moved from their locations and placed up front.

"Wow!" Daniel said as he looked around the room. "This is disturbing."

Lester began to feel weak, and Victoria rushed him to a bench near the entrance. The constant conversation was passed around the store from group to group.

A man stood by the entrance and silently watched them walk inside.

"Sir, are we good to come in?" Tawnie asked.

He smiled at them, then held a thumb up. "All good folks."

Tawnie smiled and waved at the man. His eyes watched her closely as if he was recalling something.

"Ms. Oracle?" He called out. "Ms. Oracle, what are you doing here?"

Tawnie's eyes grew as she took a deep breath. She turned around to acknowledge the gentleman. However, she inadvertently grabbed the attention of others. People began to stare and come alive upon seeing her face. The conversation shifted with the energy in the room as the crowd slowly formed around her.

"Tawnie?" Daniel called, forcing her to look back and see that people blocked the path behind them.

"Madame Oracle!" A woman shrieked from across the store. This cry startled the tiny woman but made her presence in the establishment obvious. Within seconds of their arrival, Tawnie was already being surrounded. Daniel took Milo's hand and returned to Lester and Victoria's bench. They allowed Tawnie a moment to deal with the crowd. But there was something wrong. The number of people thinned enough for Gordon to see a suspicious group. They stood away from the crowd and watched as about 95% of people crowded the Oracle. One man thumbed his nose in obvious annoyance. His jaw shifted, and his lips parted as he reached for a knife.

"Hey, hold on one second," Daniel said as he tapped Victoria on the shoulder. She nodded at him and then proceeded to tend to her weakened husband. He bent down to get eye-to-eye with Milo. "Stay here, kid," he said before getting up and walking toward the hostile patrons.

As he headed through the store, Daniel noticed a display of rage from a large portion of the crowd.

The group consisted of about four large men and a few women. They were only average citizens.

"How's it going over here, folks," Gordon asked as he jumped into the conversation. "My name is Daniel. What got you guys all worked up right now?"

As they turned their attention to him, he saw a hunting knife in the furthest man's hand. He hurried to hide it behind him, but it was too late.

They all turned to him and stared without saying a word.

"Pretty cool we have a celebrity here with us, huh?" He asked. "Someone with influence is bound to help make all this right."

One man scoffed. "Hell, all this is happening is because of

her!" The other people audibly agreed with him.

"I don't understand," Gordon replied, leaning back and placing his hands in his pockets.

"She just some disgruntled government worker that got her hands on some secrets." He yelled. "That's how she knows about stuff before it happens!" Again, the group around them cheered and nodded in agreement. "Now she got us all roped into this madness because the government thinks we all agree with her!" A woman chimed in.

Daniel nodded and crossed his arms. A look of pure confusion graced his face.

"Give me the punchline." He ordered. "Clearly, you are not saying that the government is exterminating Idaho because of social media videos."

The group began to talk again, this time to one another, almost icing Daniel out of the conversation.

"Alright, listen!" he barked. "I'm going to clarify some things for you folks you may not know. But the people attacking us, this city is not the government."

The anger faded from their faces and turned quickly into concern.

"Why are you telling us this, Man?" A guy asked.

"Because, from me to you, my friend," Daniel said as he got close. "You don't want to go head to head with her."

The people went silent and stared at him.

"Will, ya look at that." One of the men said as he approached him. "Little Oracle got herself a bodyguard."

Daniel smiled and let his eyes fall to the floor. He pressed his palms together in front of his mouth for a moment.

"Look here," He said to the man, pointing his hand into his chest. "She's our bodyguard, and if the people here are going to survive this, we need her. Now would be a horrible time to cause her to lose focus. Your life depends on it."

The man went silent and stepped back. He nodded as he stared deep into Gordon's eyes. The officer looked around at all of them before walking away. When he returned to the bench, he patted Milo on his head.

"Who are those guys?" Lester asked in a breathy tone.

"Some losers who are surely going to try and take Tawnie,"

Daniel answered. "I'm trying to figure out if I need to defend her or advocate for their ignorance when they do something stupid."

"Good point." Victoria nodded. "After what we saw earlier, God bless the next man that challenges her."

Tawnie found herself amid the crowd, shaking hands, signing autographs, and doing her best to answer questions. Victoria observed her moving through the crowd with confidence. But she could also see a glimpse of overwhelming anxiety. She shook hands with people, smiled, and laughed with them. But in between conversations, her eyes showed a brief sense of worry. Over and over, she'd try to get out of the crowd, but they were persistent. Victoria found it intriguing as she began to gain a new level of respect for the woman. After entertaining everyone in the store, she jumped on top of one of the checkout counters. Everyone calmed as they watched her.

"Ladies and gentlemen!" She addressed everyone. "I am so sorry we all had to meet this way, but we can do nothing about it now. Outside, our homes are being ravaged, and our people are being slaughtered. My home, Idaho Falls, suffered the same fate a few days ago, and the death toll there is around 98% of the population."

Everyone gasped and began sidebar conversations as she tried to continue. "Folks, despite the nature of my profession, I have no clue why this is happening. All I can offer now are speculations, and I don't do those; I only deal with absolutes. And there's one thing I'm sure of: they will come for us too. I will bleed for this country and hold to what's right. We are backed into a corner right now, and that's not our fault, but I will not die without a fight!"

The crowd cheered her on as she jumped from the counter and returned to the bench where the others sat. Daniel's face said a lot. His eyes were wide, and his mouth was opened slightly.

"You just promised to keep all these people alive," Daniel said. "Why would you promise something like that?"

Tawnie looked at him and raised her chin with confidence. "Because, for the first time in my life, I am done running from who I'm supposed to be."

Daniel looked at Victoria, who was also confused. "And who is that?" She asked.

"I guess we'll all find out together, won't we."

Chapter LV

Tawnie had excused herself from the crowd at the front of the store and slipped away to clear her thoughts. She left Milo with Lester, Daniel, and Victoria. The officers seemed unqualified for the task, but the boy appeared at ease. That was enough to comfort them. They sat next to a couple with two kids, a girl and a boy. Milo played with their children while the adults chatted about current events.

Lyric, the couple's daughter, took all of Milo's attention. She was a few years older than him, slightly taller, with long, black, silky hair that flowed down her back. Her brother was a little younger than him and had hair that looked similar. The three of them ran around and allowed the adults to talk.

"Your kids are adorable, Dina," Victoria said. The woman smiled and thanked her. She looked like an older version of her daughter. The resemblance was so remarkable that Lester and Daniel couldn't help but compare. Her husband, Pablo, watched the kids closely, ensuring they would not get into trouble.

"Lyric has always been a good role model for her brother!" her mother said. "PJ, on the other hand…" She looked at her husband with a sly grin. He made eye contact with her and proceeded to laugh out loud.

"So, do you two have any kids?" Pablo asked Lester and Victoria. The two of them paused before answering.

"No." Victoria sternly responded.

Daniel looked at her with thin eyes. She glanced over at him and looked away quickly after brief eye contact.

The man shook his head and stood up.

"Milo, I'll be right back," he said before stepping away. The kid nodded and then continued to play with Lyric and Pablo Jr.

Everyone seemed relaxed. The majority of patrons all sat around talking about various things. Most waited with their phones glued to their faces. It then occurred to the officer that the people were all waiting for a sign.

"I can't believe the government hasn't said anything yet." He overheard one woman say as he walked through.

"I tried to call 911, but it's disconnected," said a man nearby. He began to wonder if any of them truly understood the magnitude of the danger they were in. Instead of spending time teaching them, he continued to walk through the store. Before long, he walked past the guys from before. They looked at him with rage as they hid objects behind them. Daniel shook his head, trying not to appear angry, as he followed Tawnie.

Back up front, Lester stood up from the group, holding his abdomen.

"Will you guys excuse me for a moment?" He said as he limped away. Victoria's eyes followed him as he headed to the entrance. Each step caused him to buck from the injuries he sustained the night before. Victoria couldn't even hear Dina talking to her.

"Hold up one second." She said, cutting the woman off while she ranted about her troubling morning. Victoria jumped up and followed her husband.

"Lester, wait, where are you going?" She asked him.

He turned around, one hand still on his rib and the other held out to his side. Victoria noticed the blood staining his palm.

"Oh shit, Lester, let me stitch you back up!" She said as she approached him. The man held a finger to her as he took a step back.

"I'll be fine," he growled. "But I can't continue to watch the Allens give each other googly eyes and not remember what you did to me!"

Victoria quickly looked defeated. "My own wife fucking shot me!"

"It was to protect you!" She screamed.

"Protect?" Lester exploded as he turned away again. He took a few steps forward, seething momentarily. He turned around and pointed his blood-stained finger in her face as he approached.

"I faced some shit with those crooked cops that I wish I had never seen before! The entire time, I was hoping that I died because of what you did!" He roared at her.

Victoria flinched and swallowed hard as she stared into his unforgiving eyes.

"I can explain." She whimpered.

"You did already."

Victoria shook her head,

"Les, I thought they'd see you as innocent if I turned on you!" The man grinned as he looked down, his hand wiping blood on his chest. "I bet you weren't counting on that plan to backfire, did you?"

"I didn't want you to have to run into the fire with me!" Victoria said as she stepped closer to him. "I didn't have a choice in any of this. I wanted to give you the option to stay away from it all!"

Lester shook his head, still grinning. "Is that because you wanted to drag me in yourself, Vic? Because that is what you did."

Lester walked around her and headed back inside, leaving his wife alone.

Meanwhile, Gordon headed straight to the back of the store. He would find an entrance to the stockroom behind a large dog food section.

He pushed through the swinging doors and found Tawnie pacing the back room alone.

She walked in a big circle on the pavement underneath, one hand on her hip and the other rubbing her bottom lip.

"There you are," he said as he tried to smile. He approached, but she was somewhat cautious of him and moved away the closer he came.

"I need to focus, Daniel." She warned him.

The expression on his face changed to immediate annoyance.

"Well, because of you, I can't focus." He argued. Tawnie's head and arms fell. He continued to walk and went to stand in front of her.

"Tawnie." He called. Slowly, she lifted her head to look at him. His eyes stared at her with a hint of eroticism.

"Yes, Daniel?" She said.

The man shook his head and grabbed her hands.

"Tawnie, I'm not one to seem ungrateful in the light of things, but how the hell are you alive? I saw you get gunned down by dozens of police! The hospital said a body with seventy—"

Tawnie shook her head, pushing herself away from him.

"I can't honestly answer that right now." She said.

Daniel ran his hand through his hair and clenched his jaw. He could feel the rage bubbling from inside. He was about to yell at her but couldn't find a point.

"I, I just don't get it." He said, sounding defeated for the first time. "I thought you were the most intriguing person in the world and got burned for it."

She turned to face him again. Her mouth was open as if she was about to speak.

"Who are you?" He asked. Tawnie froze as she heard the question again. "Seriously, who the hell are you? Because I've been to your stash house, and Tawnie Everwood died in 2073. So who the actual fuck are you?"

The woman stared, and for a moment, she wanted to tell him everything. But there was so much to tell and not enough time to answer.

"There are so many red flags here, whatever your name is." He sarcastically said, causing her to cringe. "You have an entire career of knowing things before they happen. You weren't affected by that Anti-Caster tunnel we went through on Route 20. These soldiers have been targeting you and Milo specifically…"

He stopped what he was saying and pulled out Tawnie's tablet. He held it up, the back facing her. He held it still for a moment as if he was taking a photo. But she knew exactly what he was doing. Her head fell as if she was ashamed.

"I also learned about Kaitrons from the device you conveniently left with me. Have you heard of that?" He asked.

Tawnie muttered as if preparing to speak, but Daniel cut her off.

"Kaitrons are the measurement of life energy in an organism. Mine and Vickie's are high because we're 'Casters,' apparently." He said, using air quotes.

"But Milo's Kaitrons are 370 times higher than mine."

He stopped talking as if to give her a moment to explain, but she struggled to find the words.

"And your Kaitrons are about 500 times the amount of his."

Angry, he slammed the tablet on the floor, breaking the screen. Tawnie looked down and saw a mess of glass around it. The screen was still illuminated but unreadable.

"Who did I…" He began to ask but seemingly became choked up. Tawnie looked up into his eyes and saw the pain. She took inventory of what was happening. Somehow, she scarred this man emotionally.

"Danny, I-" She began to say, tears streaming down her cheeks.

"Who the fuck are you?" He asked again, this time seeming more aggressive. "What the fuck did I make love to last night?"

Tawnie sighed and approached him slowly. She stared into his eyes the entire time, and her face seemed to glow red as she looked at him with sorrow. The burning desire to pull her close and kiss her was masked by his unyielding desire to cast her away due to her lies.

"I see now that I hurt you." She spoke softly. "I never meant for that to happen. You're a good man that I have dragged into my mess."

"I want to know about the mess." He said to her. "What is it that you have me involved in?"

Tawnie stepped back and bent over to pick up the tablet. "This is the full extent of it for now. But the good news is, I've been here before, so I know how to exclude you."

She tried to walk away, but he grabbed her arm and spun her back around. She suddenly appeared angry.

"You don't get it. I'm in love with you, Tawnie."

She closed her eyes, and more tears poured. She prepared to speak, but there was a crash behind them.

Daniel turned around to look at the exit. To no surprise, he saw the men he talked to earlier. Each of them held a weapon in hand. He shook his head and looked back at Tawnie over his shoulder.

"What the hell?" She asked.

"Not everyone's a fan of the Oracle." He stated. "Fellas, this is a mistake. Regardless of who you're here to attack, it won't be good for you."

The men proceeded, causing Daniel to get angrier.

"Okay, if that's how you want it, let's go!"

"Actually," Tawnie stepped in front of him. "We don't have time for this, guys. There are people outside hunting people, and we have to figure out how to stop that before they hunt us."

"Yeah, they think you're somehow orchestrating it," Daniel informed her.

"Wait!" She yelped as she looked back at Daniel. "I've been attacked by these guys like six times now."

Daniel sighed. "Yeah, I know."

"Did you tell them how they just tried to kill me last night?" She asked.

"It honestly didn't come up naturally in conversation."

Tawnie's mouth clicked as she raised a finger. "What if I told you guys that–"

"SHUT UP!" The leader screamed at her, pointing a hunting knife he held. Tawnie flinched. "I'm done with all of this Oracle bull shit!"

Each man smiled as they closed in, circling the two with intense looks on their faces. Tawnie looked back at Daniel with concern.

He shrugged his shoulders. "Unlike you, I'm not knife-proof. So you need to make a decision."

Tawnie didn't answer but watched the man approaching Daniel from behind. His knife pointed straight up. His opposite hand stretched toward the officer, signifying his intent to grab him. Daniel took a deep breath and threw himself backward. His shoulder rammed the man behind him in the chest. The large man heaved as he tried to catch his breath and regain his composure. His knife fell to the floor and rolled away from him. He watched it flip away as if it was his last hope. But Gordon watched him with pure malice written on his face.

He grabbed his wrist and punched him in the bicep as he reached for the knife. The man screamed in agony. Daniel then smashed his knee into his shoulder, dislocating it with ease. Another one of the men went to attack him, hoping he was too preoccupied to see him coming. But Daniel spun the first man as if they were ballroom dancing. Attacker number two approached with a readied blade. He stabbed before even realizing what he was doing. But in the blink of an eye, the officer had gotten out of the way. The man stabbed his partner right in the kidney and pulled the knife out immediately.

Blood pooled on the floor by the man's feet. The others stopped and stared in shock.

"Dammit, Mike, what the fuck!" The leader of the bunch yelled as he backed away, inching toward the door. The man holding the knife had an immediate energy shift. His eyes thinned, and his body began to rock. Suddenly, his mouth rounded, and a projectile stream of vomit shot from his lips. The bile landed on the chest of the man in front of him.

Tawnie's eyes widened, and her mouth rounded in shock. The man who received the knife to the hip looked down at his chest, then back up to his partner. He dropped the knife and then wiped his mouth with his hand. Gordon threw the man's body and stared at the man who stabbed him.

"Good job, Mike!" Tawnie cheered. "Kevin, I bet you're proud now!"

The leader looked at her, appalled.

"How does she know your name?!" The henchman asked.

"I don't know man!" He cried as he ran away. The guys with him tried to flee as well. Tawnie looked at Daniel with a look of suggestion.

"I'll get them." He said. But Tawnie threw her arm across him, forcing him to stop.

"No need." She said to him as she waved a hand shrouded in light in front of her. Suddenly, they all appeared in front of them again and watched them collide. Tawnie took a deep breath as she shook her head. The men all groaned and squirmed as they tried to get up from the ground. Tawnie looked at Daniel, then at the man on the floor, taking his last breath.

"What do we do about that, Officer?" She asked.

"Let these idiots answer for this one." He said as he walked away. "I'm done cleaning up people's mess."

Tawnie was left standing with the men as they all stumbled to their feet. Each of them holding their heads in agony.

"I'm sorry I'm not the villain you guys thought I was," Tawnie told them. Kevin stood and wiped a dribble of blood from his nose. "Also, I'm sorry for your friend. I wouldn't wish that on anyone."

The three men looked around aimlessly during the awkward

silence. Then Tawnie walked away without saying a word, and the men turned to their fallen comrade.

"Well!" Kevin barked. "We're fucked."

One of the men cleared his throat. "Why do you say that?"

"Pretty sure that guy was a cop."

Chapter LVI

Tawnie and Daniel headed back to the front of the store. They met back up with the Frances, who was sitting atop a checkout line. Daniel recognized the distance between the two of them. Milo was still playing with Lyric and her brother. Tawnie walked to the door and looked outside. The sky had become a deeper shade of red. The usual bustle of Rexburg was silenced. There were still a few stacks of smoke on the horizon. Daniel and Victoria went to join her. Upon seeing how red the environment was, they reeled and gasped.

"Tawnie," Daniel called as they approached. She looked back at them. Getting to know her so well in the last few days, Daniel could tell that something was bothering her. She'd typically look so confident. But this version of her was afraid.

"You guys strapped and ready to fight?" She asked the officers.

Victoria nodded as she looked over to Daniel. "As ready as we can be."

Gordon stepped to her. "What are we expecting here?" He asked, staring into her eyes with fiery intensity. "And be honest with us, Tawnie!"

She sighed, keeping her eyes locked on his.

"As you remember from Idaho Falls, the power is bound to be cut. The remaining people in the city will be killed and added to a burn pile to destroy the evidence."

"Who would do something like this?" Victoria asked. "There's no way the government is responsible for this… right?"

Tawnie shook her head, allowing her head to fall once more. "The government takes partial blame for this atrocity. How much blame do we give them is a better question. Based on what Wesley told me the other day, some corrupt politicians may be working deals with the devil."

Daniel snapped his head to look at her. "You talked to Wesley?" he asked, his eyes wide as he stared into hers. "When?"

"The day before, when we stopped at that store."

Daniel's eyes saddened, and he let out a huge sigh of frustration. Victoria touched his arm for comfort.

Victoria shook her head vigorously. "I can't believe he's gone." She said as she folded her arms over her chest.

Tawnie shuffled over to her and opened her arms. The woman flinched as she approached. Tawnie put her arms around her for a moment. Victoria was apprehensive for only a moment before she realized the hug was genuine. She then unfolded her arms and reciprocated, tears welling in her eyes.

"We are the last of the 316th," Daniel announced. "So that binds us together whether we like it or not."

Tawnie let go of Victoria and turned away. She looked up into the sky again as the clouds began to spiral.

"What the fuck? It looks like a tornado is about to touch down!" Daniel said as the two of them came to stand next to her.

"What the hell is happening with the sky, Tawnie?" Victoria asked.

She cleared her throat before answering. The pause made Victoria uneasy as she waited for the answer.

"You guys remember those markings from the temple in Saudi Arabia?" Tawnie asked. The two of them nodded. "I once deciphered some text that depicted the end of the world as we know it."

The two of them looked at one another, almost skeptical.

"When I met you guys, I was tasked to find more pieces of this text and find out just how much of this prophecy was applied. It wasn't until the Massachusetts incident that we even believed it was true."

Daniel touched her shoulder gently. "We know about the prophecy already." He sternly said, urging her to get to the point.

"Yeah, there were things written in it that I'm sure the two of you wouldn't even be able to comprehend right now. Many wouldn't. Everything you know about the human race is a facade.

Fables created to give some false sense of order to humanity."

Victoria stepped forward, turning to Tawnie with a raised eyebrow. "Is the world ending at this moment?"

She shook her head and closed her eyes. "Not now. But no matter how many times I tried to prevent this, how many–." She paused, opening her eyes and giving them the sense that she was still hiding something. "The sky is the result of the Pyro Stone. It's close."

Again, Victoria and Daniel looked at one another with concern.

"Isn't that the thing you took from the temple in Saudi Arabia?" She asked.

"One of them," Tawnie replied.

"Why is it turning the sky red?" Daniel asked.

Tawnie sighed and turned to him. Instantly, the man gasped.

"Milo?" He yelled. Victoria scrunched her face as she gave him a side-eye. But Tawnie nodded.

"It turns out that each of the Elemental Cores has an anchor. These individuals usually serve as grounding rods for the relics… for all the power."

His face went pale as he looked back into the store. He could see Milo playing with his new friends—so innocent and youthful.

"Someone is looking to weaponize these powers. Thus far, they've been unsuccessful," Tawnie added as she stepped forward. "Massachusetts was a wild card accident. It shouldn't have ever happened. But everything hereafter was a fault of human error."

Victoria looked back at the kids playing as well.

"Tawnie, what's the worst-case scenario here?" Daniel asked.

She grunted and crossed her arms. "Whoever has their hands on the Pyro Stone gets their hands on my son."

"Now, you said that there are individuals that act as grounding rods to the elemental cores," Victoria repeated. "How many more of these cores are there?"

Tawnie sighed. "ten... If the Celestial and Obsidian stay separated, as they should."

Daniel stared at her, his lower lip quivering, "What the hell are we talking about here?" Victoria grunted.

Tawnie cleared her throat, "As I said before, things that humanity can't possibly comprehend."

Suddenly, the three heard a vehicle in the distance, cutting through the silence. The sound of its screeching tires seemed to increase in volume.

"Someone's coming," Tawnie said as she turned to walk back inside. Seconds later, a black SUV pulled into the parking lot. Tawnie's eyes locked onto it. "They're here." She announced.

"What the hell do we do?" Victoria asked.

"Round everyone up and take them to the center of the store." Tawnie calmly answered. "If it's anything like Idaho Falls, these guys will cut the power to the entire grid. Everyone will be safest away from walls and windows."

Tawnie walked toward the door. Daniel called to her, and she looked at him over her shoulder.

"I can't imagine you'll be staying here with us." He said.

The little woman smiled. "I need you two to take care of Milo for me."

"What the fuck are you saying, Tawnie?!" He snapped. "If you think I'm going to let you face an army again on your own, you must be out of your mind!"

"I've faced armies before," She said. "But what truly worries me is whoever has their hands on the stone."

Daniel nodded. "You can take care of your own damn son, Tawnie. Whatever you think will happen today can take a back seat to reality."

She smiled at him. The first genuine happiness he'd seen in a while. But it was short-lived. The vehicle in the parking lot was open for an attack. Daniel caught a glimpse of a shining white object. There was a loud pop, followed by a swoosh. Gordon was inside Victoria's shield within a split second, tumbling backward. They watched Tawnie jump into the air to catch a rocket. She grabbed it as it entered the store, performing a superhuman twisting motion. She snatched it to her body and wrapped herself around it.

"No!" Daniel screamed. But the inevitable explosion rocked the store. The rocket seemed to set off a chain reaction inside the building. Screams were heard everywhere. It was accompanied by the sound of twisting metal and endless explosions. Inside Victoria's shield, Daniel's ears rang, and he felt extreme pressure behind his eyes. An army of red lasers and flashlights marched through the smoke and debris. Daniel attempted to get back to his feet to fight. He rolled around and saw Victoria on the ground, holding her hand up to maintain the shield.

"Gordon!" She screamed as the soldiers began to shoot at the civilians in the store. "We have to move! GET UP!"

He did what he was told, and the two returned to Lester. He jumped from his spot on the counter, far enough from the blast to assist others through their panic. Bullets tapped the shield surrounding Daniel and Victoria and bounced off like they were hitting rubber. He looked around for Milo, but he didn't see him anywhere. He called the kid's name and listened for a response. But all he could hear was the guns and people howling with fear. Flashes of light cascaded through the cloud of dust at the entrance. Soldiers all blasted their weapons at a target. But they were countered with a ferocious offense that nobody could see through the fog. The soldiers screamed as death was being handed to them one by one.

"What's happening out there?" Victoria asked.

"It's Tawnie!" He answered as he searched for Milo.

"I lost him the moment that explosion took place," Lester said.

"Alright. It's still hot, so he can't be far."

Through the crowd, the three of them scanned. Anyone who didn't get caught in the blast ran to the back of the store. But countless bodies lie scorched on the floor. As the crowd thinned, the sound of people screaming started to fade. Lyric stood by the checkout counter, staring at the field of bodies in front of them.

The three of them ran to her.

"Lyric, are you okay?" Victoria asked her. Still sobbing uncontrollably, the little girl could only shake her head. They looked down at the bodies on the cold, tile floors—three, 90% scorched and beyond recognition. Victoria looked at them and felt her heart breaking. Daniel stepped around the little girl and moved her away. Lester, however, fixated on the bodies, shaking his head softly.

The smell was so familiar that Daniel was forced to step away, taking the girl with him.

"Lyric, it'll be okay," Victoria said. "You're fine. Everything is going to be okay."

Still shaken up, Lester only covered his mouth with his hand

and attempted to quell his emotions.

Suddenly, Tawnie ran inside. She immediately found the four of them standing there but didn't see her son.

"Milo!" She called out, looking around the destroyed store. "Have you guys seen Milo?"

"Tawnie, I don't think he's here," Gordon announced.

Victoria chimed in by waving her hand. She looked down at Lyric, and the girl spoke, hardly loud enough for anyone else to hear her. But when the girl finished, Victoria's face became ghostly. Tawnie braced herself for the bad news, wondering if she somehow already knew what she was about to say. She closed her eyes and clenched her fists.

"Milo's gone!"

Chapter LVII

Milo opened his eyes hours later inside the same tube-like structure from before. But this time felt different. He was standing. A red glow emitted from below. He looked down, and the dull light gleamed against the tears in his eyes. He tried to move, but the tight space had no wiggle room. He had half a mind to scream but thought against it. The glass was soundproof. The only thing he could hear was his pulse. Separated from his mother, Daniel, and anyone he knew, he felt his world shrink. The dull ache in his chest increased, and a lump formed in his throat, making it hard to swallow. His bottom lip wobbled uncontrollably, and the heat inside his body intensified.

He clenched his fists, nails digging into his palms, trying to hold back the rising tide of emotion. But the feeling is like a dam about to burst. Hurt, anger, and frustration all tangled together. His face scrunches up, preparing for the inevitable. A hot tear escapes, tracing a warm path down his cheek. He sniffs, the sound barely audible, willing himself not to sob. But another tear follows, and another, each one chipping away at his resolve. His breath hitches, each inhale a shaky gasp of air. His vision swims, making even the darkness outside the glass wobble precariously. He feels small, insignificant, and lost in overwhelming emotions. All he wants is comfort, a safe haven from the storm brewing inside him.

A choked sob escapes a tiny tremor running through his body. The dam has broken, and the tears flow freely now, washing away his frustration in salty streams. He tried reaching for his face. The glass swaddle surrounding him made it impossible for his elbows to bend. He tried to suppress his emotions, knowing his rage came with consequences. His level of maturity would not allow him to comprehend his issues entirely, but he wished for them to end.

His primal instinct took control. The rush of tears became steam as the salty mixture rolled down his cheeks and crystalized on his face. He could feel his veins. Every inch of his cardiovascular system burned as the glow of his limbs began to offer pain. He wanted to keep himself from exploding, but he couldn't hold back any longer. Milo screamed. His ear-shattering screech even hurt his ears as the tube filled with flames. His skin was burning. Every inch of him was in writhing pain that never affected his appearance or his clothing. As the fire enveloped him, he noticed something strange inside the tube. The flames were funneling. It was as if the red area underneath him was somehow absorbing it. Suddenly, he saw tubes outside that glowed red like a stovetop element. It started near him, and then the light inside the tube spread as if magma filled it. He watched as it happened in front of him. The flame inside the tube traveled upward across the room and disappeared quickly.

The lights turned on. Milo's eyes squinted as they tried to adjust from extreme darkness. The room was large and full of all kinds of testing equipment. Lab utensils covered one table to his left, and a desk with computers on the tabletop sat to his right. He could see the exit in the distance. He hoped his mother would miraculously open it and save him again. But when that door opened, his hopes were crushed. It was the soldiers again. There were three of them whose primary stance was holding their rifles low and ready to shoot. Milo began to squirm as his eyes became fixated on the large men. Each of them looked as if they could point their rifles and start shooting at any moment.

As he examined the brutes, he noticed something different about these soldiers. Although their uniforms and weapons were identical, these men didn't have masks on. He called out to them.

"Let me out!" He screamed as more flames filled the tube. But just like before, the residual energy was transferred through the thick tube on the floor. With the lights on, he could see what it was connected to. Men stared at him with no emotion on their faces. The tube was connected to a machine resembling a large file cabinet. The hose was attached to the side of the top section, where a small window sat. Inside the window was a device resembling a car engine's pistons. Some gears and prongs sliced through one another in a gyroscopic showcase. The energy seemed to collect in the core and secrete away after a moment of what looked to be harvesting. Milo was too young to comprehend what he was looking at. He thought it would seem cool if he weren't scared or trapped. Suddenly, a man in a white lab coat entered the room, speaking with the soldiers. One man in the middle tilted his head to the left to hear what he was saying.

When he was done, the soldier nodded, and two of the four stepped forward. They reached for the back of the tube. Milo attempted to turn his head but couldn't see what they were doing.

"Hey!" He yelled as he began to rock back and forth. The man in the lab coat faced the tube and placed his hands in his coat pockets.

"Milo, can you hear me?" The man asked. There was a silence in the room as the two stared at one another. "My name is Dr. Asahn Ashrani, and I've heard a lot about you. You're a special child indeed."

"Let me out of here!" The boy cried.

The man sighed. His hand came up from his pocket and wiped his upper lip.

"I'm afraid I can't do that now." He responded. The doctor stepped forward and kneeled before the glass chamber. He sat at eye level, looking the boy in the eyes as he adjusted his square-framed glasses.

"There is no reason for me to explain any of this to you, Milo. You are only five years old." The doctor continued. "I will say this, however…"

The man stood up and stepped to Milo's left, where a steel table stood.

Milo began to sob again. "I want my mommy!"

The man chuckled. "Even at five, I am surprised you are still thinking about your mother."

The man turned around with a long extraction needle, instantly causing the child to panic. He began to hyperventilate as the flames filled the tube again. Ashrani stepped out of his view. "Milo, I wish I could tell you everything, but it is not my place."

The tube shifted slightly, and Milo went stiff in anticipation.

Then, there was a burning in the back of his neck as the doctor jammed the giant needle down his spine. His body became numb, and his limbs became heavy. He screamed again as the strange doctor pulled the needle from his back.

"I just injected you with a drug called Felcumniacide." He announced. "It's a predecessor of the drug that your mother has been feeding you. Milo's eyes grew large, wondering what the man meant. "This will suppress your powers long enough for us to install the kaitron siphoner inside you.

"No, no, no, no!" Milo repeated. "Let me out, please!"

The doctor turned around with an even bigger needle the second time.

"Milo, outside of your flame, you are most certainly feeling the pain of this toxin tearing at your nerves. Your spectacular powers will try to save you from the pain. But I will apologize now because there will be no escape."

He jammed the second needle into the kid's spine and extracted his blood. The flames inside the tube began to die down as his mind began to lose conscience. He fought to keep his eyes open, fearing what would become of him.

Dr. Ashrani walked to the opposite side of the room and approached one of the soldiers. He held a large metal briefcase, opened it, and held it to the doctor. The inside of the suitcase was lined with black foam on one side and what looked to be a computer monitor on the other. In the foam were rectangular cutouts, and Dr. Ashrani put the vile of Milo's blood in the first empty slot. The tube glowed a bright red that shined throughout the room.

"Scan complete." An AI voice came from the computer. A lengthy, detailed analysis appeared on the monitor. The doctor raised his glasses and leaned in to get a closer look.

"Subject, The Primal Flame, Kaitron levels exceed scan range."

The doctor placed the glasses back on the bridge of his nose and looked back at Milo. He grinned as he turned to face the boy.

"Well, I'll be damned!" He barked. "That psycho was right about this!"

The group around them began speaking amongst one another as the man returned to Milo.

"Your father always said you were special, Milo," he announced. Milo's eyes grew large.

"You…you know my daddy?" He whined. With a huge smile, he nodded.

"I want my daddy!"

The man nodded. "You will be reunited with your father. But there is something else that we need from you first."

Chapter LVIII

Against his better judgment, Daniel took the time to start moving bodies. This task began as a survival hunt. Yet it quickly went south when he realized that people still on the ground were probably not getting up. Families of the fallen remained in the store. This included Lyric Allen, Milo's new friend, who was mourning her deceased family. Other survivors, scared for their lives, tried their hand at escaping. Tawnie sat in the middle of the floor with her legs crossed and eyes closed. Victoria looked at Daniel and pointed to the woman in question.

"Tawnie, what are you doing?" Victoria asked as she looked around, still attempting to understand the carnage. "Is now really a good time to meditate?"

She opened her eyes momentarily.

"Your son was kidnapped!" She continued. "How are you so calm?"

Tawnie turned her head to look at Daniel. The way his eyes followed her as she walked suggested that he was also curious.

"Daniel, Victoria, come here," she sternly ordered. The two of them looked at one another with intrigue. Victoria raised an eyebrow as her attitude began to heighten.

"I don't take orders from you!" Victoria yelled.

But before she could continue her rampage, Gordon barked her name. She paused and saw him walking toward her with caution. Reluctantly, she followed him over. Tawnie reached forward and tapped her index finger on the floor. Daniel kneeled in front of her. Tawnie looked up at the blonde, her eyes sharper with each passing second. Victoria blinked first and sat next to Daniel. They looked at one another, their heads tucked like two school kids locked in detention.

"Shut up and feel for Milo." She said. The two of them locked their heads back, appalled at her statement.

"Uh, what?" Victoria asked. "Feel for what? Tawnie, he's gone!"

Tears fell from her eyes. "No, feel for his energy!"

Daniel looked over to Victoria and tapped her arm. "She's referring to his Kaitron."

Her eyebrow raised.

"I don't have much time left, guys." She said as she wiped her eyes. "You guys are Casters, so you can feel his energy too."

Victoria squinted, "Wait, what are we talking about?"

Daniel closed his eyes and took a deep breath. He sat for about thirty seconds before determining he couldn't feel a thing.

"What's happening?" He asked. "Why can't I feel it?"

Tawnie shrugged and rested her elbows on the side of her knees.

"The Pyro Stone is clouding my senses." She said.

Daniel shook his head. "That makes sense." He stood again and looked at the sky, noticing the red aura fading.

"Tawnie," Victoria called out. Her eyes stared distantly at the bodies on the floor. "8 years later, what do we know about that stone?"

Tawnie shook her head and looked down at the floor. "I know we should have never found it." She answered. "I thought I was doing the right thing, taking those relics from that temple."

Victoria looked up at Daniel. The two of their eyes met in wonder for a few seconds.

"Tawnie, how did you know about those relics in the first place?" Daniel asked.

The woman sighed. "They are objects of pure source energy of this universe."

"Source energy?" Victoria asked.

"This universe?" Asked Daniel.

Suddenly, Tawnie's small body began to levitate from the ground and rise to her feet. The two of them stared in shock as she walked toward the front of the building.

"Did you just see that?" Victoria asked. Daniel nodded, eyes locked onto her.

"Yeah, that raises even more questions, doesn't it?" Daniel asked.

Daniel followed her, shaking his head.

"We don't have time to unpack that. We have to get Milo back." He said. "We can discuss the nuances after that."

Tawnie sighed deeply. The two of them snatched their attention to her.

"We won't be having any discussions after this." She said. "Once we find Milo, the prophecy will be in motion, and we won't be in contact anymore."

Daniel became silent, his head tilting downward as he glared at her. He closed his mouth, and his jaw clenched.

"Victoria, go tell Lester the plan." Daniel requested. "I need a minute with Tawnie."

Victoria moved swiftly to avoid hearing anything she didn't want to.

As they stared into each other's eyes, it was quiet. The wind howled as it whipped through the openings of the ravaged structure.

"Danny?" Tawnie said.

"Don't you Danny me! How dare you!" He screamed at her. "How dare you make me fall for you just to tell me the next minute that we won't see each other anymore?"

"Daniel, I–" She tried to interject.

"I've waited patiently for you to give me your reasoning, some logic, anything that makes any of this make sense! But all you want to do is keep secrets!"

"Ok!" Tawnie snapped as her lower lip quivered in anger. "You want to know what I am, Daniel? Well, it's your funeral!"

She turned and walked a few steps away from him. Then she turned to face him.

"I wanted you to stay innocent in all of this! But since you must see the truth, I'll put your life at risk then!"

Daniel's eyes widened as Tawnie raised her palm to him.

"Tawnie, what are you doing?" He asked, fear taking over his spirit. "We can talk about this like adults, can't we?"

But Tawnie ignored him. Her eyes began to glow white, and a bright energy emitted from her hand. Daniel tried to look back at

Victoria and Lester. But as he saw them moving, he saw afterimages of their figure as if they were moving slowly.

"What, Tawnie, wait!" He yelled again as he closed his eyes.

The energy changed. Suddenly, the ominous feeling of dread that Daniel had in the store vanished. There was a tranquil calm in the atmosphere. A beam of light touched his eyelids, blinding him even with closed eyes. A crisp, clean breeze swept past him, and the sound of pooling water and chirping birds filled his ears. He opened his eyes quickly. He was amazed at what he saw. Daniel found himself at a lake. It was so large that the other side was hardly visible. The water was clear, and he could see schools of different colored fish below. The sky was clear, and the sun warmed him. He recognized a small island with a stone structure and two tall pillars in the middle of the lake. From this distance, he could hardly tell what the figure was at the top. Outside the lake's perimeter stood large mountain terrains and forests beyond the clearing. Daniel looked down at his own body. To his surprise, he was okay.

Just ahead, he saw Tawnie. His eyes squinted as they landed on her because of how different she appeared. Despite seeing her in a white peat coat and leggings a few seconds ago, she was now in something different. Her entire appearance was different.

"Tawnie?" He called as he approached her. "Tawnie, where are we?"

She wore a white stola dress, lined at the edges with gold. She wore golden Olympian sandals with straps traveling up her leg, ending under her knees. Daniel could see it through the slit on the side of the garment that swept to the ground. Her black hair was straightened instead of its typical curly nature. She wore a crown laden with gold and diamonds. Gordon ran out in front of her and was shocked. The man shook his head and took a step backward.

"Who the hell are you?" He asked.

The woman turned her head slightly and stared at him with a smile. In size and facial features, she favored Tawnie, but she was someone different. She was Caucasian, and her hair was straight, voluminous, and draped to her lower back. The rings and clasps on her dress gleamed in the sunlight, nearly blinding Daniel.

"Oh, Daniel." The girl giggled. "You are so funny!"

His eyes sharpened, and his eyebrows tilted as he questioned the woman's sanity.

"I know we've had a rough landing, but we are only stranded if we believe we are?" She continued.

"What the hell are you talking about?" He asked. "Where is Tawnie?"

The young woman nodded with her eyes closed and a wide smile. "I know Daniel. But if the truth were clear, this discussion would be different."

Gordon stepped back and put his hands on his hips, watching her silently. Her smile faded as she clasped her hands over her chest.

"The balance of nature has been compromised, and now, the universe has to atone for its sins."

The man frowned, confused about her statement.

"This is what I've been dealing with my entire life." He heard Tawnie's voice. He looked to his left and saw her standing with her hands in her coat pockets.

"Wait, what?" He asked as he looked over his shoulder. "Where the hell are we? And where did you come from?"

"Unfortunately, our physical selves are still in Idaho." She answered as she approached the woman. "But I've invited you inside my subconscious mind. Which also happens to be a real place in another dimension."

Gordon's eyes widened, and his jaw fell open as he looked around the environment.

"How the hell is this even possible?" He asked as he followed. "Are Casters able to use telepathy like that?"

Tawnie shook her head slowly and turned to face him. Her eyes squinted from the harsh sunlight.

"So far, no Casters has been able to manipulate time and space." She answered.

Gordon shook his head again. "Did you just say time and space?"

Tawnie stared at him for a moment, unsure how to answer. Then she looked at the woman standing next to her. She smiled at Tawnie and nodded. Then she looked back at Daniel and nodded.

"I guess so." She casually answered. She began to stare off into the distance as the mysterious woman stared into his eyes.

The officer stood waiting patiently, looking between the two of them. "Tawnie?" He called.

"Yeah?" She responded as if she snapped out of a deep thought.

"Why the hell are we here?"

Tawnie looked back at the woman again to see her shaking her head.

"Daniel, you're inside the place that made me what I am." She explained. "I stopped time and manipulated light. So you can finally see the chamber inside my mind and meet the five entities that cursed me."

"Cursed?" The mysterious woman yelled, appalled at the statement. "You are the one who refuses to be what you are supposed to be!"

"I'd be happy if I could dodge all of your expectations of me!"

"Wait, what the hell am I missing here?" Daniel interjected. Suddenly, there was movement nearby that caught his attention. He felt something that bordered the feeling of instant dread and anxiety in his body. The figure was dark and seemed to negate any light that touched it. There were no reflections on it at all. It looked like a person's body but didn't appear solid. It was almost like smoke, and stood nearby, watching him like a statue.

"What is that?" Daniel asked.

Tawnie stepped to his side, staring at the figure as well. "That there is the being that taught me how to survive this long. She tapped his arm, signaling him to turn around. She pointed at the gorgeous woman behind them.

"This annoying woman is the one who taught me Arcanin." She continued.

Daniel threw his hands up and shook his head in disbelief as he walked toward the lake.

"Daniel, where are you going?" She asked. "I control this place!"

"Let me out of here! This isn't real!" He yelled back.

Tawnie approached him again with her finger pointing in his face.

"Danny, I need you to keep your head straight because I need your help!" She yelled at him. He could see a look in her eyes that he had never seen before. Her eyebrows slanted toward her ears, and her jaw clenched tight. She was afraid. His defenses fell as he looked at her, recognizing her internal struggle.

"I don't know if I'm the one to help you, Tawnie." He said as he turned to look at the lake.

The woman in the dress approached the water, looking past the two of them. Tawnie turned her head, watching the woman with trepidation.

"My Liege, I didn't realize you've already had your collision."

Tawnie's head fell as if she was ashamed. "I will admit I have never seen any Aetheryte in history fight the truth for so long."

Tawnie slowly picked her head up. "And I'm glad I did." She said as she approached the woman.

She reached out and placed her hand on Tawnie's shoulder. "Do you remember the life you had before?"

She nodded, staring at the water past the woman. She sighed, then made eye contact. The woman, slightly taller than Tawnie, looked down at her with an intense look. She nodded, causing Tawnie to spin around and look at Daniel.

"Danny, I need a favor, and it will sound outright ridiculous." She said as she stepped toward him. "Excuse me if I sound cliche, but the fate of humanity depends on your contribution."

The man chuckled, looking away in disbelief. "Why should I?" He asked. "I don't even know you."

Tawnie's head fell, and she cleared her throat.

"You're right, and I'm sorry." She said to him. "Nothing that I do now will change my deception., but it still doesn't change the fact that humanity is endangered!"

Daniel took a deep breath and looked to the woman behind Tawnie. "What do you need?"

Tawnie smiled and stepped back, tossing her hair behind her ear.

"Here's the truth, Daniel." She started. "I am the only person on Earth able to translate the Arcanin Text. As you know, they predicted the end of the world to the exact date."

"Yeah, yeah!" He interrupted. "We've discussed this already!"

"Yeah, but this organization targeted us because I was trying to stop something big that the government has known about for a long time. The events that ultimately destroy humanity have already begun."

Daniel was stunned. He felt ill at her words and stumbled backward a few steps.

"Daniel, I have a plan to save humanity, but we have to die first."

Daniel stepped forward, and suddenly, he was back inside the ravaged store.

"What the fuck?" He asked as he looked around.

"Daniel?" He heard Victoria call out behind him. "Where's Tawnie?"

The man looked back at the entrance and realized that she was gone.

"Uh, shit!" He grunted as he ran outside. Victoria dropped what she was doing and followed him. She found him standing in the parking lot, looking around for Tawnie.

"Did she?" She asked him after catching up.

Daniel nodded, still looking around. "She did." He answered. He turned to her, shaking his head. He reached up to run his fingers through his hair in frustration.

"You want to follow her, don't you?" She asked.

The man nodded.

"You know she can handle herself, right?" She continued.

"Yeah, but she's about to do something reckless." He replied. "And I am supposed to be there when she does."

Chapter LIX

"This is your destiny." The woman in the white dress told Tawnie by the lake. Three other individuals flanked her. One man was tall and had long black hair. He wore no shirt, and the cuts of his muscles took shape as he held his arms across his chest. He wore baggy black pants that looked like something you would see on a genie. His jewelry and gear resembled gladiator armor and Egyptian craft. The shadow stood next to him, and opposite the woman stood a mass of light that took the shape of a person.

"I want to believe," Tawnie said.

The woman nodded, "This is the only way." She stepped closer. "Tawnie, this is what the world truly is, and you were born to carry the torch. We don't have much time left to be indecisive."

Tawnie's attention snapped to her. "Indecisive?" She yelled. "Look at what you're asking me to do!"

The woman nodded. "If we had options, we would not have brought you here."

Her eyebrow raised as she leaned back with folded arms.

"What does that mean?"

The woman cleared her throat. "You are the only person in the universe able to continue our legacy."

Tawnie paused momentarily and shook her head as she let her head fall.

"You could have picked anyone to be your grunt worker! Why me?" She yelled. "I don't want to do this!"

She cut her eyes at Tawnie and stepped away toward the water. She looked out into the distance at the island, approximately a mile from the banks on which they stood.

She pointed, "You see that island?"

Tawnie walked next to her and nodded. "I do."

"Two hundred million years ago, that's where it started for us." She looked back at the people behind her.

"I had no say in my conception. Two beings of opposing forces fought tooth and nail for supremacy. The clashing of their power caused me to come into life right there."

"Where are you going with this?" Tawnie asked nonchalantly.

"You'd mind your tongue if you knew what's good for you!" The man behind them said. The woman threw her hand up, signaling him to stand by.

"Tawnie, you've read the Arcanin text by now, right?" The woman asked as she walked toward the lake. Tawnie watched as her sandals flattened the grass. The green blades overlapped onto her perfectly pedicured toes. Without hesitation, she stepped onto the lake as if it were solid ground. Tawnie grunted and folded her arms.

"We cannot tell the power of the universe what to do," she said as she turned to look at the young woman."

Tawnie unfolded her arms and squared her shoulders. Her curious eyes locked onto the woman.

She put her palms up to her side and shrugged. "It is admirable to believe that you have the liberty of choice. No one person could carry that much power and not be involved."

Tawnie clenched her fists tight as her eyes lowered. She began to grind her teeth as she stared into a patch of grass in front of her feet.

"There are many things that must take place for humanity to carry on, young one." She announced. "You were created to be one of many bridges between us and them. If the Midworld chooses to pursue things they have no business, the balance will continue to shred and–"

"Dammit!" Tawnie Interrupted. "I heard you the first time!"

She turned around and stormed off. She held her arm out and plowed through the group standing in her way. But the moment they parted to allow her through, the mysterious woman stood behind them. She looked Tawnie in the eyes.

"Oh, for fuck's sake!" She screamed.

"You think you are going to run away from your destiny?" She asked.

"The humans don't want to hear about this prophecy! I tried to save them from themselves!"

"Try harder!" She barked. The ground rumbled as her voice boomed, loud enough to echo through the mountainous lands.

Tawnie dropped her guard and turned back to face the water again.

Suddenly, she could feel a pulse of Milo's energy. She opened her eyes to the present. The sky in front of her burned with a profound red aura. The ground was crawling with soldiers searching for survivors. A temporary structure was built on the main road leading northwest toward Yellowstone. It was similar to the structure they drove through to get to Rexburg.

Like the gate from Idaho Falls, there were two sides, and this one was desolate. There were few cars in the area. All of them had already been exterminated of any passengers.

"Tawnie scanned the area, feeling for unknown energies in the facility or around it. At the moment, she could only feel Milo. But even his energy fluctuated, causing her to become uneasy. She pulled out the radio she stole and turned it on. She switched it to channel thirty-two and paused. She closed her eyes and took a deep breath. She pressed the button, causing the unit to chime. Her arm lifted, getting heavier with each inch as it reached her mouth.

"This is The Oracle," Tawnie said. "I am outside your base of operation, alone and unarmed. I am not here to fight for as long as I can get my son back alive and unharmed."

A few seconds passed, and the radio chimed as someone prepared to respond.

"Do you surrender, Oracle?" A man said.

Tawnie nodded. "I am willing to give my life for his." Not long after her announcement, the gates began to rattle as they opened. She heard men yelling and barking orders at one another as they rushed to get to her. The corners of her lips lifted as she looked around the small crowd.

She scoffed. "No masks, really?" She asked. "Are we just comfortable after eliminating the entire population? Your gift for yourself is fresh air?"

Ignoring her, one brave soldier approached. He threw his arm to his side, activating a device that glowed a white light.

"I need you to remain silent and put your hands behind your back. Quietly, Tawnie did as she was told and put her hands back. The man stepped around her to grab her arms and slapped the device on her hands and wrists. Tawnie felt the energy in her body fade. She began to feel tired, and her knees began to buckle. As she started to fall forward, the man yanked her backward. This placed her back on her feet and stalled her blackout.

"Keep moving, Caster!" He growled as he placed a gun in the middle of her back. "These handcuffs make you human, so don't make me shoot you!"

She was escorted through the crowd of men, which parted as she entered. Everything was silent except for the gravel shifting underneath her feet. She looked around at the faces of the men surrounding her. There was a burning hatred in their eyes that she couldn't possibly justify. Jaws clenched, and eyebrows twitched as she passed through their formation.

The soldiers they passed had already filed behind the man who retrieved her. But in front of her, the men began to close the space. Suddenly, Tawnie was surrounded.

"I take it that you guys don't plan to honor my terms." She said.

The man behind her chuckled. "Haven't you heard? Casters don't get to make rules around here."

Tawnie lowered her head and smiled. "Haven't you heard? I'm not a Caster."

"Wha–" The man began questioning, but she leaned against him to keep him quiet. Her hand opened, grabbing a handful of his cock through his pants. A sharp twist caused him to twitch.

"What are you doing?" He asked as he began to feel immense heat in his crotch.

"If you don't call these clowns off, you'll lose your dick before any of them gets a hold of me.

"How are you–?"

But Tawnie gripped tighter. "As I said, I'm not a Caster!"

The man waved, signaling the group to clear the path again.

"You guys know this is not how it is supposed to happen!" He yelled. "Once the boss gives the go-ahead to snatch her throat out, you'll get your turn!"

"Really?" She asked.

The man gulped. "Did you want me to tell them the truth?"

She chuckled, trying not to smile. "Good point."

The man walked her through the crowd and approached the command center's entrance. Two soldiers standing at the door opened it to allow them inside. Soldiers began to file in behind them. Immediately, Tawnie could see the ominous glow of fire down the hall to her left. She turned her attention to it, but the man pushing her moved in a different direction.

"My son!" She yelled as she attempted to grab the man's crotch again. But this time, he stepped back and swung the rifle he was holding at the back of her head. The buttstock of the gun made contact, and Tawnie went face-first into the floor.

"Not a second time, Oracle!" He barked as he jumped in celebration. Tawnie tried to shake off the attack but couldn't recover fast enough. She shook her head vigorously as the men grabbed her from the floor and took her into a room at the end of the building. She tried to struggle, but there was no use. As she was dragged into the chamber, Tawnie's arm was raised in the center and hoisted to the ceiling. She screamed in agony as her arms were rotated all the way around, but she was able to pop them out of place to reset them.

"Let me go!" She screamed. "Where is my son!"

The men all took a step back and watched her. A few of them were smiling from ear to ear as they watched her like a zoo animal.

"We just caught The Oracle!" One man said. "The boss is going to go nuts!"

"Just in time, too!" The next man added. "He just arrived for the kid!"

Tawnie lowered her head and looked at them with rage. "You will pay for this!" She growled.

They looked at her and smiled again before walking away, leaving her hanging and alone.

The Nobles mentioned in the Arcanin Text were said to protect the flame. But those from this timeline will fail to do so. Thus, the Harbinger of Chaos would be compromised in her efforts to keep the Arcanin Flame safe.

-Excerpt of the Arcanin Prophecy; Translated by the Oracle

Chapter LX

How the hell do I proceed here? From being a regular cop on the beat of a city with nothing going on. To being a noble from a prophecy written ages ago, when Earth was still young. When I met her, she seemed like a small girl in a big place she didn't belong. Now, we're going to some random ass facility on the edge of town to fight against an army for her. I don't understand why Tawnie would do such a thing. I don't know if my heart could bear seeing her in more compromising conditions.

I wish that I was stronger. There is a lot more in my tank than I can exert in most cases. On one hand, I see how powerful this woman is, but I still attempt to put my own life at risk to help her. Nonetheless, I can only fault myself for stepping in so much and getting involved. But if I'm being candid, I'm still alive because of her. Hell, we all are. The least I could do was help her get Milo back.

I keep asking myself why I bother. She's married and has a kid. She's successful and famous. I'm just a brooding beat cop. She's rich and has connections in high places. All I'm doing is holding her back, right?

"Dan!" Victoria called out to me from behind. I turned around to look toward the supermarket. Somehow, the damage from the outside of the building looked even worse. Victoria was walking through the parking lot with Lyric and Lester. The poor guy was still hurt pretty badly. He attempted to hold it together in front of her. But the wincing in his expression, whenever she wasn't looking, said it all.

I imagine that Victoria has to explain why she had to shoot him. Of course, I understand. But Lester isn't like us. Hardly anyone on Earth is as lethal as the 316th. Not the ones who survived anyway. Victoria, Tawnie, Wes, Victor, and myself. We all walked out of that temple much differently than when we went in that night. But based on the tidbits of the prophecy I read, maybe that's not the case. I've been checking behind her, attempting to understand what was happening. But now, in this moment, it all makes sense.

"You ready?" Victoria asked as she approached their SUV in the parking lot. She had tears in her eyes and wiped them away as she walked away from Lester. His eyes caught mine. He stared intensely at me, and I looked away into the distance, pretending not to notice. But he waved his hand at me to get my attention. I nodded, pretending I had just noticed him. He gestured for me to come to him. I looked at Victoria and nodded.

"Give me a second," I said as I stepped away. As I approached him, I could see the disappointment in his eyes. I could also see the little girl standing nearby, lost and distraught.

"Yeah, what's up, Les?" I said as I approached.

He shook his head, eyes rolling as he dug deep to figure out what to say. I can only imagine that he was searching for something that didn't walk the line of verbal abuse.

"Man, G, I thought we were boys, man." He grunted.

"I... Les, I didn't mean–"

"Man, shut up and listen!" He interrupted me. I could feel my eyes sharpen and anger creeping in. I clenched my fists, hoping to relieve some of the pressure. "Bro, I didn't ask any questions about your time in the Army. I didn't even ask any questions when the two of you disappeared for three months after we got married. I would say you two owe me answers, but it's too late for that, man!" He said as he stepped backward.

A sharp grunt exited his mouth as he winced in pain. "Take care of her, G."

I shook my head, looking at him from the corner of my eyes. "Les, you're talking like—" He raised his hand to cut me off. It shook in front of me as he tried his best to hold it up. "Don't bull shit me, Gordon." He snarled.

"I'm telling you that I'm good to tell her what she needs to hear." I glanced back at Victoria. She turned away quickly before getting into the passenger seat of the vehicle. I turned to look at him again. A sly smile grazed his lips as he stared at me. "It looks like that conversation we need to have is going to have to wait until another lifetime, huh?" I stepped forward and hugged him. He let out another grunt. "Not too tight, bro!" I let go of him, noticing the fading look in his eyes as he stumbled backward. He reached down for the little girl's hand and took it in his.

I smiled and nodded. "Yeah, that's fair."

He clenched his jaw and limped.

"Don't worry. I'll take care of her and make sure she comes back safe." I said as I headed back to the parking lot. I found myself calling out to the little girl. "I know it doesn't feel like it now, but you're in good hands."

The girl smiled temporarily, but it faded away faster than it had appeared. She just lost her entire family. So I can't even blame her. I turned around and headed back to the SUV. Victoria was already inside, staring out the windshield in a trance. I got in, closed the door, and started it.

"I always thought we were doing the right thing keeping all of this a secret," she announced. I put the vehicle in gear and drove out of the parking lot.

"I'm starting to question all of this," I said, looking around for any soldiers. But the roads were empty and desolate. It looked as if they had already taken this city down and slaughtered all of the civilians.

"Tawnie showed me something earlier that I'm a bit confused about," I told her. She looked over at me with her eyebrows furrowed.

"What?" She asked.

"She showed me a vision or something. Some sort of weird lake where this woman was waiting to meet me. She was… divine." I explained, expecting to be laughed at or something. But Victoria simply leaned back in her seat and sighed.

"What do you think it means?" She asked. "I could see you were being taken over because of how the two of you were staring at the entrance."

"Yeah, I can imagine that the two of us were standing still for a while."

She turned to me once more. Her eyebrow hiked again.

"Yeah, no. It was only a few seconds." She said.

I turned forward, wondering about her claim. How was that possible? It felt like I had been talking with the woman in white for at least fifteen minutes.

"You okay?" She asked.

I nodded. "I feel like there's stuff happening in this world right now that contradicts what we've learned about the past."

Victoria shrugged. "Maybe."

"Tawnie tried to warn everyone about this moment right here, shortly after Riyadh." I explained. She turned to look at me. Her eyes were wide, and a look on her face that suggested she would be sick.

"If we win this battle in Idaho, there's a battle we have to face that's much bigger than even the mission we went on years ago."

Victoria shook her head.

I sighed, not even believing the words exiting my mouth. "Is it ridiculous to believe that all of this may be orchestrated?"

She looked at me again with a blank stare.

"What if this Arcanin Prophecy that Tawnie told us about is the script for humanity? All these things are happening that the public never knows about. What if someone else can translate the Arcanin text but is working against us?"

Victoria shook her head again. "I'd say that you sound just like her."

Victoria looked at me. Our eyes met. The corners of her mouth hiked.

"I can't believe you are in love with her." She said.

"Who said I'm in love?" I asked. "I'm just really fond of her."

"So fond that you will run into the literal fire for her."

I looked down the road, seeing the burning red aurora high in the atmosphere. In seconds, everything around us was red. I began to think about why I was even traveling to this place, chasing after this woman. She's complex and challenges me in ways that only she can. From the day I met her in Riyadh, I have been fond of her. How she took charge of the most dangerous military unit in the United States Army was enticing. She's dark and scary but also the most captivating sight I have ever seen. I've always had a thing for puzzles, even as a child. But this woman, whoever she is; whatever she is, is the next puzzle I want to solve. A pit sat in my stomach as I thought about her marriage. It almost made me sick. But driving into the inferno is hardly the right time to have a moral dilemma.

"What's the plan, Top?" Victoria asked. I didn't answer her right away. I simply raised my right hand and channeled my power to it. My skin began to glow blue and fill the car with the light.

"Seriously?" She asked as she looked over at me.

"I'll bring the boom?" I said to her. She raised her arm next to mine and did the same. Her hand began to glow red, and the light inside the vehicle started to blend. A purplish color shined all over the SUV, and we both smiled.

"What is the worst-case scenario?" She asked.

I began to feel the heat the closer we drove toward the border.

"We go in, rescue Milo, and find Tawnie," I said. "Anyone in the way will be flattened."

I smiled at her once more, and she laughed. "I'll bring the boom," I said again with widened eyes.

"And I'll lock the room!" She responded.

408

Chapter LXI

Victoria and I reached the city limits and the literal end of the road. The sky here was the reddest I'd seen. The color was so vibrant, making the world appear as if I had a welding mask with a red lens. My eyes burned as they attempted to focus on nearby objects. We stopped shy of seeing the gate and the structure they built beyond it.

"What are you doing?" Victoria asked.

"I can't see a thing, Vic," I said as I turned the vehicle off. "If we need to shoot, I will need some distance."

"Understood." She said as she opened her door and walked to the front of the truck, waiting for me. I followed and saw that she held her finger up as if she had an idea.

"What is it?" I asked.

"Come here," she said as she grabbed my hand and pulled me close to her. A red shield surrounded us, and I could see my own color again.

"I can imagine this bubble isn't so obvious when everything else is red anyway." She suggested.

"Good point."

We walked toward the gate. It was the first time I had walked straight into danger without a gun in my hand. It felt uneasy, but I knew I had to trust my abilities. Victoria walked with her chin high as if she had no worries. She looked at me with a grin on her face.

"Practice any?" She asked.

"Uh… What?" I replied.

"Have you done anything since our last mission?"

I turned forward and sighed. "Not as much as I should have," I said. "With everything happening today and Casters getting all this bad press, I've tried not to use them."

She smiled and shook her head. "I guess it's good that I'm the Racket."

"Well, I'm not going to be just a ball for you to serve whenever you need," I growled.

Again, she shook her head. "That's what you think." She put one hand on her hip as the other moved before her as if she were drawing something.

"We are only here to save your girlfriend and her kid from this shadow op. You are out of practice, and I'm not. Do the math here, Top." She explained with a smile.

"We are here to save the world, Vic!" I yelled. "Don't you understand, if we screw this up, then humanity as we know it will suffer!'

Victoria relaxed and went silent for a few seconds.

"You sipped the Kool-Aid, I see." She growled.

"If we don't save her and Milo, then our world falls into chaos," I argued. "I don't know what it means, but dammit, I'm not ready to find out!"

Momentarily, I stopped walking. Victoria stopped a few paces ahead and turned around with an attitude. "You are stretching my bubble." She said, rolling her eyes.

"Look!" I growled, holding my hand up straight, pointing at her. "You may not want to believe this is real, but it is! Tawnie's existence spits in the face of your beliefs and scares you! I get it! But we still have a mission to accomplish!"

Victoria's eyes perked, and her body convulsed as if she would be ill. Again, she reached for her golden cross.

"Dan, what the hell are you saying right now?" She asked.

I shook my head and continued toward the gate. She followed to keep from breaking the bond of her shield.

"I have a theory, Vic, and if I'm right, then we are all in trouble," I told her. My mouth salivated as I said it out loud. I didn't even want to believe it. But there was too much evidence. Vic's head tilted as she looked at me side-eyed. I could barely see the glow of her pupils as she pursed her lips.

"What exactly is this theory of yours?" She asked.

I took a deep breath, getting ready to say something completely inconceivable. But we heard something pop in front of us.

"What was that?" She asked, looking at the gate. I looked and didn't see a thing.

"I don't know," I replied. But before I could say anything else, I heard a rifle fire.

"Run!" I yelled as a second gun fired, then a third. We ran to a corner in the gate structure that covered us from fire. Just as we exited the blast zone, a beam of white light hit Victoria's shield and canceled it. The break in her shield caused an implosion that whipped us against the wall.

She screamed, unable to brace herself from impact. The front of Victoria's body slammed against the steel structure.

My chest tightened as I watched her body fall to the ground. "Vic, you okay?" I yelled as I ran to check on her. She lay on the ground, her body contorted in a way that no human should lay. I carefully grabbed her, feeling for anything out of place. Her eyes were open, but her body was limp. I dragged her toward the corner as the bullets were now coming in masses. So many rounds hit the steel wall that it ripped to shreds.

"Vic, are you okay?" I asked. Suddenly, she gasped for air.

"What the hell was that?" She asked.

I looked up, and my eyes caught a round of what looked to be a white laser hitting the wall along with a slew of bullets.

"They have Kaitron Suppression Blasters," I said as I looked down at her. "Are you good?"

She nodded, a grimace on her face as she tried to pull herself up using my hand.

"I have to take them out," I said as we stood.

She stepped to the corner and tried to look around, but it was too dangerous.

"Fuck it!" She said. "You ready?"

I got into a running position and faced the wall on the opposite side of the gate. "Ready."

Victoria held her palm toward me and motioned as if she was throwing something out to her side. I felt the tug on my power. A force so great pushing me forward like a catapult. I generated my energy from within. Something that I have done numerous times before, and my body shot toward the wall ahead. I slammed into it before bouncing away and heading straight for a group of about twelve soldiers. They were all still pointing in the same direction. But in the breath it took me to reach them, many of them had their eyes on me and prepared to switch targets. But there was no use. I slammed to the ground, going through four of them, completely decapitating the first man, and thrashing through the others. As I touched the dirt, my blue energy whipped to the ground and caused a wave of blue light. It spanned the ground about twenty feet away. The men caught in the ring were amputated on contact, and the force blew away others outside. Even the small gate to the side of the road was destroyed, leaving a gaping hole open to see the building behind it. I grabbed a rifle that sat at my feet from one of the men and killed the remaining soldier.

"Clear!" I yelled to Victoria as I turned the rifle at the opening of the building. An alarm began to sound as she ran over.

"Talk about making an entrance she said with a smile.

I turned toward the entrance and tilted my head back, signaling her attention away to the compound. "Yeah," I said. "Grab a gun, and let's get this over with."

We took cover on both sides of the gate. We waited for the inevitable wave of soldiers to exit the facility.

"Let's move!" We heard someone yell. I looked across the opening at her, and she nodded.

"Out here!" Another man yelled. Victoria dropped her rifle and pointed her palm to the ground at the opening. The first man that exited the gate stopped. I could see him convulsing as he tried to proceed. Also, Victoria's face soured as the strain took its toll on her. The other soldiers behind him attempted to push past, and the man began to scream. His battle buddies crushed his body as they pushed him against nothing. They had no idea he was being crushed. I stepped into the doorway before the men behind could get around him. Immediately, I was thrown into the cluster of soldiers trying to exit the building. Blood splattered everywhere as I plowed through dozens of them. I entered the facility and bounced against the walls. This caused me to plunge deeper into the space and still topple the soldiers. With each bounce, my momentum was cut. Brisk flight quickly turned into sluggish rolling. After clearing a path for Victoria, I heard her entering with her rifle blazing. She killed the remaining disoriented soldiers before they could regain their composure. I let down my shield and began to shoot as well. We proceeded through the building with ill intent. Our goal was to kill anyone who wasn't Tawnie or Milo. We cleared room after room until we approached an open door that felt different. It was like a familiar presence was pouring from the threshold, or something was guiding me. I stepped forward and pointed my gun inside, and ran in. There were no armed men—just men in lab coats and goggles. Instinctively, I shot one in the head.

"Fuck!" I yelled as I ran in. "Everybody, hands in the air!"

Victoria ran in, and her eyes grew wide as she looked around. She aimed her rifle at the engineers in blinding white lab coats. Her eyes were continually drawn to the center of the room, where a glass tube was full of light. We could both feel the immense energy cascading through it. It was astonishing, yet horrifying. But in addition to that, a woman's body dangled inside, being drained of the very energy I felt from before. It was Tawnie, and she was unconscious. Her arms were up, and her legs were bound. Each vein inside her body illuminated and shone through her skin. Victoria looked at me with fear in her eyes. I sighed as I looked away at the case. It didn't take a genius to know what she was thinking. The sight of her hanging inside the tube was familiar, making all of this too real.

"What the fuck am I looking at here, Top?" She asked me.

"I think they're–" I began to say but stopped to look around for more evidence. "I think they're draining her energy."

"For what?" She yelled in response as she raised her rifle to the lab personnel again.

"No, please don't shoot!" They all yelled as they threw their hands up.

"What the fuck are you doing to her? Why are you draining her?" Victoria asked.

One man put his arms down and took a deep breath. Victoria watched him closely, prepared to turn her gun to him if she needed to.

"It's too late, Victoria France, Daniel Gordon." He said. "He has already succeeded in his plan."

My eyes bulged from my head as I stared at the man. I walked to him and raised my rifle, pressed it into his chest, and pinned him against the wall.

"Who the fuck are you talking about?" I growled. But before he could answer. Each of the lab workers turned their attention to the door. Victoria and I looked over our shoulder. My stomach turned as I saw a man in a suit. His hair was slicked back, and he wore glasses. He was a skinny fellow who seemed calm in his demeanor. His eyes locked on mine as he popped the collar of his tailored blazer. Behind him, more soldiers who already had the drop on us. I raised my rifle and pointed it into the air, slowly surrendering to them. Victoria did the same. Two soldiers walked over to us and snatched the weapons from our hands. They pulled us back and made us kneel in front of Tawnie's tube. We faced the man in the black suit on our knees and a rifle to the back of our necks.

"Did you really think you could take us out here?" he asked with a smile. I immediately recognized his voice. Anger filled me as I looked him in the eyes.

"Who the fuck are you?" Victoria asked. "And what do you want from us?"

"Vic!" I yelled. "This is Milo Simms Senior," I announced. "Her eyes widened as she looked over to me. "And he already has a checkmate."

The man smirked as he stared at me. "Now that the introductions are over, I need to speak with you, Mr. Gordon. Because this is the last time you'll meddle with family business."

Chapter LXII

"What the hell did you just say?" Victoria asked. "Milo Senior? As in, her son's father?"

The soldier behind her jammed the barrel of his weapon into the back of her neck. She screamed.

"Hey!" I yelled. But something blunt struck me in the back of the head as well. The headache started, bringing along a loud ringing in my ears.

"Shut the fuck up! The man yelled as he tugged on the collar of my vest to hoist me back up. My vision was blurry. I tried to lay my eyes on Milo again; he had the biggest grin.

"You wouldn't be smiling so big if you knew what was coming to you," I said, hoping to piss him off. A butt stock swang and hit me across the nose, knocking me into the guy behind me. He extended his arm and threw it around my neck. He squeezed as tight as he could, cutting off my circulation. Blood pooled in the back of my throat, making even gasping for air impossible.

"Please, don't kill him!" I heard Victoria. I grabbed the man's arm, hoping to pull him off, but the hold was too tight. I tried to get leverage with my legs, but there was far too much blood on the floor to get traction. Then I saw Milo signal for him to stop. The man's hold was released, and I began to choke on the blood.

Milo's eyes seemed cold, almost penetrating the heat in the room. He locked onto me without even blinking. His hands slowly went into his lower back, and his chest inflated as he lifted his chin.

"Mr. Gordon," He called out as he slowly walked in. "Born and raised in Boise. Graduating top of your class in high school. To graduating top of your class from Iowa State with a degree in Digital Engineering."

I watched him closely as he walked to the glass container holding his wife.

"Joined the Army to participate in the war and became First Sergeant of the most elite military company in the history of the armed forces. At such a young age, I might add."

He turned around and looked down at me with resentment in his glare.

"You have to help me understand something, though." He requested as he walked back to the entrance of the room. "As smart of a man as you are, how could you be so stupid as to fall for someone like Tawnie in the first place?"

I chose to remain silent. The man behind me pushed his rifle into me a little more. I did my best not to allow my expression to reflect my level of discomfort.

"If any situation, your partner, Victoria France, should have talked you out of, it should have been this." Dr. Simms continued.

"Let me ask you something, Simms!" I growled. His eyes lowered as he looked at me again. It was as if he was appalled that I was speaking to him.

"You have a family that is your responsibility to serve. How do you call yourself a man if—"

"If what?" He cut me off, walking toward me. "If I can't protect the woman I made vows with! Or were you going to suggest that I was a bad father, Mr. Gordon? Either way, I don't think you understand the position you are in right now!"

He stood before me, cracking his knuckles. His bottom lip was tucked underneath his front teeth for just a moment. I swallowed hard as I felt the climbing of energy that wasn't my own. It was like a cold chill was coming, or what it would be like if every nerve in your spine was vibrating. It was intense, so this man was mighty in multiple ways.

I quickly glanced at Victoria; she looked like she had a plan. They took our guns, but we still had our powers. I could see her hand making a symbol. It was subtle, and I hardly caught it, but I knew the premise: Prepare for takeoff.

"I'll kill you myself, Officer Gordon!" Simms yelled.

As he pulled his fist up, preparing to throw it down, a veil of red appeared before me. The force of the violent pull sent me shooting through the room. My blue energy surrounded me as I headed directly toward Victoria. She jumped down to the floor and allowed me to blow through the men holding her. I hit the wall, my energy compressing like a rubber ball bounced from the floor. The force sent me back toward Simms, and I knew for sure that I would bowl him over or go through him. I felt accomplished. But for a split second, I could see a sick, sadistic smile. Instead of bowling him over, his forearm flew up, guarding his body. He punched back, breaking through my barrier. The cascade of blue energy shattered like glass.

I flipped over his arm like a horseshoe hitting its target. I landed on the floor near him and slid on my back. He spun around to stomp me, but I evaded by rolling out of the way. His heel slammed into the floor, breaking through the metal underneath. Immediately, Simms pulled his ankle from the ravaged steel and smiled. We watched one another closely as the hall started to fill with soldiers. He pulled his foot from the hole he made in the floor. The metal was at least two inches thick. Still, his heel was able to penetrate it like foil.

"Gordon, we're out-gunned," Victoria said, grabbing her rifle again and pointing it at the door.

"To be expected when you run into the base of your adversary," Simms said.

"You pretentious piece of shit!" I snarled at him. "What do you want with us?"

The man smiled again as he wiped his collar, eyes locked onto me the entire time.

"Mr. Gordon. If I'm being completely candid, I want the two of you eliminated."

The room went silent for a moment. I looked at Victoria, and she trembled with worry as the soldiers by the door pointed their rifles at her. It appeared that they would try to take her out while the boss kept his eyes on me.

"I don't suppose we can renegotiate a treatise?" I suggested.

Simms turned his head and snickered. "I don't think my boss would approve of that plan."

There was a pause. The moment just before the storm whipped up in the room. It was now or never. Just past Simms, I could see a soldier at the door struggling. He trembled as he reached to his side. His face showed a hint of frustration and fear, and his teeth clenched in his open mouth as if he were distressed. I looked back at Victoria and saw her fingers moving. It was like she was manipulating a puppet. Her eyes were distant and empty. She was tuned out of reality and somehow in pain. I could see it in her face. But if memory served me correctly, she was in danger.

One drawback to her abilities is that she risks having an aneurysm if she over-exerts herself. The man pulls out a couple of grenades from the crowd and activates them. A bead of crimson falls from her nose as she releases and passes out, allowing her body to fall to the floor. Simms immediately recognized the danger and jumped to the floor. The bombs exploded, engulfing the hall and doorway where dozens of soldiers gathered.

I shrouded myself in my energy to shield myself from the blast, and I was immediately shot away. I bounced around the room from the kinetic energy and hit every obstacle around me. This caused my weakness to be fully exposed. I'm safe from the explosion, but now I'm a weapon I can't control, and I have to stay in the ball of energy until I slow down. Otherwise, I'm dead too.

I couldn't take control of the sphere like before because the hits were too close together. With each bounce, it was almost like a plane smacking a building at high speed over and over again. Each hit disorienting me more than the last. Finally, I smashed the glass into Tawnie's containment tube. Luckily, I missed her body. The entire tube shattered, and I was on a crash course with Simms as he got back up from the floor. His glasses were broken, and his suit was torn and dirty. The look on his face was intense.

His eyes were demented and full of rage as he reached forward and caught me in midair. He held me like a giant medicine ball and squeezed until the veil of energy shattered again. This time, I was ready. The pause allowed me to get my bearings and prepare for offense. The bubble broke, and a wave of converted energy traveled through him. This threw the man backward. His clothes waved like he was trapped inside a vortex of wind. Most of it ripped away before he was slammed against the wall behind him. He peeled away from the wall and landed on the floor, seemingly unresponsive.

Here is my chance to correct all of this. I looked over at Victoria; luckily, she was still alive and getting back up on her own.

"Vic!" I yelled as I ran to her.

"I'm okay." She said. "Just a mild migraine. That's all."

"You little reckless whore!" I said with a smile. She looked up at me with a smile on her face as well. "We have to get Tawnie and M.J. and get out of here."

Victoria's attention snapped over to Tawnie, and I could feel why. Her energy was increasing. It was climbing so high and so fast that it made me dizzy. I looked back at her and noticed that the light gathered inside the tube was flowing back into her body.

"What the hell is happening?" Victoria asked.

"That machine was designed to take Tawnie's power," I answered. "But now, she's taking it back, and she's pissed."

Suddenly, her eyes popped open. They glowed a bright white but immediately sharpened as she saw her husband's body lying on the floor. I turned to look at the soldier's body behind Victoria. Special Anti-Caster handcuffs were attached to his utility belt. I grabbed them and calmly walked to Milo's body and whipped the cuffs on him. The light on the lining of the bands went from red to blue, and I released a sigh of pure relief as I stood. I looked back at Tawnie and noticed that her anger and power increased by the second.

"Tawnie, relax!" I yelled at her, but the energy around her continued to flare. She pulled her arm down, breaking the mechanism bounding her to the ceiling. Shredded metal, parts, and wires were pulled down and tossed to the side. The mangled mess of debris looked like a car totaled in an accident. Her hands began to glow white again, and I intervened.

"Tawnie," I called her again. "It's over."

Miraculously, she floated off the pedestal and hovered above my head to land behind me. My eyes grew large as they followed her.

"What the fuck is happening?" Victoria asked. "Did she just fly?"

I backed up against the remainder of the tube that she was trapped in, holding my head in my hands. I had to be seeing things, right? There's no way I just saw this woman fly. But if I did, it only proves my theory.

As she walked toward her husband's body, I began to feel his energy increase as well. It was then that I came back to reality.

"Hey, Top, am I going insane?" Victoria asked. "I can swear that dude's power level is increasing."

"Danny," Tawnie called out to me. "Go get my son."

I froze momentarily, thinking about something the woman in the vision told me. A chill entered my body, momentarily causing me to forget the intense heat. Victoria ran over to me and snapped me out of my stupor. We ran out of the room and headed down the hall, hopping over bodies along the way. We looked inside each room, attempting to find the boy, but he wasn't in them.

"Where is he?" Victoria asked. "I can't even feel his energy. Is he even here?"

I stopped to look around. Tubes were lining the ceiling—the same metal ones connected to the container we found Tawnie in. A set traveled in series but entered the wall without a door.

"Alright, Vic, throw me in right here," I said, standing before the wall as if I was about to run into it.

"What?" She asked.

"Trust me." I simply said. She sighed as she looked at the wall, then back to me. Her hand raised, and I slammed against it. Instead of bouncing away, I went through, breaking a secret door. I entered a dark room with an ominous glow toward the back. The light cascaded into the room from the hallway, but I couldn't see anything but the darkness. My mind immediately shifted to our last mission with Tawnie in Riyadh. I pulled out a flashlight to look around and quickly realized it was a lab just like the one Tawnie was being held in. But this room was certainly much bigger. We walked toward the glow with caution. We constantly looked around for threats that could have been hiding in the shadows. But the closer we got to the area where the light came from, the more we grew to realize what we were approaching. It was a podium-style device that held a small item with a tremendous glow. An orb that had the glow of magma inside glass.

"It's that orb," Victoria announced. I began to look around the room again and caught a visual of another containment chamber nearby. The control panel at the base had the same lights as the one Tawnie was inside. I shined my flashlight over to it and recognized the feet inside. As my light slowly rose, I sighed in relief as I verified it was little Milo. He twitched softly as the light shined over his eyes. Suddenly, a crash was nearby, and the ground shook violently, almost knocking us from our feet. Victoria and I stood fast as the wave passed, waiting for an aftershock.

"What the hell was that?" She asked, "An earthquake?" I shook my head as I felt Dr. Simms's energy climb, then Tawnie. I braced myself just before another crash was heard, this time sounding like thunder in the distance. The ground shook again, this time with much more intensity. "Let's get the hell away from here!" I yelled to her as I ran to Milo's confinement. Victoria ran to retrieve the relic.

422

Chapter LXIII

We broke the kid out of his imprisonment and headed to the exit. I carried him in my arms, following behind Victoria. The crashes continued, and the quake went from intermittent to continuous.

Just as we reached the door, Victoria stopped and held her hand up so I could stop walking. Her other palm whipped forward as if attempting to use her powers on something. But a large blast of fire entered the room and enveloped us. Luckily, she blocked it with a perfectly timed shield. I looked up as the flames surrounded us, completely encapsulating the spot where we stood. When it was over, a man stepped in, pulling off a white lab coat, throwing it aside, and revealing his slender frame. He wore square-framed glasses on his face and pulled them off as well.

"I can't allow you to leave with my test subject." He said.

I stepped in front of Victoria and handed Milo off to her.

"Alright, your call, Doc." I confidently replied as I threw my fists up. "If I gotta fight you to get out of here, let's make it a date!"

The man rushed toward me. His arms began to blaze. He stepped in to punch me, but I ducked and used my energy only in my fist to punch him in the gut. He groaned as he doubled over and immediately tried to get back up to keep fighting. I could hear his wheezing and panting as he fought the pain in his abdomen. He was sloppy. I could tell he was never meant to be a warrior, but that didn't mean he wasn't dangerous. To my surprise, he threw a backhand at me, and a wave of fire blasted from it. Again, I was able to get out of the way. The intense heat stole the oxygen from the environment as it went over me. I reached forward and grabbed his right leg behind the knee. Then I put my other arm around the left side of his waist and hoisted his frail body into the air. After holding and falling backward, I pulled his leg toward me and pushed up on his back to slam him down on his face. I was hoping to compound any damage made to his abdomen. The impact caused a puff of flame to excrete from his body. It was almost like a balloon that had released some air. But despite his demise, the man continued to get up.

I shook my head and reached up to wipe sweat from my face. I looked at Victoria, and she stared at the man in wonder.

"What the hell is happening to his skin?" She asked. Focusing so much on defending Milo, I hadn't even noticed the lesions on his body from the flames. His skin was charred in some places but had burned entirely off in others.

"Woah!" I said. "Sir, you may want to give it a rest!"

But the man continued up to his knees, panting like a dog. "All I have to do is defeat you. Then the boss can heal me with her blood!"

I was perplexed by the statement. I looked up at Victoria; her face showed she was just as lost. Hell, at least I wasn't the only one.

"Vic, get out of here," I said to her.

She became worried. The ground rumbled again, followed by yet another explosion in the distance. "Are you sure?" She asked.

I reached into my pocket and threw her the keys. She caught them, surprisingly not waking the boy.

"Take Milo and that thing far away from here," I added.

"No! I won't allow it!" The man said. His voice began transitioning about halfway into the sentence, and his body changed. The lesions on his skin began to bubble. It was almost like the heat was escaping through the folds of his skin. Cracks began to appear all over his body like segments of the Earth after a volcano erupts. His body seemed to become unstable as he stood to his feet. He was turning into lava. Victoria stood in front of the door, shocked at what was happening.

"Vic, get the hell out of here! That is an order!" I screamed at her. Without words, she ran outside. When I looked back at the man in front of me, he appeared larger. His entire head became engulfed with magma, and the smell became infallible. A body was being burned. This man was a goner. Whatever he had become was now the new threat. I stood before it with my chin up, trying to figure out how to stop it. He made the first move. A quick jab of his arm sent a magma plume in my direction. I rolled to the side and generated a shield of my own. I looked at the lava and noticed the floor underneath us was melting.

"Alright, Igneous Hulk, you want to fight. I have one for you!" I ran away, needing to see if he would follow, and he did. Not only did he follow, he did it faster than I imagined he would. The stumpy legs of the golem were moving in a way that seemed impossible. I created enough momentum to send me into a recoil. I ran to the wall directly before me and powered up when I hit it. The impact was enough to send me barreling back into the monster. Bits of magma chipped away from his massive body and splattered. The remnants landed all over the support structures above. The rafters began to snap, and the sounds of bending metal filled the room. After landing, I looked back at him and saw he was already coming back for me. His shoulder was exposed. A large portion was missing from it. But embers burned bright as it seemed to regenerate on the spot.

"Fuck this," I said to myself as I ran toward the wall behind me. I dived into the bottom of the wall and bounced back again. This time, I bowled through one of his legs. Again, the magma splattered, degrading more of the structure around us. A support beam broke and swung into the room, hitting the golem. It had gotten stuck momentarily, and I felt like this was my opportunity to finish the fight. While he was stuck under the fallen rafter, I ran to him at full speed. It roared at me as it reached to eat away at the steel beam holding it down.

I jumped into the air near it and dived head-first into the floor. I popped up at an angle that sent me right into his chest and ultimately split the beast from its hip to its head. In addition to destroying the golem, I removed an integral support beam as I exited the building. I never thought I would be so happy to see the red sky. I landed on the main road near our parked area and saw that the France's SUV was still there. I stared at it, wondering if Victoria had made it inside. But she quickly opened the door and called for me. I looked back at the building, and the entire thing collapsed. But there was yet another explosion, followed by the ground shaking.

I looked around for the source of the noise but saw nothing. I looked back at Victoria and noticed her stepping outside the vehicle. Her eyes were locked to the sky. Daniel followed her gaze to see what was so fascinating. Then, he recognized the war happening above. A veil of white light filled the area like the sun as a giant stream blasted across the sky. Suddenly, something stopped the energy from moving further. It was as if it slammed into a solid object and caused another shockwave. The blast was torn apart, split into dozens of spark-like beans that shot down to the ground like a meteor shower. I ran to the SUV and jumped into the passenger side. I looked back for Milo and realized his eyes were open but still groggy.

"He put up a little of a fight, but we're ready now," Victoria said as she put the vehicle into gear and began to drive. She turned around and headed back toward Rexburg.

"Do we even have another route out?" Victoria asked.

I shook my head. "I guess that depends on what kind of blockades they set up."

She sighed.

"We'll go get Lester and Lyric, then head West," I said. "At least if there are any blockades, we can take them out."

"But what about–" Victoria began to ask as a giant beam of light slammed into the ground, shaking the world underneath us again. Up close, it looked like pure light energy. There were rays of the rainbow inside of it. Chunks of Earth were tossed into the air as the beam moved from right to left, cutting through the road like a hot knife. Victoria slammed on brakes, attempting not to barrel down into the ravine that was created. But there was an explosion. The force rocked us, the flames engulfed us, and the vehicle spun through the air. We flipped inside the firestorm for what felt like hours. Completely ravaged, our truck landed upside down. I'm not sure how, but we survived. My body was hurting, and I'm pretty sure I had a broken rib.

"Vickie," I called out. "Vickie, you okay?"

I could hear her moving around. But I wasn't sure if it was gravity settling her body or if she was conscious. I was so bad off that I couldn't even look in that direction.

"Milo, you good back there, kid?" I yelled.

"Yeah." He whimpered.

"Everything is going to be okay, kid." I heard myself say it. It was my instincts speaking for me. But I don't think I truly believed that we would. There were flames all around us, and I began to smell the gasoline from the vehicle. I raised my hand and pressed against the car's roof, slightly relieving the 247lbs pressing on my neck. I tried using my other hand to undo the seat belt. But upside down and disoriented, I realized that I used the wrong hand. I attempted to switch but was too exhausted, and using my powers was out of the question. It was then that I heard footsteps. I looked forward and saw sharply creased pant legs and expensive dress shoes.

"You gotta be shitting me!" I growled. The toes bent as the person kneeled to the ground. As I suspected, it was Dr. Simms.

"Daddy!" Milo called out, full of excitement. "Daddy, back here!"

"I'm here, Spud." The man said with the same energy. "I'll get you out of there!"

He walked around to the back door and ripped it off the hinges.

"Daddy!" The boy cried as he stepped out of the vehicle.

"Milo, no! Don't go with him!" I screamed. But there was no answer. I could only imagine his confusion.

"He's a bad man, Spud," Simms said. "We don't trust the bad guys, do we?"

"You son of a bitch!" I screamed again. Then, a hand reached into the vehicle and grabbed the Pyro Stone.

"I'll just be taking this back." Simms chuckled.

"You'll pay for this," I growled, trying to free myself from the upside-down seat. He laughed.

"Well. It's a good thing I'm rich."

He and his son walked away with me still inside the vehicle. The flames burned along the grass, inching its way toward me. After realizing that I didn't have the strength to get out, I had no choice but to accept what was coming. The smell of gasoline became more potent, and I began to panic. Again, I called for Victoria, hoping she would answer this time. But there was no answer. Finally, I could work my neck to look at the driver's seat. My heart sank, realizing that she was gone. The A-pillar that separated the windshield from the door was stained with her blood.

"No, no, no!" I screamed as I suddenly got a rush of energy. Again, I tugged at the seat belt retainer. I pushed myself up from the ceiling, hoping to release the latch. To my surprise, it did. The smoke filled the vehicle, mixing with the smell of gasoline and making it hard to breathe. I grabbed the door handle and rammed my shoulder into it. It opened, but there were flames already working its way inside. I realized I had been too focused on freeing myself that I took my eyes off the environment—a costly mistake.

I slammed the door shut again, forced to look for another way out. But my pool of options was drying out. I crawled to the driver's side, feeling the sharp pain in my neck and back as I struggled to move. I was sluggish, but I made it to the other side. I pressed out on the door, but it was stuck. I tried to crawl through the compacted window, but there wasn't enough clearance. The flames immediately swept into the openings. The headliner, the doors, and the carpets above me caught flame instantly. My opportunity to escape had vanished in a heartbeat. With one final look around, my only option was to watch as the fire consumed me.

The Noble of Clarity has a specific place in the timeline. This person is integral to the survival of our message and thus shall be protected at all cost, even by the universe itself.

-Excerpt of the Arcanin Prophecy; Translated by the Oracle

Chapter LXIV

"Daniel!" I heard someone yelling. My body was numb, but I felt no pain. I tried moving my extremities, but no luck.

"Daniel, wake up!" The voice yelled again. It was Tawnie. She asked me to do something I didn't know how to do. I couldn't see anything, not even the light of the red sky. I couldn't feel my body at all. I wasn't even breathing. But the more she called my name, the more my senses returned, followed by just one heartbeat. It pulsed through me. Something that I took for granted before, but now I truly understand its importance.

I heard her calling me over and over, thinking that, at some point, she would give up and move on. But she didn't. She kept pushing me to–

"Wake up!" She screamed. The faint heartbeats turned to small, shallow beats of a drum. Or maybe it was her beating on my sternum.

"I'm going to say something, and I don't want you to take this the wrong way," she said as she continued pressing on my sternum. Each press brought back a little more feeling in my body. However, I still couldn't wake up.

"I thought you were a means to an end. For that, I'm sorry. But now, everything is different, Danny!"

A few more presses to my chest opened my airways, almost making me feel like I could breathe again. But still, I couldn't move.

"Daniel, the prophecy may need you for the moment. But I need you to live."

I could feel the wetness of her tears falling on my cheek. The warmth seemed to travel through my entire body. It was like the blood was rushing through my veins for the first time. I was starting to feel alive again. Her hands cuffed at my chest, and she pressed hard, repeatedly.

"Come on, dammit!" She screamed. "I need you to wake up!"

"Oh my God, Oh my God!" I heard another voice yell, accompanied by footsteps that grew louder. "Daniel!"

It was Victoria. Thank God she's alive.

"I got him!" Tawnie yelled. "He's going to wake up for us. Aren't you, Danny?"

Everything in me wished that I could open my lips and answer her. But I couldn't. For a few minutes, she pressed down, almost throwing the world down into my body. But the feeling started, and her voice began to fade over time. Another tear hit my body, and it would send a surge of energy through me. However, not enough to wake me up. Suddenly, She placed her lips to mine, and everything stopped momentarily. The sounds of her whimpers had subsided. No more tears were falling onto me. The warmth I felt had gone cold again, and the thumping subsided. Then, I was able to open my eyes.

"Hello, Daniel." I heard someone say. The light was blinding, but I felt my eyes getting adjusted to it. My eyes… they worked. I was breathing again. I bent my knees and felt my legs, and I was standing. After a moment of wincing in place, my vision was finally restored, and Tawnie stood in front of me. We were back in that place by the lake. I spun around to verify and found the woman in the white dress staring at me. The crystal blue waters behind her sparkled against the light from what I thought was the sun. However, I looked up and saw no source of light, just an open, blue sky. I looked at the woman again, and she smiled at me.

"You're lucky, Mr. Ricochet." She said as she stepped forward and walked around me. My eyes followed her in awe.

"Wh… why?" I asked, clearing my throat afterward.

She stopped next to Tawnie and looked at her with what

seemed to be disappointment.

"I used up my last favor to abolish him from the River Styxx." She said to her. The smile that she wanted to have, realizing that I was alive, was now masked with indifference.

"I understand." She said as she turned to the woman. "How can I make this right?"

The woman shook her head. For the first time since I met her, she seemed worried.

"You need to get the flame away from Milo, both of them." She answered. "The fate of our worlds hinges on that."

She looked at me, and she seemed just as angry. I took a step backward for caution.

"You may have realized this already, Mr. Ricochet. But you died." She said. My head fell. "Time moves at a different rate in the Underworld. So you will probably feel a lot more experienced at times. But that will pass when you are back inside your body where you belong."

I shook my head in disbelief. "Are you saying I've been dead for a long time?" I asked as I approached her. Suddenly, a veil of darkness shot up from the ground before me, erasing everything from my view.

"Primordeus!" She yelled. "Heel!" The darkness fell back to the ground and dissipated at our feet. It appeared like we were all standing over a pitch-black hole for a moment.

"How long have I been dead?" I continued, still watching the inconceivable darkness until it faded into the ground like rainwater.

"In the Midworld, it has been about twenty minutes." She answered. My mouth fell open with disbelief. "But you were in the River Styxx for years."

"The River Styxx?" I asked, feeling like there was no way I heard her correctly. "Like the place from Hercules that drains souls?"

The woman looked over to Tawnie. "Are the mortals not versed on this topic?"

Tawnie's cheeks hiked, but her lips remained flat as if embarrassed. "Exactly, Danny." She answered me. "You were a lost soul for about twenty-three years in the underworld. That time, you will remember. But your soul has been out of your body for only twenty minutes."

For a moment, I felt like I was dead again. I was so appalled that I forgot to breathe. My head turned to side-eye her.

"I understand how shocking this all could be at this moment. You are learning much about the universe you shouldn't know." She continued.

"I don't!" The other woman yelled. Causing Tawnie to sigh in frustration. "Are the mortals not teaching this to their children?"

"They don't even know!" Tawnie turned to scream at her. "Now, could you relax and stop shellshocking him?"

"Tawnie?" I called. "What the hell is happening here? And why is this lady acting so holier than thou?"

"Holier than thou?" The woman asked. Tawnie slowly turned to her, eyes widening and head tilted. "He says things like this, making it seem like humans don't know anything!"

Please, stop!" She yelled again.

The woman looked forward, staring out into the lake again. "Tawnie, they don't remember."

"Huh?" She asked. "The humans?"

"Humans can't remember what happens when the universal balance is disrupted."

Tawnie nodded. "Yeah, I know, and I'm working on it."

But she shook her head. "No, if the entire race is lost, this problem is much bigger than we could have imagined."

Tawnie looked down. "Yeah, but we'll reassess after we retrieve the Pyro Stone."

She grabbed my arm, and we began to step away from the woman.

"But, My Lady, the flame!" She called out. Tawnie turned around and smiled at the woman.

"I'll be alright, I promise."

Suddenly, I gasped for air for what felt like the very first time. My eyes were open, and I recognized the red and gray colors alternating against the overcast. I could smell the wonderful scent of Tawnie's hair on my face and felt her body on mine.

"Dan!" I could hear Victoria yell. "Thank God!"

Tawnie quickly jumped to her feet and reached down to help me up.

"If you want to thank God, then we have much to discuss," I

told her. Tawnie waved her hands across one another, signifying that she wanted to move on to the next topic.

"Are you okay?" She asked me. Her eyes locked into mine, glossy and innocent-looking. Her lips were drawn back at the corner of her mouth from discomfort and uneasiness."

"Yeah," I answered as I grabbed her hands. "I'm fine,"

That's when I looked down to realize that my clothing was singed. Most of the skin on my body was exposed, but there were no burns. I was amazed.

"I want to know how I walked away with no burns or bruises, but I'll save it until after we go and get MJ."

"Good idea," Tawnie said. She stepped away and looked in the direction where the red in the sky was the most prominent. "I'm not sure where Milo is taking my son. But either way, I don't think he plans to let him live much longer."

"Then let's go before we run out of time,"

Chapter LXV

Tawnie flew across the sky, carrying Victoria, who also pulled me along with her powers. Up ahead, the sky had darkened as if it were nighttime, but it was smoke. The red aura in the atmosphere was now swirling as if it could form a tornado at any moment.

"What's happening here?" Victoria asked.

"This is what it looks like when the balance of nature is beginning to unravel." She answered.

"I'm sorry. What did she just say?" I interjected.

Tawnie looked down at us for a moment. "I have to place you two before going any further." She said as we began to descend.

"What?" I said. "We can't let you go alone."

She shook her head as my feet swept across the snow in the barren field. Shortly after, Victoria was placed in front of me. Tawnie landed next and turned to look at the two of us.

"Danny." She said.

"Don't you dare!" I cut her off as I approached. "If you are going there, then we will be right behind you on foot. The best thing you could do is tell us how to help you. Because we are not leaving you to fight this alone!"

She sighed.

"Steer clear of the field until the time is right." She quickly answered before blasting off into the sky again. Then, she made a 90-degree break into the direction of the central area of the red energy. All we could see from here was a golden glow in the distance. I began to walk in that direction. My arm was pulled. Turning around to see the look of fear on Victoria's face almost reminded me of how serious it was.

"Now, I remember scuffling with terrorist organizations and corrupt politicians. But this is too much!" She said.

I nodded. "Vic, I completely understand that you're worried. But this outcome will be much worse if we don't do anything!"

She approached me and jabbed me in the chest with her straight hand.

"You will not stand here and pretend you don't feel their power!" She continued. I turned away to look down at the veil of light again. I could see Tawnie land near it, and my toes shifted toward that direction again. She was right about that. I could feel their powers in my soul. All three energies surged through me like invisible electricity. Without warning, I began to walk. Victoria ran out in front of me.

"Vic!" I screamed. "I have to get down there!"

"And do what?" She roared. "You'll just be in the way!"

Suddenly, a pulse of energy spanned the land, akin to the shockwave of a large explosion. It came toward us fast, whipping up a cloud of dust and rocks as it approached. Victoria used her quick thinking to deflect the debris.

"What the hell was that?" She asked.

I shook my head, still staring down range. But there was an object coming toward us. It moved fast, somewhere in the range of 100 miles an hour. The object angled downward and fell to the grassy terrain. It landed with the force of a comet landing from the atmosphere. The land shook underneath us, and a wave of debris accompanied the crash.

"Get down!" I yelled. But Victoria grabbed me and raised a shield to deflect the rushing dust and wind. When it settled, I ran toward the impact site.

"Daniel!" Victoria screamed for me. But I ignored her and kept running, knowing what I'd find at the bottom of that crater. I reached the edge of the massive hole and looked over it. That's when I saw her. Her body twisted and contorted in ways that no human should be. In addition, I felt the very power fading. I jumped over the ledge and slid the wall of the crater.

"Tawnie!" I screamed. My heart pounding faster the more I think about her not getting up. I kneeled next to her and rolled her body over to her back. She felt soft, softer than usual. I took a hard swallow. I lifted her arm to get it from behind her, and it felt light.

There were no bones. Her skeleton was shattered.

"No, please, no!" I said as I leaned over her face. The closer I got, the more I realized her eyes were slightly opened. I leaned toward her nose and open mouth to feel for air, but there was nothing. In addition, her power level continued to fall.

"Oh fuck!" Victoria said. She clasped her hands over her mouth and took a step back. She looked toward the area underneath the red spiraling aura. The monstrous energy coming from underneath it was sickening.

"Tawnie, please wake up!" I said, feeling a rush of emotions sweep over me. My heart grew heavy, and the image of her mangled body soon became hazy due to the accumulation of my tears.

"Top, we have to go!" Victoria yelled as she grabbed my shoulder. I rolled it back to brush her off. Then I clung tighter to Tawnie.

"I can't," I muttered with closed eyes. "Tawnie, please!"

Everything went silent for a moment. I opened my eyes to see the green grasses by the lake. The woman in the white stola stood before me with her back to me, staring out into the water. I looked down at my hands. Tawnie was gone. I immediately jumped to my feet.

"Uh… Miss?" I called out. All logic flew from my mind as I attempted to actualize my thoughts.

"Yes, Daniel?" She replied, not even bothering to turn around.

"Where is Tawnie?" I asked as I approached with caution. The woman pulled her hand from the small of her back and pointed a finger into the lake. I lifted my eyes across the blue water and landed on the small island in the center. A woman was kneeling in front of a structure that looked like a piece of a wall. But it was too far away to make out what it was exactly.

"She's alive," I said with a sigh of relief.

"She's present," Aphrodite said. "But as long as she repairs her physical body in time, she will be."

Suddenly, I was back in the real world, hearing the eerie whirring sound of the energy in the atmosphere.

"Gordon!" I could hear Victoria screaming and feel her tugging on me. "What the hell is wrong with you? We can't stay here!"

I swung my arm back and pushed her away. I lifted Tawnie's

body, and she felt less dense. I smiled as I looked down at her.

"Hey, Vic, if you're not with me, I need you to get Tawnie out of here," I said.

"What!?" She screamed at me. "You want to help me understand what kind of drugs you got into on the way here?"

"Look, I can't expect you to understand what's happening here," I said to her as I handed Tawnie's body off. "I just need to stall until she awakens."

"You handed me off a dead body, Daniel!" She assured me. "God has his plan for her already!"

I thought about Tawnie's videos, posted online shortly after we returned from Riyadh. She stated that manufactured gods would threaten to unwind the coils bound by deities. The world thought she was nuts; others understood.

"Dammit, Vic! Don't you get it yet?" I roared at her. "The God you serve is..." I bit my tongue and sneered as I walked away from her.

"Get out of here, Victoria."

"What are you going to do? It's too dangerous to face this guy alone!" She said.

"This guy is a fake deity. I only have to hold him off until the real one wakes up."

I didn't allow her to respond. I just sent myself blasting off toward the eye of the swirling storm. As I barrelled deeper into the vortex of crimson-red energy, I began to see the man standing in the field next to his son. Milo was still inside the glass tube. As I passed overhead, I realized the energy surrounding him was dark. Purplish swirls emanate from the soil, and rocks hovered above the ground. The Earth around him seemed like a wildfire had charred it. At that moment, I wondered what I truly got myself into. I flew over him initially and hit the ground. I bounced back toward him, wanting to take his head off for what he did to Tawnie. But despite how fast I approached, he still turned to look at me with a smug grin. As we collided, I could see into his eyes as he blocked me with his forearm only. I was appalled. I've taken out tanks with my ability. I've pierced through buildings, smashing them to rubble with a single pass. This man stopped me with his forearm. His body didn't even budge. He shifted his eyes in my direction and suddenly punched upward into my shield. I dodged it and fell to the ground. I took a quick look at Milo, but he was unconscious. However, I could still feel him. I looked back at his father, who was holding the Pyro Stone.

Instead of paying it any attention, I commenced the attack. I shrouded my arms in my energy, allowing my hands to become lethal. I slammed my fist against his face, and he was sent flying backward. He hit the ground and rolled in the ash.

"Hey, Lab Coat, I'm gonna need to talk about your wife some more," I said, feeling foolishly confident. "I think she deserves better."

The man said nothing. He thumbed his nose and proceeded to approach. I stepped forward onto my right foot while blocking my face. He stepped forward onto the same foot and leaned in to take the first swing. I dodged and sent my left fist flying toward his jaw again. He used his other hand to block, then attempted to knee me in the abdomen. I was able to get my arm down and block his knee as he began to levitate, completely catching me off guard. He spun and kicked me in my shoulder. That's when I heard the pop.

I howled in agony as I soared across the burnt Earth and landed just yards away. He landed and arrogantly popped his collar. The smile on his face filled me with rage as I hoped that massaging my shoulder would help. But I quickly lost faith as I began to lose feeling in my fingers. After one pass over the mounds of my upper arm, I realized the bone was broken. I howled, the pain shooting through my entire body like lightning.

"You have some nerve, Daniel Gordon." He said as he circled me like a predator in the wild.

"Yeah, I know," I said to him. "How dare I attempt to keep the world safe from scumbags like you?"

He stopped walking and looked forward to the container holding his son.

"You're keeping the world safe." He muttered. "You are dabbling in affairs that you can't possibly understand!"

His power flared before he stomped over to me. He hammered his fist down on my head, sending me straight to the ground. My body immediately seized. I couldn't move. The pain from my shoulder had now radiated to all of my extremities.

"I was supposed to be the hero, dammit!" Simms roared. "If we don't kill her, we're all dead anyway, Daniel!"

He kneeled next to me and stared down at my helpless body. My fingers inched toward him, hoping that I could at least anchor him somehow.

"You thought she was our savior. But the Arcanin Prophecy starts with her."

Wait, he knows about the prophecy? If Tawnie wasn't the only person able to read it, we are in trouble. It also means that I was right. But I wasn't getting any answers out of this guy. I'd be lucky enough to leave with my life.

"The Harbinger of Chaos is what I believe the prophecy calls her. If she dies today, we live to see another."

At that moment, I could feel something in the distance. Yet, another power rivaling his in mass. Simms felt it and lowered his head as his evil eyes glared across the plains.

"Here it comes." He muttered. A wisp of wind buffeted us, giving a refreshing, cool whip across my body. But as I blinked, something was happening that sounded like a train wreck. The force of the impact caused ripples in energy to span across the land.

There she was, alive and strong as ever. Tawnie was back to her feet.

Chapter LXVI

Tawnie and her estranged husband continued to fight, going blow for blow. Each strike was like an explosion of C4 at close range. Victoria joined me on the battlefield, regretting her decision with each thunderous collision. Tawnie managed to signal me during her fight. But I translated the message as 'Release Milo.'

I could be wrong, but that seemed like the best-case scenario at the time. The Pyro Stone sat on the charred ground in front of me. Behind it, I could see the kid in his enclosure, still unconscious.

"Vic, we gotta get Milo and get out of here," I said.

She nodded. "That sounds like an amazing idea!"

I nodded back and proceeded to run. She followed closely behind. My eyes were locked onto the Pyro Stone. The orb seemed to glow brighter the closer I got to it. But before I could reach it, I was attacked from behind. I heard Victoria screech as I collided face-first with the charred Earth. Ash plumed around us, creating a light smokescreen. Someone was pulling at my legs. I looked down to see a soldier trying to finish me off. I managed to roll to my back and proceeded to plant the sole of a boot into the man's face. He stumbled backward, just missing the guy who held Victoria. He slipped to the ground, attempting to roll backward to his feet. He gained enough momentum to pop onto his hands. His head dangled between his shoulders for a split second. I ran over to kick him in his face. I enjoyed seeing the anticipation in his eyes as I approached. He dropped from his hands and landed on top of his head. I quickly pushed his body aside. Before I could get to her, Victoria wrapped herself around the man, pinning him in a standing armbar. With his arm behind him, bent in a compromising position, she was able to reach one hand to the man's neck. The sound of his bones snapping sent shivers through me. Yet, somehow, it excited me even more.

"We got company!" She said to me as she stood. In the distance, there were dozens of headlights coming toward us.

"Get the fuck out of here!" I snarled as I reached for the rifle from the dead soldiers. I stood and handed one to Victoria. She took it with a grin. But without a second thought, she tossed it aside. My eyes grew wide, "What the hell?" I asked.

"It's time to acknowledge that we are the weapons now!" She growled back at me.

I smiled and sighed deeply as I tossed the rifle aside as well.

"Mr. Ricochet, are you ready to soar?" She asked with a fist extended toward me. With a massive smile, I reciprocated and gently bumped knuckles with her. She began to glow red, which meant only one thing. Before I knew it, she had already launched me across the field. The soldiers stopped about seventy-five yards away. They all dismounted their vehicles to attack us. Their line was massive. We were faced with what looked like almost two hundred men. I slammed down into a car, causing an explosion that tore a hole in their defenses. A wave of my energy spanned the ground, disrupting the others around. It eliminated three of their vehicles and a good number of their men. I was whipped to the left and crashed like a wrecking ball into every vehicle.

Once Victoria's energy faded, I unleashed another wave of energy. This time, it was forward momentum. The wave blasted like a cannon, with enough force to pierce the vehicles ahead and rip them inside out. Blood, body parts, and debris splattered all over. The flames from the explosions covered me. I was sent flying upward. Suddenly, I was blasted by a beam of light. I knew exactly what type of weapon sent the round because I was utterly vulnerable the moment it hit me. My power stopped as if someone had hit a switch to disable me temporarily. I would need a few seconds to regenerate. But at about one hundred feet in the air, I'd probably hit the ground before that could happen. I stayed completely still as my body rolled in the wind like a rotisserie. With everything under the red glow, seeing the world spinning around me was difficult. I barreled to the ground, wondering how

I would survive this. Just before I landed, Victoria broke my fall. She ran to my side, still holding the shield up.

"It's not time to relax, Top!" She said, holding her back to the bulk of the gunfire. But I could see a white beam charging in the corner of my eye. I got up from the ground and tackled her. The shield broke, briefly exposing us to the gunfire. But it disappeared long enough for the Caster Neutralizer to pass by, and her shield was back up. I looked down at my hand and realized that my power was good to go.

"Alright, Vic!" I called. "End of both sides, Neutralizers. We have to take them out, or we're dead."

She nodded, and we stood back to back momentarily, calculating the next move. I ran out of the protection and jumped to the ground like I was performing a cannonball into a swimming pool. Just before I landed, I executed my powers. Inside my blue bubble, I launched myself into the sky. I could feel my connection to Victoria reestablished before I was deployed to neutralize the formation below. The impact felt more aggressive. It was as if Vic was somehow getting stronger and angrier. The shock wave was emitted, and she sent me barreling through the line of soldiers. This attack quickly eliminated all of them in one swoop. The cavalry was gone, and Victoria reeled me back in. I landed just yards away from her and saw that her eyes seemed distant, and her body swayed from side to side. I ran to her and grabbed her by the shoulders before she could fall.

"Hey, hey, take it easy." I calmly said as I guided her limp body to the ground safely.

"We need to keep going!" She growled as she struggled to fight gravity.

"Okay, that's cool, but you gotta hang back."

Victoria shook her head in defiance. "I can't rest now." She said as she pulled on my arm to help herself up.

"We have to go get the kid!" She yelled. I nodded, looking at the distance between Tawnie and Milo Sr. at the showdown. "Yeah," I answered. "I may need to handle that on my own. You get some rest."

I patted the back of her hand and stood up. I looked down at her again. "Good work, soldier." I complimented. She looked up at me and smiled.

"Don't get yourself killed, Top."

I paused, coming to realize the genuine danger of death at the hands of Milo Sr.

"Yeah." I simply responded before stepping away and jumping toward the primary fight. But more importantly, where Milo Jr and the Pyro Stone sat. I soared into the vicinity of the battle. As I approached Milo and the Pyro Stone, the two powerhouses fought above me. It was like stepping underneath a roller coaster. The wind-cutting sounds of their flight and the impact of their strikes were intimidating. The Pyro Stone sat in the scorched grass, and I walked toward it. I noticed the ominous and tremendous power it emitted. No matter how high the kaitrons of Tawnie and Simms were, neither of them were more than the four-inch ball. The flames inside were captivating but horrifying. I kneeled to grab it, trying to determine if it was too hot to touch. I flicked the ball with my index finger. To my surprise, despite being the source of the immense heat, it was not hot. I opened my grip and wrapped my fingers around the sphere. I could feel its energy surging through me. It was like my body was focused on the power, but my mind was focused on rescuing Milo. I turned toward him, my muscles fighting me the entire time. It felt like gravity had been increased. I tried to let go of the orb, but in defiance, my hand did not cooperate. Pain filled my body, and I tried to suppress my reaction.

"Top?" I heard Victoria yelling for me from behind. Suddenly, I recognized her little blonde head at the bottom of my eye line. I tried to adjust my eyes to look at her, but I couldn't even do that.

"Victoria, I can't move!" I grunted, hardly able to use my mouth.

"What the hell?" She asked as she stood back to examine me. That's when she discovered that I was holding the Pyro Stone.

"Oh shit, Dan!" She said as she became focused on the arm holding the ball.

"I'm not trying to scare you, man, but there might literally be fire in your veins right now!"

"Yeah!" I agreed, trying to smile.

"I can't imagine that feels good, Battle." She said as she stood upright.

"Victoria, go free, Milo," I ordered. She limped over to the container and pressed some buttons at the top of the unit. There was a beep, followed by an airlock. Then flames began to spew from underneath the lid as if gas ignited inside. Milo immediately awakened. His eyes were shifty and unsure of his environment. Once the flames subsided, Victoria finished removing the lid. Milo quickly jumped out of the tube.

"Officer Gordon!" The kid said with glee as he ran for me.

"I'm glad you're okay now," I said.

"Where's my mommy?" He asked, seeming to ignore me.

"She and your dad are a little busy at the moment," Victoria answered. Suddenly, there was silence amongst us. But high in the sky, there was another explosion. The kid looked up, concerned and afraid.

"Milo, let's go," I said, holding my extended hand out to take his.

"Hey, Top, what about–" Victoria began to ask.

"We'll discuss whatever it is later," I told her. "But right now, we have to get out–"

Before I could finish my statement, something crashed into the field. Dust plumed into the air. I raised my arm to cover my face before Victoria raised a shield over the three of us.

Suddenly, another crash happened in the same spot.

"What the fuck?" Victoria asked.

"Vic, there's a child here!" I yelled, tapping her shoulder.

Suddenly, we saw a figure hovering out of the newly formed crater.

Victoria stumbled forward with her mouth open. "No way!" She breathily said in disbelief. "Is that–"

"Daddy!" Milo screamed.

My heart sank. I could feel the bile building up in the base of my neck, and my body grew cold as he spotted us and hovered toward us. Milo tried to run to him, but Victoria grabbed him by the collar and pulled him back.

"Aaaah! I want my daddy!" He cried out as he began to fight her.

"Milo, you can't!" she said to the boy, but it was as if he didn't hear her. His eyes remained locked on Dr. Simms, and his loud cries echoed through the fields.

"Milo, your father is a dangerous man!" Victoria yelled.

"You're a liar! I want my daddy!"

"Spud, stop!" A voice screamed from the distance. It was Tawnie, yelling for her son as she crawled from the crater.

Chapter LXVII

"Tawnie!" I yelled over all the madness. I could see her bloodied, battered face even from this distance.

"How could you!" I yelled at her estranged husband. I approached him, ready to fight. "I'll kill you myself!" I said.

"Will you now?" He asked me. "Because I'm willing to bet you don't even believe what you said. Do you?"

"Danny, just get out of here!" Tawnie said as she finally stood. Her clothing was torn entirely, and her body was covered in purplish-blue spots. Half her face was bruised and nearly unrecognizable.

"Take my son and leave, now!" She continued.

"Mommy! No!" Milo screamed as he attempted to run for her. But I grabbed him and assisted Victoria in keeping him contained. "Tawnie, are you sure?" I asked, wanting her to say no, hoping she would ask me to stay by her side.

"Yes." She said as she looked at him. I could see her disdain for him in her expression. Her jaw flexed as she stared at the side of his face with devilish eyes. She was confident she would teach him a lesson, but her kaitron levels were dropping fast.

"Alright, kid, let's go!" I yelled as I pulled on his arm. As expected, he screamed for her like a banshee.

"Mommy! Daddy! I don't wanna go!" He screamed. But neither of them acknowledged his blight.

He proceeded to sob as I jerked him away from the two of them. Suddenly, Simms was in front of me. His eyes burned with hatred. A red ring appeared where a more human color would usually glow in a person's eyes.

"Holy shit," I muttered unintentionally.

"Noo! Milo, run!" Tawnie screamed from behind us. With one brisk motion, Simms raised his arm, and a large beam of scattered light and aura blazed out of his palm. The light was red and seemed to have another white glow to it. I couldn't believe what I was seeing. I'd think I was losing my mind if I hadn't felt the energy. The blast soared across the field and clipped the ground at the crater's edge, right in front of Tawnie. There was the faint sound of her screaming. Then, it was immediately masked by the roar of pure power. I was frozen in fear for a split second before reaching my breaking point. Milo screamed for his mother as I stared at his father. I felt her energy fade fast, but I could tell that she was still alive. How long was the real question? I was angry, and I had no idea what to do. I could run, but apparently, this dude flies. His son is squeezing my hand as I stare into his emotionless eyes. He was as cold as a soldier who had come from war. There was only one option for me.

"Milo, come here." The man said, holding his hand out for his son. But the boy pulled away, looking back for Tawnie.

"Milo, come here!" He said again. But the boy continued to pull away.

He stepped forward, and I stepped in front of him.

His head fell, and his hand raised to thumb his nose. "Daniel Gordon, I was going to allow this all to blow over, and you would have been able to walk away with your life." He raised his head again, and his eyes seemed to glow brighter. "Now, I'm not so sure I can entertain the idea of your survival any longer."

There's the confirmation. He was about to kill me, so there was no need to be cautious. I threw all the energy I had into my fists. My hands glowed blue, and I punched him with the most power I had ever sent. The punch connected, and it seemed to affect him. Simms stumbled, and I followed him like a heat-seeking missile. The second punch was sent from underneath, forcing his head up. I temporarily sent my energy to my feet and kicked him in the side of his knee. He went down, kneeling before me. I rained down on him with continuous punches, hoping that he would just die. Wouldn't that be poetic? As bad as I wanted to keep going, my shoulder would not be able to keep up with the demands of this fight. Unfortunately, the transfer of energy does not make a body invincible. The pain intensified the longer I continued. But eventually, I broke, literally. I landed a punch, and the swing caused my entire shoulder to give out. He used the opportunity to strike back. Simms delivered a straight punch to my chest that was so intense that I felt pain in my entire body. How the fuck is he so strong?

"You thought you could get the drop on me?" Simms said as he slapped his knee. He stood and stomped his foot, and I could hear his bone pop before I landed on the ground, flat. That escalated quickly.

"That was admirable, Mr. Gordon." He acknowledged as he approached. I looked around to find him, and somehow, he was fine. Even if he were taken out, I would still be flat on my back from exerting that much energy. But this man survived my deadliest strikes. He came to stand over me.

"I almost want to use you as an example officer." He said as he fixed his clothing. When he finished, he gave me a sick, sadistic smile, and then he stomped on my shoulder. The pain was extreme, causing me to yell in agony.

"You thought you could stand up with her without preparation, Mr. Gordon?" He asked. "I've worked for years to gain the power she has and some!"

He stomped again. This time, digging his heels into me. He smiled at my pain and gnashed his foot down.

"Is that the pain you were hoping to inflict on me?" He asked. "Sorry to disappoint."

Simms removed his foot as he locked eyes with his son. The boy began to crawl away from him.

"Daddy, no!" He whimpered.

"Come now, son," Simms said as he extended his hand toward Milo and walked toward him. There was nothing I could do but watch and squirm. Hell, I could hardly even speak. I wanted to tell the kid to run. But the strike to my sternum did more damage than I thought. I began to taste blood in the back of my throat. Suddenly, I could see light rays shining from the crater's bottom. The beams drew Simms' attention to the sky.

"Well, hello Tawnie!" He yelled, sounding excited about her recovery. There was an explosion, and giant rocks from underneath the surface flew everywhere. Simms took to the sky, levitating slowly as he waited for Tawnie to emerge. Her power seemed higher than before; when she emerged, he seemed worried.

Suddenly, I felt something on my leg. It was a hand wrapping around my ankle.

"Not how I saw any of that going." I heard Victoria's voice.

"Ye...yeah." I chuckled back. The pain in my chest overwhelmed me. "We did the best we could, huh?"

"Shut up!" She said, forcing herself to a knee to look down at me. She was bloodied. I can see the bruising on her face as if she was burned. Then I realized she was caught by the light beam that Simms shot from his hand.

"What... are you okay?" I asked her.

"Don't worry about me!" She growled as she began to feel around my body.

"You have broken ribs and a punctured lung." She said. "We need to get you out of here!"

I managed to grab her wrist, but the pain of moving my arm prevented me from speaking for a moment.

"Where are we going?" I asked. Victoria stared at me. She looked as if she wanted to spring into action. But the question seemed to have stunned her.

"Top." She cried.

I nodded with a smile. "I'll be fine. But Tawnie can't lose to this guy."

She looked at Dr. Simms as he stared down at her. Little Milo innocently watched as his parents engaged in this supernatural battle.

"If this man defeats Tawnie, God won't be able to help us survive what's coming."

Victoria's eyes went sharp as she stared at me.

I smiled again. "What?" I sarcastically asked. "Figured I meet you halfway with that one."

She shook her head as she patted my leg. Then, running her hand along my pocket, she felt the curve of the Pyro Stone. She reached in and pulled it out. Her eyes grew in size as she stared. It was as if it was the first time she had seen it.

"It's so beautiful." She said as she began to marvel at it. Based on what I knew about that orb, it could drive ordinary people insane. It gives them an unquenchable thirst for power. From the moment Victoria touched it, I could physically see her mind beginning to warp. I squeezed her leg as hard as I could.

"Victoria, listen to me!"

Her head flicked as if she wanted to look at me, but she couldn't take her eyes off the sphere.

"Vic, I know what you're thinking, and I understand. But if you act on this, you'll become another case of what we're fighting right now!"

Her eyes popped open, and she looked down at me.

"You're right." She muttered. Her body relaxed as she shook her head in denial. "That's not me."

I let go of her leg, and my hand hit the ground, now completely unusable. I slowly closed my eyes, knowing that I was done for. The sounds all around me became muffled, like I was underwater. My voice even sounded muffled and unrecognizable.

"Get the kid and that stone out of here, Vic," I told her. "It's humanity's only chance for survival."

The stone was placed in my hand, and I immediately felt my body wake. It was like life had been restored inside me. My eyes popped open, and Victoria stood by, watching with a face full of concern.

"You alright, Top?" She asked. My body went from lifeless to fixed within a matter of seconds.

"I'm getting there," I answered as I got up. "Now I'm starting to understand how this all works."

Victoria stood up from the ground and wiped herself down. The bruises she had were gone as well. "You want to help me understand it?"

I looked down at the Pyro Stone in hand as I stood back up on my own. My body was completely healed from the attack by Simms earlier. Milo ran behind me and hid. I looked up at the continuous battle above. Meanwhile, another group of soldiers traveled across the plains to reach us.

Suddenly, there was a continuous beeping sound coming from Victoria. I looked over at her with an eyebrow raised. She stared at me, dumbfounded, before remembering that she had Tawnie's tablet. She hurried to retrieve it from her coat and activated it.

"What is it?" I asked. Her eyes grew large as she peered at the screen. She turned it about as if attempting to look around the cracked screen.

"It says, sorry for the late response, Agent 0, but we have arrived at the rendezvous point to assist."

Suddenly, a jet flew overhead, speeding past in a literal blink of an eye. They reached the line of soldiers and pulled upward into the atmosphere. They disappeared into the clouds above. Suddenly, explosions were happening everywhere. Three carrier aircraft descended, barely making it through the fight in the sky. Their wings sported two large thrusters and a smaller pair mounted underneath. The force they exerted on the ground was almost crushing. It was as if hurricane-like winds were pushing down on us. Victoria covered us with a shield as the vehicles descended to the ground. Armed men dismounted all of the carriers even before they touched down.

"Shit, it's more soldiers!" Victoria announced as she prepared to run toward the group. But something was different about these people.

"Wait!" I yelled, stepping forward out of the circle. A man approached me and lowered the weapon he carried.

"Officers Gordon, France, we're here to help!" the man said as he spun around to wave for his comrades to follow. He stepped backward past the three of us and yelled to the others.

"A big group is heading this way from the East! Let's move!" He barked.

"Top, look!" Victoria yelled as she tapped my abdomen repeatedly. "The symbol on his shoulder. It's the same as Tawnie's computer!"

I caught a glimpse of it. Which was pretty easy, considering the bird was gold and stood out against his black shirt.

"Holy hell, I see it!" I replied. "Hey! sir!" I called him. "Who are you guys?" I asked. "Who Are you here to help."

The man nodded as some of his cohorts began to run across the tundra.

"We're here to help the people who don't want the world to end."

Hearing him say that added some relief.

"Agent 0 vouched for you guys, so you're good with us."

Chapter LXVIII

"Agent 0 vouched for us?" Victoria asked. "When did she have time to do that?"

My eyes widened at her question. "As I said, things are happening that neither of us will ever comprehend."

She nodded and rolled her eyes. "Such as how we were on death's doorstep just moments ago, and now we're alive and well."

I shook my head. "I'm pushing my luck." I smiled. "That's the second time today."

There was an explosion in the sky behind us. We both turned our attention to it, verifying that it was Tawnie and her husband again. A bright light shined down on the land, cutting through the red that had become normal. They were so high up that we couldn't see them from the ground. But there was something up there that made me quiver with fear. Another blast was unleashed, like the one that Simms attacked Tawnie with earlier. The explosion traveled upward and had multiple streams of fire extending from it. They were all on a trajectory to fall to the Earth's surface. The entire thing looked like a comet passing by the planet in orbit. Suddenly, something crashed into the ground behind us. Soldiers swept in and cleared the space just before the object landed.

"Make way!" One soldier yelled to the others.

"Enemy overhead!" Another screamed.

I looked up, and he descended into the battlefield like an evil version of Superman. At this point, his eyes glowed even brighter as he stared at the ground. Soldiers began to aim and fire at him without cease. Guns blazed to the sky, but he was still hovering there, unphased.

"What the hell?" Victoria yelled. "He's impervious to guns?"

"He is now!" I said as I ran to the crater. Victoria called for me, but I kept going. I knew what I would find at the bottom of it. I immediately jumped to the ground, activating my abilities and shooting at my target. But the closer I got, the slower I moved. I went from a 200-mile-per-hour rush to zero in almost an instant.

"Fuck!" I yelled as my eyes caught his. He held his palm toward me, clenched his fist, and my powers stopped. My energy field popped like a bubble, and I began to fall out of the sky. I wanted to scream as I tumbled to the ground, but there was no point. The distance was small, maybe one thousand feet. Either way, I had no faith that I would escape falling to my death. The ground got closer until I recognized the detail of every pebble, blade of grass, and snowflake. But my fall was broken. I stopped mid-air but still thought I hit the ground. It felt like I hit a flat surface, but I couldn't see anything with closed eyes. I believed that if I opened them, I would see the goddess looking at me and shaking her head. Instead, I heard Victoria.

I opened my eyes and looked around. I was suspended over the crater. It was horrendous in size. Somewhere around a football field in length and just as deep it seemed. Below, in the center of it, was Tawnie, beaten, battered, and unable to move again. Her eyes caught mine, and I could see the defeat in hers. I shook my head as I was released from the bond that held me up. I looked back at Victoria, and she gripped Milo tight around his shoulders for protection. The little boy stared up at his father in disbelief.

More of the invading soldiers approached, causing there to be a lot more gunfire in the air than I could imagine. It reminded me of World War III. It's not as big of a scale, but a battlefield is always at the bottom of the list of places I want to be. I looked up at Dr. Simms. His attention was stuck on the outfield, watching his soldiers fall victim to the forces that came to aid us. He was plotting. A grin crossed his lips, and he looked down at his hand. A ball of orange light formed in his palm. He popped it up, causing it to levitate.

"What the hell?" I yelled as I watched the ball float away from him. He raised his arms to his side as if he was about to hug it, and then it grew larger. I could only stand there, wondering what devastation this blast would cause. There was nothing I could do. I ran down into the crater.

"Tawnie!" I called out. She had just enough energy to pan her eyes to me. I reached her and kneeled, immediately sticking my fingers into the dirt to dig her out. Once I believed I had dug enough, I began to tug at her extremities. Her entire body was flaccid and lifeless again. She was no match for the strength of Dr. Simms.

"Spud," She muttered.

I nodded. "At the moment, he is with Victoria," I said as I gently squeezed her hand.

"The relic?"

I pulled it from my pocket and showed it to her. A tear formed in her eyes as she stared at it. I reached for her face and wiped the moisture from her cheeks.

"What's wrong?"

"She warned me about doing it my way, Danny." She admitted. "I thought I could make all of this right on my own. But I never would have guessed my husband would be my greatest adversary."

I nodded and looked back up at Dr. Simms.

"He's long gone." She continued. I looked back down to acknowledge her again. "The moment he absorbed the energy from the relic, he was a dead man. We are now looking at a weapon hell-bent on destroying the universal balance."

"We just have to kill him before he gets out of Idaho and take his act on the road."

Miraculously, she was able to make it back to her feet. She was healed already, mostly.

"How do you suppose we do that?" I asked her.

She looked back at me and rolled her shoulders and neck to relieve pressure.

"The prophecy said we must do this, but I swear I tried to keep it from happening." She answered as if she was still thinking about another plan. I pursed my lips to ask for clarification, but I chose to keep quiet.

"The prophecy explains that the Primal Flame will reawaken if the Relic of Fire is reunited with its master."

I shook my head in shock. "There's more to this prophecy?" I asked.

Tawnie smiled as she looked down at the ground. "I wish I could say there wasn't, but I can't possibly lie to you now."

I sighed as my head fell in defeat. She approached me and placed her hand on my arm.

"Hey, it's going to be okay." She assured me. "This will all be over before we know it."

I grinned and cut my eyes at her. "Yeah, but at what cost?"

Her eyebrows furrowed, and her jaw clenched. "It's gonna cost us everything!"

I nodded, signifying that I understood. I'm a soldier who has not only heard this speech but has given it multiple times also.

I went to stand in front of her and opened my palm, exposing the Pyro Stone. "Before you continue, can I ask you something?"

She appeared perplexed as if my timing could have been better. Her eyes scanned the environment for danger.

"Something gives me the impression that you are older than you seem. Where did you come from?"

Tawnie's eyes bulged from her head. "I promise, we have lots to discuss. Whether it's in the afterlife or we survive this all. I promise I will explain, but now isn't the time." She reached up and squeezed my hand, enclosing the Pyro Stone in my fist.

"We need to get that stone to Milo." She said, pointing to it casually. I looked down at the relic with a perplexed stare. I'm not one hundred percent sure about the prophecy itself. But I wondered if I could trust her judgment at this point. That's when she spun around to look at me. She shook her head.

"You feel the difference in our power levels. Don't you?" She asked.

I nodded.

"Well, my good-for-nothing baby's father has siphoned energy from his son, me, and that relic. Do you know what that makes him?"

Again, I nodded. My eyes fell to the ground, then back up into hers.

"It makes him a False God."

"Exactly!" Tawnie growled as she clutched my free hand in hers.

"So, wait, I'm confused," I said, stepping away from her momentarily. "You want Milo to kill his father?"

Tawnie smiled and shook her head. "No, but you know he can't control his powers."

She approached me once more. "If he touches that relic, he gets all that good power that has healed you from the brink of death twice now. It also comes along with the chaos of Idaho Falls. Senior will perish in the Primal Flame."

"That means that all of us will suffer the same fate!" I yelled, pissed that she would even suggest that. "There has to be a better way!"

She calmly shook her head. "There's a plan to get you all out of here to safety, but I must stay here with Milo and my son. I have already contributed too much to the universe's imbalance, trying to save everyone, including myself. She told me that I had to follow the plan, but it was my defiance that caused this. So it'll be my sacrifice to make."

I bit my lower lip and bowed my head. I understand now who Tawnie is... what she is.

As I lifted my eyes, she stared at me. The glare from above highlighted the golden sparkles deep in her eyes. Her gaze made me want to defy her orders, knowing her sacrifice was the next step.

Chapter LXIX

"I can't!"

She looked at me and tucked her lower lip as her patience receded. I could feel the spike in her energy. I took a step back, her eyes watching me closely.

"You have to understand why I can't do what you're asking me!" I yelled. "You can't make me fall in love with you then expect me to watch you die!"

She nodded slowly and closed her eyes.

"I understand, Daniel." She said as she stepped toward me. "How can I expect to be what I am and expect someone like you not to be negatively impacted?"

"I thought I was helping a defenseless mother and her child. My involvement was my fault." I admitted as I looked up. The ambient sound of gunfire subsided as Dr. Simms eliminated Tawnie's reinforcements. The man stared down at us with folded arms.

"What the hell do we do here?" I asked.

Tawnie grunted. Suddenly, I could hear her voice again, urging me to pay attention.

"I believe he is going to target my son, and I'm going to hold him off while you get that to Milo."

I shook my head. "I don't think you understand me. I won't do it!"

"You don't have another option. I won't last forever," she said as she squatted, curled her arms upward, and clenched her fists.

"Tawnie! Please don't say it!" I said, inching my way towards her again. I had spent so much time attempting to make a point that I didn't account for the change around me. I wanted to run to her, but it was too late. Her power blazed. The ground appeared like a giant spotlight shining inside the crater. But the only thing shining downward was the glow from Dr. Simms' ball of energy. The power that Tawnie generated swept me from my feet and blew me out of the crater completely. I rolled and tumbled back to the top like a plastic bag moving across a windy parking lot. Eventually, I hit the ground, landing hard on my shoulder, yards away from the hole. But I had to get up. I looked around and noticed the carnage that was created above. There were still soldiers shooting at Simms, but they had no clue that their efforts had no effect.

I looked in the distance and saw Victoria's energy shield. I looked back up at Simms, who seemed to be making eye contact. His movements were swift. It was like I had lost the time it took him to move. But it didn't take long for me to realize that Tawnie was wrong about his motives. I saw her take off from the crater and blast into the sky toward him. But he avoided the attack and appeared in front of me. I didn't bother stalling. I still had the Pyro Stone in my pocket and channeled every bit of power I could from it. I used my power to encase my fists again and attacked him repeatedly. I scouted his counter. His hand vaulted upward as if he wanted to grab me by the neck, but I somehow felt it coming. I stepped to the side and jumped behind him, holding his wrist. The torque cranked his shoulder, and I spun around. I stepped close to his backside while attempting to rip his arm from the socket. He roared in pain, which gave me a bit of relief for a moment. But then, his painful cries slowly transitioned into laughter.

"I wish you truly understood how pathetic you look right now." He growled.

I sent my knee rocketing into his lower back. The anger boiling inside me was masked with a hint of fear.

"Maybe you're the pathetic one," I replied. "Thinking I would go down without a fight."

Suddenly, Simms began to levitate, taking me to the air with him. I lost my footing and stumbled onto him as my feet left the Earth below. So I found myself dangling from his arm that was still wrenched over his shoulder. Then, suddenly, I was soaring upward. The force felt like I was in a rocket, blasting off toward the atmosphere. I had no control of my body at this point. I wiggled and flipped like a ragdoll until I felt a sharp pain in my back. Just as fast as I went up, I returned to the ground. The impact was enough to break the soil underneath me. My body practically embedded into the cold, icy tundra. The pain was unexplainable. I laid on my back with my head bowed and looking downward. I could see my legs sticking up from the Earth, facing in unorthodox directions. They reminded me of dying plants growing in unfertilized soil. My arms were contorted over top of me. My right arm completely shattered from the bicep to my fingers and folded over on itself like a limp water hose. I wanted to scream, but the most I could do was tiny whimpers. The mad doctor landed before me, looking down at me with satisfaction etched in his face. My eyes inched up to his face, taking a final look at my killer before he would inevitably deal the final blow.

"I can't believe she thought you were a better fit." He growled. "That's always been her problem," He bent down to look me in the eyes. "She was always underestimating me!"

The red in his eyes began to grow brighter. I knew his kaitrons were increasing, but I started to lose my ability to feel anything.

"I spent eight years since you idiots raided that tomb absorbing the power of the Pyro Stone. So, could you rub it for a few minutes and match me, Sergeant Gordon?"

With shame, I let my eyes fall away from his, attempting to conserve my dignity. I could see Victoria in the distance, still hurt. But back to her feet and holding on to Milo, who watched his father as he prepared to kill me.

"Milo," I muttered.

"What was that?" Simms yelled at me. But I couldn't respond. The only thing I could do was look at the kid. The maniacal man followed my eyes and turned around to look.

"Right." He said as he stood up and turned around to take a few steps in their direction. Victoria clutched the boy tighter and took steps backward.

"I bet you're wondering if I would have the heart to kill you in front of my son," Simms announced. I couldn't even tell him that he was right at this point.

"Milo Simms Jr. may have my name, but he is no son of mine!" He roared. The young boy's face went pale. His eyes widened, and his mouth gaped as he stared at the only man he knew to be his father. Victoria told the kid to run, but he was frozen in pity, staring at the mad doctor.

"I don't know if you understand yet, Officer Gordon. Tawnie never needed a man to create the reincarnation of the Arcanin Flame."

Simms made solid eye contact with his namesake as he threw his palm toward me. Slowly, a light appeared in his palm, like sunlight. I looked into it, feeling a bit of the warmth against my shivering skin. I closed my eyes to accept my fate. But suddenly, the heat was more intense, and the bright light faded. I opened my eyes again and saw flames roving over me. The Pyro Stone began to react. I remember Tawnie saying that we had to get it to Milo. But it appeared to be responding to him all of a sudden. I called his name as the flames dissipated. The doctor was gone. Suddenly, I could hear the clashing happening again. The impacts sounded like continuous explosions. Victoria and Milo ran to me.

"Mr. Gordon!" The kid yelled as Victoria looked around to figure out how to help me. Tears welled in her eyes as she began digging with her hands to clear the dirt surrounding me. Milo jumped in to help. I looked at the boy, trying to call his name again, but this time, nothing came out.

"Don't worry, Top, I'll get you to safety. Just hold on!" Victoria screamed. But I didn't even have the energy to tell her to give up. She continued to dig until her hands bled from the fingertips. In the middle of her tirade, Tawnie landed nearby, taking the mad doctor to the ground.

"You useless piece of shit!" We heard Tawnie yell. "Was it all about power to you?"

Her hand pressed into his neck. The force shook the ground like an earthquake. Milo fell, and Victoria stumbled into me, dislodging The Pyro Stone and causing it to roll away. Suddenly, it was being picked up by one of Dr. Simms' soldiers. Tawnie turned her attention to him. Then she glared at Vic.

"Victoria, get that relic to Milo now!" She yelled.

She stared at the man in shock as he ran away from us. All I could see in front of me was Tawnie struggling to keep her husband down. He fought back, but she created a response with each urgent movement he made. But that would have no use as he was still overpowering her. I could hear footsteps coming fast. Victoria called for Milo as she approached. Dr. Simms began to succeed at removing Tawnie, and I saw Victoria running past me to get to Milo. My vision blurred, making it impossible to see. The last thing I noticed was Simms countering Tawnie. Somehow, he reached his feet and threw his fist at her. There was another explosion of energy, followed by a trail of blood. Suddenly, a calm swept over the land, and a bright, white light illuminated the distance before turning a deep shade of red. Then, a wave of power expanded from where Milo was recently seen. I couldn't move, forced to witness the wall of fire spreading over the land. Then, I started to understand something I read from Tawnie's Arcanin research: The Arcanin Flame will burn the land, ridding us of all sin.

464

Chapter LXX

Three months had passed since Milo touched the Pyro Stone for the first time. The world was different. Though the red aura that loomed over Rexburg, Idaho, had dissipated, there was still a hint of chaos. The city had since been evacuated due to the radiation in the area. Kaitron levels were so rampant that the home I knew was now just as dangerous as Chernobyl. It took almost one hundred years to repopulate the city ridden with nuclear energy. But it may take much longer for anyone to be able to go back to Rexburg.

The unknown soldiers working with Tawnie swooped in to pick up Milo and me after the explosion. The poor kid was sitting in the barren, charred field with the sphere in his hand and his body changing before his very eyes. His father was gone. But what remained of Tawnie's body lay wasted in the fields, unidentifiable, but certainly her. She was skeletal, the remains of her charred skin stuck to her bones. Her hair was singed but still partly intact. It looked like she attempted to protect herself. I couldn't get to her and Daniel fast enough.

I lost everything. I watched my best friend get burned alive after being broken and mangled. I couldn't help anyone. Completely broken and alone, we returned to the store to find Lester. He was already gone. The building and everything around it was destroyed and burned. But there was one survivor. That little girl, Lyric. She refused to leave her family's bodies. A sentiment I understand, but a costly mistake. She, too, was severely injured and in a coma.

I agreed to go into the custody of the soldiers who rescued us.

In those three months, I had only lived the same day on repeat. I would awaken in some kind of dorm room that overlooked New York City. I'd silently eat breakfast in a fancy dining facility and walk around aimlessly for a few hours.

Then, I would head back to my room and sit silently for the rest of the day. Occasionally, I would train in a large, empty room filled with targets and mannequins. I waited for their military-like organization to interrogate me or lock me up, but they never did. I was free to go, not knowing who this group was that housed me this long. Nobody had ever told me who they were or what they wanted from me. Occasionally, I would see Milo around. The poor kid was lost. His mother and father both perished in the fire. Even worse, he was aware of why they died. He knew it was his hand that caused the explosion. The only sound that I've heard him make since coming here was his sobbing on his sixth birthday. My heart aches to see him like this. I wanted to console him, but he was still dangerous. On day ninety-four of my stay, I stood in my room, looking out onto the illuminated city below as nightfall approached. The large windows of the dorm looking out onto the city only serve as a space to think. An activity I should honestly do less of. It could ease the hurt a bit.

I heard the clicking of high heels echoing through the halls, getting louder by the second. I held my breath, attempting to keep my anger under control. I just wanted to be alone, but they wouldn't honor that. Someone was always in my face, pretending to be helpful and offering fake smiles.

"New York City." A woman said. "City of mystery and mystique."

She came to stand next to me, leaning her back on the giant glass window.

"You know what I love about this particular spot, Fixer?" I asked. The petite brunette with sharp eyes looked at me with her head turned slightly.

"This spot is quiet, and nobody needs to talk here," I explained.

She turned to face me. A smile on her face that seemed a bit devious and mysterious.

"I want to leave you in your quiet place to wallow in your pity. But I have a job to do. I turned toward Fixer and took a step back.

"What could you possibly need from me now?" I asked her. "I

don't have the mental fortitude to deal with you people right now!"

Fixer rolled her eyes.

"Victoria, you went through something traumatic. I completely understand your apprehension about associating with us," she said.

I allowed my eyes to fall from hers and looked down at the black, skin-tight suit she wore. I then looked at her shoulder where the same crest etched in Tawnie's tablet sat. She looked down at it and smiled. Her hand wrapped around herself to touch it.

"Do you know what this emblem represents?" She asked. I shook my head. "This emblem represents the Phoenix that is reborn from death and torment. That's who we are."

I turned, looking out onto the dark city full of twinkling lights.

"I know you are having a hard time trusting us." she continued, reaching to touch my arm. "But we are the best thing for humanity as it is."

I couldn't stand her pretentious frame of thinking. Immediately, I threw her arm off of me. I stepped forward, red light shining from my fingertips. But she seemed unphased. She stood with her head held high and maintained eye contact. The grin on her face made me feel like she didn't take me seriously. I had the advantage and could show her what I'm made of if I just surprised her.

"I am not the enemy, Ms. France." She said as her head lowered, and she took a step forward. Her hands were behind her. "Those are the powers the world has turned against, remember?"

I sighed deeply and let my energy fade, clenching my fists until my nails dug into my palms.

"Yeah, you're right." I acknowledged.

"Look, I have the first mission for you if you're okay with it."

My mouth clicked. It wasn't even intentional, but it certainly matched the annoyance I had in my spirit.

"I am not one of your agents, Fixer. I don't answer to you."

Immediately, she glanced past me and smiled. There was someone there. I spun around, and my heart sank. I wanted to scream from fear and jump for joy simultaneously.

"What the hell?" I exclaimed. "This can't be!"

A large, solid man stood before me. A man that I was for sure was dead, yet here he was.

"As you were, Sergeant." He said with a huge smile.

"General!" I shrieked as I ran to him with open arms. He wrapped his big gorilla-like arms around me and pulled me close. "How are you alive?"

He grinned. "A magician never shows his hand, Vic." He said as he let me go.

He pushed away, holding me at arm's length, examining me with squinted eyes. His gaze went toward my hair, and a hand was raised to comb through a fire-red loc hanging over my face.

"Had an experiment with hair dye, Vic?" He asked.

"No, this was my gift from nature and its illustrious Pyro Stone," I explained. "Apparently, I was cursed with its power during the explosion."

His eyes popped open, and he gulped. "We'll have to discuss that later."

"Anyway, how are you here, alive?" I asked as I broke away from his hold.

In an instant, his demeanor changed. His eyebrows furrowed, and his eyes went to the floor. "Vic, it was Tawnie." He announced. "She helped us scout all of this before it came. "I didn't want to believe her, but my cabinet was responsible for trying to assassinate me. It's not too much of a stretch to believe they were responsible for Idaho."

I turned to look at Fixer. "Three months," I said to them.

"Vic…" Wesley called me, forcing me to cut him off.

"Three months, I've been thinking I was alone. That the only survivors from this ordeal were me and those damned kids!"

Wesley winced. "Yeah, I can see how that can become a problem." He smiled as he rubbed the back of his head. "I needed to ensure that every stone had sunk before I came out to take down my old Vice-President publicly."

I lowered my head and folded my arms over my chest.

"Victoria," Fixer called to me. "I understand your frustration. But you need to understand that this is not over. In fact, we are just getting started."

She caught my attention, and I looked at her with intrigue. Behind me, Wesley cleared his throat and touched my shoulder.

"Please tell me that Tawnie was able to teach you how to read

Arcanin." He said. I shook my head in disbelief. I turned to look at him with annoyance in my stare. He stepped back as he began to feel it bubbling over from my spirit.

"Why the hell would Tin Hat need to teach me Arcanin?" I asked. "I never want to hear about that damned prophecy again!"

Wesley peered past me at Fixer. "So we have not a soul able to decipher that shit?" He asked.

Fixer slowly shook her head. The look in her eyes predicted the fate of the world. But I didn't allow it to bother me at all. I turned around and softly punched Wesley's shoulder.

"I'm glad you're all good, General." I smiled at the man. "Link up with me after all of this nonsense is over." I walked past Fixer, causing her eyes to follow me down the hall.

Wesley cleared his throat again and stepped next to the mysterious woman. "As I stated before, Vic, we are not done with the mission."

I threw my hands up in frustration and spun around. "What the hell do you need from me?" I asked. "Tawnie is gone, so that prophecy stuff can go to hell with her!"

The two looked at one another, then slowly back at me.

"Vic," Wesley said. "The prophecy only started with Tawnie. It ends with everyone else."

Chapter LXXI

The world moved on from Nathaniel Wesley's legacy. Hawthorne McTierman, once his trusted adviser turned vice president, had taken the Oval Office. His cabinet evolved drastically over those short months. This made him more bulletproof. Due to the recent tragedies, he would have leverage to gain more power than any president before him. Of course, the world views it now as a necessary action. But for some reason, the people who rescued us from the devastation had a different opinion of him. I asked for clarification, but they were cryptic. Especially Fixer, who planned a mission for us to make a surprise visit at a gala in honor of this new president.

"Why is this necessary again?" I asked, interrupting a conversation between her and Wesley. "We don't have any evidence that he did anything! For all we know, we get there, accuse him of this, and he has a solid alibi."

"All the evidence we need will meet us there," Fixer answered. She sat at the desk in her corner office with the perfect city view. She brought us here to finalize the plan before we departed. She looked down at a paper covered in Arcanin. Her body tensed as her foot began to tap underneath the glass table.

"Fixer," Wesley called out to her. She looked up at him with frustration in her eyes. She took a hard swallow and stood from her chair.

"It has to be right." She said as she slammed her palm down on the paper. "If it's not, the director will have my ass! He's already losing his confidence in me as is!"

Wes shook his head. "I don't think that's true." He said to her.

"He knows this is a complicated matter, just like the rest of us."

"And where has this director been?" I asked, looking up at my old general. "Seems to me that if he wanted it done right, he should be here leading."

Wes smirked and shook his head, maintaining eye contact with me.

"The director is still researching how to contain the power in the relic that Milo has awakened."

Immediately, my body seized in agony. I was removed from the room entirely and stared at sheer darkness suddenly. Fixer and Wesley continued the conversation as I stood there, paralyzed. My mind recalled the scent of smoke and dead bodies as I could see the literal flames in front of me. My body heated as if I was in the hot deserts of Saudi Arabia again, and my stomach prepared to send the roasted chicken and potatoes back to my mouth. The fire grew closer, and I tried to step away but couldn't move. The closer they came to me, the color shifted, and the flames gave off a purple hue. It was almost like a black light. All I could do was tense up and prepare for impact. I felt my knees fall from underneath me, and I was caught before I could fully collapse.

I blinked and realized that I was looking at Wesley's barreled chest. I reset my legs and pushed myself off of him, shaking my head and gasping for air. I sat in the chair across from Fixer, who only stared at me.

"Still happening, I see." She retorted as she pulled her dark hair back into a ponytail.

I shook my head again. "I'm fine."

The room went silent, and Wes came to sit next to me in the other chair. He stared in wonder and reached for me to touch my arm gently.

"I can only imagine what you're going through, Vic." He said, slowly shaking his head. "I've seen you in some tough spots during our time in the service. But this fire has done something to you I've never seen before."

Fixer nodded. "It's one thing to be trapped in the fire." She said. "But being trapped in the Arcanin Flame, " she paused and looked away, almost seeming uncomfortable. "...is something different."

I leaned forward in my seat, staring into her eyes. "How would you know?" I asked.

She trembled as if she wasn't expecting the question.

She cleared her throat. "I've had many experiences I wish I could forget, just like you."

My eyebrow hiked as I looked at Wesley, hoping he would interrupt the awkwardness.

"Well, ladies, are we ready to go?" He asked with a grin on his face. He stood from his chair and tugged on his white dress shirt collar. "We have a party to attend."

Fixer jumped from her seat as well. She scrambled for a few items on the tabletop before she headed to the door. "Wait, I have to change into my dress!"

Wesley opened the door to her office and allowed us through. Before they could exit the room, they noticed I hadn't moved.

"Victoria, what's wrong?" Wesley asked me.

"Why does this mission feel like we have no direction?" I asked as I stood and joined them. "Why am I going on a mission to a party and have no other orders?"

Fixer looked over her shoulder to answer. "Our orders are to attend this event and get our orders from there."

She left the room, and I headed to the door where Wesley stood, watching her walk away.

I punched his bicep. "Wes, what the hell is she talking about?"

He turned to look at me as if he had something to say but shook his head. "I can't say right now. But we were all briefed a while ago about what would happen."

My eyes narrowed at the bullshit answer he gave me. "Am I not worthy of the truth?"

Suddenly, he looked fearful and stepped closer to me. He raised his arms and placed his hands on my shoulders. "Do you trust me?"

The question halted me. Instead of continuing my conversation about the mysterious woman, I was forced to look at him objectively. I stared at him with my lips slightly parted, indecisive. But he squeezed my shoulders gently and looked into my eyes. The same considerate eyes that led me into many battles and assuring we would be safe. Promises that he had fulfilled every time.

"Victoria?" He called out, sounding slightly concerned.

"Yeah." I quickly answered. "Of course, I trust you, Wes."

He closed his eyes and nodded as he let me go. It had gotten quiet, and the sound of Fixer's heels had faded in the hall outside. Wes opened his eyes and sighed as he looked down at me, nodding.

"I trust them, Vic." He said. "It's the only organization in the world that Tawnie would trust with her secret."

Hearing her name made my mouth twist with disgust. But I did my best to show some discretion.

"What secret are you referring to?" I asked.

He stayed silent long enough to raise red flags within my psyche as we stared into each other's eyes.

"Victoria, you are about to learn some things about human life that you probably weren't ready to learn." He said to me.

"How do you know?" I quickly responded as I stepped closer and looked up at him. His eyes thinned as if he was getting uncomfortable. "Where the hell did you go to learn anything before anyone else?"

Wesley cleared his throat and began to explain where he truly was. But he was right. I wasn't ready for his answer.

Chapter LXXII

Not far from Fixer's headquarters, the ceremony was just starting at the infamous Gotham Hall. We pulled up in our black SUV, and the driver stopped outside the door. The walkways were crowded, and people were flooding inside.

"Agent Dimios," Fixer called out to the front. "Stay close in case we need a quick getaway."

"Roger that Agent Fixer." He answered. Sitting up front with Dimios, Wesley jumped out and returned to open the rear door where I sat.

"My lady." He looked at me and smiled. I smiled back, "Thank you, sir."

I stepped out of the vehicle, tugging on the hem of my dress and being careful not to let it slide underneath my heel. I stumbled slightly as I stepped away. It had been years since I had worn a pair of heels, so I was shocked I made it this far without falling over. Fixer stepped out of the SUV behind me, and her index finger pressed on the tragus of her ear.

"Eagle Team 1, report." I could hear her inside my ear.

"Eagle 1 is in position, Commander." A man responded. "Your six is covered and clear."

"Alright, let's head inside," Fixer said as she held her arm out in front of her, guiding us toward the building. I couldn't help but notice how clean she was. Her skin seemed flawless and shiny almost. Her long, dark hair was curly and voluminous, making the blue in her eyes pop. She wore a form-fitting black dress. On her feet were fine-strap heels that accentuated the muscles in her calves. She was toned and ripped but still seemed feminine.

"You look beautiful tonight," Wesley said to me. Appalled at his statement, I dragged my eyes away from Fixer to look at him with concern.

"What?" I asked.

"Don't make this awkward." He said with a smirk. "I just thought you needed to know."

He stepped ahead of me and grabbed my hand to pull me along. Wearing a dark blue dress and leather boot heels, I could hardly walk in. I wondered what he saw, and I didn't.

The building had columns on the second level with bright red lights shining behind them. The entrance was upon a broad set of stairs with a row of glass doors at the top. We hiked up the steps and made it inside. The lobby was round, with shiny white, tiled floors reflecting the colorful lights above.

"Hard to believe this building is still here," Wesley said.

"Yeah," I replied as I looked around in wonder. "It does look pretty old in here."

"Considering that it's been here since 1924, it should look old," Fixer added.

We could see the entrance to the banquet hall. The inside was filled with beams of light that waved around the room. Staff members dressed in suits were inside, sending patrons to the show. Fixer ominously stared at the entrance.

"Are we ready for this?" Wesley asked her.

She shook her head. "How could anyone be ready for what's about to happen?" She asked. I stepped into their conversation. "What the hell is about to happen?"

"Something that wouldn't happen in normal laws of reality," Fixer answered as she walked towards the hall. "I wish I could logically explain, but I don't have all the details myself."

"Yeah, the fact we're even here is outside logic," Wesley added. I looked at him with an eyebrow raised.

"What the hell are you saying?" I asked.

"We're here because of something that Tawnie told us years ago. We don't even have a concrete reason to be in attendance tonight."

I shook my head. "Then I'd much rather be back in bed right now."

"Except for the fact that we received letters from Tawnie with an invitation to this very event."

I stopped walking for a moment. The two of them stopped as well. People in the crowd were forced to stop behind us or go around.

"What the hell?" I asked. "I watched her burn alive in the Arcanin Flame!"

Fixer shook her head and touched my arm. "Learn not to ask questions; this will all go much smoother for you."

"But I don't trust any of this!" I yelled at her.

She sighed. "I understand, Racket. But whether or not we have faith in the plan doesn't mean a lick of difference to the prophecy."

Hearing that word again made me cringe. "Not with this fucking prophecy again!" I yelled, shaking my head with disapproval. "Everyone seems to be hiding behind this prophecy and using it as an excuse not to give any answers."

Fixer opened her mouth, readying herself to speak. But the second I noticed the twitch in her eyebrow, she walked away, following the crowd again. Wesley nudged me from behind, forcing me further into the building.

"You're out of line here, Vic." He said to me. At that moment, my eyes locked onto a banner with Hawthorne McTierman's face on it. Just as much a problem, people began to recognize Wesley. People who were in a rush to find their seats stopped to stare at him.

"Yeah, I need to make it to the stage before this plan blows up in our faces." He said, stepping off into the busy crowd and hiding his face behind his hands.

"Wait!" I yelled to him. But he had already gotten too far away to hear me. I hurried to look for Fixer in the opposite direction and noticed her heading to the seating area. I hurried to reach her, nervous that she would vanish in the crowd.

"Cleaner, you up?" Fixer called into the radio. I paused to recall this agent. But this was my first time hearing that name.

"Rags are down." A deep, bassy voice responded. I could see her as she looked back at me. Her eyes shifted, and her neck puffed as she swallowed hard.

"So far, she is two for two, Wes." She announced. "Cleaner, what you got back there?"

The man chuckled as if he found something to be funny. "We

got guys in black riot gear, full armor." He replied. "Looks like they were getting ready for something. At least twenty-five of these fuckers here."

Fixer clenched her jaw and looked at me. I walked over to her as she found a table to sit at. The lights began to dim, and a spotlight shined on the nearby stage as a small Asian woman walked out to a podium. The crowd started to cheer for her. Fixer gave me a look of concern, then she looked past me, down toward the stage. Her eyes squinted at the realization of what she was looking at. Or, better yet, who? Hawthorne McTierman. He sat at the head of a table in front of the stage. With him sat a group of billionaires that, at first glance, gave me chills. One is the CEO of the world's largest tech and weapons company, Jacob Maxwell. The others were members of leading industries of the world.

Fixer collapsed in a chair. "There's a lot of political power at that table."

"I'd like to know how the Fixer will fix this scenario," Wes interjected.

The woman smiled. "Let's not forget why we're here, Mr. President." She said. She leaned back in her seat and crossed her legs. She cockily rested an elbow on the table and began to twirl her hair.

"Tell me, are you in position Wesley?" She asked.

He chuckled. "Just say when."

The room went dark, and the brightest light shone on the center of the stage.

"Ladies and gentlemen, welcome to the Fifteenth Annual Magnificence Gala!" The woman announced. The crowd began to cheer. "I am your host, Lana Sui-Lin. For those who don't know me already, I am the governor of Washington State. I am glad to be here with you all in the presence of such greatness. Included in that group is our United States President, Hawthorne McTierman."

The crowd began to cheer again, but I turned to Fixer.

"What the hell is this ceremony?" I asked her.

She grunted, and the smile on her face faded. "It's a ceremony designed for the most vile people in the world to pat themselves on the back and make them look like saints, which is why we're here. To display the truth about at least one."

I looked back at the table up front, realizing Fixer was fixated on something. However, I couldn't tell who. I turned back to her, raising an eyebrow.

"Why exactly do they call you the Fixer?" I asked.

Her eyes cut to me. "Because I'm here to fix history."

She pointed to the stage and stood to her feet. She became fixated on Governor Sue-Lin. There was a sense of hesitation in her eyes until she closed them and took a deep breath. Her eyes opened as she continued to the stage, and her confidence sounded off in the echo of her heels.

"Now, ladies and gentlemen," Sui-Lin said. "I am honored to welcome…" But she paused as she realized Fixer was stepping onto the stage. Sue-Lin looked around, expecting security to come out. Fixer smiled at her and waved at her concern. She stepped to the woman and faced the crowd. She grabbed the microphone off the podium while staring at the table before the stage. McTierman stood from his seat. It was as if he knew who she was already. She offered him a devious grin just before leaning toward Sue-Lin's ear. She whispered something to her, and I could see the governor's face begin to express fear. She stood up straight and looked back down at President McTierman. Fixer jolted the microphone into Sue-Lin's sternum. The governor grabbed the microphone and shakily turned toward Fixer. I could not read lips well, but I'm sure Fixer leaned again and whispered, "Do it."

Sue-Lin raised her hand and put the microphone to her lips.

"Ladies and gentlemen, please welcome to the stage, the President of the United States." From my seat, I could see McTierman look around for confirmation. The showrunners and producers were just as confused. He buttoned his blazer and headed to the stairs. But there was a surprise waiting in his path. Just before he touched the first step up, the curtain at the edge of the stage was thrown back, and out came Wesley. McTierman paused, foot still pending the ascent to the first step. His shocked eyes watched his former president as he took center stage. The crowd realized who they were looking at. The whispers made the room sound like a pit of hissing snakes. The crowd became a box of mixed emotions.

Nathaniel Wesley headed to the glass podium at center stage. He stood next to Governor Sue-Lin. He looked at her and grinned big. The woman looked at him in horror. She couldn't move.

"Preh...preh... President Wesley!" She said as she tried to catch her breath.

He nodded at the woman, "Sue-Lin."

Fixer approached and snatched the microphone again. "Ladies and gentlemen, if you are confused about what you're seeing, let me assure you that a crime has been committed," she said to the crowd. Everyone gasped in disbelief. "But it is not our mission to speak the truth. We are only the messengers."

Suddenly, every phone in the building vibrated, including mine. Then, there was a long beep that filled the entire room. It seemed to pour from every speaker in the hall. The crowd began to panic like a swarm of mutts sent into a craze by a dog whistle. People started looking around as they reached for their devices, hoping for an explanation. I pulled mine out and stared at it as the vibration continued.

"What?" I thought out loud as I saw a symbol on the screen. It was an inverted, white cross with two rings encasing it like cross-hairs.

"What is this? I asked. The room finally went dead silent as everyone stared at their phones. Finally, the emblem cut away to an image of a Tawnie. She was sitting at a desk with many papers hanging on the walls and Arcanin markings drawn on them. There was also a calendar. The days on it were marked off. According to that, this video was recorded on March 13, 2073. That was the same year we went to Riyadh. I looked back up at Fixer, standing beside Wesley, staring down at McTierman.

"If you are watching this, I died before achieving my mission of correcting the past and future," Tawnie said, playing from every phone in attendance. The video also played on the hidden screen at the back of the stage and through the hall's sound system. "The Arcanin text was left here to teach us how to protect our planet, cultures, and race. My mission was to be able to teach this forbidden, sacred language to others who would join the fight to stop humans from doing the things that the Arcanin told us would disrupt the balance of nature."

Her head fell as she leaned forward in her chair. She placed her elbows on the desk surface and interlocked her fingers in front of her.

"I want to be angry with humanity. But they already said what would happen if mankind stumbles onto power they should never have."

I stood and walked to the back of the room near the stage and found a hallway. I stepped through the double doors, thinking I could escape the noise. But it still played through my phone. There was a room with a sign next to the door that read, "Green Room."

I knew that I could go inside and find somewhere to hide and calm myself. I looked into the open door and saw men lying all over the floor. The carpets on the floor were drenched in blood, and the room smelled of iron. Indeed, I recognized their armor. The only man standing in the room, however, was looking at his phone as well. He raised his head to look in my direction. His golden hair flipped over his forehead. His piercing, blue eyes glared at me, warning me to stay away. He was tall, around six-foot-three, and slender. But his body seemed fit and muscular. I felt that he somehow looked familiar. I stepped closer to him, and his gaze followed.

"I take it that you're Cleaner," I asked.

The man nodded and looked down at his phone, continuing to listen to Tawnie. "Have we met before?" I asked, turning my head to the side to look at him. "You look familiar." I looked around again, wondering if any other agents were with him. But he was alone.

"Where's your team?" I asked.

"What team?" He replied casually. "You took them all by yourself?" He held a finger up to me. "Lady, please, I'm in the middle of something." Appalled, I backed out of the room in silence.

"By now, you've probably witnessed a good share of chaos." Tawnie taunted from beyond the grave. At that moment, I was intrigued and walked back to the auditorium. Tawnie's face filled the screen on stage. A smug grin sat against her lips, causing even more distrust from me.

"We have seen many tragedies in history and tend to ask the wrong questions. That even applies to our current reality. Humanity will discover things, powers, and objects that will make those tragedies more horrific. Starting with the assassination of our United States President by our Government."

Her words gave me goosebumps as I stared at Wes, still standing on stage, glaring a hole into Hawthorne McTierman. The rest of the crowd began to whisper again, pointing at the man before them.

"But as many of you can see, it didn't quite work, did it?" Tawnie mocked as she pretended to rub her eyes before laughing maniacally.

"This text." She continued, suddenly becoming more serious. "This text was found in the world's oldest book, left to us by an ancient civilization. In it, they laid out, in detail, every tragedy we've faced as humans. This includes events that have yet to come."

Fixer clenched her jaw as she looked at Wes. I walked to the stage, hoping to snap them out of their trances, thinking the goal was to spectate. The guests in attendance became flustered with curiosity as Tawnie continued. Outraged, people stood from their chairs and began to uproar.

"Trust me, people, you are not ready for what is about to happen. I tried to warn you all of what's to come, but they silenced me. Why? Because they don't want you to know the truth!"

Tawnie roared, and her inner eyes began to glow. She stood silent for a moment, watching the camera. There was a long, awkward moment when I felt like I was looking into her eyes, and she could see straight through me. She got up from her chair and walked off-screen.

"Shut this off–" Governor Sue-Lin began to shout. But Fixer grabbed the woman by the collar and pulled her close. She whispered something to the woman that appeared to strike the fear of God into her.

"9-11, the pandemics, France, Saudi Arabia, World War III, Idaho… all tragic events. Billions of people… dead. But none as bad as what's to come and whose responsible."

Tawnie grabbed her camera and pointed up toward her face. Through the dark, you could make out her eyes as the glow inside them faded.

"I tried to tell you all, but you wouldn't listen. But the people you listen to are the ones responsible. Which ones?" Tawnie playfully asked as she sat on the surface of her desk, casting herself back into the dim light.

"Who? You ask. I could tell you, but what's the fun in that? Don't fall for the distractions people, and trust no one. Especially those in politics."

The crowd in the hall gasped. I was appalled, mostly because I knew the type of press this video was about to get. Finally, I walked up to the stage to grab Fixer.

"I wish I could simply tell you what happens next. But I tried that already. So I'll be with you in spirit as you try to figure out what the Ancient Arcanins were trying to tell us all along." She laughed again, this time more sinister. The look in her eyes spooked me. "Also, you may think that this is all a coincidence. But it is no coincidence that Nathaniel Wesley thwarted his killer's plan to take his seat at the head of the table. This was only one of The Ancient Arcanin's teachings. And they have already predicted the end of humanity as we know it. The clock is ticking. So figure out what they're saying or else… well, you see what happened to me."

The camera got closer to her face, looking into her eyes.

"If you keep your eye on the truth, the lies will never distract you."

The video ended, and my phone screen went back to normal. So did everyone else's. All eyes landed on the stage. Wesley stood tall with his hands behind him and smirked as he stared at all the people in the crowd. He began to walk to the side stage, and the eyes of the crowd followed him. He walked down the steps and approached Hawthorne McTierman. People raised their phones, ready to capture the moment. But when they did, Fixer snapped her fingers. Everything went dark, even the phones in the room. When electricity was restored in the city, we were already back on an unknown aircraft.

"Mission accomplished?" Cleaner asked, looking back at Fixer from his seat near the front cabin. The woman closed her eyes and sighed. "The seed of doubt has been planted." She mumbled, wiping her face over with her hand. "Now, here's where the real challenge begins. Failing our next mission will undermine all efforts that Tawnie has made thus far."

"What will happen then?" Wesley asked.

The woman shook her head and clamped the bridge of her nose

with her fingers.

"History will repeat itself… the world will fall victim to this damned prophecy."

Chapter LXXIII

The jet carried us back to headquarters. The skyscraper in the city's center was taller than the other structures. We headed for the top, giving us a full view of the Happy House Inc. logo at the top corner of the building. An overturned ice cream cone replaced the 'A' and 'O' on the first and second lines. The entire ride was silent. Fixer stared out the window blankly, contradicting her previous bravado. Cleaner sat meditatively, staring forward without even a blink the whole trip. Wes looked as if he had something heavy on his mind.

"Who the hell posted that video?" I asked. Everyone looked at me as if I lost my mind.

"Uh… what?" Fixer asked.

I shifted in my seat and turned toward everyone. "Tawnie's dead, so who posted the video?"

Fixer sighed as she shook her head. "I don't know."

She turned to look out the window again as if she was dismissing the conversation.

I exploded from my seat, "How the hell do you not know?"

"Vic, hold your shit together, please," Wes commanded me. "The last thing we need is a meltdown."

I turned, pointing my finger at him. "Meltdown?" I yelled. "Do you people not understand the magnitude of what just happened at that gala? Do I need to give a lesson about what Tawnie is attempting to dig up… General Wesley?"

"We need to stay out of it," Fixer suggested.

"That implies that there is something to stay out of, Fixer!" I turned to her and placed my hands on my knees. She looked at me side-eyed and clenched her jaw. "What exactly happened? And I ask again. Who the hell posted that video?"

She sat silently and closed her eyes for a moment. Then, taking a deep breath, she turned forward in her seat to face me.

"Would you believe me if I told you we were all brought to this moment because we received orders."

"Orders?" I flinched with squinted eyes. "From who? Your organization?"

She shook her head. "By the Arcanin Prophecy?"

I stared at the woman in front of me. Unconsciously, my mouth clicked in frustration.

"You can't seriously be telling me that you believe the prophecy told you to go to that Gala."

Wes nodded. "Vic, it's true. Tawnie read it to us."

I felt my skin begin to crawl as my body temperature climbed. My eyelids itched, and my mouth dried as I heard her name. "I'm so sick of people talking about Tawnie! She ruined us all, and she's dead! Why are we still talking about her?"

"Because we have no one to translate the Arcanin Prophecy," Wes added. "You may not want to hear about her, Vic, but the fact is, Tawnie knew all of this was coming. Believe what you want, but I'm more open to believing that she read us all our future. I would be dead if it weren't for her!"

I shifted in my seat. My face was so scrunched that I could feel the skin on my nose overlapping. "Are you telling me that she had all of that planned?"

"In a way, yes," Fixer answered. Tawnie helped the three of us in some significant ways," Wes added.

Fixer smirked. "Yeah, I would be dead, too," she announced. The woman paused again as she stared distantly. I waited for her to speak again.

"Fixer," Cleaner called to her. The woman shook herself back to reality. "Don't go there right now."

"Can you guys be a bit more specific?" I asked.

Wes shook his head. "Can't." He barked. "We don't even understand how it happened. All I know is you are also one of us because she spared you as well."

My eyebrows fell as I stared at him. "Who?" I yelled.

"Are you dense?" Fixer yelled at me. She stood from her seat and approached me with a hint of malice in her expression. "Instead of defaming the only person who could save this shitty rock, you should be focusing on what's going to happen next!"

Her words stunned me, and I realized she may be taking offense to my stand. I looked at Wes and then Cleaner. Their expressions shared her sentiment.

She straightened her hand, pointing her fingers into my chest as she gazed into my eyes. "I don't want to hear shit else about Tawnie from you until you learn how to read Ancient Arcanin and zip through time."

My eyes grew large for a split second. "Wait, what?" I asked. "Say that last part again?"

Suddenly, I could feel the ship descending.

"Alright, Lieutenant, we have arrived at Happy House." The pilot announced.

"Thank you!" She replied as she walked to the front where the exit was, just behind the cockpit. The plane touched down on a helipad at the top of the building. A silent moment passed as the pilot left his seat to undo the latch on the door. The cool winds of the spring evening swept inside the jet, immediately cooling the inside. I looked down the corridor and watched the others as they left me standing there alone. I suddenly wondered if things would change for the worse once I stepped off. I'm unsure how to explain it, but something felt wrong. Then again, for the last eight years of my life, things have always gone wrong anytime that woman's name was involved. I felt the heat on my face and clenched my jaw so tight that my eyes hurt as I stormed to the door.

"How many people need to die following her wild, conspiracy-charged nonsense?" I asked the two of them as they casually stood to leave the jet. "I've lost Gordon, the 316th, and my damned husband! Why are we still doing this?"

They stopped walking, and Fixer turned to look at me. Her stare displayed her annoyance.

"Because Tawnie has been right about everything that was ever going to happen." She said as she inched closer to me. "All the government betrayals, assassinations, the wars!"

I shook my head and squinted. "Wars? With an 'S'?"

She jammed her finger into my chest again, in between my

collarbones, and sneered at me.

"All of us are alive because Tawnie was the only one who read that prophecy. And now she has said that the world as we know it is about to end!"

I couldn't tell if it was the fact that she seemed utterly upset or if there was a hint of fear in this powerful woman. But something about what she just said resonated.

"We owe her our lives, Vic," Wes said as he shrugged. "Ever since Saudi Arabia, she's been our guiding light, and now she's gone."

Fixer pulled her finger back and stepped away from me with her hands up. Still, she shook her head in disapproval.

"I have done the unthinkable to get us here today." She said. "I have given my life to maintain order in the world. Hundreds of thousands fall under my command, and the thing I couldn't prepare for was that woman."

Her eyes softened for just a moment. "I completely understand your frustration, Victoria. But the numbers don't lie. Had I gotten to Rexburg thirty seconds sooner, I would still have my strongest warrior here to help. Milo would still have his mother, and you would still have your husband. But now, the world wouldn't be facing sudden death!"

My head fell. That last sentence was like a gut punch. I was talking down about someone who was genuinely revered like a god. Maybe she was more than just the kid who screwed up our mission years ago. But how much more?

"We just need to be able to decipher the Arcanin on our own," I suggested.

Fixer raised her hand and slightly turned her head as if she were prepared to scream. But she started to chuckle, which worried me even more. As she placed her hands across her chest and folded her arms, I understood the message clearly.

"Have you ever looked at the Arcanin language?" She asked me.

It was then that it occurred to me that I had never actually had. I glanced at it a few times in Riyadh or inside Tawnie's hideout in Rexburg. But it dawned on me that I never actually looked at it objectively. She pulled a piece of paper from her jacket's interior pocket and handed it to me. My eyebrow raised as I watched her step backward away from me. Eyes locked on hers, I unfolded the sheet and saw it covered in symbols. I stared at it for a while before Fixer finally came to take the page back.

"I've stared at this page that Tawnie wrote and told me that I would have to figure out what it said on my own." She explained. It's my own personal prophecy."

"Do you really believe that?" I scoffed. "How do you know she wasn't just baiting you?"

Fixer's head tilted with disbelief, and she turned away to leave. Cleaner followed behind her, then Wes.

"Am I the only one that believes it is possible to learn the language?" I asked them.

"Yeah!" Wes chuckled. "Archaeologists and historians have worked tirelessly to decipher these alphabets for years. There has been no progress."

"Well, if Tawnie knew so much about the Ancient Arcanin, then why didn't she teach the language to anyone?"

"Because knowing the language itself makes you powerful. Look at what happened when humans got their hands on the Pyro Stone." Fixer answered. "She never wanted the world to be in this type of danger in the first place."

I threw my hands up and started for the door, passing the three of them. Before I reached it, one of Fixer's agents rushed outside. The clash startled me, and the man ran out to meet them.

"Lieutenant!" He called out. "Come quick. There's been a development!"

Moments later, we found ourselves watching the news inside an office. The headline on the screen read, "New Conspiracy Threatens World Order."

"It's 2 am, and we're seeing a breaking news report," Wes said as he looked down at his watch. "This can't be good."

"The video heard around the world." The news anchor said. "World-renowned conspiracy theorist Tawnie Simms stirs the world even three months after her death. The young tycoon's video surfaced last night warning people to be cautious of the government."

The other anchorman looked at the camera and swallowed hard.

"In addition to this video, an official document went out from the same anonymous source that leaked the video. The file lists those allegedly linked to the crisis that ravaged Idaho three months ago. The FBI has–" The man paused and just lowered his head.

I looked up at Wes with a raised eyebrow.

"Paul, what's wrong?" The anchorwoman asked.

The man ripped away the microphone lining his clothing and stormed off set. The anchorwoman watched him in horror.

"Paul, please don't do this right now!" She continued.

"No, fuck this, Carol!" He yelled. "And fuck all of you who said that racist shit before the cameras started! Don't you people understand what's happening here? This empire is crumbling beneath us!"

People behind the camera stepped on the screen to assist the man, pushing and attempting to calm him. But the more they moved him, the louder he got. Carol Tyus, the anchorwoman, seemed troubled as she watched her partner break down. She usually looks so poised and confident. Something about this turned her into a school student with stage fright.

"Uh… okay." She shuddered. "The FBI has initiated an investigation to determine where the confidential information was sent. But there have been no known suspects so far."

Suddenly, a crash was heard in the background as the anchorman began to fight with the station staff.

"Influencer Tawnie Simms is said to be responsible for hundreds of reported riots occurring worldwide. The most notable location is the White House in Washington, DC. There is no clear motive at this time. Nor is there any logical reason these groups are congregating. But officials are working to extinguish the influence these groups are having."

Suddenly, the screen transitioned to the multicolored test screen with a message in the center that read 'signal interrupted.' This was accompanied by the long beep that would soon become the dreaded tone of worldwide panic. Then, another video of Tawnie. She was in the same room. This time, it seemed darker. Her face could hardly be seen, but she looked at the camera with her head tilted.

"Let me guess," she said with arrogance. I looked at Wes and Fixer, and they seemed just as confused. "Someone is attempting to discredit my movement. I'm willing to bet Carol Tyus is the first to stomp on my grave."

I immediately felt a cold chill, and a surge ran through my body, filling me with dread.

"She has to be still alive," I muttered. "There is no way."

"Before I died, I wanted to make sure that everyone sees the truth. Because 'THEY' are not going to tell you the truth, are they, Carol? But what you aren't saying is the released list has one name at the top! And I'm going to give you all a teaser of the horrors to come!"

Somehow, every time she screamed a sentence, I could feel remnants of her kaitrons still surrounding me, horrifying me as I watched her enticing rant.

"Because every United States government organization is going to lie to you and pretend that we are the problem! Let me tell you, folks, if you suspect it, then it is real, and we are the ones who will see through the shadows and find the truth in the darkest of times!"

A light turned on and illuminated Tawnie's face. Her eyes were angry and demented looking as she stared at the camera. It felt like she was looking into my eyes.

"The names on that list were actively responsible for what happened to me. They invested a lot of money to make sure that I was dead, and they thought they won. But here it is, checkmate."

She squatted out of her chair and moved closer to the camera. I found myself stepping back as if she was in front of me.

"Mr. President, you may think you won!" She snarled. "You thought you could get Nate Wesley out of the way and step up without us knowing? You must be stupid!"

She stared into the camera and smiled momentarily before flipping her hair back. "McTierman, here is your warning: run. To everyone else, good luck. The government will take drastic measures to combat this one… and believe it or not, that was always bound to be part of the problem. A government so destructive that it destroys the rest of the world attempting to protect itself…And the prophecy said that we would all die because of their insecurities…The world will perish because of the men who helped build it."

The flames of our sins will burn the lands we walk, smothering our consciousness. The waves of our debt will wash them away, leaving the world with nothing else. One woman could change this: an unlikely hero. I, the Harbinger of Extinction, was not the hero that humanity deserves.. But my mistakes will pave the way for her ascension.
-Excerpt recovered from the journal of the Oracle, Via Lt. Victoria France

Chapter LXXIV

I opened my eyes, and light penetrated the edge of my soul as I became blinded. I raised my arms to my face and groaned. My body felt weak and sluggish, making it seem like there was a delay from my brain to the movement itself.

"Ugh, where am I?" I asked. "This isn't my bed!"

I could hear something that resembled wind chimes in the distance, and the air felt pure. I didn't know where I was, but I knew I wasn't in Oxnard, California, anymore. My eyes finally adjusted to the immense light, and I found myself… Wait, this has to be a dream. I looked up and saw that I was in a cylindrical room. The walls looked like some sort of whitish-colored crystal, like selenite. Light poured through the crystal formation, illuminating the room like a stadium. The geodes were incredible, nothing like I had ever seen before. But now wasn't the time to admire. I looked down and found that I was also standing on dirt and rock.

I looked back and noticed that the ground had ended a reasonable distance behind me. I walked back toward the end of the platform and watched as it dropped off the ledge. I shrieked in horror as I attempted to stop quickly to prevent falling over myself. I looked down into what turned into sheer darkness. The rocks underneath me disappeared into nothing at all.

"Holy shit!" I said.

Suddenly, something moved behind me. I spun around to see what was there. Or, in this case, who?

Six women were standing before me, all staring.

"Who are you?" I asked. "Where am I?"

The women all remained silent for a moment, watching me. One woman stepped forward. She was the smallest of the bunch. She wore a black, armored, skin-tight suit that accentuated her curves. Her eyes were bright green as if they were glowing. Her hair was golden white. I couldn't tell if she was reflecting light or emitting it. She had a black cape draped down her back and attached to a gold buckle on her collar. She approached me. A pattern on her chest resembling a thunderbolt glowed, casting light into my eyes as she drew near.

She stopped in front of me, looking up at me. A devious smirk cast on her face in silence.

"Can I help you?" I asked. The woman flipped her hair behind one ear and crossed her arms.

"My Lady, are you positive this is the one?" Another woman asked the blond as she stepped forward.

"I don't know." The blond answered. "The Tribunal said this is the one."

The taller woman and a woman who looked similar to the blond came to stand on both sides of her. One woman was a spitting image of the blond, except her eyes were hazel, and she was a brunette. Her power suit was different, though. She seemed to have the same pants, boots, and gloves. The difference was in the leather jacket she wore. It donned a white thunderbolt pattern emerging from the collar. The zipper was integrated. The other woman wore a casual blouse with pants, heels, and a cotton-down jacket.

"Madame First Lady?" I called, staring with my mouth open like a fan girl. The woman blushed and turned away slightly. It was her, a personal hero of mine since her husband was elected president. I even did last year's Social Science project on her efforts to garner world peace.

"Uh oh!" The remaining two women cheered as they stepped forth. One stepped in front of the blond and examined me briefly. She looked at me from head to toe as if she was searching for something in particular. This woman was a brunette as well, standing at around five-five, a bit taller than the blond. Her eyes were dark brown, and she wore a long black trench coat. She had what looked like a white bodysuit underneath, full of zippers and buckles. She also had on white, finger-less gloves with armored knuckles.

"I told you she'd recognize you first, Madeline!" She said.

"Well, that's obvious, Berserker!" She argued. "I'm the only one from her time period!"

"Time period, what the hell does that mean?" I wondered.

The other woman stepped forth to examine me as well.

"Carrigan, what do you think?" Berserker asked the woman as she studied her. Carrigan stepped forth and glared at me in the same fashion.

"You also share a face with one of her heroes." The woman said, appearing to be the bad-ass of the group. She wore a black belly shirt with shoulder holsters and short shorts. She also had crossed straps across her sternum. This attached a plate to her back where she mounted two swords and one rifle. Madeline Wesley smiled and nodded at the statement. She then turned to the blond woman.

"My Lady, why did you gather us here today?" Madeline asked. Everyone separated and turned to the small blond woman, waiting for her to respond. The little lady smiled again, not taking her eyes away from me. She placed her arms behind her back and cleared her throat.

"I didn't call this meeting." She announced.

"Meaghan?" Berserker asked. They all turned to look at the last woman in the group. She appeared young and was also slender in her build. She was a bit taller and had her brown hair in a ponytail. She wore a white cotton coat and a turtleneck underneath. She also wore black pants with boots. She was a biracial woman with facial features that seemed familiar to me somehow.

"Close," Meaghan said, crossing her arms. "But it wasn't me either."

"Well, that presents a problem, doesn't it?" The taller, thunderbolt-clad woman stated. "There's a mortal in the Sacred Chamber."

"That's worse than all of us being pulled from our timelines?" Carrigan asked.

"Everything is good in our time." Berserker taunted as she flipped her hair. "And don't hate on the mortals."

"Was it anyone here right now that called me here?" The blond woman asked, seeming to get impatient. But there was no response from the other women. "Well, if it wasn't us…"

The six of them turned to look in one direction. Another woman stood in the distance, watching all of us in silence. It was yet another familiar face. My eyes bulged, and my mouth opened wide with excitement and horror.

"M… M… Madame Oracle!?" I announced. Four of the six women in front of me bowed to greet none other than Tawnie Simms. The blond smiled as she approached.

"Nice of you to join us, Gen. 3." The blond said to her. Tawnie chuckled as she approached the woman with open arms. The two of them shared a lingering hug. I could see stress fall away from Tawnie in that instant.

"It's good to see you too, Skyvolt," Tawnie said. The blond woman nodded. "I haven't heard that name in a long time."

Tawnie stood silently for a moment, staring at her. "I hope you are enjoying your retirement," she stated.

"Cut the shit, Oracle!" The other thunderbolt girl said to Tawnie.

"Rayna, you really need to learn to respect your elders." Tawnie joked as she pointed her finger toward her face.

"I gathered you guys here today because I miscalculated the outcome of my last ordeal. It has opened up a bit of a weak spot in our defenses." Tawnie explained. "So I had to find our next hope."

Skyvolt raised her hand, pointing at the girl. "She's a baby!"

"She's sixteen!" Tawnie revolted. "The same age I was when you made me remember all of the chaos we lived through!"

Skyvolt raised her hands and shook her head. "It's not my fault that we're bound by fate."

Tawnie swiped her hand toward the blond, trying to move on.

"In fact, you may be more responsible for that than I am… Right, Great Grandmother?"

Rayna laughed at the joke, and Meaghan swiped at her arm.

Rayna flinched and got herself together before Tawnie looked at her with thin eyes.

"You guy's family are annoying." Said Carrigan.

"What do you need us here for, Tawnie?" Berserker asked. "The two of us aren't really part of this."

Tawnie smiled at Carrigan and Berserker. "There is a personal favor I need from the two of you in order for our new friend here to accomplish her mission."

"Hello?!" I yelled, cutting them off. "Why are you talking around me?"

"Uh…" Tawnie started.

"Tawnie Simms is dead, so this must be a hallucination or a bad dream!"

The other women looked at Tawnie in shock.

"Dead, huh?" Skyvolt asked.

Tawnie closed her eyes and shook her head, "As a door nail."

"What is this all about?" Meaghan asked. "You couldn't have called us here for idle chit-chat. I have a nation to rebuild."

Tawnie looked at Meaghan and sighed.

"The prophecy is unfolding." She announced, catching everyone's attention. "The Tetra Sphere has been stolen, and I believe it is in the wrong hands."

The mood quickly sobered.

"This means our greatest fear is becoming a reality," Skyvolt said as she stepped forth. "We are stuck in our own times and can't do anything about it."

Tawnie nodded.

"You must get the others involved!" Meaghan commanded.

"Hmph." Was all that Tawnie could say about that statement. She raised her hands to her head and walked away mid-conversation.

"Madeline, talk to her, please!" Meaghan continued.

Madeline shook her head, "I can't. I serve her."

"It's funny you say that, Madeline!" Tawnie said as she spun around and threw her hands down. "So does she!"

Meaghan approached her. "You need to summon her!"

"Dammit, Meaghan!" Tawnie yelled. "If we do that, we'll risk universal collapse. Is that something you want?"

The woman stared at Tawnie for a moment before roaring into

the void "There has to be something we can do!"

"There is something we can do." Tawnie said as she pointed at me.

"Right, I can't wait to hear this," Skyvolt said. "What brilliant plan has my namesake cooked up for us today?"

Tawnie lowered her head, eyeing me like a hot meal. She rubbed her hands together and stepped toward me.

"I want all of you to pay attention to this one. She will be our champion." She announced.

"Tawnie, what can this child really do for us?" Madeline asked.

"This is no ordinary child, folks…" Tawnie continued.

"I know who she is," Carrigan announced. "She is the Obliterator."

"Not yet." Tawnie smiled as she stepped closer to me. She looked me in the eyes and grabbed my hands. I wanted to ask questions to understand what they were talking about. But I continuously remained silent.

"We don't have much time to explain. Just know that you'll learn everything when the time is right." She said.

My head jerked, attempting to understand where Tawnie was going with her message.

"Do you understand?" She asked me.

I nodded timidly, "I think so?"

Tawnie closed her eyes and tilted her head back to take a deep breath. It was like she was meditating.

"Are you ready?" She continued, letting my hands go free. One of her brows hiked as she attempted to fully grasp the situation. I nodded, "I am."

Tawnie smiled, cleared her throat, and took a step back. She looked around at the others. The six of them gave their nods of approval. Though some were reluctant to the idea.

"There is no life without balance," Tawnie announced. "So let this era bring us balance and peace."

Everyone stood straight and focused on me.

"It's time," Tawnie told me. She snapped her fingers, and suddenly vision went black.

"The fate of the world is in your hands… Laura."

Author's Note

If you've come this far, thank you for reading! There are many wonders about the Ancient Arcanin, aren't they? They are the exact reason I had to rewrite the series. I felt that my original, as good as it was, did not convey the series and background the way it should have. The Aether Universe is vast, with more history and chronicles than one could imagine. The first book should convey that properly. If you couldn't tell, there was another story told just like this one before. If you have read that story, don't worry; it's still relevant.

If you have the original, physical copy of The Gem State Siege, hold on to it! It'll be worth it one of these days! Congratulate yourself as well. If you've read the original series, things will become much clearer as we traverse deeper into our heroes' journey. This series will be full of mystery and darkness! In the first installment, you meet Tawnie and are introduced to the Arcanin Prophecy. In the next book, you'll be introduced to a whole new world that will leave you fascinated and in wonder. Those of you who have been previously introduced to the Arcanin Calamity, you may already have an idea of where we'll visit next. But whether you are new to Aether or a returning reader, get ready for the next chapter of the Arcanin Calamity! The flames have burned our sins, so now the waves shall cleanse.

Join The Mailing List:

Uncover the Secrets of the Universe

Craving more cosmic conspiracies, mind-bending twists, and heart-pounding action? Join our exclusive community of insiders and get:

- **Early Access:** Be the first to know about new releases, pre-order bonuses, and exclusive excerpts.
- **Behind-the-Scenes:** Dive deeper into the Aether Universe with author interviews, character breakdowns, and worldbuilding insights.
- **Exclusive Content:** Unlock bonus short stories, deleted scenes, and never-before-seen artwork.

Don't miss out on the chance to explore the galaxy with us!

Scan the code:

[illegible]